CAST ME NOT AWAY

CAST ME NOT AWAY

A Window to the Future

By

Zara Heritage

Cape Arago Press
P.O. Box 771
North Bend, OR 97459
www.capearagopress.com

Cover: Wind dispersing dandelion seeds ©Shutterstock, Inc.

ISBN 13: 978-0-9825949-6-4
ISBN 10: 0-9825949-6-8

1. Fiction: Contemporary Women
2. Fiction: Alternative History

Cast Me Not Away is set in sight-saving Georgia 11 point type for reading ease.

*Cast Me Not Away is dedicated to
the countless women and girls who fell victim to society's lies
and had God's most precious gift wrenched from them.*

And

To the memory of all the baby girls and boys who never had a
chance to make this world a better place.

Foreword

"The truth is incontrovertible. Malice may attack it, ignorance may deride it, but in the end, there it is." ~ Winston Churchill

Reading this entertaining and perceptive novel will give you a glimpse of what awaits us. And knowledge like that will make it impossible to ever view the world in quite the same way again. This is perhaps the most profound aspect of a book like *Cast Me Not Away*. Fiction such as this has a curious way of becoming fact.

For validation, one only has to look as far as George Orwell's classic novel, *1984*. It was, of course, written in 1948. The date was reversed to place the events about a generation or so into the future. Many people looked around in 1984 and noticed that many of Orwell's expectations had gone unfulfilled.

On second glance we see that the problem was the amount of time he allowed for these changes to occur. Very few people would dispute that we are now deep in the throes of Orwellian chaos. *Big Brother* is clearly recognizable in the Presidential cult of personality we experience in the U.S.A. Listen to any news conference if you want to hear *Newspeak*. The *Ministry of Truth* is alive and well in the meaningless drivel and outright lies coming out of most governmental agencies. And we encounter Orwellian thought control in the Mainstream Media every time they respond *en masse* to a *Thoughtcrime,* or *hate speech* as it's now called.

Needless to say, Orwell would feel right at home within the cabal surrounding Planned Parenthood and the Pro-Abortion movement where euphemistic language masks an ugly reality. After all, the Pro-Aborts can hardly shout, "We demand the right to decide if and when to kill our children!"

As this is being written, a major scandal has erupted over undercover films documenting Planned Parenthood negotiating to sell organs and body parts of aborted babies. This aspect of their business is apparently so profitable that the clinics develop a daily want list of desired parts/organs and plan their day's work around it to maximize profits. One is reminded of the adage of a slaughterhouse selling every part of the pig but its squeal.

Whether we acknowledge it or not, the *After-Birth Abortion* is a reality. Everyday infants born alive during an abortion are routinely dispatched. Many hospitals set aside children born with severe deformities, consigning them to a prolonged and agonizing death. News reports of the bodies of newborns and young children found in a dumpster, or abandoned in a field, have become commonplace.

This constant exposure to such unimaginable horrors is desensitizing many people. We cannot allow this to happen; too many lives hang in the balance. For if apathy replaces empathy, we have lost the battle.

What to do? Take to heart the underlying messages of *Cast Me Not Away*. First and foremost, recognize that our nation and our world are in a crisis situation. Then, rather than freeze like a deer in the headlights, do something about it while you still can.

E. G. Lewis
Author of the Seeds of Christianity Series

CAST ME NOT AWAY

CHAPTER ONE

"It's a matter of taking the side of the weak against the strong, something the best people have always done."
~ Harriet Beecher Stowe

Three-year-old Robbie was tired of crying. It felt like he'd been doing it forever. He lifted his arm and wiped his nose on his sleeve. He knew he shouldn't, but he couldn't find any tissue boxes here like at Gramma's house. He missed Gramma. He wished she'd come get him, take him home and tell him everything was okay.

The tiny room was dimly lit and nearly silent. A low murmur of mournful sobs and soft moans filled the dismal space where other little kids like him waited. Several toddlers slept on the cold cement floor. No one played with anyone else. Somehow the children understood this was a time to be afraid.

Robbie wrinkled his nose at the dank, musty odor pervading the room and wondered what smelled so bad. Spider webs dangled in the corners and dark roaches scurried in the shadows feasting on the occasional cookie crumb the mice missed.

The room's only table had hunks of laminate chipped off its surface. Remnants of its original tabletop had stains where spilled liquids dried into sticky circles. Child-sized chairs formed a haphazard pile in one corner, their broken legs and missing seats rendering them useless.

A rickety bookshelf held the only toys. A pathetic fleet of trucks and cars with no wheels sat parked beside the frames of puzzles without pieces. Naked baby dolls leaned against each other as if attempting to hold in one another's stuffing. The tears of a thousand terrified youngsters had washed away their painted faces.

Robbie sniffled. He tried his best not to start crying again, but it was nearly impossible when surrounded by the sobs and hiccups of other weeping children. A single window, its lower half mostly boarded over, provided the room's only light. The boards weren't there to stop the children from looking out, but rather to prevent people on the outside from seeing their unhappy little faces pressed against the window glass.

He noticed two kids standing side by side staring out through a narrow crack in the sheets of plywood. Their expressions were as miserable as he felt. Robbie wondered why they appeared so much alike. And why these two held hands when everyone else huddled alone casting sidelong glances at the strangers beside them?

Slipping off his dilapidated wooden bench, Robbie walked over beside the twins to peer through the crack with them. The sad trio stared down at a nearly empty parking lot far below. Robbie marveled at how the car shadows had changed. He always wondered about stuff like that. They were different now than when his father brought him here. It had been early morning and the shadows were off to one side of the cars. Now they'd moved to the other side.

At daybreak Robbie's father had stood at the toaster grumbling under his breath. "Quit dawdling. Drink your milk and finish your toast. We've someplace to get to."

Robbie remembered picking up the dry, shriveled toast when Father plopped the plate in front of him. It reminded him of the half-burned wood in Gramma's fireplace. He took a bite. It tasted like half-burned wood too.

"Gramma always puts butter and jelly on my toast."

"Well, I'm not Gramma, am I? You'll eat it and be glad you did. Now shut up."

He ate it because Father told him to. But that was a long time ago and his stomach growled from hunger. Robbie closed his eyes and thought about Gramma's kitchen, always filled with wonderful food smells. Thinking about it made his mouth water.

"Robbie, honey," Gramma would say, "Have I told you how much your mother loved you?"

"Yes, Gramma, over and over." He munched another chocolate chip cookie. Her cookies were the best.

"I don't ever want you to forget how much she loved you."

"And you loved her and she loved you too, didn't she Gramma?"

"Yes, Sweetheart, your mama was wonderful. She didn't want to die. She'd be with us right now if she could." Then she hugged him and kissed the top of his head. "I love you just as much as I loved your mama, Robbie."

"I know. She was your little girl and I'm her little boy." Robbie frowned. "A car akkadent happened to her, right?"

"Yes, honey. Now eat your cookies and I'll tell you another story about your mama."

"What about my papa?"

"You should love everyone, especially your papa. Always be careful to do whatever your father tells you." Robbie thought that wouldn't be a problem since he rarely saw his father. Father didn't live with Robbie and Gramma. Father never gave him hugs or kisses the way Gramma did. That's why he was so confused when Father came and took him away from Gramma's house.

Robbie studied his fingers and tried to count the nights he'd spent at his father's. Whenever Robbie wanted to keep track of how many days went by, he did it by remembering what Gramma fixed for supper each night. That didn't work after his father took him away because he mostly fed him toast. He wasn't sure if he counted all the days, but he knew they didn't go all the way to his baby finger.

Father seemed angry this morning when they came to this place. Robbie didn't know why; he'd tried to do everything Father wanted. He couldn't remember ever being afraid like this before. Something awful was about to happen to him and all the other little kids here. He didn't know what or why and couldn't explain his feelings, but – like the bad smell – evil seemed to ooze out of the ugly gray walls.

Robbie sat down on the cold floor, pulled his knees to his chest and wrapped his arms around himself.

He started to cry again.

CHAPTER TWO

The children jumped when the door flew open and slammed against the wall. They shrank back, staring at the open doorway and blinking at the sudden brightness. Robbie's heart raced.

A short man wearing olive-green coveralls entered the room. He sneered at the cowering children and waved his arm, motioning a young woman to enter. When she hesitated, he shouted, "C'mon. I ain't got all day. Pick one!"

She stepped into the room wearing tan slacks and a white blouse covered with an olive-green apron that matched his coveralls. She clutched a broom in her left hand reminding Robbie of one of the characters from a Cinderella cartoon he'd watched with Gramma.

Lingering in the doorway, she tugged at her lip as her gaze flitted from one child to the next. She sighed. "Oh, how can I choose? I want them all."

"Well, ya ain't gettin' 'em all. Hurry yap, or yur not gettin' none of 'em." He pulled her into the room. "And remember, since there's so few this time it's riskier for me. The price of this un ain't 500 no more, it's gonna be 700."

She frowned. "Yes, I know, I know. Somehow we'll get the extra 200 to you next time."

He held out his hand, grinning and rubbing his fingers together. "Right, and in cash. That means you better bring me 900 for the next kid after this un."

She nodded and started across the room toward the twins.

"Hey, what d' ya think yur doin'?" The loud man stomped his foot. "Get that crazy notion outta yur head. This ain't the Bargain Mart where we have two-fur-one Tuesdays. Ya can't have either of 'em two. Somebody'd notice if one of 'em was gone. Pick another one."

"Okay. Then give me the list."

He reached in his back pocket and pulled out a crumpled

sheet of paper. Unfolding it, he handed it to her.

She gazed heavenward and moved her lips in a silent prayer. A moment later, she stabbed the page with her finger and tipped her head down to see where it landed. "Robert Wilson." Her eyes darted around the room of terrified youngsters cringing on the floor and against the wall. "Who is Robert Wilson?"

No one responded.

"Yuh heard her. Which one of youse kids is Robert Wilson?" The man circled the room pulling at the name tags pinned to each child. When he reached Robbie, the man's scowl made the boy shrink back. He grabbed Robbie's tag and yanked it off. "It's this un. He's Robert Wilson."

Too late, Robbie remembered his whole name *was* Robert Wilson. He knew that. He recognized it after the man said it. But, no one ever called him that and he wasn't used to it. He gawked at the glowering man and tried very hard not to sob.

The young woman quietly crossed the room to reach Robbie. She knelt in front of him and took his hand. "Little guy, would you be willing to come with me?"

Robbie looked into her kind eyes, then over at the mean man who slouched against the doorway picking his teeth. It was an easy decision. Anywhere would be better than here, wherever *here* was. He nodded.

She rose. Placing a hand on his shoulder, the nice lady guided him to the door.

He felt the other children watch him as he crossed the dimly lit room. Robbie shot them a quick backward glance. If they'd met at a park playground he'd have made several new friends. But they hadn't met in a park, and he wondered if he'd ever see any of them again. He caught a whiff of urine. Someone had peed their pants. He was glad it wasn't him.

The man reached down and seized Robbie's hand. Lifting it in the air, he drew a large knife out of his side pocket. Robbie saw the approaching blade and flinched in fear. He tugged with all his might, trying to pull away. But the man was too strong. The room's gray walls suddenly seemed even darker and scarier than they had moments before.

"Wait!" the woman shouted. She pulled at Robbie's arm to get it away from the man, but she didn't succeed. "Let me at least get the ether out and put a tourniquet on it."

Hurriedly she clamped a white handkerchief over Robbie's nose and mouth. His face scrunched up at the smell. He squirmed and kicked for several seconds before collapsing against her. The rest of the children watched wide-eyed as the man raised Robbie's arm and splayed out the fingers of the boy's left hand.

"Not yet, it needs a tourniquet," she shrieked.

"I ain't got time." The man placed the knife between Robbie's fingers and, in one quick motion, sliced through the knuckle of the smallest digit.

The children cried out in horror as blood sprayed across the floor. Whatever fear they felt before increased ten-fold.

Color drained from the woman's face. "Couldn't you have waited until we were out in the hallway so the other children didn't have to witness that?"

"Oh, don't gimme none uh yur bleedin' heart crap, Miss Goody Two-shoes. Life's tough. Sugar coatin' everthin' don't make it better fur them urchins." He guffawed. "B'sides it ain't like it's gonna scar 'em for the rest o' their long lives now, is it?"

The woman shook her head and cradled Robbie's unconscious form. "How can you be so heartless?" Taking Robbie's hand, she bound it tightly in clean linen to staunch the bleeding.

Meanwhile, the man retrieved the end of Robbie's finger from the floor and popped it into a plastic bag. Pulling a dirty rag out of his back pocket, he tossed the rag in the direction of one of the girls who looked like she was about to be sick. The tallest in the room, she appeared to be almost four years old, probably the oldest child there. Her blond curls were tangled and her blue eyes brimmed with tears.

"You! Wipe up this blood and don't leave none. Hear me? Do it now. I'll be back for the rag and that floor better be done good."

She began to sob. Crawling over on her hands and knees, she picked up the rag and started wiping the floor as the adults left the room. The hinges of the heavy iron door squealed as he slammed it shut behind them.

℘ℭ℞

The woman gently laid Robbie in a rolling laundry hamper. Lifting his hand, she carefully placed it across his chest and pulled the clean laundry around him. The hamper was a molded polyethylene tub attached to a wooden platform with casters on each corner. It had a matching lid that she snapped closed over its rounded rim concealing the laundry inside, as well as Robbie.

"Why are you so callous and careless? My apron is splattered in blood. You know a tourniquet makes it less messy and is better for the child."

He scoffed. Holding the bag up to the light, the man stared at the piece of Robbie's tiny digit through the clear plastic. "You know, these finger ends ain't very big; mebbe I should get somethin' bigger."

"That's all the lab requires. It's awful enough as it is. Leave us alone. You've got your money and your DNA proof; he's mine now." She made shooing motions with her hands. "Go away."

"Listen, and listen good, ya better show me more respect than that. You be nice to ol' Giles, or you won't be gettin' no more of these little discards."

"They aren't discards. They're sweet children who have as much right to a good life as you or I do."

"Ha! Speak for yourself, Missy. At least I'm useful. What do you do around here, huh? Sweepin' floors at a FFU ain't no big-time job."

The woman bit her tongue. FFU indeed ... an acronym everyone used for *Facilities For the Useless*. She threw her shoulders back and glared at him. "Do not call me Missy. You know my name." She turned her back on Giles and lifted the hamper lid to check Robbie's breathing. She adjusted the laundry to further conceal his unconscious form before snapping it shut again.

"Right you are, Aranda Blackthorn." Leaning his shoulder against the wall, Giles savored the feel of the crisp bills passing through his fingers as he counted them a second time. Yep, he had a good racket going here. He could just keep raising the price and there wasn't a thing pretty little Aranda could do about it. If she refused to pay, he'd threaten to make a visit to the security office. Not that he ever would, of course, but she didn't know that. He stuffed the money into his pocket.

With the child hidden, Aranda bent at the waist and grabbed the sides of the heavy laundry hamper.

Giles studied the tan slacks stretched across her round bottom with a smirk. Believing they were alone in the hallway, he gave her a slap on the backside.

Aranda did a startled stutter-step and scampered away from him. She stopped a few feet away, exhaled loudly and frowned back at him.

"Transporter Giles!"

They both jumped.

The Director's shout echoed down the corridor toward them. "What did I just witness?" Director Mira Hastings had rounded the corner in time to see the slap and now placed her hands on her slender hips and glared at Giles from the other end of the corridor.

He stood at attention and self-consciously brushed at smudges on his coveralls. "Sorry Ma'am. Just a friendly gesture between two co-workers," he hollered down the hall to her. "Won't happen again, Ma'am."

Under his breath he muttered to Aranda, "Bit 'ov a bitch, ain't she? Deserves t' be put in 'er place, is what I think."

Ignoring him, Aranda pulled off her soiled apron and bunched it up to hide the blood splatter. She'd have to pass the Director and hoped she wouldn't notice the missing apron. Best do it quickly. She hastily pushed her laundry hamper away from Giles and prayed the unconscious child inside remained quiet. She gave the Director a passing nod as she hurried past and continued on.

The wheels of her hamper wobbled and squeaked as Aranda scurried down the narrow hall. She moved at a steady, deliberate pace toward the elevator, trying not to appear rushed or nervous. A bell chimed and the elevator doors parted. Heart racing, she rolled the hamper in. As the car descended, she lifted the lid and listened for Robbie's heavy breathing under the white towels. Reassured, Aranda let out a sigh of relief and sagged against the wall.

CHAPTER THREE

"The only thing necessary for the triumph of evil is for good men to do nothing." ~ Edmund Burke

The elevator's car lurched as it slowed. Aranda gripped the hamper's handles tightly. Looking down, she was surprised to notice her knuckles had gone white. She took a deep breath and forced herself to relax.

Something didn't feel right. What was Mira Hastings doing there? It wasn't like the attractive, business-like Director to leave her office and wander the halls. If this continued, it would make Aranda's retrievals more difficult.

Giles criticism of her janitorial position still smarted. She'd foregone other opportunities and applied at several FFUs specifically because of the children. But, like all opportunities, this one came at a price, a high price. Taking a job at FFU-1116 put her at the epicenter of this chaotic enterprise. She'd immersed herself in its evil and some days it draped itself around her like a damp cloak, weighing her down until she felt like it could bury her.

But, there was no way she would share her motives with the likes of Giles. The very thought of him made her shudder. He was a barbarian who derived pleasure from the disgusting sexual remarks he made about every woman he saw, treated the children he tended callously, and happily pocketed the fees he extorted from her.

Well, not really from her. An anonymous donor provided the funds. All she knew was that they didn't come from *Life Chances*, the underground organization she belonged to. She offered a silent prayer for her benefactor, whoever it was.

Some people are blind to the evil around them, she thought. Otherwise, places like this FFU couldn't exist. She didn't want to hate anyone; it wasn't in her nature. Giles, however, was a special case. She found it difficult *not* to hate him.

Her eyes went to the covered hamper beside her. What of this little boy she'd so carefully hidden? She didn't know whether to feel elated for him, or to weep for the ones left behind.

As she exited the elevator, the back wheel caught in the track. When she jostled the load to free the wheel, Robbie moaned in his sleep. Aranda glanced left and right, then stepped up her pace. She had to get him outside and off these grounds before he woke up. If he started to cry, all would be lost.

৪০জ

Grayson Stevens slowed his jog and settled into an exhausted walk. A casual observer would think he was taking a break, cooling down. He was more than ready to rest, but that wasn't why he'd slowed his pace.

He ran a hand through his hair and perspiration darkened the slight graying at his temples, blending it into his short brown hair. He was too warm. The weather report had predicted a cloudy day with wind and he'd chosen to wear his navy blue jogging suit and running shoes. The dark color absorbed heat from the bright sun making him wish he'd put on the silver and white outfit instead. He stopped under a huge oak, grateful for its circle of dark shade. The big tree grew across the street from an old multi-storied red brick structure.

Like many abandoned inner city schools, they'd converted the old building into a Facility For the Useless. This one was designated FFU Eleven Sixteen, officially written FFU-1116. The walls of the brick edifice once echoed with the sounds of happy children, laughing and playing. No longer. Now, the only sounds those walls echoed back were the mournful cries of weeping children held captive inside them.

Stevens bent his knee and grabbed his foot, stretching. It provided justification to remain there a little longer. He repeated the motion with his other leg. Keeping his face aimed straight ahead, he cast surreptitious peeks at the building across the street through the tall chain link fence surrounding it. He took pains not to appear to be watching. He was merely out for a jog.

The sign over its entrance read *A Planned Society Makes Good Sense*. That was the mantra the government used to justify its madness. And what of those deemed useless, Stevens asked himself. Where did they fit into the system's omnipotent plans?

Out of the corner of his eye, he caught movement in the parking lot and straightened. *There she is again.*

He felt he was viewing a movie he'd already seen. This same young woman had rolled a similar laundry hamper across the parking lot several days earlier. Today, just as before, she cast cautious glimpses to both sides as she walked. Why?

Stevens slipped behind the giant oak. Unable to see what she was doing, he relied upon his other senses. He heard the metallic clink of a car door opening and chanced a quick peek. She stood with her back to him at the passenger side of an old dark blue, two-door sedan. Time and weather had turned its once shiny finish dull and drab.

He watched her transfer a bundle into the car. Perhaps she was nothing more than a common thief stealing supplies from her employer. As a public prosecutor, and therefore an officer of the Court, he should report her suspicious behavior. However, something about her made him think she wasn't an ordinary thief.

He disappeared behind the oak when she turned. Leaning back against the tree's rough bark, he tried to make sense of the situation. Suppose it wasn't cleaning supplies she was stealing? What if she was doing something else entirely?

He stroked his chin and took a deep breath. One way or another, he needed to quit killing time and make up his mind. If someone was watching her, they might have seen him as well. What would a man out on jog be doing hiding behind a large tree?

He rolled his eyes and chuckled. People didn't take kindly to men relieving themselves in public places. He hadn't, but someone who chanced to look in his direction might mistake what he was doing.

Stevens pulled a pen out of his pocket and came out from behind the oak. He stretched and rolled his shoulders, then bent to grasp the strings on his shoes as if to retie them. While he fiddled with the shoelaces, he scribbled her license number on the palm of his hand.

Ever since he'd noticed her, he couldn't get the woman out of his mind. He wouldn't sleep until he found out what she was up to. But he didn't want to frighten her off either.

As he stood up, he felt someone's eyes on him. His gaze darted instinctively to a window on an upper floor. A woman peered at him through a lifted slat in the blinds and quickly released it. Why was she staring down at him? She'd no doubt seen the young woman loading the car. What part did she play in the mystery?

He resumed his jog, hoping neither woman suspected he'd been paying them any attention.

೫ೞ

Mira Hastings lifted the window slat again and watched the man who'd stepped out from behind the tree jog away. He made a final backward survey at the FFU's parking lot before disappearing around the corner. She frowned. Something about his presence gave her an uneasy feeling. It was impossible to tell much about him from up there. She wished she'd been able to get a better view. If only he'd not realized she was watching him and the young woman in the parking lot.

While Aranda pushed the hamper back into the building, Mira remained at her office window like an unseen guardian angel monitoring the old blue car with a child stowed in the front seat. She stayed there until Aranda drove away. Sighing, she released the blinds and let them close.

The position of Director of an FFU was more title than power. Mira came into FFU-1116 with expectations of righting wrongs and changing the system. Instead, she encountered a hidebound monolith that resisted the slightest change.

Even her smallest attempts raised the ire of her District Supervisor. When she ordered the holding room repainted and the purchase of toys and games to make the children's short stay less traumatic, they accused her of wasteful spending. So, it never happened. She attempted to circumvent the restrictions by instituting a *Bring a Toy to Work* day. When word reached the Regional Office, it earned her a formal reprimand.

Mira had given up trying to transform the system. Instead she found consolation in covertly aiding Aranda's rescue efforts by turning a blind eye to her activities. But she found this passive stance less than satisfying. This occasionally led her, at great risk, to personally snatch a child herself.

☙❧

Bundled up in laundry, Robbie remained hidden and unconscious on the car seat beside Aranda. A few blocks later, she slowed for a stop sign and leaned over to recheck him. He seemed okay. She heaved a sigh of relief and smoothed a lock of hair from his forehead. She gently caressed his pink cheeks. He was such a cute little fellow.

A jogger in a navy blue jogging outfit crossed in front of them. She didn't give the man a second thought as she drove forward, wondering why someone didn't value the precious little person beside her.

CHAPTER FOUR

Rebecca Stuart paced her kitchen, weeping. She circled the room, alternately wringing her hands and running her fingers through her gray hair.

The house was quiet, too quiet. She could hear birds outside and the usual traffic noises. What she missed was her grandson's *varoom, varoom* as he drove one of his four-wheeled plastic toys across the floor. Her eyes roamed the adjacent living room. Trucks and race cars remained where he'd left them, a heartrending reminder of his absence.

Where is Robbie right now? Is he okay?

She'd been shocked and frightened when Frank Wilson, her daughter's ex-husband, burst into her house and demanded Robbie. She'd trailed behind him pleading for an explanation. "I don't understand. You've always been so good about providing support money every month ... first to Veronica before she died, and now to me. I thought you were satisfied to let me raise my grandson."

When they reached the kitchen, Frank jerked a chair out from the kitchen table and plopped down. "Yeah, well the cost doubled after Veronica died, didn't it?"

"That's nothing Robbie or I did. The state sets the amount." She studied his face, trying to discern his motive. If he resented the increase, it wasn't her fault. "If it could be changed—"

He cut her off midsentence. "Yeah, well it can't, can it? And, there's no way I can make you his legal guardian." He paused long enough to shout to Robbie that he'd better hurry up. "So, I'm stuck providing for him. Do you know how much I'd be fined if we tried to pull a fast one and the government learned you were the one paying for his upkeep, not me?" He extended his hands and shrugged. "There's nothing else to do; I'm taking him."

Her daughter, Veronica, divorced Frank shortly after Robbie's birth and moved back in with Rebecca. When his mother went back to work, Rebecca became Robbie's caregiver. Then Veronica died in a traffic accident a few months later, and Rebecca continued to care for Robbie full-time after his mother's death. Until now, his father had been okay with that arrangement.

Like it or not, Frank could do whatever he wished with Robbie. They both knew the state always sided with a child's parent, even if he'd never shown any interest in his child.

But why the sudden interest now?

Frank seemed to read her thoughts. "So, since I've gotten married again, I thought it time to bring Robbie back into my world. You see?" He hesitated, waiting for a reaction that didn't come. He began to tap his fingers on the table impatiently. "You got any coffee or something?" Frank craned his neck and glowered at the stairway. "The kid's taking forever to pack his stuff."

Rebecca stiffened. It took all her resolve not to pour hot coffee over him. She filled a mug with shaky hands and thumped it down in front of him. "You know where the sugar and cream are. I'll go help Robbie pack."

She paused at the door to Robbie's bedroom and watched him lift clothing from his dresser drawer one piece at a time and carefully place it in the carrying case his father had shoved at him the moment he came through the door.

Robbie heard everything we said, she thought. Rebecca tried to will away her tears, but couldn't. Robbie looked so confused. She couldn't frighten him further by letting him see her cry. She stepped away from the door and into the bathroom. Wetting a cloth, she washed her tear-stained face. Nothing about this made sense. Okay, even if Frank resented the increase, did he think it would be cheaper to raise Robbie himself?

Rebecca shook her head, bringing herself back to the present. That was days ago and she'd heard nothing from him since. She desperately wanted to know that Robbie was all right.

At first, she'd hoped he'd tire of Robbie and bring him back. What if his new wife didn't want to raise someone else's child? It happens. Rebecca blew her nose, wiped her eyes, and sighed. The questions kept coming. What if they had a child of their own? Poor Robbie would always be the one who didn't belong. Would they still want him then? Being a woman, his new stepmother might be kinder than Robbie's father. She wished for that, even allowed herself to hope for it. More than anything she wanted Robbie to be where he was loved and happy.

Then a terrifying possibility crossed her mind. Families were limited to only three children. If his new stepmother wanted them all to be her own, where would that leave Robbie?

The color drained from her face. She suddenly felt very cold. Rebecca buried her face in her hands. It was too awful to think about. Even Frank wouldn't do *that*. Would he? If he did, how would she ever know?

She recalled that China's experience with limiting families to only one child had proven disastrous. With so many couples aborting girls in order to have a boy, a generation of young men grew up without enough women to marry. As a result, China's problems were legion. The best educated men left China to seek their livelihood elsewhere. Some imported mates from neighboring countries. Others, angry and frustrated, turned to criminal violence.

As more countries decided to limit population growth in order to control the masses, they hoped to avoid what happened in China. Most decided to recommend only two children per family and allow no more than three. Rebecca hadn't expected that proclamation to affect her as it now seemed to.

She ran to the computer screen in the corner of her kitchen and clicked the "FIND" button. When a box appeared, she entered the correct town and typed *Frank Wilson*, searching for his address. As the computer searched local databases, she realized how much of a stranger he was. Other than the general area, she had no idea where, or how, Frank lived.

She wanted to check on Robbie's new surroundings and make sure he was okay. She knew Robbie's father would be hostile to visits, but she didn't care. Robbie was *her* grandson. Frank had no right to keep them apart. One way or another, she'd find a way to see Robbie and lay her fears to rest.

ℰℭ

Eileen Abramson swept her blond hair behind her ears, grabbed a tissue and dabbed at her eyes. She picked up the offending test stick and held it up for another check. She sniffed, blew her nose, and left the bathroom holding the pregnancy test results in front of her. At the door of the master bedroom she paused to watch her husband tickle their twin boys as they rolled around their parents' bed. The toddlers laughed and giggled.

"Jacob, here it is." She held it out to her husband.

He squinted at it for a moment. "The lines are pink. What does that mean?"

"It means you picked the wrong day to feel amorous. We should have considered the time of the month before going to bed instead of thinking about it the next morning." She toppled into his arms. Tears brimmed in her eyes. "I'm pregnant, Jacob." She sniffed. "What are we going to do?"

With the children still squirming on the bed, he wrapped his arms around his wife. He cradled her head against his shoulder as she softly wept, and patted her back to reassure her. "A new baby is meant to be a blessing and should always bring joy. I'm so sorry it doesn't right now, Sweetheart."

"Like it or not, I seem to get pregnant every 18 months," she said into his shoulder. "But, in spite of everything, there's part of me that's elated." Eileen leaned back and considered her husband's kind face. She placed a hand on his cheek and let her fingers run up through his dark brown hair. "Our children, Mandy, Nathan and Noah..." She rubbed her eyes. "What are we going to do? I won't contemplate an abortion. It's too horrible to consider."

Jacob held her at arm's length. They locked eyes. "I'd love to have as many children with you as possible. If only our society wasn't in such a mess." He sighed and fell back onto the bed, pulling his wife down beside him. The twin toddlers immediately crawled in between them.

Eileen wrapped her arms around 18-month-old Noah. "These two are inseparable. We can't—" Her voice trailed off, leaving the thought unspoken.

"You're thinking it should be Mandy?" He frowned. "I can't imagine that either."

Hearing her name, three-year-old Mandy came flying through the doorway and leaped onto the bed. She shouted, "Group hug, group hug!"

The toddlers left their parents' arms to crawl all over their big sister.

Eileen picked up Jacob's hand and placed it on her abdomen. "This baby is a living human being with every right to life," she whispered. Her eyes went to the raucous trio giggling and laughing as they rolled around the bed hugging one another. "Just like our three there. So, how do we reconcile having four children, when we know the state will demand one of them be sacrificed?"

He swallowed hard and shook his head; he had no answer. Putting his arm around Eileen's shoulder, he hugged her to him.

CHAPTER FIVE

"The test of the morality of a society is what it does for its children." ~ Dietrich Bonhoeffer

Giles raised his eyes when he heard the elevator's doors open. He frowned as Director Hastings stepped into the hallway. He hated it when she showed up unannounced. *What'd the bitch want now?* He shut the door to his storage room and headed down the corridor to meet her.

He forced a crooked smile. "Good afternoon, Ma'am. It's good t' see ya again. Always at yur service. What might I do fur ya, Ma'am?"

"I wondered if I might see today's children."

He started to roll his eyes, but caught himself. Straightening, Giles gave a sharp nod. "You betcha, Ma'am. After all, yur the boss, ain't ya?" He gave a self-conscious giggle. "If ya wanna see the kids, I'm ready 'n willing to show 'em to ya. They'd be down there in the holding room."

"Don't you mean the corral?" Mira asked, with an eyebrow cocked upward.

He swallowed hard. *How did she know that's what he called it?* "Oh no, Ma'am. Regulations say it's the holding room. That's where we hold the incoming tots until, well...um... Right this way, Ma'am."

Giles spun on his heels and headed down the hall at a brisk pace. He needed to get there before her in case she planned on whipping out her white gloves and doing some kind of impromptu inspection. He was breathing hard by the time he reached the holding room.

The heavy door creaked when he threw it back. A few children turned and blankly peered in his direction. He ran his eyes around the room, checking to make sure nothing was out of order. Two little girls sat huddled together in a corner, one dozing against her new friend's shoulder. The other kept an arm around her and stared listlessly at the ceiling. Some youngsters were sleeping on the bare cement floor, while others aimlessly wandered the empty space.

He smiled to himself. The valium-laced cookies had taken effect. Let 'er inspect her heart out. All was as tranquil as could be.

"So, this is everyone taken in today?" Mira asked.

Giles gave a start at the sound of her voice.

Icy fingers clutched his stomach as she scowled down at him. A bead of perspiration formed along his lip. Giles licked it away nervously while doing his best to appear nonchalant.

"Umm, yeah...sure. Just a typical day, ya know. Nothing out of the ordinary. No more than usual. No less than usual. About the same number of kids as always, actually." He was saying too much, and knew it. Short of grabbing his jaw and holding his mouth shut, there didn't seem to be a way to stop himself. He took a deep breath and wiped the back of his sleeve across his forehead. "Just as I said...a typical day."

He hated the idea of answering to a woman, especially one who towered over him. He'd been here longer and knew the protocols better than she did. He should have her position. Then *she* could answer to *him*.

"What about the realignment charges for each child? Did everyone pay promptly? Any fees still outstanding?"

Giles jabbed a thumb into the chest of his olive-green uniform. "I know how to do my job. Everyone paid a fee fur their kid upfront."

Mira's brows furrowed. If someone failed to pay the FFU she might be able to develop other options for the youngster. At the very least, she could suspend the process due to nonpayment which especially benefitted an older child.

She gazed around the room and her eyes landed on a little girl with curly blond hair. She was leaning against the wall with her legs tucked under her. Although Mira couldn't know it, she was the same girl Giles forced to clean up Robbie's blood.

"What about that one over there." Mira pointed at the

lethargic youngster whose eyes were red and swollen. "She looks too old."

"Naw, I checked. She's less than four years. All of 'em had their birth certificates when I registered 'em. They got her here just in time. If her auntie'd waited another week, it'd been too late." Giles began tapping his foot.

"She could be especially bright. If my hunch is right there's an advantage in saving her for the children's Foundling Home of Future Contributors." She turned to Giles. "I think we should have her intelligence tested."

Giles gritted his teeth. "And if she ain't particularly bright, which I don' think she is, then she'll be past four-years-old and too late for the FFU. You thought about that?"

Of course she had, that was the point. But, she'd never return a youngster to a family that didn't want her either. When tested, this child's intelligence would rank high enough to ensure a place at the Foundling Home of Future Contributors.

Mira walked over to the little girl and reached for her nametag. *Emma Jane Spencer.* She wanted to talk sweetly to Emma, reassure her. But with Giles in the room she hesitated. If he started talking about her being softhearted toward the children, it could jeopardize her job.

Mira reached down and took the little girl's hand. "Emma, I'm Ms. Hastings. I want you to come with me."

Emma pulled away from her. She'd seen what happened when a woman came to take a child away. She gave Giles a terrified sidelong glance, rolled her fingers into tight fists and held them at her side.

Mira took the girl's hand and tugged her closer. "It will be all right." With her back to Giles, she smiled at Emma and winked encouragingly.

Giles watched the back of Director's head, scowling. Every time he turned around, she was sticking her nose into his business. She had too much power. If you asked him, her *High and Mightiness* was out of control. Why spare a child who would take years to develop? It made no sense. Wards of the state were a drain on society, everybody knew that. Obliterate unwanted children. That's what the FFUs were for. He had parents who wanted and raised him, didn't he? Well, they should too.

"You sure you wanna do this?" Giles called from across the room.

His question went unanswered.

Giles revulsion grew as he watched the Director interact with Emma. Didn't she have work to do? Why was she down here touching and fawning over the kids? It's not like they were worth anything. You'd think she was choosing a pet kitten to take home. My 'us well drown 'em all like kittens in a sack. They're worth 'bout as much, he thought.

Mira walked little Emma to the door without a word. They left the holding room hand-in-hand and walked to the elevators.

There were times when Mira could barely tolerate being in the same room with Giles. Even though he made her skin crawl, a part of her pitied people like him. She'd always told herself that any person, regardless of their moral status, had the potential to rise above their past and reorder their life. Since meeting Giles she'd begun to wonder. Perhaps some people had sought the low and base so long they'd stunted their spirit and built an unbreachable wall between themselves and what was good and noble in life.

Mira inspected the little girl at her side and gave her an encouraging smile as they waited for the elevator. A pair of red-rimmed blue eyes lifted to meet Mira's. The child made a weak attempt to smile back. If I'd spent my morning in that holding room, I wouldn't feel much like smiling either, Mira thought.

When the elevator doors rattled open, she gave Emma's hand a gentle tug, and they stepped inside. The elevator slowly rose and Mira began to plan. She could delay testing and wait until Emma turned four, or go ahead with testing immediately. Either way she'd ensure Emma went to a Foundling Home to be cared for, trained for an acceptable profession, and allowed to grow up.

CHAPTER SIX

The large garage door was open when Aranda pulled into the driveway. She drove right in and, as soon as she did, a young man sprinted out to close the heavy door behind her.

It pleased Aranda to know Jonathan Bracken had been watching for her. When the garage's side door opened, she watched Jonathan enter and hold it for his mother, Carolyn. Sunlight funneled through the open door filling the garage with brightness. A light breeze whistled in behind them, tousling his dark hair and ruffling Carolyn's skirt.

A walled courtyard spanned the space between the house and garage, offering complete privacy.

By the time Aranda slipped out from under the steering wheel, the two were at her side. Jonathan hugged her first and then Carolyn pulled Aranda into a one-armed hug. Aranda had long since stopped noticing the older woman's missing arm. She was simply Carolyn, a warm and loving grandmotherly type who helped rescue children.

Carolyn hurried around the car and opened the passenger door. The seat was reclined to cradle the bundle lying there. She undid the seatbelt and folded the laundry towels back. "Oh my, he's such an adorable little fellow." She stroked his cheek and smiled.

Robbie thrashed and moaned in his sleep.

The young man crowded in behind her for a peek at their newest charge and grinned. Raising his head, he stared across the roof of the car at Aranda. "We were worried. What took you so long?"

"I'm sorry. Giles arrived late today. He arranged for the previous shift to stay and cover for him, but no one bothered to tell me. I had to wait until everybody else went home and Giles was alone." She sighed. "To make matters worse, Director Hastings almost caught us."

Aranda rubbed her temple as she circled the car. At the other side, she leaned against it, sighing. "Carolyn, will you and Jonathan take care of his hand? It's bad enough to witness such brutality. Seeing it again would bring it all back."

"We'll take care of him." Carolyn studied her with concern. "Are you getting another migraine?"

"I drove home blinking through bright spots and flashes. Thankfully, God answered my prayers and got us here safely." She turned to walk away then hesitated. "I had to give him a second whiff of ether to be sure he slept. He might be under longer than usual."

Jonathan leaned around Carolyn and lifted the child's hand. A blood-stained towel covered the injury. "The bleeding isn't excessive. You did a good job staunching his wound. What's his name?"

Aranda squinted and kneaded her fingers over the pain on the side of her head. "I can't remember. Giles wasn't exactly patient." She shook her head. "There were so many children there. It's always heartbreaking. I feel like the Grim Reaper deciding who lives and who dies." Aranda pressed a palm against each temple. "I think the FFU roster said Robert something or other. Giles kept his tag."

Jonathan went to her and patted her back. "Go lie down and sleep away the headache. We'll take care of your precious cargo."

"Thank you." Aranda reached up and gently touched Jonathan's cheek. Their eyes met and she smiled for a second before going into the house.

Jonathan crossed his arms and watched her go, his eyes lingering wistfully.

His mother nudged him, and he gave a surprised jerk.

"Sorry if I'm intruding," she said, with a grin and a wink.

His cheeks colored. "I don't know what you mean. Was there, uh...something you wanted?"

"I want to be sure you secured the garage door. There have

been more break-ins in the neighborhood lately."

"Got it covered," he said with a nod. "Let me carry little *Robert* inside for you, Mom."

"Thank you, sweetheart, I always appreciate your help." She tugged her sweater up over her left shoulder. With no arm to hold the sweater in place, it kept slipping down. Now in her sixties, Carolyn Bracken had never married or given birth to any children, but Jonathan and several other young adults owed their lives to her. She considered them her children, and liked it when they called her *Mom*.

෴

Jonathan laid little Robert down on the bed that would be his for the next several days. He filled a syringe and handed it to Carolyn. Gently lifting the boy's hand, Jonathan cradled it and extended it toward his mother.

The youngster tossed and turned in his sleep. He whimpered in pain when she injected the numbing solution into his tiny hand. The anesthetic would help him feel better and, when he awoke, they'd offer him a tempting meal.

Many of the new arrivals didn't want to eat. For all a child knew, they could still be in the FFU. She enticed the frightened children with lots of tempting choices. Carolyn grocery shopped with them in mind, trying to create menus a child would like.

Jonathan's gaze moved from the child to Carolyn. "I hope Aranda's okay."

"I'm sure she will be. You know, you can go talk to her. She won't mind."

He shrugged and stared at the floor. "What Aranda said didn't make you feel bad...did it, Mom?"

"Why? What did she say that might have bothered me?"

"About them lopping part of this boy's finger off. That's nothing compared to losing an arm."

She dropped the empty syringe into a biohaz container and

laid her arm over Jonathan's shoulders. "Honey, don't worry. I've never known anything else. I'm grateful for my life, even if I do only have one arm." She smiled at him and caressed his jaw. "I feel very blessed. We weep for those who are lost, but I'm grateful to be able to save even a few of these little ones."

"No one else feels like you do."

She stepped back. "How can you say such a thing? Of course they do. Many people oppose what's happening in our nation." She took a deep breath, "...and in our world."

"Yeah, well then, why aren't more people doing something about it?"

Carolyn sighed deeply. "Who can say? We're placed here to do what we can. As for those who don't care as much as they should, well, they have to deal with their own consciences."

⁊ʘ

Little Robbie sat up. His vision was blurry, his ears were ringing and he felt sick. Memories of the cold room he'd been in slowly materialized. Prickles of fright danced in his stomach. He gradually became aware of two people standing next to him. The woman spoke to him in a kind voice the same way Gramma did. As his sight cleared he peered around the room. It was pretty, with nice furniture. Not like the ugly room he was in before. And it wasn't cold here either.

Maybe this was a safe place.

He wobbled from side to side, leaning precariously toward the edge of the bed. Both adults scurried to catch him. Unable to stop himself, he threw up on their shoes.

Feeling better, Robbie sank back into the pillows, closed his eyes and went back to sleep.

CHAPTER SEVEN

The blond, blue-eyed child silently waited on a couch in Mira's office. She flinched at a rap on the door.

"Come in," Mira called.

Carolyn Bracken entered the Director's office and Mira crossed the room to greet her. When the door closed behind them, Carolyn put her one arm around Mira's shoulders and gave her a hug. "Is everything okay?"

"As okay as anything can be at an FFU." Mira relaxed in Carolyn's presence. "Did Aranda arrive home safely?"

"Yes, she's fine and so is the little boy. We couldn't manage without your help. And now with Giles demanding more cash..." she sighed. "That places an additional burden on you."

"No one else needs to know I provide the money to pay the ransom he extorts." Mira clasped Carolyn's hand warmly between both of hers. "Thank you for coming on such short notice."

"Your call was unexpected. What's up?"

Mira smiled at the older woman. "We got a twofer today. Come meet Emma." She gestured across the room. The little girl's eyes were downcast and she'd pulled her legs under her. She appeared lost on the oversized couch.

"Hello," Carolyn said, dropping onto the couch beside Emma.

The child's eyes darted to Carolyn, then to Mira, and back to the hands in her lap. She was sniffing, trying not to cry.

Mira knelt in front of her and took Emma's hands into her own. "Emma Spencer meet Carolyn Bracken." She turned to Carolyn, still holding the child's hands. "Emma will be four next week, so we should move her into the Foundling Home of Future Contributors as soon as possible." Mira cupped Emma's chin. "I'm sure Emma's very smart, but she'll require verification from *Bright Minds*."

"We'll certainly test her," Carolyn said with a knowing nod. "I realize your position here requires you to distance yourself from any resistance to FFUs. But, you're very effective working behind the scenes. You've saved many little lives passing through this facility and at high risk to yourself."

"It's nothing compared to what you're doing. It took a great deal of effort to convince government officials they might be losing potential geniuses. You pointed out the loss of any exceptionally bright child is a waste of resources that can negatively impact a nation's future."

"They eventually relented. Thankfully all senior managers at FFUs have the discretion to decide if a child brought to their FFU merits testing as a potential genius. There are a few other Directors like you, Mira, who send children to Bright Minds." She smiled, "We help them become geniuses."

Carolyn studied the nervous child beside her. She appeared to follow the conversation, trying to make sense of it. *Maybe she's not a genius, but she is intelligent. That will make it easier to help her pass Bright Mind's tests.* "Come along, Emma, it's time to leave."

Mira walked Carolyn and Emma out of the building and across the parking lot to Carolyn's car. She waited as Carolyn belted the little girl into the back seat.

When they were out of Emma's hearing, Carolyn turned to Mira. "As an abortion survivor, I can't thank you enough for each and every life you save." She reached out and took Mira's hand.

Mira raised her eyebrows. "Abortion survivor? You?"

"Haven't you ever wondered how I lost my arm?"

"It was none of my business."

Carolyn shrugged. "It's more your business than anyone else's." She cast her eyes skyward before continuing. "Fortunately for me, a sympathetic nurse assisted the man doing the procedure. She carried me out of their *killing room.* That's what I choose to call it. When I was born there was still a legal requirement that any child born alive had to be cared for. Most abortionists didn't observe it, but this nurse did. She phoned for emergency back-up. Something in her conscience made her keep me from bleeding to death from the loss of my arm. She saved my life."

"But, you were only a newborn. How do you know that's what happened?"

"From my mother."

"You've got to be kidding. She went in for an abortion, yet claimed you when it failed?"

"She told me when she heard my weak cry she had a change of heart. She yelled at the nurse, 'save my baby.' Maybe that's what impelled the nurse to act." Carolyn reached to touch her empty shoulder and smiled at Mira. "My mother never lied to me, and I'm here."

"She raised you?"

"Yes, and told me over and over how much she regretted her attempt to get rid of me. I'm convinced she suffered from the loss of my arm far more than I have."

"It's a miracle you were spared. Most abortionists won't quit hacking away until the baby's ripped to pieces. The fact that you only lost an arm is a miracle. No wonder saving children is so important to you."

"I hope it would be important to me regardless."

Carolyn opened the car door and leaned in toward Emma. "Sweetheart, I'm going to take you home with me until your birthday next week. We'll have cake and ice cream, and then you'll go to a brand new home with lots of other children. I'm sure you'll like it there."

Emma released the latch on her seatbelt and tossed it aside. She climbed out of the car and trotted over to Mira. "Can't I go home with you?"

A look of surprise filled Mira's face. She stooped down. "Emma, I can't keep you. I wish I could. There are other children I have to help. Understand?"

Emma shrugged and turned her gaze to Carolyn. "Will I have a bed, or do I sleep on the floor like at my aunt's?"

Carolyn laughed. "You'll have a bed in a very nice room with a window. We'll even bake a cake for your birthday."

Emma smiled and took Carolyn's hand.

৪০৫৪

Robbie sat at the table in a booster seat, absentmindedly watching Aranda at the stove while Jonathan moved around him arranging silverware on placemats. He wanted to tell them to call him Robbie, not *Robert*, but couldn't muster up the courage.

When the kitchen door opened, they all turned in its direction. Carolyn entered the kitchen with Emma in tow.

"Perfect timing. Dinner is almost ready." Aranda grinned at Emma. "We'll set another place. Are you hungry?"

Emma nodded. The delicious food smells swirling around the kitchen were enough to make everyone's mouth water.

"You can sit here." Carolyn said, pulling out a chair.

Robbie watched Emma climb up beside him. "You w-w-ere th -th-there t-t-too," he stammered.

Emma recognized the boy who'd lost his finger. Her eyes went to the bandage around his left hand. "Does it hurt?"

Robbie peeked at his hand, but didn't answer.

"My name's Emma. What's yours?"

"Rrrr-ooob-b-b-bi-bi-biee..." He frowned. He'd never had trouble saying his name before. Something happened to his mouth while he was in that bad place. It didn't work right any more. Afraid to say anything else, he stared at the table.

Jonathan sat a glass of milk on their placemats. "I helped Robbie take a bath and put on some clean clothes from our donation cupboard. I want you to see the bruises on his upper arms, Mom. I think someone shook him."

Robbie's head popped up, his face fearful.

Carolyn sat beside him and looked into his eyes. "Robbie, no one is going to do that to you here. Will you tell me who did it?"

Robbie turned away.

"Was it the man who was in charge of the children?"

Robbie's chin gave a slight movement from side to side.

"Who then?"

He studied his plate, pretending not to hear. He remembered when Father grabbed him by the arms to shake him. He'd cried for Gramma, and it made Father even madder. He quit asking for her after that. He tried to stop crying too, he really did. He knew if he didn't stop crying, Father would stay mad. But, the more Father yelled, the harder it got not to cry. No one had ever yelled at him like that before.

The very next day Father woke him early. He shoved dry toast at him and told him to hurry up and eat it. Having missed dinner, Robbie was hungry. He had no trouble eating the plain toast and drinking the milk. He would have liked more, but was afraid to ask.

"I'm disgusted with you," his father said.

He remembered; that was exactly what Father had said, *"I'm disgusted with you."* He definitely said that. Robbie searched his memory trying to remember what else he said. *"You qualify as useless."* Yes, that was it.

When the wheels came off his toy truck Gramma said it was kinda useless without wheels, but she knew he liked it so she let him keep it anyway. What did it mean if *he* was useless?

CHAPTER EIGHT

Robbie lay in his bed weeping. It was dark outside and everyone else was asleep. He wasn't afraid in this new, strange place. The people here were kind. He wept because his hand throbbed. Why did it hurt so much underneath the wrapping, and why wouldn't they let him see it?

Just enough light filtered in through the curtains for Robbie to make out objects in the room. He stared at the large, white bandage wrapped around his hand. He wiggled his fingers a little and moaned in pain. Even having Gramma take that big splinter out didn't hurt this bad. If Gramma was here she'd make it better.

Did he fall and hurt his finger? He didn't remember falling. In fact, he couldn't remember anything after Aranda asked him if he wanted to come with her. He was glad to be out of the other place, but wished his hand didn't hurt.

Deciding the way to find out why it hurt was to unwrap it, Robbie began picking at the bandage. He worked slowly, trying not to make it hurt more than it already did. The tape didn't want to come off, but he kept at it.

೮೦೧

Emma heard Robbie's sobs through the wall and wondered why no one else did. She couldn't sleep either, but she knew better than to cry. Crying always made her aunt angry.

When she couldn't stand the weeping any longer, Emma got out of bed and slipped on the pink slippers and bathrobe they'd laid out for her. The slipper's soft fleece hugged her toes, making her smile. They were much nicer than anything she'd had at Aunt Reeta's.

Emma quietly opened her bedroom door. She peered up and down the hall before stepping out. Robbie's room was right next to hers, and it only took a few steps to scurry over. She reached his door and hesitated. She knew she should knock, but that might wake everybody up. She gently turned the knob, eased the door open and hurried inside. Robbie's head jerked toward her.

She closed the door softly behind her and tiptoed over to sit on the edge of his bed. "Robbie," she whispered, "are you okay?"

He held out his hand. He was half way there. Strips of tape and bandages dangled down. "It h-h-hurts."

Emma shivered. The image of Giles slicing off half of Robbie's little finger remained all too sharp in her memory. "I hope it gets better real quick."

"Why does it h-h-hurt so b-b-bad?"

"Don't you remember?"

He shook his head. His lips puckered up and he sniffed.

Emma took his elbow. She didn't want to touch his hand. "I don't think you should do this. It needs to stay covered up to get well." *Did fingers grow back?* They must because she'd never seen anyone without a finger. But, Mrs. Bracken, Aunt Carolyn, didn't have an arm. Maybe Robbie would never get his finger back either. "Robbie, lay down and close your eyes. In the morning, you can tell Aunt Carolyn it hurts and she'll make it better."

"I w-w-want it b-b-better now!" Robbie shouted. "It h-h-hurts awful!" He started wailing.

Emma jumped up. Someone would surely hear him now and come into the bedroom. She started for the door, but heard footsteps thumping down the hall. Spinning, she spied a chest of drawers and ducked behind its farthest end.

The door opened and Carolyn Bracken walked in. "Robbie honey, what's wrong?"

Sniveling and hiccupping, Robbie held out his hand.

"Oh dear, you've been playing with your bandage. That's not what you should do." She went to his side and took his bandaged hand in hers. "I'll get Jonathan to help me rewrap it." As she turned she saw Emma out the side of her eye. "Emma, it's okay. I'm sure you were trying to help. Knock on Jonathan's door and tell him I need him in Robbie's room."

Emma nodded and headed for the door.

"Be sure to knock and listen for his answer."

Emma scooted out of the room as fast as her legs would carry her. As soon as she woke Jonathan, she headed back to her own bed. This was too much excitement for the middle of the night, besides she'd already had more than enough stress for one day.

෨ශ

Jonathan and Carolyn stepped out into the hall and he quietly closed Robbie's door behind them. "That didn't take long. He's sound asleep already."

She sighed. "I should have realized the Novocain would wear off before morning and given him another shot at bedtime."

"He was a brave little sport, though." Jonathan ran a hand through his hair and yawned. "Good thing you warned him about his damaged little finger before you unwrapped it."

"He'd have been more shocked if he'd seen the exposed tendon and bone before we worked on it." Carolyn tightened the belt on her robe. "Cutting back the tendon, removing the bone chips and filing down what was left of the proximal phalange would traumatize any child."

Jonathan yawned again. His mother expected him to understand, and he did. Her nursing skills led him to study medicine. All he'd ever wanted to be was a doctor and he was excelling in his university pre-med classes.

"He can tell we want what's best for him," Carolyn said. "Unlike so many of the children we get, I think someone loved and cared for him. Otherwise, he wouldn't be so trusting."

"I could make a prosthesis for his little finger. I bet he'd like that." Jonathan stifled another yawn. "Sometimes one evil parent attempts to punish the other by disposing of their child. He might still have a parent who loves him."

"Try to find out. I'll check on Emma while you put things away." She stretched up to kiss her son's cheek. "See you in the morning."

ം⊃ൟ

Emma's soft snores told Carolyn she was sleeping soundly. She eased the bedroom door closed and went back to her own room. The children were her responsibility for now and it weighed heavily on her. Soon enough they'd go to the local Foundling Home of Future Contributors, but until then she had to keep them safe and show them all the love she could.

A familiar fear gripped her. She wasn't a young woman anymore. Who would take over if anything happened to her? There were many who secretly rescued children, but she was the only contact for FFU-1116.

To accomplish what she did, she couldn't allow herself to become discouraged by the multitude of deaths every year at the local facility; or the enormous number *every day* nationwide. She had to focus on those she could save, did save. She knew in her heart that every life was precious.

Denied access to medical training because of her disability, Carolyn had sought out caring doctors as mentors and read everything she could about the care of the sick and injured. Out of necessity, learning to care for amputated fingers became her specialty. When Aranda wasn't available to help with a surgery, Jonathan became her extra pair of hands.

She wanted the children who lost half a digit to have as much mobility as possible and did her work with meticulous care. Most of them never experienced any loss of sensation in the remaining stump, or in their palms. What they felt in their *phantom finger*, however, varied from child to child.

She prayed her health would hold out until Jonathan, or someone like him, could take over.

CHAPTER NINE

"Perhaps it is impossible for a person who does no good to do no harm. ~ Harriet Beecher Stowe

While Robbie and Emma remained safe and sound at Carolyn Bracken's home, new groups of youngsters continued moving through FFU-1116.

Frightened and physically stressed, they were left without toys or entertainment. Alone in the holding room, they only had each other. Some wept, others tried to play together, creating make-believe race tracks or castles with princesses. Giles allowed them out of the room only for designated bathroom breaks, and several of the children experienced accidents. Most toddlers wore soiled diapers, but Giles wasn't about to change them.

After what seemed like forever to the children, the room's only door screeched open. The loud clatter of a cart preceded Giles as he wheeled it into the room. It held plain, dry bread and pitchers of water.

Driven by hunger, the children ran to the cart grabbing for the bread. The shy ones held back for a moment then quickly joined the others. Toddlers too small to get to the food, watched and wept.

Like ravenous animals, Giles thought, shaking his head in disgust. I might as well be on a farm dumping slop in a trough for hogs. He turned when he heard the door open behind him.

Aranda Blackthorn entered the room. "You're relieved of this responsibility. I've been told to serve the children their water." It wasn't true, but she expected him to be happy about it.

His brow furrowed. "At's odd."

"Would you rather do it yourself? I assumed you'd be happy to take off early, given the chance." She turned to leave. "I can find something else to do and be glad for it."

He wrinkled his nose at her. "Naw, the stinky things are all yours. Why waste good food on 'em is what I say."

"You begrudge them stale rolls donated by a neighborhood market and a few sips of water? Bread and water doesn't sound like a banquet to me." Turning her back to him, Aranda walked to the cart and began pouring water into paper cups and handing them out to the children. Many of those who'd been crying were headachy from dehydration.

Giles slouched with his hands on his hips, watching her work. He particularly liked studying the sway of her hips as she moved from child to child. "Yeah, well, as long as it ain't wastin' no more money. Givin' 'em somethin' to stuff in their mouths keeps 'em quiet. With any luck they'll stop their whining 'til their time comes." He turned to grab the door handle, stepped out and slammed the door behind him.

The children jumped.

Aranda scanned the room and sighed. "You all deserve better than this, sweethearts. I'm so sorry." Seeing their condition tore at her heart, but salvaging even one, made it worthwhile no matter how much it hurt to be there. She stroked a little toddler's sweaty brown curls as she held the cup so the child could drink.

Even condemned prisoners get a last meal, she thought, *but look at what these children have.*

෨෬

Glad to be home early, Giles marched up the sidewalk toward the door of his duplex. He had the key in his lock when the landlord called to him from next door. He rolled his eyes and ground his teeth. *Ah geez, what's the old coot want now?*

The elderly gentleman took a step away from his own door in order to see Giles better. "I'm sorry to bother you, Mr. Giles, but it's your dog again." His voice trembled as he spoke. "He spends most of the day barking and people in the neighborhood are complaining to me about him."

"How many times we been over this? I ain't gonna have surgery done on *her* so *she* can't bark. She's supposed to bark. *She's* a *guard dog.*" His lips curled into a snarl. "Now, I don't wanna hear no more about it, ya hear me?"

Giles punched his fist into the cedar siding on the wall, splitting the board. He opened his door and went inside, allowing it to bang closed before his landlord had a chance to say any more.

The moment Giles entered his side of the duplex, a white pit bull leaped at him, tail wagging. She wasn't tall enough to reach his face, so he knelt down and let her lick him.

"How ya doin', Bella Baby? Bet you're sick and tired o' bein' alone all day. I don't blame ya." He ruffled the dog's ears. She whimpered in approval when he scratched her back. "Let's get outta here. I'll take you out t' do yur bizness, 'n then we'll hightail it over to the park. Maybe get us a coupla hot dogs from the cart for dinner, okay?"

The dog woofed and leaped in the air.

Giles laughed. "I'd rather have dinner in the park with you than with any other selfish, 'spensive bitch of a broad." He snickered, "Hey, Bella, did ya hear the joke I jus' made? Called all women bitches, when you're one too." He grinned. "I'm a pretty funny guy, ain't I?" He continued chuckling to himself as he lifted the dog's leash off the door handle where he'd draped it that morning.

A tremor of fear rippled through his landlord as he watched Giles depart. He rued the day he'd ever rented the duplex to Giles. But he didn't dare evict him. Who knew what a person like him was capable of?

℘☙

In the park, Giles bought four hot dogs, sat on a bench and watched Bella wolf down two of them before he'd even taken a bite. He cracked open the over-sized can of malt liquor he'd carried from home and guzzled half of it before attacking one of the hot dogs.

All was quiet except for laughing children on swings at the other end of the park. "Damned kids," he snorted. "Bad enough I have to deal with the little buggers at work. Oughtn't to have to hear 'em the rest of the time."

The dog lifted her ears, tilted her head and stared at him.

"Aww here," he tossed her another bite of hot dog. "You're my girl, ain't ya, Bella"

"Hey mister, is your dog friendly?"

Giles slowly turned, giving the two young boys a quick once over. "Why not find out for yourself."

They took a step closer and Bella started to growl. She leaped at them, straining against the leash and snarling.

The boys turned and ran. Bella tried to chase them, but Giles held fast to her leash.

"Useless bastards. I wish I could let you have a go at 'em. Bet you'd tear the little jerks limb from limb. But, that'd get us in trouble. They prob'ly got parents what don't think they're useless." He patted the dog. "Good girl. Settle down now. You done good ... just relax."

Bella laid down at his feet, head up and ears erect. Giles finished the rest of his malt liquor and pitched the empty can over his shoulder. It clanked on the sidewalk before rolling onto the freshly mowed grass.

"Let's take a walk, Bella? There's someone I wanna check back on."

෧෬

Giles stood outside Mira Hastings's residence searching for a window where the curtains weren't drawn. He knew where she lived and had followed her home several times. From what he could tell she lived alone. The situation posed some interesting possibilities.

He'd had tempting thoughts about her for weeks now. He wouldn't need much, a way in, a ski mask and a knife. Watching her squirm would be half the fun. She'd never know the person she browbeat by day used her like a cheap hooker one night.

Yup, he liked thinking about that...a lot.

He circled her house in the dim evening light, surveying potential entry points. If he was discovered wandering in her side yard, or anywhere else, he had an excuse. He'd simply say he had to retrieve his dog. Giles grinned. He was smart; he always had an answer.

He skulked past each window, lurking in the shadows, hoping to watch her. But, try as he might, he'd never been able to catch a glimpse of her. Didn't matter, he'd find a way in. He always did.

One of these days, Mira Hastings, you'll get yours, he thought, smirking.

He walked back to the front of the house and onto the sidewalk. "Let's head home, Bella. It's gettin' breezy out here. We'll catch some sports on the TV. Think I'll pick up another six-pack on the way."

Then he heard Mira's voice at the back of the house.

"Here kitty, kitty."

His skin prickled. If he'd been in the backyard when she opened the door to call her cat, she'd have recognized him. He breathed a sigh of relief, and a wicked gleam lit his eyes. Some dark night he could crouch behind that bush with the giant blue flowers by her front door and wait for her to come home. Then he'd rush up wearing his ski mask, knife in hand.

"If she'd caught me 'n you in her backyard, Bella, I might've had to kill her. I could do that, but it's too quick. I'm gonna cut her and make her pay. Watch her suffer."

He kicked leaves off the sidewalk as he walked. "Next time I'm here, Bella, you'll stay home. I'll be geared up and ready for her." He snickered when a new idea formed in his mind. "Why should I be the only one having fun with the Director? Maybe I'll bring her cat back for you to play with. How'd you like to eat her cat?"

Giles giggled with anticipation. Yup, he was clever all right.

CHAPTER TEN

"Can a woman forget her nursing child and have no compassion on the son of her womb? Even these may forget, but I will not forget you. Behold, I have inscribed you on the palms of My hands; Your walls are continually before Me..."

~ Isaiah 49:15-16

Grayson Stevens entered the courthouse a half hour before the trial began. He'd prepared a solid case against the man accused of drowning his two-year-old son in the family bathtub. As distasteful as the crime was to him, he sought the case. He wanted to put the defendant behind bars.

Although considered a possession of their parents, the government frowned on the wanton destruction of a child without due process. Current government directives stipulated that children under four years of age could be *humanely* disposed of, but only when turned in at a licensed Facility For the Useless.

Sanctioned by law, like abortion clinics, the FFUs operated as independent entities. A few national chains controlled most of them and enriched themselves by killing unwanted children. However, unlike abortion clinics an FFU required no skilled medical staff, making the profit margin that much higher.

Each FFU contributed a set fee per child to a national association which represented their common interests. Hired lobbyists, directly or indirectly, funneled huge amounts of money into politicians' pockets. Bought and paid for, they quickly squelched any legislation that limited the power of the FFUs. Those at the top were fat and happy. The last thing they wanted was people killing their own kids. Where was the profit in that?

The defense planned to claim the man on trial had returned home drunk, and acted impulsively. His motivation? The child wouldn't quit crying and made his aching head feel like it would explode. They'd argue he could have taken the child to an FFU the next day. That he had, in fact, been discussing the option with his wife. But given the circumstances, one could understand how he might take matters into his own hands. They'd argue for a fine and probation as fair compensation for this *mistake*.

As prosecutor, Stevens would do everything in his power to send the man to jail. But he wasn't hopeful; time in jail represented an expense to the government, whereas fines generated revenue.

Stevens rested his briefcase on the prosecution's table and scanned the empty courtroom. He sat down, interlocked his fingers, and stared at the dark wood ceiling. As often happened, his thoughts returned to issues he'd been concerned about since law school. It wasn't just about taking children's lives anymore. If the *powers-that-be* didn't care about life, then maybe they'd care about the economics of what they promoted.

He'd developed an argument they could understand. Allowed to grow to maturity, the children the government so carelessly destroyed would contribute to the economic prosperity of the nation. Taxes from their salaries would help fund the high-minded social programs the administration prized. Deductions from their paychecks could close the existing gap in retirement benefits and health subsidies.

The planners ignored demographics used by previous generations as a basis for those program strategies. Instead, this government derisively referred to the programs of earlier eras as *Ponzi schemes that ran their limit.* He shook his head. Such talk made for great sound bites; but it overlooked previous generations' rational expectations for an increasing population. If those in power hadn't plundered trust funds and destroyed potential contributors, the balance sheet of the economy would be very different. The country could maintain roads, bridges, sidewalks, street lights, libraries and parks...all for the want of generations of babies and children not allowed to survive.

A door opened and the clatter of people entering the courtroom echoed off the walls. Time to go to work. He sighed, whether in resignation or disgust, he wasn't sure.

ଯ୍ଜଓୠ

Jonathan Bracken entered the small conference room of Bright Minds and leaned over to kiss his mother on the cheek.

He ruffled Emma's hair. "Are you ready, kiddo?"

"It has to be today," Carolyn said. "We don't dare put it off any longer. Too many delays and the state might decide to eliminate Bright Minds."

"How could they do that?"

"Simple. You've no idea how hard it was to sell the idea of salvaging children of superior intelligence. Given the slightest justification, many high-ranking officials would happily pull our permits."

Jonathan glanced at Emma. She'd scrunched up her face into a worried frown. He nudged his mother.

Seeing Emma's distressed expression, Carolyn patted Emma's hand and smiled at her.

Jonathan put his hand under Emma's chin. Tipping her head up, he gave her a reassuring smile. "Do your best, Ems, okay? We know you're smart. All we want you to do is prove it." He left them alone in the leased office space Bright Minds kept to appear legitimate and professional.

The room was stark, nearly bare of furniture except for a long table with chairs. Three fire-proof file cabinets sat against one wall. Every government contractor was required to maintain them for record storage as a backup for overburdened computer systems that often locked up. The files housed the official exams for rescued children. To keep them alive every child passed their exam at Bright Minds. Therefore, the cabinets also contained bogus exams to make it appear as though some had failed.

A computer keyboard and screen sat at one end of the table ready and waiting. As required by law, an immediate transfer of data followed every exam. Using the numbers Bright Minds sent to the government, a program calculated means and medians, variances, standard deviations and confidence intervals for each group, toddler to four years of age. It automatically added each new test to its database, updating its records and providing a percentile ranking for each child tested. Recording equipment was the only other electronic device in the room. Government regulations required them to record all oral exams.

Emma sank lower in her chair. She hoped she remembered all the things they quizzed her on at the house last night. *I'm supposed to be ready and it's supposed to be easy.* She chewed her lower lip. *But I'm not smart; Aunt Reeta always told me I was stupid.*

ഇൽ

Carolyn sat down beside Emma at the long oak table. "Honey, don't worry. Just answer as best you can. Remember last night when I talked about a lot of things and asked you to try to remember them? Well, those are the same questions I'll ask this morning. It's okay if you don't remember all the answers. Just tell us the ones you do, okay?"

Even though she didn't feel ready, Emma nodded. There was something significant about this test. She didn't know what it was all about, but she sensed it was very important.

Carolyn reached across the table and pushed the *Record* button on the machine. A green light flickered on. "This is Carolyn Bracken of Bright Minds. Today, we are quizzing a female child, almost four years of age, named Emma Jane Spencer. She was delivered to Facility For the Useless number eleven sixteen by an aunt who accepted guardianship after the disappearance of the child's mother."

Emma sucked in her breath and stared at Carolyn. She started to tear up and sniffle. Carolyn shut off the recorder. "What's the matter dear?"

"My mama..."

"I'm sorry, Emma. We only know what your aunt put on a form. Maybe we can help you find your real mother someday, but I can't promise." She stroked Emma's silken hair with her hand then laid her cheek against the soft curls. "Meanwhile, you'll have people who love and care about you at the Foundling Home.

Everyone who works there is different from the ones you encountered before. You'll like it there."

Carolyn handed Emma a tissue. She swiped at her tears, straightened in her chair, and took a deep breath. "Okay. I'll try to remember what to say."

Carolyn gave her an encouraging smile before reaching for the recorder. She hated having Emma listen to this, but it was required. Maybe it would answer some of Emma's questions about why she was here and not back at the place she'd lived in and thought of as her home.

Carolyn pushed *Record*. "The aunt is expecting her third child and prefers to keep that child instead of her niece. As permitted by law, she brought the subject, Emma Jane Spencer, to FFU eleven sixteen prior to her fourth birthday. Upon observation, Facility Director Mira Hastings noted the child was particularly alert and astute. She ordered this evaluation. Her exam follows."

They'd reviewed all the questions ahead of time. This, of course, violated all protocols and if the state knew, it'd mean the end of Bright Minds. However, it was imperative that Emma pass this intelligence test with flying colors. For her, it was literally a matter of life or death. If necessary, Carolyn could wipe the tape, give her additional prompts, and start again.

Emma tried to appear confident, but her thoughts wandered back to what she'd heard about her aunt. When Aunt Reeta got pregnant, she said there wouldn't be room for Emma anymore. The rule was three kids per household, Emma knew all about that. Raylene and Rhonda were Aunt Reeta's real kids. Emma was only the daughter of Aunt Reeta's little sister. Her mama wasn't supposed to get pregnant, but did anyhow, and didn't tell anyone until she gave birth in her bedroom.

Emma wasn't sure what became of her mother. Over and over, they told her that her mother wasn't married and too young to be a mother. But she *was a mother*. It'd been almost four years. Her mother would be older now, maybe old enough to take care of her so she could have a real mom like other kids.

CHAPTER ELEVEN

"Once you bring life into the world, you must protect it. We must protect it by changing the world." ~ Elie Wiesel

Carolyn returned the recorder to the cabinet and smiled. "You did very well, Emma. You remembered all the answers and passed your test. You won't have to do it again."

Emma grinned.

Carolyn lifted a bubble gum dispenser out of the cabinet. Its clear glass globe sparkled as she set it on the table. Filled with sweet multi-colored gum balls, it never failed to excite every child who saw it.

Emma's eyes glittered in anticipation. Carolyn placed coins for the dispenser in Emma's hand as a rapid series of hard knocks rattled the office door. Gumballs forgotten, they spun around and stared at the door. The frantic pounding continued.

Carolyn always locked the door during tests to avoid unplanned interruptions. You never knew who might come barging in and she wanted to feel safe with the children.

"Who is it?" she called.

"Please," a female voice implored. "Please, I need to talk to you. It's very important." The woman sounded close to tears.

Carolyn turned to Emma. "Go into the bathroom, shut and lock the door. I'll tell you when you can come out."

"Coming," she shouted as she waited to hear the bolt on the bathroom door slip into its mortise. When it did, she opened the door, but left the chain engaged.

A pretty young woman peered at her through the narrow slit. She held the hand of a little girl whom Carolyn guessed to be about three years old. A young man with a double stroller stood behind them. The woman peeked right and left before whispering, "We're searching for Bright Minds. Please tell me we've come to the right place."

"What do you want?"

"My name's Eileen Abramson. This is my husband Jacob and our daughter Amanda. We need your help."

Taken aback by the similarity to Aranda's name, Carolyn gazed down at the little girl with curiosity. "You've come to the right place," she said, releasing the chain.

The girl and her mother stepped in. The man rolled the stroller forward a few feet then stopped. The child's mother released the girl's hand and eyed the width of the stroller against the doorway. "It should fit. There's a bit of space on the left."

The little girl peered around the drab room while her parents eased the stroller through the narrow doorway.

Carolyn noticed the child's wide-eyed gawk and wished the room could be more welcoming. It would be better to have the walls painted in bright cheerful colors with a few pictures, but she didn't dare. The expectation for a quasi-government office, like this one, was for it to remain plain and utilitarian.

Once the stroller's rear wheels cleared the opening, everyone gave a collective sigh of relief. The stroller held twins about 18 months old. Both toddlers were dressed in blue. One look at the woman told Carolyn why they'd come. They'd reached their limit of three children, and the woman was obviously pregnant.

"What is it you want from Bright Minds?"

"It's about Mandy. She's very bright. We thought maybe she could qualify as a *Contributor*."

"So you want me to test your daughter and see?"

The woman's eyes were red and swollen from crying. Clearly, she'd settled on this possibility rather than abort the child she carried.

"It was careless to get pregnant again, but I can't destroy the life within me." She bit her lip. "I don't know how you feel about the directive on family size, but we don't believe in exterminating children. They have as much right to be here as we do. I'd sooner die myself than allow one of my children to be killed."

Carolyn took her hand and gave it a gentle squeeze. "It's all right. I can't openly agree with you, but I won't give you any argument either. I can test Mandy, but not right away. Would you be willing to leave her with me for a few days? There are preparations that have to be made."

Fear clouded the woman's face.

Carolyn noticed and crossed the room to peruse the twins, giving Mandy's parents a moment alone. Carolyn tickled the boys under their chins with her single hand, making them giggle. "Who are these handsome little fellows?"

"They're Nathan and Noah." Eileen leaned toward her husband and whispered, "She seems friendly; shall we trust her?"

Jacob gave his wife a slight nod before speaking up. "I know it's presumptuous of me, but can we see where Mandy will stay?"

Carolyn understood their concern, but she also needed to protect the location of her home. The safety of the children who passed through there depended upon it. "There is a problem—"

A creaking noise stopped her midsentence. Everyone turned toward the bathroom door. It continued to open, creaking as it went. A little head popped around it. "Aunt Carolyn, can I come out now?"

"Oh Emma, I'm sorry. I got so busy that I forgot you. Of course, sweetheart, come on out."

"I could hear you talking and knew there were other kids out here, so I thought it would be all right."

Carolyn gave Emma a hug. "You thought right. This is Mandy. I think she's going to go home with us for a few days. Then maybe she'll move to the Foundling Home of Future Contributors when you do." Carolyn turned to the couple again. "Emma just passed her Bright Minds test."

The young father looked down at his sons in the stroller. "What if Mandy doesn't pass?" He already knew the answer. Everyone did. Deciding which one of his four children to sacrifice would be heart wrenching.

Eileen Abramson placed a hand on her husband's arm. "We've been tutoring her ever since I realized I was pregnant. It seemed like the best alternative."

Parental pride aside, they both knew their daughter was no genius, and all the tutoring in the world wouldn't make her one.

Another tear slipped out of Eileen's red-rimmed eyes.

Carolyn touched Eileen's shoulder. "I don't think you need to worry. Mandy appears exceptionally *bright* to me."

The couple studied the elderly woman in front of them. They saw only kindness in her eyes.

Eileen licked her lips and sighed deeply. "Ma'am, I'll trust you. How soon can we see Mandy again?"

"You can be present during her oral exam if you like, although the twins probably shouldn't come. I have to record everything and the sounds of them in the background could be a problem."

"We can leave them with my mother," Jacob said. "When should we come back?"

"I need a few days with Mandy. Let's say 1:30 next Monday. We'll begin the test at 2 p.m."

Jacob reached into his back pocket and pulled out his wallet. He offered her several bills. "We don't have much money, but this should cover the cost of her food."

Carolyn's raised hand stopped him. "I take monetary donations, but only from people who can afford it. Keep your money to feed the other children. We have enough food at my house."

Eileen knelt and pulled Mandy into her arms. "She seems like a nice lady, Sweetie. She's going to take you home with her for a few days." Eileen caressed her daughter's cheek and stared into her eyes. "We'll see you real soon. Okay?"

Mandy began to sob.

Emma walked over and put her arm around the girl's waist. "Mandy, it's all right. Honest. Aunt Carolyn's place is really,

really nice. You'll like Jonathan too. He makes great pancakes and plays *Go Fish* with us. He can teach it to you." Emma looked up at Carolyn. "Can Mandy have some bubble gum too?"

Carolyn reached into her pocket for more coins to give the girls.

Mandy quit crying when she saw the red gum ball machine with its glass globe full of bright colored gum balls. She watched Emma put a coin in, slide the handle, and take out a red one. She followed Emma's example. When a blue one came out, she grinned and held it up for her mother to see.

Eileen smiled and pulled a valise out of the back of the stroller. "I packed some of Mandy's clothes just in case. Her nightgown, robe and slippers are in here, along with a couple of outfits. I can bring more on Monday."

Mandy took the valise from her mother with Emma watching.

I wonder why Aunt Reeta didn't pack anything for me, Emma wondered shaking her head. *I'll think about it some other time.* She grinned at Mandy. "It'll be fun spending the night together. Sorta like a pajama party."

CHAPTER TWELVE

Exhausted, Mira Hastings eased herself into the living room rocker and reached into her knitting bag. Lifting out her most recent project, she laid the half-finished baby blanket across her lap. She tucked the pastel ball of variegated yarn in beside her and picked up her knitting needles. The multi-colored strand of yarn hurried through her fingers as she knit her way across the blanket, willing away the day's tension. Despite her best efforts, her stress remained.

How could anyone sanction FFUs? Didn't they know what happened to the little ones? She stared down at the blanket in her lap through tears. She caressed the soft yarn, imagining a tiny infant wrapped up in it. Knitting sweaters for little children made better sense, but creating baby blankets spoke to something deep inside her.

Unbidden, her mind wandered back to her own child. She was 17 and in a stark room with a middle-aged, heavy-set woman in a starched uniform. "Lie down on the table, Suzie, and put your feet in the stirrups. The doctor will be here in a few minutes."

Being called Suzie sounded odd. She'd used a false name when filling out the forms so they wouldn't know who she was. It made her feel like less of a person, unimportant. Mira felt alone and abandoned. The air conditioning vent spewed out cold air and she shivered in the thin gown they'd given her.

She stared at the ceiling. *Were those spots of blood? God, what am I doing here?*

If only she hadn't given in to Clayton. She was too young to have a baby. She couldn't support herself; how would she support a baby? Her parents counted on her graduating from high school next spring.

Mira placed her hand on the tiny rise in her lower abdomen. She wondered about the baby inside her then quickly banished the thought. This problem was about to go away. It occurred to her that Clayton hadn't asked her out since she'd told him she was pregnant. She swore to never make that mistake again.

The door opened and a bear of a man with a graying beard walked in. "Okay, Sweetie, let's get on with this. It'll all be over before you know it." The doctor stepped between her feet and picked up an instrument.

"Before you begin, may I ask a question?"

"The time for that was with the nurse. Don't worry, Sweetie. It'll be over before you know it."

He'd already said that. She realized he must call all his patients *Sweetie*. She'd overheard jokes about all women looking alike from where he stood. Was she just an anonymous nobody without a name or feelings? She winced when the cold metal speculum entered her. "Wait! I've changed my mind."

The doctor clucked his tongue and shook his head. His eyes remained between her legs; he hadn't looked her in the eye even once. A chilling thought occurred to her, the women and girls who came in here had no identity, any more than the babies he killed.

It wasn't the pain or discomfort of the abortion she'd remember. It was the fear and the questions that flooded her mind. *Was she doing the right thing? How big was the tiny person inside her? Would she even know whether she carried a boy or a girl?*

She'd struggle with those same questions all her life. If only I knew then what I know now, Mira thought. I was so young. I viewed the baby I carried as a liability, not an asset. They'd called it a *product of conception*. If only they'd told me the truth, told me of the risks, told me of the pain the baby would feel. Instead of sparing myself a temporary inconvenience and embarrassment, I gave myself guilt, regret and sorrow forever.

She blew her nose and wiped her eyes. She had to let go of this. Think of Emma instead she told herself. She's one of those rescued. The staff at the Foundling Home will be good to her and enable her to grow into a responsible adult.

Mira heard scratching at the back door and went to open it. A long-haired yellow tabby cat wandered in and wrapped itself around her ankles, purring loudly.

"Well, I wondered when you'd come home you disgraceful creature." She reached down to pet him. "I can scarcely believe I took in a stray cat. Your persistence paid off and here you are bold as brass." She chuckled. "Maybe I should have called you *Brassy* instead of Butterscotch."

Butterscotch looked up at her and meowed. He whipped his long fluffy tail against her knee and continued making circle eights around her ankles.

"Okay. I'll get you some canned cat food. Heaven forbid you have to survive on the dry stuff." She reached down and lifted the big yellow cat into her arms. "Butterscotch, I'd trade you in a minute for a child of my own, but since I don't have one, you'll have to do."

She stroked the cat's back, tracing the intricate pattern of his fur while he ate. Her heart quit racing. The cat accomplished what knitting had not. Focused on his well-being, she relaxed and her sorrows faded into the background.

స౭ఴ

The next morning, Mira treated herself by stopping at a deli down the street from her office. She breathed deeply, enjoying the yeasty smell of rolls fresh from the oven. She didn't often eat pastry for breakfast, but today she craved comfort food. Focusing on the chocolate drizzled croissants, she jumped when someone tapped her lightly on the shoulder.

"Sorry," he said. "I wondered if you'd step a little to the left so I can see around you."

She glanced up at him as she stepped aside. His masculine good looks sent an unexpected quiver rippling through her.

"Thank you," he said, and smiled. "I'm fond of the apple Danish, myself, but I like to view everything before deciding. What about you?"

"Umm, yeah, Danish are nice." Feeling awkward, she added, "But I'm crazy for anything chocolate." There was something very familiar about him. His dark hair, slightly graying at the temples, was thick but conservatively cut. He wore a suit and tie, very different from the jogging suit he wore when running past the FFU, so she didn't make the connection.

The young woman behind the counter grinned up at him. "Hiya, Gray. The usual?"

Mira gaped at the young woman. She was obviously playing favorites. Why not? She would've too.

"Yes, my regular, plus two of those chocolate croissants. Bag the croissants separately, please."

The young woman handed him two white sacks. After he paid, he turned and handed one to Mira. "You were here first. Accept these as my apology for cutting in."

Mira took the bag he offered. Resting her elbow on the counter, she watched him head out the door. The young woman lingered at the register, also watching as he left.

Hmmm, so his name is *Gray*, Mira thought. Is that his first name or his last? Does he work around here?

When he faded from sight, the girl behind the counter turned her attention to Mira. "What can I get you?"

Mira gave a start. She remembered the teabags in her desk and said, "Nothing, thank you." She left with a smile swinging her bag of croissants.

At the office, Mira clicked on her computer and waited impatiently for the screen to flicker to life. *What kind of name is Gray? He probably has a brother named Brown and twin sisters Puce and Chartreuse.*

Mira rapidly tapped computer keys as she thought about *him*. She wouldn't be worth anything this morning with his handsome face floating around in her head. She grinned. Maybe the deli should become a regular stop.

CHAPTER THIRTEEN

Loneliness drove Robbie's grandmother, Rebecca Stuart, to loiter near Frank Wilson's house hoping to catch a glimpse of Robbie. Seeing no sign of the boy, she grew increasingly concerned.

Head down, she slowly crossed the street to the park and checked the playground. No Robbie. She found a bench with a view of the front of Frank's house. Sitting down, she waited, hoping Robbie might appear. Rebecca hesitated to approach the home. If they knew she'd been watching, they could have her forcibly removed. Then she'd never see Robbie.

The sun began its slow march to the horizon. Shivering on the bench, Rebecca tightened her coat and lifted her collar. The few remaining children left the park as shadows spilled across the playground. Rebecca remained and watched porch lights blink on up and down the street.

It was dark by the time Robbie's father returned from work. He parked in the driveway and jogged up the front steps. His new wife met him at the door and took his coat. Before the door closed, Rebecca had a brief chance to see inside. Robbie was nowhere in sight.

She rose from the bench and made her way to the bus stop. As she walked, she vowed to return the following day and every day thereafter until she knew Robbie was okay.

ᔕᗯᑕᖇ

The following morning, Rebecca caught the earliest bus. Exiting the bus, she hurried to her park bench across from the house and pulled her dark wool coat tight around her. As she shivered on the cold bench, her worries ratcheted up. Who did she think she was kidding? What were the chances of ever seeing Robbie through a crack in the door? If she wanted to see her grandson, she'd have to quit being such a wimp and walk right up to the door and knock on it.

Rebecca had never met her grandson's new stepmother, but

any woman had to be less intimidating than Robbie's father. She watched Frank leave and head off to work. Mustering up her courage, she went to the door and pushed the com button.

A young woman's voice came over the speaker in the door. "Yes?"

"I'm Rebecca Stuart."

The woman said nothing. Rebecca wondered if she'd ever heard her name before. Didn't she wonder where Robbie had been the first three years of his life?

"Rebecca Stuart, Robbie's grandmother. He used to live with me."

The door opened and the lingering smells of breakfast wafted around her. The young woman slouched against the doorframe. "What do you want?"

"I'd like to visit Robbie for just a few minutes. May I please come in, dear?"

The young woman's eyes turned cold and flinty. "My name is Denise."

"Please. I won't bother you. Just give me a few minutes with Robbie. That's all I ask and then I'll leave."

"He's not here," Denise said. She put a hand on the door, preparing to close it.

"Then tell me where Robbie is, or when he'll be back."

"You'll have to ask his father. He was here for a couple of nights and then left with his dad and didn't come back."

"When is Frank coming home?"

"He just left. He won't be back until this evening."

"Then, I'll come back."

"Whatever you want," she said and slammed the door.

Rebecca descended the steps wondering if there was a library nearby, or at least a coffee shop. Maybe a small mall to window shop and stay warm. It promised to be a long and dreary day.

৪৩৫

It was dark and Frank's car was already in the driveway when Rebecca returned. Her joints ached from sitting in the library's wooden chairs. A vise seemed to grip the back of her neck as she ascended the steps. She whispered a prayer. *Be with me Lord. Help me relax and be confident so I can see my Robbie again.*

"Oh, it's you," Denise said answering the door. She led her into the entryway and instructed her to wait there.

Rebecca could make out Denise's voice in the other room. "Frank, there's a woman here to see you about the boy you brought home the other night."

"A woman?"

"She says she's his grandmother."

He stomped down the hall to where Rebecca waited. "What do you want?"

His tone raised goose bumps on her skin. "I came to see Robbie. I need to know he's all right."

"He isn't here. Now, go away."

"What do you mean?"

"He was my child, not yours. Until I took him back, you got paid. Your involvement in my life and Robbie's has ended. Go home and leave me alone."

"What have you done with Robbie?"

"Whatever I did, I had a legal right to do. We have nothing else to talk about." He gripped her arm and pushed her in the direction of the front door. Swinging it open, he shoved her out.

She stumbled down the steps and grabbed the railing to avoid falling. Upset as she was, Rebecca somehow managed to make her connections on unfamiliar bus routes and find her way home. The lamp she'd left burning shone through the doorway like a welcoming beacon.

She tossed her coat over the back of the sofa and collapsed into her rocking chair with a sob.

She'd made it back safely. If only Robbie was safe too.

Frank's behavior convinced her he'd taken Robbie — his very own son — to one of those detestable Facilities for the Useless. She brushed aside a tear and pounded her fist on the arm of the chair. How dare he? Her Robbie was not useless.

She never knew what Veronica saw in that man. Her chin sank to her chest. She'd not only lost her daughter, but now, thanks to Veronica's lout of an ex-husband, she may have lost her only grandchild as well. Robbie was all she had, all that mattered.

She moaned, "Why euthanize a child when there's someone who'll love and care for them?"

Beginning early the next morning she vowed to begin visiting FFUs to inquire whether they'd taken in a Robbie...no, a Robert Wilson. She had to know for sure.

With a plan firmly in place, her pent-up tears flowed freely. Rebecca spent the night pacing, crying and praying that she was somehow wrong about what happened to Robbie.

CHAPTER FOURTEEN

Aranda's mind raced as she pushed the laundry hamper down the corridor. As usual, a sleeping toddler lay hidden within the towels. She guessed the pretty little girl with dark eyes and curly brown hair was about two years old. The child remained still and quiet even though she'd had less ether to give her this time.

The creak of the hamper's wheels echoed in the empty hallway. Aranda's hands clenched the rim of the hamper and her eyes darted everywhere. She'd done this numerous times without a problem, yet she couldn't shake the niggling feeling that something wasn't right.

Giles? No, he'd been the same disrespectful, greedy oaf as always. Each time she performed a rescue she grew uneasy, but today felt worse. Try as she might, Aranda couldn't dispel her heightened sense of impending danger. She continued casting nervous sidelong glances up and down the hallway as she hurried toward the elevator.

Slow down. You're walking faster than normal.

But she couldn't help it. Every nerve ending tingled with apprehension. It took every ounce of will power she had not to break into a run. She took a deep breath and let it out slowly.

You can do this.

Then she heard footsteps behind her, and the sound of approaching voices. Her heart pounded. The corridors were normally empty at this time of day. Should she turn to watch or pretend not to hear them?

The footsteps grew louder the nearer they came. Her pulse throbbed in her ears. Her whole world seemed to reverberate to the drumming cadence of those approaching footfalls. The end of the corridor was just ahead, only two more corners to reach the elevator. With luck, she could get around the corner and clear the connecting corridor before they caught up.

She broke into a run as soon as she rounded the corner.

Glancing warily over her shoulder, she rolled the hamper as fast as possible. She clipped the corner as she careened around the second turn. The cart wobbled momentarily then skidded to a stop as one of the front wheels broke loose and folded under. Aranda tugged and shoved the hamper, but couldn't make it budge. The jostling woke the toddler and she whimpered.

Taking a deep breath, Aranda moved to the front of the hamper and hefted the corner with the broken wheel. She lugged it toward the elevator, one hand supporting the corner, the other arm extended toward the elevator's down button.

We can still make it, she thought, taking a deep calming breath. *I'll pull the hamper into a custodial closet and transfer the baby and towels into a new hamper. We'll make it...we will.*

She smacked the call button so hard she feared it'd break. Aranda nervously rocked from one foot to the other. Her eyes flicked back and forth between the adjoining hallway and the elevator's dull gray doors. "C'mon, c'mon, c'mon," she begged.

Voices reached her from around the corner. After what seemed like an eternity, the elevator chimed. The doors slowly parted displaying a tantalizing bar of light. Aranda struggled to raise the hamper's damaged corner and pull the hamper into the elevator. For a few brief seconds escape was in view.

Two people, a man and a woman, both wearing the dismal gray-green uniforms of the FFUs Security force rounded the corner. Ugly uniforms, Aranda thought, just like their jobs.

"Barnard, go help her." the heavy-set woman said.

The big guard lumbered over, grabbed the bulky hamper and jerked the front wheel across the elevator's threshold. The jostling caused the hidden toddler to release a single wail. Barnard dropped the hamper and stepped back. Both guards stared at Aranda.

"It...it has a broken wheel and I'm taking it down to exchange it for another. It needs oiling too; it squeals like that when I roll it." It was a long shot, but the only one she had.

"Don't you take another step." The woman rested her hand on her nightstick as she mulled the situation over. Stepping closer, she loomed over Aranda. "It didn't sound like a squeaky wheel to me."

Tremors of fear threatened to overwhelm Aranda. She forced herself to take slow, calming breaths. She must appear innocent. Her palms grew damp and sweaty. With effort, Aranda managed to control her shaking.

Things seemed to happen in slow motion like when you trip, know you're going to fall, but can't stop yourself. Aranda's thoughts jumbled together as she slowly shook her head. Her eyes darted from the woman to the large, intimidating man beside her. An involuntary shiver rippled through her.

Feeling trapped, outnumbered and alone, she forced a smile and extended her hand. "You're Helen, aren't you? I'm Aranda."

Helen sneered, ignoring the gesture. "That look on your face says you're afraid of something. We've heard rumors about a discrepancy between the number of children coming in and going out of this facility."

Going out? What sort of euphemism was that for killing children? Aranda shook her head. "I'm just a janitor; I wouldn't know anything about rumors."

"You're lying!" Helen shouted, and droplets of saliva sprayed Aranda's face. She poked Aranda with her night stick. "What are you hiding in that hamper of yours?"

Oh, God, Aranda begged, *don't let them search it.*

She'd no sooner thought it than Helen said, "Barnard inspect the inside."

Barnard shoved it back into the hallway and lifted the

hamper's lid. The toddler remained safely hidden under a stack of towels. Meanwhile, the elevator chimed a second time. Its gray doors trundled toward each other, eliminating Aranda's only means of escape.

The squinty-eyed female security guard smirked as her male counterpart began jabbing the pile of towels with his night stick. He shoved them this way and that, lifting them up and tossing them back down. By some miracle, the tot remained quiet.

Helen leaned over and peered in. "Instead of flipping the towels back inside, throw them onto the floor." Stepping back, she crossed her arms with smug expression.

"Those towels are clean," Aranda said, "fresh from the laundry."

"I want to see what's at the bottom of this thing."

Panic seized Aranda. What could she do when they found the baby? Act surprised and pretend she didn't know the child was there?

Piles of towels soon littered the floor. Helen reached in and grabbed the toddler by an arm and yanked her up. The baby's head lolled to one side and the woman's rough treatment made her whimper. She swung the youngster in Barnard's direction. "What do you make of this bandage on her finger?" When he answered with a shrug, Helen began picking at the wrapping.

Aranda grabbed the child away from her. "Leave her alone. She's been through enough for one day." She cradled the youngster and smoothed her hair. "She's done nothing wrong. If you take the bandage off, she'll start bleeding again."

She'd given herself away. Aranda had always known it could happen. Sometimes she speculated on how it might come about and what she'd do if it did. No matter what, she must not expose anyone in the Life Chances organization. Focusing on Jonathan's kind heart, she threw her shoulders back and resolved to face with courage whatever lay ahead.

CHAPTER FIFTEEN

"...the moral test of government is how it treats those who are in the dawn of life, the children; ... those who are in the shadows of life; the sick, the needy and the handicapped."

~ Last Speech of Hubert H. Humphrey

In the dim holding room, the children gulped down the pitiful snacks Giles brought them. The contents on his cart quickly disappeared, and he pushed his food cart out of the holding room, happy to get away from the children. The little buggers had their food. He'd done his job.

He attempted to whistle as he ran a damp sponge over the cart's stainless steel top. His tune, off-key and unrecognizable, echoed down the corridor while he speculated on how to spend the booty Aranda paid him.

He dipped the sponge in his bucket and wrung it out with an exasperated sigh. What difference did it make if the little brats got a few germs with their food? As much as he hated the routine, he did everything by the book. That bitch Hastings might drop in on him at any time for an unannounced inspection.

He chuckled to himself. Let 'er get the rule book and try to nail him. She could run down the *Regs* all afternoon and never catch him in a violation. He'd beat her at her own game. An evil grin lit his sallow face. When he got her alone, she wouldn't be so high and mighty.

He stopped whistling and cocked his head to listen. He heard approaching footsteps coming down the hall. Giles stepped behind the corner and peeked around to see who it was. The color drained from his face when he saw Helen marching toward him with a little girl under her arm. He gulped. It was the same child he'd sold Aranda.

Giles squeezed the sponge so tightly it dribbled disinfectant on his shoe. Cursing, he tossed it aside and bent his leg behind him to dry the shoe on the back of his pant leg. They musta nabbed Aranda with the goods. She'd probably already spilled her guts and told them all about him.

He licked his lips and swallowed several times, trying to wet his dry mouth. He painted on a crooked smile. "Hiya, Helen. Whatcha got there?"

"Never seen a kid before?" she asked with a scowl.

"More of 'em than I wanna think about. So, is she yours?"

Helen snorted. "Mine? Are you crazy? We caught Aranda trying to slip this kid out in a laundry hamper." She shoved the little girl at him. "Here, take the little snot; I don't want her."

Giles quickly decided his best defense would be to play dumb. "What am I supposed t' do with her?"

"The same thing you do with all the others."

"But shouldn't we have paperwork or somethin' authorizin' it? We can't jes go killin' 'em on a whim. It's against regulations."

"She's one of your useless children, you dolt. Aranda had her."

Giles thrust the groggy toddler into the holding room with the other children and watched her crumple into a heap on the floor. "What makes you so sure she came outta my holding room? Aranda coulda got her anyplace."

"We found one of your name tags in the bottom of her cart. It fell off in the search."

His blood ran cold. A quick review of the day's dispatch records would show his initials on her check-in slip. He needed to stall for time. "Okay, let's go to Accounting and check the day's records."

Helen fell into step beside him.

Giles twisted to look over at her. "How did you...um, catch Aranda with the kid?"

"What's it matter to you how we caught her?"

"It doesn't. I was just curious, that's all."

"We're security guards; we do our job."

Entering the Accounting office, Giles pulled down the clipboard with the day's list and handed it to her. "Check it yourself."

Helen's finger stopped halfway down the page. "Here she is, just as I thought."

Giles snatched it back. "Why that little sneak! Tryin' t' steal a kid right out from under my nose. How did she think she'd get away with somethin' like that? I'd uh caught it when I did the final census."

"The better question is how she got her to begin with."

"That's easy enough to figure out. Aranda's been comin' around on her breaks. You know, acting all flirty like and tellin' me we oughta go out after work and have some fun. At first I ignored her on account of the no fraternizing during work hours rule. But when she kept it up, I figured there was some reason for her newfound friendliness." He gave Helen a knowing wink. "I mean ol' Giles has been around the block enough times not to fall for that."

Helen returned an uncomfortable nod.

Giles lowered his voice to a conspiratorial whisper. "I've been watchin' her...knew she was up t' somethin'. I see it all now. She kept hangin' around so I'd get used to her. Then when I wasn't lookin', Zip! She up 'n' thieved one of 'em."

"If you've been watching her, how did she swipe the kid?"

He ran a hand across his face and swallowed hard. "Musta been while I was in the can. That's the only time she was alone down here."

"You went away and left her alone?"

"Hey, don't use that tone with me. People come and go all the time. Ain't never had anyone snatch a kid on me before. What ya want me t' do, strip search everybody who comes down? I got as much right as anybody t' use the john."

"What about the little girl's finger?"

"What about it?"

"Half of her baby finger is missing."

The plastic bag with half a finger in it was still in his pocket. Pretending nonchalance, he said, "I cut off the little finger of every dead kid before Benjamin pitches 'em into the cooker." He crossed his arms and pretended to mull it over. He snapped his fingers. "Ain't she the crafty one? Aranda musta done it herself. It was her way of coverin' up."

He ran to the other side of the room. Surreptitiously plopping the bagged finger into the lab's box, he pretended to find it. He held up the bag and waved it at Helen. "Just like I said, here it is in the box already. When I dumped all the others in on top of it, I'd have never seen it."

Helen slapped him on the back. "Good work. Then we got to her before you did."

"So, umm, where's Aranda now?" Giles asked as they walked back down the stairway.

"Barnard took her to the Security Office for questioning. I'm going to get some truth serum and go back up there. We'll get to the bottom of this."

Giles scratched his chin in what he imagined to be a thoughtful manner. "Truth serum, huh? You know that stuff can't be trusted."

"Since when?"

He shook his head and raised his hands protectively. "You're the expert. It's just I've read it makes people loopy 'n' they say all kinda crazy stuff that ain't true."

Helen stopped, looking intently into his face. "You're worried she'll implicate you, aren't you?"

"You're damned right I am. She's gonna be tryin' t' shift the blame t' anyone she can. This is how it always happens. A fella's minding his own business, following regulations 'n' doin' his job...the next thing ya know someone's draggin' him into the middle of somethin'."

"You can trust us to do a thorough investigation."

Giles dug a rag out of his back pocket and wiped his brow. "Fair enough. Let's keep it that way."

After Helen left, Giles nervously paced the hallway ticking off possibilities. Sooner or later, Aranda was bound to talk. She could tell them exactly how much she'd paid him. He patted the folded bills in his pocket. If Helen came back and found the cash on him, his goose was cooked. He nervously scanned the room searching for a safe hiding place. That money was the only thing tying him to Aranda. He needed to get rid of it.

He raced down the stairwell to the basement. The incinerator was already blazing. Giles dashed over to it, glanced both ways, and flipped open the door. Heat roared out, forcing him back. He hesitated for a second, swallowed hard and then pitched the money in. The fire flared for an instant as the damning evidence vanished in a puff of smoke.

There, he thought as he closed the door, the problem's solved. Without evidence there could be no charges. By sacrificing his ill-gotten gain, he'd bought himself immunity from prosecution ... clearly a bargain in any man's language. Now that he'd prepared himself, Giles patiently waited for the inquiry he was certain would follow. When it didn't immediately materialize, his feelings of cleverness began to sour.

CHAPTER SIXTEEN

"Of all tyrannies, a tyranny sincerely exercised for the good of its victims may be the most oppressive." ~ C.S. Lewis

Mira closed her office door behind her. *I need some time away from this awful building. A short walk around the block will lift my spirits.* Bright sunshine and a gentle breeze greeted her when she opened the front door.

As she descended the steps, she saw a young woman sitting on the brick wall near the base of the stairs, her shoulders slumped forward. The woman dabbed at her eyes with a tissue. A little girl sat at her feet. The child used her finger to absentmindedly make circles in the dust on the sidewalk.

Something drew her to them. "Hello. Is this your pretty little girl?"

The woman lifted her chin, but didn't reply.

Mira gestured toward the imposing building she'd just exited. "Are you thinking about taking her in there?"

The young woman sobbed. "Wendy's pediatrician diagnosed her as autistic. He says she'll never learn to call me Mama, or even hug me." As tears rolled down the mother's cheeks, her daughter began to sob in unison. The woman bent to blot away the child's tears. "There, there, Darling, don't cry."

She turned back to Mira, trying to control her sobs. "Her doctor asked me if I believe in God. When I told him I do, he said she'd be happier with God than here with me."

Mira placed a hand on the woman's arm. "People make mistakes, not God. Wendy's just exactly the way he wanted her. And if she was supposed to be with God, wouldn't he have already taken her?"

"But the doctor's a professional, he's studied these things. He knows."

"Sometimes physicians know what's best, and sometimes they're merely acting on their own prejudices." Mira took a deep breath. "Dr. Temple Grandin was autistic and grew to successfully deal with it. She made many valuable contributions to society."

"Temple who?"

Mira swept her skirt around her legs and sat beside the woman. "Dr. Temple Grandin. She was born autistic just like your Wendy. She went to college and earned a PhD. She gained worldwide respect and is still quoted today. You can find her on the internet. Who's to say what Wendy will be like as an adult, or what she could eventually accomplish?"

The young mother quietly mulled over what Mira said. "Doctors can't know, can they? Only God knows how each of us fits into his plan."

"That's the spirit. Take Wendy home and continue to love her."

The woman's face lit up when she smiled. "Oh, thank you. I don't know who you are, but God surely sent you. You've spared Wendy, and saved me from a life of regret." She hugged Mira, then took her daughter's hand and led her away.

Mira watched them go. *There's more than one way to save a child's life.* Glancing skyward, she whispered, "Thank you."

  

While Helen returned the child to Giles and went after the truth serum, the hulking Security guard, Barnard, folded Aranda's arms behind her back and led her into an interrogation room. The two guards had outfitted a small conference room off their office for something like this.

Doing her best to appear confused about the circumstances, Aranda crumpled into a chair and choked back her fear as he secured her.

Barnard flipped a switch and a bright yellow light shone down on her. The click of his shoes against the dark linoleum floor echoed in the small space. "So, Aranda Blackthorn, is it?"

"Yes sir. But, I haven't done anything, sir."

"We'll see about that!" His hand flew out, slapping her across the face.

Aranda's head snapped to one side and her eyes watered. Stunned, she blinked back tears. She wanted to reach up and touch her face, but her hands were bound to the back of the chair. Bile rose in her throat.

She watched him clenching and unclenching his fists, and stole a glance at his face. Nostrils flared, he stared down at her without emotion. She shivered. *He enjoys hurting people.*

Aranda prayed for the inner strength to maintain her story and not give him any information that could implicate others. She called to mind the children she'd rescued. Focusing on those she'd saved gave her peace.

Barnard paced circles around her, smacking a fist into the palm of the other hand with each step he took. "I could make this easier for you if you cooperate."

Where had she heard that before? This guy watched too many old gangster movies. "I know it was wrong to steal the child. I just wanted to keep her for myself. I don't have any children of my own." Aranda lowered her eyes. "I, I thought she'd make a sweet daughter."

"And how did you think you'd pass her off as yours without a birth certificate or any papers?" He planted his hands on the desk and glared down at her. "Why risk it? The kid's a non-entity. She has no future."

"I didn't think ahead. It was a spur of the moment thing. I just took her without considering the ramifications." Tears streamed down her cheeks. She was powerless to wipe them away. "I regret my selfish, foolish action."

"Hah! You had accomplices, I'm sure of it. You were going to get papers for her, weren't you?"

"No, no, I didn't, I only—"

The punch came out of nowhere. Aranda shut her eyes against the pain; red spinning stars enveloped her vision.

"I'm tired of your lies. Tell me the truth," he shouted. Her head had barely stopped moving when Barnard hit her again with his other fist.

"I told you everything," she whispered.

Left then right, then left again, he hit her over and over.

She heard her teeth crack against each other and tasted blood. Aranda's tears flowed freely. She blinked her puffy left eye again and again, but couldn't focus properly. The right one had swollen shut. She longed to wipe her nose, but couldn't. Mucous and tears mingled with the blood dripping from her cracked lips and trickled onto her blouse.

Barnard backed away. His breath came in quick huffs. Sweat stains darkened his shirt and his hands shook with frustration. The skin on his knuckles showed several bloody cracks. His eyes flicked around the room as he massaged his battle-weary fists. Without warning, he sucked in a deep breath and rushed at her again, pummeling Aranda as he spewed curses.

ഇരു

When the door flew open, Barnard stopped and Helen walked in. She took one look at Aranda and screamed.

"What have you done?" She barely recognized him when he spun to face her. Never in her life had she encountered such rage in someone's face.

"She had it coming to her," he muttered. "She wouldn't tell me who was helping her."

Walking over, Helen gently lifted Aranda's sagging head off her chest and cupped her battered face in her hands. Pushing matted tendrils of hair aside, Helen gasped at the damage Barnard had inflicted.

Aranda's head lolled when Helen released it. She gave a painful groan then lapsed back into unconsciousness.

Helen frowned at Barnard. "I hope you're satisfied, you big lummox. Look at her! She can't even hold her head up. It's too late for truth serum or anything else now. I left you with a suspect, not a punching bag."

He twisted in Aranda's direction and cringed. "I didn't mean to hit her so hard, honest."

"You're easily twice her size. If you need to punch someone, go to a boxing ring. " She slammed the bottle of sodium pentothal and syringe down on the table. "These won't do us any good now. Thanks to you, we'll probably both lose our jobs."

"What are we going to do?" Barnard meekly asked.

"Help me move her onto the table before she topples over. Then let's go back to the office. Give me time. I need to think this through."

Leaving an unconscious Aranda sprawled across the table in the interrogation room, Barnard and Helen sat across from each other at a desk.

"Were you able to figure out what's been going on?" Barnard asked.

"Giles has been selling her kids. I'm sure of it."

"How do you know?"

"There's no way little Aranda's going to lop off a kid's finger. He's terrified we're coming after him next."

Barnard grinned. "Well, what are we waiting for? Let's go get him."

"Not so fast. We'll take this one step at a time. Besides, it's better to let him stew in his own juices for a while." Helen slapped her hand on the desk. "We've got a bigger problem to deal with. Aranda's got to disappear. There's no other way out of this."

The color drained from Barnard's face. "What do you mean *disappear*?"

"Just what I said. Go get one of those laundry hampers. We'll toss her in it and dump her in the Goodbye Room." Helen smiled and rubbed her hands together. "From there it's into the cooker and up the smokestack."

Barnard worked his hand around his jaw. "I'm not sure that's a good idea."

"You didn't leave us any other option. Do you want the Director to see Aranda? We've got to get rid of her now and pretend this whole thing never happened."

"What about Benjamin and Giles? They'll both see her when they go back in."

"Benjamin's not going to see anything. I'll send him home early and tell him I'll clock him out at his regular time. And we don't have to worry about Giles if we send him home early too. We'll clean out the Goodbye Room and pitch her into the fire with the kids."

Barnard's hands went to his face. "Oh, good gawd, the thought of handling all those dead kids gives me the willies. Besides, it doesn't take two people to pitch 'em into the fire. Why don't you take care of it?"

"I'm not going in there alone. You have to help. I can't lift Aranda's body into the incinerator by myself."

When she reached for his arm, Barnard shook her off. "I don't care what happens to us, I'm not doing it."

She bit her lip. "Okay, I'll take care of it. After we get her in the Goodbye Room, I want you to move her car out of the parking area." She tossed him a ring of keys. "Take it down to the Mall and park it where it won't be noticed. Be sure to wear gloves and if you move the seat, put it back where it was. You'll have to walk back. We don't want any record of you having been there."

Helen checked her watch then slid her chair back. "It's almost time. Giles will be taking the kids down in a few minutes."

CHAPTER SEVENTEEN

Helen held the elevator door open and Barnard wrestled the hamper into it. Aranda lay inside unconscious. "She's a lot heavier than a kid would be. You sure you can handle her?"

He scowled at her. "What if she wakes up while Giles is there?"

"You saw her, she's out of it."

"Well, she better stay that way."

The elevator descended to the basement and she gave Barnard a shove as the doors opened. "Hurry up. We need to hide before Giles shows up with the kids." Helen cocked her head, straining to hear. "That's the freight elevator on its way down," she whispered. "He'll have the useless kids with him." She and Barnard pulled the hamper around a corner and ducked out of sight.

Giles exited the freight elevator with a row of small children in tow. He literally had them roped together and, thanks to his valium-laced cookies, they followed without complaint. The front of their rope was tied to the handle of a shopping cart. It held three youngsters too young to walk and keep up. He gave the cart a shove toward the basement door, yanking the children behind it.

"Hurry up! Git goin' you useless critters."

Once in the basement, he moved his charges to the Goodbye Room and pushed the heavy door aside. He thrust them in and swung it shut, forcing the latch down to secure it tightly. A heavy bolt ensured an airtight seal. He tested it a second time before leaving to attach the canister of gas to a connection from the floor above.

Helen gave Barnard a poke in the ribs. "After you dump Aranda in with the kids take the hamper and hose it down inside and out. Then go move her car. I'll go upstairs and stall Giles so you have plenty of time to dump her body in the Goodbye Room."

She raced away without a backward glance.

Grumbling at her under his breath, Barnard wheeled the hamper to the Goodbye Room and unlatched and unbolted the door. He pulled Aranda out of the hamper. She groaned when he dumped her on the floor. Ignoring her moans, he propelled the hamper out of the way. Before he could slam the door behind him, he had to force some of the children back inside as they made wobbly, confused efforts to escape. He leaned into the heavy door, re-latched and bolted it.

෪෬

Aranda gave a start when the door slammed shut. Her throbbing head felt as if it might explode. She held it with both hands. After a few moments she eased her hand over and touched her swollen mouth. She could feel the stubby remains of broken teeth with her tongue.

Where was she?

Though her eyes were nearly swollen shut, she strained to see into the gloom surrounding her. She had no memory of them taking her to this place, this cell, this dungeon. How did she get here?

With effort, she dredged up dreamlike memories of being stopped by Helen and Barnard. He took her upstairs while Helen did something... she couldn't recall what. Despite the pounding in her head, she closed her eyes and forced herself to remember.

The little girl!

Other things started coming back. Barnard asking questions... over and over, so many questions...and his clenched fists with the beating that followed. She remembered being woozy, laying on a tabletop and blackness following.

Oh God, what did I tell him?

She recalled focusing on the children she'd saved and, despite the pain, thoughts of those she'd rescued gave her strength. Maybe she hadn't told him anything.

Aranda heard movement beside her. Fearing a rat, she

quickly wrapped her arms around herself. The room's only light came from an opening near the ceiling. It wasn't much, but it was better than total darkness. She squinted, forcing her eyes to focus, and noticed children in the cell with her. Some were sleeping on the bare cement floor. Others had formed a circle around her.

She felt a light touch on her arm. It kindled memories of carefree days as a child when she giggled at butterflies walking along the back of her hand. Looking down, she saw the little girl she'd tried to rescue. Awareness of where she was crept into her mind and she shivered. The youngster wriggled under her arm and Aranda pulled her into her lap.

The little girl held out her hand still swaddled in the cloth Aranda tied around it to staunch the bleeding. "Owwie."

"Yes, I'm so sorry." She kissed the toddler's forehead.

The little girl reached up with her uninjured hand and softly touched Aranda's swollen face. "You owwie too."

"Yes, but it will be okay. Don't worry, Sweetheart." She began to rock the child and softly hum a tune she remembered from her childhood. Neither spoke. She continued to croon so the children would know they were not alone. The little girl drifted off to sleep in her arms. She wished they were all asleep. *They soon will be*, she thought. An involuntary spasm coursed through her.

She was rubbing the gooseflesh on her arms when she heard the raspy grate of metal against metal. Aranda raised her eyes to the ceiling and watched in horror as the small circle of light that illuminated their cell became a shrinking crescent. Like a waning moon, the arc of brightness grew smaller and smaller. An instant later a heavy metal cap clanked into place, plunging them into total darkness.

Someone up above had cut off their only source of light and ventilation. The fetid smells and dampness of the cell became stifling. Humidity gathered around her. Her skin felt clammy. Even breathing became difficult. Hearing muffled weeping in the gloom, she grieved for the children.

For their sake Aranda tried to shut out the sounds of impending death by singing *Brahms Lullaby* against a background of bangs and clanks. The children quieted as she sang. Following the sound of her voice, they inched toward her in the darkness and clustered around her seeking comfort.

She knew the delivery pipe was now attached and began taking deep breaths, filling her lungs while there was still adequate air to breathe. She'd just begun *Silent Night* when she heard a hissing noise. She sang louder, and encouraged some of the older children to join her, in hopes of drowning out the sound of noxious gas entering the room.

All around her little ones began to cough and sob as the stinging gas enveloped them. Aranda's own breaths came in gulps and gasps. Determined to outlast the children, she wadded up the front of her blouse over her face and gulped in all the air she could. Then she held her breath.

She scooped them into her lap and reached out to console as many as she could touch. She hugged them tightly and pressed their little bodies close against her, soothing them when they shook and convulsed. Her hands moved from one to the other, caressing tiny faces, brushing away tears, and smoothing sweaty hair.

She gritted her broken teeth so she wouldn't weep. To weep would be to breathe. And she couldn't allow herself to breathe so long as the children needed her. She bit her lip, reopening earlier wounds and tried not to listen to their gasps and groans, whimpering and wheezing.

Death, she realized, was now only moments away. She felt no fear, only peace and acceptance. Aranda silently prayed, asking forgiveness for her failings and begged God to take her and all these beautiful children into his everlasting kingdom. She asked for mercy on her captors and all of the employees working in FFUs. For the most part they were well-meaning, but misinformed people entrapped by evil. The few who truly understood the impact of their actions she left to God's judgment. Lastly, she prayed for, as she called him, poor pathetic Giles.

Though her lungs felt like they'd burst, she continued to comfort the few children who hadn't succumbed. Most of them, thank God, had already lapsed into unconsciousness. Heavier than air, the gas gathered around her like a smothering pillow. It irritated her skin and burned her eyes. She wanted to tear at her eyes and scream, but forced herself to remain quiet for the children's sake.

The last child slowly sank against her. The sounds of sobbing, coughing and wheezing had ceased. A dark envelope of silence surrounded them. Her time had come. Aranda's head swam. The room faded away and she began to sway. She continued to pray while holding the children's small, limp bodies pressed against her. She'd managed to outlast them all.

Aranda released the stale air in her lungs. She reflexively took a deep, coughing breath. Choking as killing gas flooded her lungs, she mentally recited the 23rd Psalm.

CHAPTER EIGHTEEN

Giles spent time straightening and arranging things in the storage room while waiting for the gas to do its work. Then he'd go in and collect the children's fingers for DNA proof of their demise before Benjamin incinerated their bodies. He'd already mopped-up the corral, as he called it, and made ready for the next day's victims.

"Transporter Giles report to the Security Office ASAP," boomed the loud speaker.

He gave a sudden start and muttered a curse.

"Transporter Giles report to the Security Office ASAP."

"I'm comin' already." Giles practiced an alibi as he walked to the Security Office. As much as it hurt, he was glad he'd burned the money. He'd known this was coming. Aranda must've ratted on him. What was her problem anyway? A few pats on the rear never hurt anybody. She pretended to be upset, but deep down he knew she liked it.

He briefly considered running. He could go somewhere else, get another job. He shook his head. Nah, no matter where he went they could track him down. And running would only confirm his guilt. Better to deny everything and hope they believed him and not Aranda.

ഇൟ

Giles stood in front of Helen, eyes wide, mouth gaping open.

"Do you understand what I've told you?" Helen asked.

His head snapped up, he closed his mouth and willed his thoughts back to the present. "Yeah, I got it. You want me to go down to the basement and burn up the kids 'cuz Benjamin had t' go home." He cocked his head to one side, and lowered his eyebrows. "What am I gonna get for doin' it?"

Helen leaned back and crossed her arms. "That little girl today wasn't the first one. I know you've been selling kids to Aranda."

The shocked expression on Giles face told her all she needed to know. He opened his mouth, ready to deny everything, but she waved away his rebuttals and told him to save his breath. Her gamble had paid off; she'd been right about him all along.

"I'll tell you what you're going to get for doing this little favor. You'll get my silence." She tossed her hand in the air. "I don't know anything about the arrangement you had with Aranda."

Giles let out an astonished sputter of relief.

"After all, we're co-workers. We need to stick together, look out for each other." She shrugged. "If someone accidentally breaks a regulation now and then, there's no sense in being hard-nosed about it. We're all human aren't we?"

Giles nodded in agreement. "I hear what you're sayin'. One hand washes t' other, don't it? All for one and one for all, as they say."

"I'm glad you understand. Now you'd better get downstairs. This requires your immediate attention."

"I'm on it." Giles unconsciously rubbed his hands together in relief. He paused at the door and gave her a little salute. "Anything for a friend," he said.

Helen snickered as he raced away.

৪০৫৪

Giles took the basement steps two at a time, chuckling to himself as he hurried down the stairway. It couldn't have worked out better if he'd planned it. When he reached the landing, he gripped the baluster and spun around it like an excited child.

The lights were on when he opened the basement door. He scurried through closing and locking it behind him. Benjamin routinely allowed him into the Goodbye Room long enough to gather his genetic evidence, the children's fingers, before securing the door. Regulations restricted anyone else from being present during the incineration process.

Death held no fear or revulsion for Giles. He'd spent several summers during High School working at a local mortuary.

Although he'd only been hired for yard work and janitorial tasks, he found the surroundings interesting...especially when left alone in the building.

Inside the basement, Giles unlatched and pulled aside the heavy door to the Good-Bye Room. He stepped through and stopped in his tracks when he saw Aranda. His newfound friendship with Helen instantly soured.

All for one and one for all like hell!

She'd blackmailed him into doing her dirty work knowing she had enough to insure he'd keep his mouth shut. Helen's little game had cost him every penny Aranda paid him. He seethed. If it was the last thing he did, he'd get even with Helen for making him pitch that wad o' dough into the fire.

Forgetting the money, his eyes returned to Aranda. She appeared to be sleeping. Tip-toeing over, he knelt beside her. After a moment he softly touched her hand.

Still warm.

An evil grin curled his lips. He flicked tangled and matted hair aside from her face and blanched at the sight. "Man, you look awful. They really worked you over, didn't they?"

Disentangling the children's bodies and shoving them aside, he grabbed her under the arms and dragged her out of the Good-Bye Room. "It wouldn't be polite to take care of things in front of the little kiddies, now would it?"

He laid her on the floor and stood up. Hands on his hips, he gazed down at her and shook his head. "Was it worth this? In the end you told 'em what they wanted to know. These kids were destined for the oven. There's no way you or anyone else is ever gonna change it."

Gazing around the room, his eyes settled on a wooden table. It held several canisters of lethal gas for future use. He strode over and carefully set them aside on the floor. Then he leaned over, lifted Aranda's body off the floor and carried her to the narrow tabletop.

Gently laying her on it, he began unbuttoning her uniform, talking to her as he worked. "They messed up yur face, but it looks like they left the best parts for ol' Giles." He snickered. "Maybe it's a good thing yur eyes are swollen shut. Least ways ya don't have t' be makin' a face like yur about to toss yur cookies. You think I didn't notice? Every time I as much as smiled at ya, you gave me *the look*. Don't pretend you don't know what I'm talkin' about. You think I'm stupid or somethin'?"

He ripped off her blouse and began tugging at her waistband. He stopped and frowned. Glancing around, he spied a dirty towel a custodian had dropped. He crossed the cold cement floor and picked it up.

"I gotta tell ya, 'Randa, I hate seeing ya like this. You went and got yourself killed for nothin'. I used to think you were a pretty little thing, but nobody'd know it now." He spread the towel over her battered face, hiding it.

He'd incinerate Aranda and the rest of them like the old battle axe wanted. But first he intended to collect his bonus. This was an opportunity too great to pass up. All that friendship crap aside, Helen surely didn't expect him to do this for nothin'.

Giles removed the last piece of Aranda's clothing and tossed it into the incinerator. He ran his hand along her bare thigh. "You're even prettier than I imagined."

He unbuttoned his coveralls, stepped out of them and tossed the heavy garment aside. Sneering he uttered, "Ya won't turn me down this time."

CHAPTER NINETEEN

"Any mind that is capable of real sorrow is capable of good."

~ Harriet Beecher Stowe

Mira snapped off her desk lamp before heading for her office door. Her hand was on the knob when the phone rang. Her first impulse was to let it roll over to voicemail; it could wait until the following morning. Yet, something told her not to ignore the call. She hurried back, sat her purse on the desktop, and grabbed the receiver. "Mira Hastings."

"It's Carolyn." Mira heard tears in her voice. "Aranda hasn't come home. Did you see her this afternoon?"

"No. I try to avoid unnecessary contact with her so I don't compromise her efforts." Mira inched over to the window as she spoke. She lifted a slat in the blinds and peered down at the parking lot. "Her car isn't anywhere in sight."

"She took money with her this morning intending to rescue a child. Her shift usually ends at 3:00. She should have been home hours ago."

"Let me check our time clock records." Mira clicked on her computer and waited impatiently for it to boot. When it did, she quickly toggled through the personnel files and opened up the day's time clock entries. Scanning the list, she highlighted Aranda's name. "I show her clocking in at her regular time. She clocked out again at 3:00 p.m. on the dot."

"Oh my heavens. Have you any idea where she might be?" Carolyn sucked in a breath. "Is there any way to question Giles without making him suspect your involvement?"

"I was on my way out." Mira quickly scanned the day's records. "Everyone on the day shift has already gone home, including Giles. But, I'll ask the night crew if they passed her when they came in. I'll let you know if I learn anything."

"Thanks, Jonathan and I are beside ourselves."

࿇

Carolyn placed the platter of French bread in the middle of the table. Plates of spaghetti and steaming bowls of broccoli sat in front of Robbie, Emma and Mandy. Jonathan said grace and picked up the platter, offering it to the children. Each took a slice of the warm bread.

"Thank you," Emma said. "When Aunt Reeta made spaghetti, she never made anything else with it. This spaghetti is yummier too." She took another bite and glanced at the empty chair across from her. "How come Aranda's not here? She promised to teach us more songs after dinner."

Carolyn's eyes turned to Emma and the others. "I'm sorry sweethearts. Something has detained Aranda."

Robbie's head shot up. He put his fork down and gaped directly at Jonathan. He'd come to depend on him as the answer man. "What's d-d-detain m-m-mean?"

Jonathan swallowed hard. "It means something's kept her away, made her late."

"Will you teach us songs instead?" Emma asked.

"Not tonight, kiddo. I don't feel much like singing."

Carolyn gave Jonathan a sympathetic look before turning back to the children. "Perhaps the three of you can play a board game tonight. Jonathan and I have other things to occupy our thoughts."

"What's oc-oc-occupy m-m-mean?" Robbie picked up his glass of milk and took a sip, watching Jonathan.

Jonathan didn't answer. He rose and left the table, wiping his eyes.

Carolyn reached over and patted Robbie's shoulder. "We need to leave Jonathan alone for now."

"He looks sad," Emma said. "Is something wrong with Aranda?"

"I don't know, Honey, but we can pray for her. Okay?"

"I don't know how to do that."

Carolyn blinked. "After dinner is cleaned up, we'll sit down and talk about prayer. And pray for God to watch over Aranda." She blotted her mouth with a napkin and, not wanting the children to notice, swept a tear from the corner of her eye.

ಬೊ೧೪

Once the children were safely tucked into bed that night, and all was quiet, Carolyn tapped on Jonathan's door.

"Come in, Mother."

She opened the door and found Jonathan atop his bed, an arm draped across his eyes, fully clothed with his shoes still on.

"Have you moved from that spot since dinner?"

"Guess not." He removed his arm and gazed at the ceiling.

"We need to consider our options about Aranda. After she's been gone 24 hours, we can file a missing person's report, but having the children here creates a problem for us."

"How so?"

"If the police want to inspect Aranda's room, the children can't be present. It's easier to hide children's clothing and toys than the children themselves. We need to move them to the Foundling Home before I can file a report."

"Then I'll help you get them ready first thing tomorrow morning."

"It's going to cause them added stress to be hustled out so quickly."

Jonathan lifted his eyebrows. "I know we typically let the kids visit the Foundling Home once or twice before a permanent move, but with Aranda overdue everything's topsy-turvy." He bit his lip. "This isn't like her. If we only knew where she is, why she's so late."

Carolyn simply nodded. "As soon as we've moved the children we'll go directly to the police station to file a report. I want to find her too."

Jonathan's brow furrowed. "Have you thought about the

money she was carrying? Someone could have attacked her for it."

"I know." Carolyn took a deep breath and laid her hand on Jonathan's arm. "Should we tell them about the money? They'll want to know why she was carrying so much cash."

"How can we not? It may be why she's missing."

"But will knowing about the money help them find her? We can't jeopardize Director Hastings or our rescue program."

Jonathan sat up and stared into his mother's eyes. "Program? What program? Without Aranda we have NO rescue program!"

"Lower your voice or the children will hear you." Carolyn hung her head. "I don't want to believe Aranda is gone for good. We need to act as if she's coming back and preserve all she worked to accomplish."

"Okay, Mother. I'll go with you to file the report. If they have any suggestions, I want to hear them."

Carolyn patted his arm. "Try to get some sleep. That's where I'm headed." She got up and walked to the door. Turning, she said, "You know, you've yet to search Robbie's background to see if you can find a contact person who might have loved and cared for him. Doing that while we wait for word of Aranda would give you something else to think about."

Jonathan sat up and swung his feet over the side of the bed. "Unless she comes home, I don't expect to sleep tonight anyway," "I might as well start my search with Robbie's birth records," he mumbled to himself. Jonathan stood up, trudged across to his computer, and sighing, clicked it on..

Carolyn silently closed the door behind her.

CHAPTER TWENTY

Robbie, Emma and Mandy were roused out of their beds as soon as the sun peeked over the horizon the next morning. The children took their seats around the kitchen table, squinting at the morning sun and rubbing sleep out of their eyes.

Jonathan sat boxes of cereal down in the center of the table and gently touched his mother's shoulder before turning to the kids. "I know it's early, and I'm sorry about that. But Mom and I need to get to work finding Aranda. She's still missing."

When Emma gasped, Carolyn reached over and patted her hand.

"A policeman may come to the house, so we need to move you to the Foundling Home of Future Contributors right away." Her eyes moved over the children. On this, their last day in her home, she wanted to fix a permanent memory of each of them in her mind.

Jonathan placed a small glass of orange juice in front of each child. "We'll be packing your things right after breakfast and loading them in the car."

Mandy reached for her glass. "Tell us what it's like there again."

Carolyn gave her an encouraging smile and began describing the Foundling Home of Future Contributors to the children one last time, hoping to relieve any fear they might have.

"It's a, it's a...uh, I can't remember that long name," Emma said. "I'll just call it *The Kids Home*." She smiled when Robbie and Mandy began to giggle.

Carolyn let out a sigh of relief.

Jonathan filled the children's bowls with cereal. "Let's all eat our breakfast and get started. You'll have lunch in a wonderful new place."

℘☙

A few hours later, Robbie found himself at the Foundling Home and alone. Right after processing, they led him off in one direction and the two girls in another. He stared out a window at the rain that'd begun when they arrived. As he watched raindrops splash on the playground below, he acknowledged the place was nice enough, just like Aunt Carolyn and Jonathan promised. But boys were all in one wing of the big old building, and girls were way off in another. He wondered what Emma and Mandy were doing. Would he ever see them again? Or even Aunt Carolyn and Jonathan?

Robbie started to think of Gramma and hiccupped, trying to stifle a sob. There were other boys walking the halls, but they were strangers and mustn't see him cry. More than anything he really, really wanted Gramma. He longed to hear her soft, kind voice and eat supper with her. Gramma made special dishes just for him. She always told him a story at bedtime, and gave him a great big hug and kiss before tucking him into bed. He always felt safe with Gramma, and never *alone* like he did now.

Better to focus on other stuff than think about Gramma, he decided. Whenever he thought about the way things used to be, he couldn't hold back the tears that followed. He sniffed as a drop ran down his cheek and settled in the corner of his mouth. He caught it with his tongue. It tasted salty and he wished he could ask Jonathan about it.

Why does everybody I care about go away?

෨෬

Carolyn sat down and laid a photo of Aranda on the desk in front of the brawny detective. Jonathan stood behind her resting his hands on her shoulders.

Brow furrowed, the detective scribbled a few notes before folding his huge hands on the desk.

A russet-colored glass ashtray sat on the corner of the cluttered desk, overflowing with cigar butts. The stench drew Carolyn's gaze and she blanched.

"Something the matter?" the detective asked.

"I'm surprised they allow smoking in this building."

He chuckled and stuffed a well-chewed stogie between his teeth. "They do in here. Anytime the mayor wants to run my beat, I'll go sit in his plush office. And I promise not to smell it up with cigar smoke."

He unfolded his hands and lifted the photo. He worked the cigar around as he studied the picture of the young woman sitting at a picnic table. "Pretty girl," he said and sat the picture aside. "So, you're telling me this gal ain't your daughter, or even a relative, but you want to file a missing person's report on her?"

"Yes sir. I've been her guardian since Aranda was eight years old. Her mother died of cancer and I was the woman's caregiver in her last days. She asked me to raise Aranda for her."

The man scratched his chin. "So, there's no other relative she could've taken off to see? Her father, maybe?"

"Aranda and I are very close. She wouldn't leave without telling me."

"Perhaps she decided it was time to reopen a connection with the man who sired her and she was embarrassed to tell you."

"Now see here!" Jonathan stamped his foot. "Aranda never showed any interest in the man who abandoned her dying mother. Mom had medical training as a nurse and she made the last months of the poor woman's life tolerable. Mrs. Blackthorn knew she was dying and begged Mom to care for Aranda after her death, and she always has."

The detective's eyes left Jonathan and moved to Carolyn. "That how it was?"

"Yes sir, officer."

He scowled. "Name's Brinkman, Detective Brinkman."

She wanted to run, but stood her ground for Aranda's sake. "Of course, *Detective* Brinkman."

"And, this is Aranda." Picking up the photo, he turned it to the light. "She's over 21 and has every right to go where she pleases, whenever she pleases."

Carolyn frowned. "She didn't return from work yesterday. She always comes straight home. Something must have happened to her. Please, you need to look for her. She could be in terrible trouble. Injured, or kidnapped, or—"

His raised hand stopped her. "Okay, okay. I get the picture. I'll see what I can do. Describe her car and I'll send out an APB to keep an eye out for it."

"What will the APB accomplish?" Jonathan asked.

"It will notify other departments throughout the state that we're looking for her and what she was driving. If someone spots her, or her car, they'll let me know." He touched the phone as if to answer it. "Then, I'll contact you and we'll all be happy."

$$\mathcal{EO CR}$$

Jonathan edged his computer mouse to Shut Down. He leaned back and crossed his arms with a satisfied smile as the screen went black. He'd done it. With no sign of Aranda, he'd thrown himself into a project he could control. And, amidst all the sorrow over Aranda's disappearance, something finally brought a spark of light into the darkness.

He went into the kitchen where Carolyn was one-handedly loading the dishwasher. "Guess what Mom?" He pretended to tip a hat he didn't have. "I found Robbie's grandmother."

The spoon in Carolyn's hand fell to the floor with a clatter.

Jonathan bent to pick it up and popped it into the dishwasher. "You're surprised. Didn't you think I could do it?"

"I've always believed you could do almost anything you set your mind to." Rising on her tip-toes, she kissed his cheek.

Jonathan pulled back a chair and sat at the table. "First, I searched for Robbie's birth record. Locating his records gave me his parent's names, and I started tracking them. Robbie's mother divorced his father. Not long after, she died when a car struck her. She was living with her mother at the time."

Carolyn's eyebrows shot up. "That's telling isn't it? So the Gramma Robbie talks about is his maternal grandmother. And he lived with her, probably spent most of his life with her."

"Exactly. I ran a search for Robbie's mother's parents, and came up with a Gerald and Rebecca Stuart. Gerald is deceased, but I located a woman by that name whose birth date matches the one on Robbie's mother's record." Jonathan rapped his knuckles on the tabletop. "I'm pretty certain she's Robbie's Grandma."

Carolyn slid onto a kitchen chair beside him. "Let's talk about how we're going to approach this. We don't know for sure where she stands regarding Robbie. She might have agreed with his father. Perhaps she'd grown tired of caring for a small child and his father didn't want to take on the responsibility."

"The way Robbie talks about her it sounds to me like she loves him. I don't think she'd agree to his trip to an FFU."

"I suppose not, but if we're wrong about her affection for Robbie ..." She opened her empty hand, palm upward.

"I think it would be best if you contact her, since you're a woman. My voice on the phone might frighten her." Jonathan reached across the table and took his mother's hand. "I know you can sound her out and determine how she feels about Robbie; maybe find out what you need to know *before* telling her he's still alive."

"If you have a phone number, I'll call her right now."

CHAPTER TWENTY-ONE

"It is a law of nature we overlook, that intellectual versatility is the compensation for change, danger, and trouble." ~ H.G. Wells

On their first morning at the Foundling Home of Future Contributors the three children awoke to a bell's deep, mellow dong, dong, dong.

Robbie opened his eyes and rubbed them. He shared a room with three other boys. They were crawling out of bed, so he did too.

"Does it d-d-do that every m-m-morning?"

The boy in the bed next to Robbie's sneered, not bothering to answer.

From across the room, five-year-old Charlie said, "That's to wake us up, silly. Dress quick. The faster we get to breakfast the better chance for seconds."

Robbie smiled at Charlie and peeled off the yellow flannel pajamas Carolyn left with him. Each boy had a small chest of drawers by his bed and they were pulling out fresh clothes. There was one beside Robbie's bed too, but when he checked, it was empty. His clothes were still at the foot of his bed where he'd put them the night before, so he put them back on.

He didn't want the other boys to leave him behind on his first full day so he rushed to dress. Hurriedly making his bed like the others did, he raced out of the room on Charlie's heels. Childhood banter and laughter echoed through the hallways as Robbie and his roommates joined the flow headed downstairs.

Robbie stared in awe as they entered a large open space bustling with activity.

"We call this the *coffee-to-ya*," Charlie said, nudging Robbie in the ribs as they entered. "Get it?" He didn't, but laughed anyway.

Rows of children funneled past counters of steaming food

taking what they wanted before carrying their trays to long tables framed by benches. Robbie was captivated. When he glanced around again, the boys he shared a room with had joined the buffet line, and a dozen others had crowded in behind them.

He understood the rules of *cut-zies* and didn't dare push back in. He hurried over to catch up with the line. Others queued up behind him. Despite laughter and activity, Robbie felt isolated and homesick. It was awful to not be with anyone. Looking at the floor, he tried not to cry.

"Hey Robbie!"

Emma! A shiver of excitement ran through him. He saw her farther back in line with Mandy. He motioned the children between them to hurry past him so they could be together.

"Emma, I was 'fraid I'd n-n-never f-f-find you again."

She leaned forward and hugged him. "We'll get to see each other at meals."

A girl with red braids asked, "Who's the little boy, Emma?"

Looking up, Robbie suddenly realized he'd moved into the center of a group of girls. When his face reddened, they started giggling.

Mandy spun around. Putting her hands on her hips, she glared at them. "Stop that! This is our friend, Robbie Wilson. A mean man already chopped his finger. Don't make him feel bad."

Properly chastised, the girls quieted.

Robbie leaned toward Emma and whispered, "My n-n-name's Robert M-M-Morgan now."

Emma remembered Aunt Carolyn's explaining the Kids Home would need to change Robbie's name, but she and Mandy could keep theirs. She spun around and introduced Robbie to her roommates. "He's Robbie *Morgan* now." Turning back to him, she smiled. "Maybe we'll get some classes together."

"I, I, h-hope s-s-so." He'd added a mumble to his recent stammer. Robbie had never been to a *class* before. He wasn't even sure what it was. But if Emma was there it wouldn't be scary.

Someone at the back of the line gave the person in front of them a shove. It rippled through the group, throwing Emma against Robbie. He turned and saw the line had moved forward leaving them behind. He hurried to catch up and found himself at the beginning of the serving line.

"Oh Robbie, see all the food," Emma said, pointing. "So many things to choose from. Pancakes, sausage, eggs, milk *and* juice... we're going to eat better than I ever did at Aunt Reeta's."

Robbie watched the other kids move down the line picking and choosing as they went. Some didn't even hesitate to ask for a bigger portion of the food they liked best. He swallowed hard. *There's plenty to eat here; but it's not the same as when Gramma makes something just for you and says she put love in it.*

Everyone was laughing and happy. He wondered what it would feel like to be so confident.

When they exited the line, rather than sit with either the boys or the girls, the three musketeers staked out a table for themselves.

Robbie began to feel better than he had since they'd arrived. He munched a piece of crispy bacon and whispered, "Emma, is what M-M-Mandy said t-t-true? Is that what h-h-happened to my f-f-finger? A mean m-m-man c-c-cut it off?"

Without lifting her eyes from her plate, Emma gave a quick nod. Robbie shivered and plopped a bite of syrupy pancake into his mouth.

೮೦೦೪

Carolyn sat at her desk nervously tapping her pencil. They'd had no word about Aranda, and she worried how the children were transitioning to the Foundling Home. As if that weren't enough, now Rebecca Stuart had entered the mix.

Jonathan noticed his mother's frowning face. "You okay, Mom?"

She looked up and shook her head. "Despite Detective

Brinkman's assurances, I can't accept that 'no news is good news.' I want to hear something about Aranda. And, did you notice the expression on the children's faces when we arrived at the Foundling Home?"

Jonathan nodded. "They were apprehensive. That's to be expected."

"I couldn't spend enough time preparing them for their transition to yet another new location. There are so few employees at the Home. No matter how hard they try, and they do try, they can't possibly give each child enough attention."

"Mom, they'll be fine. It's Aranda we need to focus on. We can't let her case grow cold. I don't want her to become a dog-eared file folder languishing in some musty file drawer."

"I'm not downplaying the importance of finding Aranda, but there are other concerns too."

Jonathan walked over beside her. "I'm sorry. Aranda's disappearance is all that's been on my mind. We'd begun to care a lot for each other."

"Yes, I know. And as much as it hurts to say it, there's not much else we can do except wait. I just hope we haven't created other problems. For instance, when I phoned Robbie's grandmother. I'm worried I told her too much. Or maybe not enough..." Carolyn gave a disheartened shrug. "I emphasized not to let anyone know how she learned about Robbie, but I didn't explain everything to her."

"Well, you couldn't exactly tell her how he got there. You told her enough so she could visit him, and he'll be thrilled to see his *Gramma* again. What harm can come of that?"

"There's something about this that makes me uncomfortable." She shook her head and frowned. "I wish I could put my finger on it."

Jonathan placed a hand on his mother's shoulder. "It's time for lunch. I'll warm up some of yesterday's vegetable soup. It'll make us both feel better."

CHAPTER TWENTY-TWO

Jonathan and Carolyn were clearing the lunch dishes when they heard a sharp rap on the front door. Jonathan pulled the curtain aside and peeked out the window. "It's Detective Brinkman," he said, hurrying to the door.

Brinkman stood in front of Jonathan chomping on his cigar. Carolyn arrived and gasped. Jonathan was frozen in place. In the detective's hand was a blue purse.

Crossing the room, Carolyn stepped between the two men. Her eyes were fixed on the handbag. Looking up, she frowned at Brinkman. "You should know I don't allow smoking in my house."

"It ain't lit." Brinkman extended the cigar for Carolyn to examine. He stepped inside and closed the door behind him. "Found Miss Blackthorn's car parked in a shopping mall a mile or so from the FFU. Locked, but the keys were on the floor. Otherwise, it was empty except for this purse. ID in the wallet says it's hers."

Carolyn took the purse Brinkman offered her. "Yes. It's Aranda's." She clutched it to her chest, trying not to weep. "May I go through it?"

"That's why I'm here. We didn't find any notes or other items that might explain her disappearance. Maybe you'll catch something we missed." He gave a half-apologetic shrug. "After all, we don't know the young lady's habits."

A tear rolled down Carolyn's cheek. A woman might leave her car somewhere, but never her purse. She carried it into the kitchen and put it on the table. One by one she carefully removed Aranda's personal effects, comb, powder, lipstick, pen, blank notepad, some hairpins. She pulled a cell phone out and turned it over in her hand.

Hands in his pockets, Brinkman slouched against the doorjamb, watching. "We checked the calls made on the phone, all to this house."

Carolyn placed it on the table with the other items. "She usually called home before she left work...except for the day she disappeared."

Carolyn spread the sides of the purse apart as wide as they'd go and peered in. She unzipped an inside pocket and removed tissues and half a pack of butter rum Lifesavers. *Where was the money?* She'd taken a sizable amount to pay Giles, and it wasn't here.

She sent a fleeting glance to Jonathan. He responded with a quick nod.

"Officer Brinkman..."

"That's Detective Brinkman."

"Of course, I'm sorry. *Detective* Brinkman, there's something you should know. Aranda had a large amount of money with her the day she went missing. It was in a white envelope. Neither the money nor the envelope are here."

Brinkman nearly swallowed his cigar. "What?" He slammed his fist down on the counter. "Why are you just now telling me this? You should have said something right away."

Carolyn winced. How much could she say without jeopardizing Life Chances? "You didn't ask and, and I was very upset."

"Isn't that great? I didn't ask if she was a certified helicopter pilot either. Should I have?"

"Oh, no. Aranda was afraid of heights. She didn't like flying."

He put his hands on his hips and glared down at her. "Marvelous. You've really simplified my job. Now I won't have to call the FAA after all."

Carolyn bit her lip. "The memory of the money surfaced when I saw her purse."

"How could you overlook something that important? We can't find her if you don't tell me everything you know."

Afraid to respond, Jonathan and Carolyn remained mute.

Brinkman spun a chair around and straddled it. Planting his elbows on the table, he looked her straight in the eye. "All right then. How much money did she have?"

"I never saw it." Carolyn turned to Jonathan. "Did you?"

Jonathan shook his head.

Brinkman mirrored Jonathan's head shake with one of his own. "But you know it was there and it was a lot?"

"Yes," Carolyn said with a nod.

"I don't suppose you can hazard a guess how she accumulated *a lot of money*?"

"I'm sorry," Carolyn whispered. "I've no idea."

"So where are we now? Did someone rob her, or did she plan to skip town all along? Have you considered that maybe the money was ill-gotten?"

"Aranda would never do anything...uh, immoral." Carolyn chewed her lower lip. She'd almost said *illegal*, but anyone who was part of the Life Chances movement, including herself, frequently did things considered illegal, but never immoral.

Brinkman continued punctuating his questions with jabs of his cigar. "How does an FFU janitor come by *a lot of money*? Care to speculate on that?"

"I told you her mother died. She inherited whatever her mother had; perhaps she sold some of her things."

"Okay. Let's say she did. What did she plan on doing with the money?" Carolyn began to form an answer, but Brinkman's raised hand stopped her. "Never mind, she probably didn't tell you that either."

Eyes downcast, Carolyn sighed.

Jonathan stepped between his mother and the detective. "Why is all of this relevant?"

Detective Brinkman stared hard at the younger man. "Because a young woman with a dead end job, living with a couple of people unrelated to her, might decide she'd had enough and wanted to see what life had to offer somewhere else."

"That's crazy! You didn't know Aranda. She was kind and thoughtful and considerate." Carolyn touched his arm and Jonathan lowered his voice. "She cared for us as much as we cared for her."

"Uh-huh," Brinkman stroked his chin, "and where were you all afternoon on the day she disappeared?"

"We were together here at home waiting for Aranda," Carolyn quickly answered.

Carolyn watched as Brinkman scooped up the items from the table and dumped them back into the purse. *How could Aranda's life be reduced to a handful of trifles?*

He tucked the purse under his arm and headed for the door without a word.

Jonathan followed at his heels with Carolyn trailing behind. "That's it? You think she just up and left without telling anyone?"

"Yeah, that's about it kid. Unless you can think of anything to add..." When neither Jonathan nor Carolyn replied, he jammed his cigar back in his mouth, opened the front door, and stormed out. "I'll be in touch if anything surfaces," Brinkman muttered over his shoulder.

Jonathan dropped onto the couch. "What a condescending jerk."

Carolyn frowned. "I don't think we handled things very well. For a moment I thought he might arrest us." Unable to wring her hands like most people, Carolyn rubbed her thumb repeatedly over her fingers.

"He didn't exactly seem on fire to locate Aranda."

"I hope we told him enough. I don't want to hinder his investigation."

Jonathan grimaced. "We can't jeopardize Director Hastings and the others."

Carolyn picked up her son's hand and pressed his fingers to

her lips. "Like you, I wish there was more we could do."

Jonathan's brows furrowed in concentration. "Let's go over what we've learned and do some brain storming together. Okay?" He stood up and began to pace. "The money is gone. Did she pay Giles off? If so, what happened to the child she was supposed to get from him?"

"I don't think Giles would risk giving up his steady flow of cash by hurting Aranda. Suppose she was robbed *before* she met with Giles." She frowned. "Yet, we know she got to work safely and clocked out again on time."

"Maybe something prevented her from getting a child like she planned. She could have stopped at the mall with the money still in her purse and was mugged. Or, maybe she got the child and was on her way home when something happened to her *and* the child."

Carolyn sighed. "Question after question and no answers."

"Someone needs to check with Giles and find out what he knows."

"The police already questioned all of the FFU employees."

"But they don't know what we do about Giles."

"Giles may have suspected Aranda had help, but approaching him now would verify it."

Jonathan slumped back down onto the couch beside his mother. "Someone has to know something."

CHAPTER TWENTY-THREE

"Man cannot live without joy; therefore when he is deprived of true spiritual joys it is necessary that he become addicted to carnal pleasures." ~ Thomas Aquinas

Frank Wilson scowled at the caller I.D. on his phone. "What in the world can that stupid old woman want now?"

Denise bit her lip. "I'm sure it's nothing. Don't be upset."

He punched the answer button. "What do you want now, old lady?"

At the other end, Rebecca winced at his tone. She drummed the fingers of her right hand nervously holding the phone in her left. It wouldn't do for him to be angry. Not when she so desperately wanted something from him. "Frank, I'd like to settle things between us, so we can part on good terms and let bygones be bygones."

When he didn't say anything, she hurried on. "I found out what you did with Robbie and I want to thank you from the bottom of my heart. You're a good man and God will bless you for it."

Frank's answer came out as sputters instead of words. He finally mumbled, "Thank me? Me?"

"There's no need for false modesty. You did a wonderful thing. Not many men today would step up to the plate and take the initiative the way you did. You know, Frank, I have to confess there were moments when I thought ill of you. Now I understand what Veronica saw in you."

"Have you been drinking?"

Rebecca chuckled. "A friend told me where you took Robbie."

"You know? And you're happy about it?" Frank gave Denise a puzzled look and made crazy circles with his finger pointing to the side of his head.

"I know his support was a problem for you and Denise."

"So you approve of what I did?"

"Yes, but I still want to bring Robbie back home where he belongs, and need your permission. Of course I won't ask anything of you. Robbie and I can manage just fine on what I have. As for the state, you make the support payments and when they come, I'll send them back to you."

"Is this some kind of joke?"

"I wouldn't joke about anything as serious as Robbie's welfare. I always knew he was a bright little guy and I'm glad you agree. But, when I visited him at the Foundling Home of Future Contributors he said he wanted to come home with me."

"You *saw* him? You saw Robbie...where?"

A shiver ran up Rebecca's spine, making her flesh crawl. The intonation of Frank's voice told her she'd made a terrible mistake. She'd already said too much.

"Where is he?" Frank shouted.

"Um, oh dear, someone's at the door," she stammered. "Let me get back to you." She hurriedly jabbed her finger down on the disconnect button. Rebecca's eyes darted about the room fearfully. *What had she done?*

೮೧೪

Frank jammed the phone into his pocket. "That loony old broad says the kid's in one of those Foundling Homes. How can that be?"

Denise shrugged. "He must be really bright."

"Are you kidding? He's three years old and didn't even know his full name. Bright?" He shook his head. "No way." Frank combed his fingers through his hair as he paced. "I need to check this out and get to the bottom of things. I'm driving over there right now."

"Shall I come with you?"

"Better you don't. You won't want to hear what I say to them if Robbie is there."

ဆာ

Several hours later Denise heard Frank's car screech to a halt in the driveway. She hurried to meet him. "Was he there? At that Foundling place?"

"He's there all right. I saw him out in the playground, but no one would tell me why or how he got there." He slipped an arm around her shoulders as they walked up to the front porch.

"Does it matter? You aren't going to have to pay for his support any longer, right?"

"Who knows? What if the old lady gets him back and files for support. What will our rights be as far as having more children? I think he still counts no matter where he lives."

"I hadn't thought of it like that. But, we can still have two children. Isn't that good enough?"

Settling into his favorite recliner, Frank fidgeted. "I went to see an attorney. He's going to file a suit against the FFU. Do you know how long it could take to get a mess like this straightened out?" His voice shook with anger. "Meanwhile, Robbie could turn four. What then?"

He pounded on the arm of the chair as he spoke. "Somebody has to pay, and it needs to be that damned *Facility*. Talk about useless? None of this would've happened if they'd done their job."

Denise stepped behind him to massage his shoulders. "You need to relax."

"That old lady thinks it's about money, but it isn't. If that's all it was..."

She went rigid. Moving to the front again, she dropped onto the arm of his recliner and stared into his eyes. "What else is there? Tell me."

He exhaled loudly. "Honey, I don't share a lot about where I work because I can't. I'll tell you something, but keep it to yourself." He watched her nod. "Working in Public Relations gives me access to things that the general public won't know."

He took her hand. "We're working on a PR campaign to sell changes to the public on how many children they're allowed. Telling people how fewer conserves resources, is better for the environment and so on." He gave her a cynical frown. "The same old BS they use to justify everything. Having Robbie around means our child won't have a sibling."

She shrugged. "I can live with one if I have to."

He sighed. "That's not all. With Robbie alive we might not even be allowed a kid of our own. In spite of the disastrous economics and what happened in China, our government's goal is to eventually get it down to one child per couple."

He began to pace. "Anyone who already has more than one child will have to pay a fee of some kind...a tax or a fine. That's income for the government. As more people try to avoid annual fees, FFU businesses will boom."

Denise touched his cheek. "Now I understand why you needed to take Robbie to an FFU. C'mon, kiss me."

He gave her a half-hearted peck on the cheek. It would take more than a simple kiss to erase the image burned into Frank's memory as he watched Robbie and other children laughing and having fun on the playground.

CHAPTER TWENTY-FOUR

A file folder thudded onto Grayson Stevens' desk. "What's this?" he asked, glancing up at his supervisor.

The heavy-set, gray-haired man flipped the folder open and spun it around. "This was forwarded to us this morning. It appears there's a problem at one of the FFUs."

He gave Stevens a knowing look and thumped his knuckles on the wad of papers stuffed into the gray-green folder. "Since you have more interest in FFUs than anyone else here, I'm giving it to you. Have at it."

Stevens picked up the file, frowning as he opened it. The comment implied his supervisor had noticed Gray's opposition to the euthanasia program, a view which could jeopardize his future. Anyone who didn't agree with *A Planned Society Makes Good Sense* was branded a malcontent. That was an automatic career ender.

As he scanned through the file's top pages, his frown deepened. An attorney filing a lawsuit against the local FFU didn't concern him. He dealt with nuisance suits every day. However, this one came with an unusual twist. It claimed a child destined for euthanization wasn't killed after all. If true, it created the potential for all sorts of repercussions.

Stevens stopped reading a few paragraphs later. Rocking back in his chair, he let his mind wander back to the date of the alleged incident. Coincidentally, the same day Robert Wilson arrived at FFU-1116 was also the last time he'd seen the suspicious young woman transferring something from a laundry cart to the front seat of her car.

He took a deep breath and let it out as a slow sigh. Instead of stolen goods, could she have been putting Robert Wilson into her car? He recalled the mysterious woman at the window. She'd seen the young woman too. Where did she fit into this puzzle?

೮೦೧೪

The Head Mistress of the Foundling Home of Future Contributors stared across her desk at the sullen young man. "Inspector Jensen, I already told you we don't have a Robert Wilson enrolled here." She moved her chair aside so he could see her computer screen. "You're welcome to check the rolls yourself."

"Just because his name isn't on the list, doesn't mean he's not here."

"Would you recognize him if he was sitting in the chair next to you?" She watched him lower his eyes. "Mm-hmm, I thought as much." She rose and gestured toward her office door. "I've done as much as I can do. I'll escort you out."

"Suppose you rounded up all the kids who've come in over the last three months. I have a pretty good description of him."

"Only boys or girls too? Perhaps Robert Wilson is a code name and you're really searching for a *Roberta* Wilson."

"That's ridiculous."

"You being here is what's ridiculous. We have rules and regulations that limit what we can share, and they restrict the type of search you're suggesting. I will not allow you to disrupt our Future Contributors in a frivolous quest for a needle in a haystack."

Inspector Jensen glared at her before stomping out of her office. "This isn't over," he shouted over his shoulder, "the dad says he saw him here. I'll be back with a picture and a warrant."

Quickly rounding her desk, she fell into step beside him.

He glared at her. "I can find my own way back to my car."

She gave him a sweet smile. "Perhaps, but visitors are not allowed to wander the halls unescorted."

He checked his watch as they traversed the long hallway. "It's too late to do much this afternoon, but you can count on seeing me bright and early Monday morning. I'll have a court order *and* a recent photo of little Mr. Wilson.

Continuing to smile sweetly, she held the exit door wide open for him. As he marched down the front of the facility's wide stone steps, she released the door letting it slam shut behind him.

ହେଉ

Rebecca laid her dish towel down on the counter and crossed the kitchen to answer her phone. The old-fashioned touch-tone rested on a credenza outside the kitchen door. She'd had it for decades and refused to give it up. It reminded her of when her daughter, Veronica, drug a chair over and whispered confidences to high school girl friends.

She was surprised to find Grayson Stevens from the County Prosecutor's Office on the line. "I've done nothing wrong. What could you possibly want from me?"

"It's about your grandson, Robert Wilson."

Her heart skipped a beat. "Robbie's my daughter's son. When she divorced his father they lived with me. He was just a baby when a drunk driver ran her down in a crosswalk. I kept Robbie, until his father took him away a few weeks ago. I saw him again a few days ago."

"Where did you see him?

"At the local Foundling Home."

"The one for Future Contributors?"

"Yes. Is there another kind?" She bit her tongue. She should know better than to be flippant with a government employee. "Is anything wrong?" A sob escaped her lips. "He's okay, isn't he?"

"Whoa, slow down, take a deep breath. As far as I know Robbie's fine. My office is investigating how Robbie got into the Foundling Home in the first place."

"Well, that's easy enough, his father took him there." Steven's tense silence set off alarms for Rebecca. "Frank did take him there, didn't he?"

He ignored her question. "Has anyone else contacted you about Robbie recently?"

"It's strange you should ask. A young man came by a while ago, an Inspector Jensen. He said he was from the police department and wanted a picture of Robbie. He said his father didn't have one. Can you imagine a father not even having a picture of his own son? I thought it was odd, but Frank Wilson doesn't like talking to me, so I assumed he sent someone else to request a photo for him."

Stevens didn't comment.

"That young man was a policeman like he said, wasn't he? Oh dear, I shouldn't have been so trusting. I never thought to ask for identification." Rebecca's thoughts trailed off in multiple directions. "I took him at his word."

"He probably was," Stevens said. "So you gave a picture of Robert...er, Robbie, to this Inspector Jensen?"

"I had extra photos from his third birthday party. The picture was for Frank, wasn't it?" Her voice betrayed her rising panic.

"I'll follow-up on it and get back in touch." Stevens ended the call and dialed the police department.

CHAPTER TWENTY-FIVE

"Courage is resistance to fear, mastery of fear—not absence of fear." ~ Mark Twain

Monday morning arrived cloudy and cold. The sun wasn't yet over the eastern horizon when the mellow dong of the Foundling Home bell woke Robbie. He rubbed his eyes and peered out the window. Reluctantly he threw his feet over the side of the bed and watched his roommates do the same. "Why are we up when it's still dark?"

Before anyone answered, their door opened. A night monitor stuck his head in the door. "Hurry up guys, early breakfast this morning."

"How come?" a chorus of young voices asked.

"They'll explain in the cafeteria. Today's an unusual day. Now hurry up!" The monitor shut the door and moved to the next room.

The boys looked at each other, grabbed their clothes and began dressing.

ഇരു

While the other boys loaded up food trays, Robbie stood aside waiting for Emma and Mandy. When Emma waved he ran to her. "G-g-girls are always s-s-slower than b-b-boys." He grinned.

Mandy smiled at him. "That's because we dress better."

"And our hair's longer and takes time," Emma said, yawning. "I'm not hungry. It's too early."

The food smells made Robbie's mouth water. He couldn't imagine ever not being hungry. Grabbing Emma's hand, he pulled her toward the end of the line with Mandy hurrying to keep up.

The sound of children's voices, laughter and clinking plates and silverware echoed through the cafeteria as everyone ate.

When a whistle blew, the dining room went silent. Everyone's attention shifted to the Head Mistress at the front of the room.

"Children, the inspector we talked about is coming today." The room buzzed with frightened gasps, furtive whispers and hushed conversations.

"Quiet everyone! Quiet!" The Head Mistress blew her whistle again. The noise stopped. "We've practiced and prepared for this. All will be well. It's also why we got you up early for breakfast."

"She's w-w-worried 'bout us," Robbie said. "She m-m-must know the 'spector is l-l-looking for us kids from the FFU."

Emma put down her spoon. "Where did you hear about the FFU?"

"A b-b-big kid t-t-told me. He s-s-said we're lucky. Other kids t-t-there were all kilt."

"That can't be true. They probably got sent someplace else."

Sometimes Emma could be so smart, Robbie thought, but this time she was being really dumb.

The whistle blew again. "You have another fifteen minutes to finish eating and then we'll break into two groups. You all know which group you're to go with."

Robbie frowned. He knew. But going with them would separate him from Emma.

The Head Mistress circled her hand above her head. Her baby finger was folded forward at the middle joint and held down by her thumb. "Those of you who have a shortened finger go into hiding. After clean up, everyone else go to your classrooms as usual."

She paused and ran her eyes over the children. "Your classroom will look different. We removed the extra desks and chairs and put them out of sight. Your bedrooms have now changed too. The mattresses are slightly smaller than the bed frames, so extra mattresses were slipped under the other beds. Empty bed frames went into a closet. Nightstands are now two per bed instead of one."

Robbie crossed his arms and turned to Emma. "W-w-where will my s-s-stuff go?" He swallowed, hoping to control the stutter. "Will I g-get it b-b-back?"

Leaning close, she whispered, "Hiding is more important than your stuff."

He looked at the floor and nodded.

"I don't want you to be afraid," the Head Mistress continued. "As long as those in hiding remain quiet, this will all be over quickly and things can return to normal. When the bell rings, form into your two lines and follow the designated matron. Thank you all for cooperating." She turned and headed for her office.

Robbie gave Emma a sad look then glanced at the table behind them. His classmates, twins Sarah and Samuel, were eating together.

Sarah has to hide too. If I go with her, I won't feel so alone.

"I don't want to go to class without you," Robbie heard Samuel say. "I'm going where you go."

"Sam, you can't," Sarah said. "That will change the head count."

Samuel began to whimper, but Robbie smiled. He leaned back and touched Samuel's shoulder. "Hey S-S-Sam, you wanna t-trade p-p-places with me? Then you can g-g-go with S-S-Sarah and I'll g-g-o to class instead of you."

Samuel's eyes brightened. "That's a great idea!" He hesitated a moment. "But your finger?"

Robbie patted his pocket. "I got this great pretend finger that Jonathan made for me. See."

"Cool," said Samuel. He held up his hand for a high five, but before Robbie could respond the bell rang to get them moving.

There was a noisy stampede of little feet, crowding and pushing, and also a lot of thumps on the backs of those missing parts of their finger.

A matron quickly assembled the children who were going to hide and led them out. The remaining children busily gathered up plates, utensils and trays and returned them to the kitchen.

Robbie filed into the classroom with the other children. A

hand on his shoulder stopped him. He looked up at his teacher. She dropped to one knee. "Robbie, what are you doing here? You know you're supposed to be hiding."

"It's okay, Ma'am. Samuel w-w-went with Sarah 'stead of m-m -me."

"It doesn't matter. They'll recognize you."

He held out his hand. "No they w-w-won't. See, I got my pretend f-f-finger. They won't know."

She started to explain that he was the purpose of the search when footfalls coming down the hallway silenced her. "There's no time to find a place to hide you." Placing a hand on his head, the teacher mussed his hair and brushed it down over his forehead as far as it would go. "Take Samuel's seat and try not to be noticed. Just rest your hands lightly on your desk. Don't try to cover up your finger; it might draw attention. And stay still."

"I'll t-t-try," Robbie said. He now regretted he didn't go into hiding with the others. Head down, he hastened to the desk. Before sitting down, he cast a frightened look at Emma in the back of the room. She sat two rows behind him and off to one side. She could see him, but he had to turn around to see her. He reminded himself not to look toward her while the inspector was there.

As Robbie slid into Samuel's seat, a young man in a dark suit shoved the door open and entered the room. The Head Mistress followed behind him.

The teacher turned to face them. "May I help you?"

The young man ignored her and walked down the first row of desks. Holding a photograph of Robbie in one hand, he paused to study the first boy.

"This is Inspector Jensen," the Head Mistress said, gazing around the room. Her eyes widened when she noticed Robbie. They darted away quickly and she gave the teacher a look that asked, *How did this happen?*

CHAPTER TWENTY-SIX

Robbie couldn't resist turning to watch Emma as the inspector passed her by. She gasped and pulled back from him. Emma's eyes met Robbie's and he read fear in them.

Why?

In the row beside him, the inspector lifted a boy's chin and held the photo up. For the first time, Robbie got a clear view of the image.

How did that man get my birthday party picture?

Robbie suddenly realized why his teacher was so upset. No wonder they wanted him to hide. The man wasn't inspecting, he was searching. For *him*. He'd made a terrible mistake switching places with Samuel. Robbie tried hard not to cry; it'd only draw attention to himself.

☙❧

Emma saw Robbie's face register shock, then terror. She remembered what he'd told her about the other children with them at the FFU. Could it be true? Was that why Robbie looked so scared?

Emma bit her lip as the inspector turned to go down Robbie's row. He passed over two little girls and stopped beside a boy sitting two desks in front of Robbie.

Emma watched Robbie duck under his desk when the man wasn't looking. She frowned. Did he think that made him invisible? Wasn't it just like a little kid to try hiding under a desk? She'd have laughed if it wasn't so serious.

The inspector was at the desk in front of Robbie's now. Adrenalin shot through Emma. She knew she had to do something and do it quick. She picked up her yellow pencil and flipped it onto the floor.

"Oh no!" she yelled. "It's broken!" She leaped up, toppling over her chair with a terrible racket.

Inspector Jensen zipped past Robbie without any notice and rushed over to see what caused the commotion. "Okay, young lady, what's all the fuss about?"

Emma looked up at him, dread obvious in her face. "It's my pencil. The lead broke because it fell on the floor. It had such a nice point, and..." She ducked her head, afraid he might strike her.

Instead, he gave her a look of disgust. "This is a waste of time, and I've got other rooms to check."

The Head Mistress came down the aisle and touched Inspector Jensen's elbow. "Let me escort you to the next room."

Sweet relief flowed through Emma and, as if one, the entire classroom seemed to release pent-up sighs. He was going to leave without finding Robbie.

But Jensen glared at the Head Mistress. "I never made it to the end of the last row." He marched back to Robbie's aisle. "Now, where was I?"

He appeared to ponder for a moment before resuming his search at the desk of the boy behind Robbie. Jensen held the photo up to the child and shook his head. He'd have moved on if something hadn't caught his attention. The edge of Robbie's red and brown plaid flannel shirt peeked out on the floor between the desk and chair in front of him.

Robbie remained under his desk, trembling.

Jensen stamped his foot. "What are you doing under there?"

Robbie was too frightened to answer.

"I believe he's tying his shoe," his teacher said.

Taking her cue, Robbie untied one. But in doing so he knocked off his artificial finger.

"Forget about the shoe and get out here."

Robbie slowly emerged from under the desk and slumped into his chair.

Jensen lifted Robbie's chin and held the photo beside his face.

Robbie held his breath as the man's eyes moved from the photo to his face and back again.

"Bingo! We've got a winner." He grinned and grabbed Robbie's arm. For the first time he noticed Robbie's balled fist. "What's in your hand?"

Robbie sniffed back a tear. "It's my finger."

"I don't have time for games—" The man gripped Robbie's hand and forced his fingers back. He froze, trying to make sense of the artificial finger in Robbie's palm. His eyes moved to Robbie's other hand then to his missing digit. "I think there is more to your story than meets the eye, isn't there little man?"

Tugging Robbie by the collar, he tried to drag him out of his seat, but Robbie desperately clutched the desk top. Annoyed, Jensen roughly jerked him into the aisle.

Robbie started to sob.

Emma leaped out of her seat. She shook her finger at the inspector and shouted, "Stop it, you big bully! You'll hurt him!"

Ignoring her shouts, Jensen drug Robbie up the aisle.

Emma stood by her desk yelling, "Stop! Someone stop him!"

Jensen cursed under his breath and continued lugging the squirming child up the aisle.

The other children began banging their fists on their desktops shouting, "Stop!... Stop!... Stop!" Someone wadded a piece of paper and threw it at the inspector. Suddenly a snowstorm of paper descended upon him.

Jensen scowled at the teacher and snarled, "Can't you control the little cretins?"

The teacher tapped a fingernail on her desk and softly said, "Now, now, children." When they didn't respond, she turned to Jensen and shrugged.

Meanwhile, children in rooms up and down the hall began drifting into the corridor to see what was causing the ruckus. When they saw the inspector emerge from the classroom with

Robbie in tow amid a hail of paper, they joined in, chanting, "Stop!... Stop!... Stop!" Others ran to wastepaper baskets for more ammunition.

Emma raced into the hallway and shouted, "He's trying to take Robbie away to kill him. We have to stop him!"

Head bent and shielding his face with one arm against a continuous onslaught of wadded paper, Jensen pushed his way through the mob of outraged youngsters. A boy emerged from the crowd and kicked Jensen's shin. Soon children on both sides began kicking him as he passed.

Wincing and stumbling, Jensen soldiered on.

Children shoved in at him from every side, grabbing at his clothes and clinging to his legs to slow him down. One particularly aggressive youngster ran up beside Robbie and sank his teeth into Jensen's hand.

He yelped in pain and released his hold on Robbie.

Momentarily freed, Robbie sprang to his feet and ran down the corridor. The milling mob of children parted to let him pass then quickly closed ranks.

Jensen muttered to himself as he wiped his bleeding hand on the tail of his shirt and headed down the hall after Robbie.

Youngsters buzzed at Jensen's heels like a swarm of angry hornets. An older boy who'd been leaning against the wall suddenly popped out his leg as Jensen passed, sending him sprawling.

A little girl tried to pry Robbie's picture from his grasp.

"Hey, let go of that. It's mine." He took a swing at her, but missed when she ducked back into the throng. Children raced forward and jumped onto his back, pinning him down. Jensen shook them off and wearily pushed himself up onto his knees.

Robbie reached the end of the hallway and turned right into an intersecting corridor. Too late, he realized it was a dead end. He skidded to a stop and curled into a ball beside a radiator. A second later, a pack of his classmates careened around the corner after him and formed a protective barricade. The stairwells filled with children from the second floor coming to see what caused all the commotion. They flooded into the corridor ahead of Jensen stopping him in his tracks.

Jensen paced back and forth for a moment looking for an opening. Without warning, the children surged forward, forcing him to retreat into a doorway. Cornered, Jensen swung his leg out trying to drive them back.

Each time he did, the youngsters attacked from the opposite side, kicking and clawing at him.

Jensen sank against the wall. He was out of breath and sweating. The children had pulled on his shirt until it ripped and blood still oozed from his hand. He knew Robbie was somewhere beyond the wriggling mass of shouting youngsters waving their fists at him. But how to get to him? They'd already drawn blood and he had no doubt that, like the Lilliputians, they could overpower him despite their difference in size. He was still mulling things over when his cell phone rang.

"Inspector Jensen?"

"Yeah. Who's this?"

"It's Grayson Stevens from the District Attorney's Office. I can hardly hear you over the background noise. Are you at a circus?"

"Oh, I'm at a circus all right," he shouted into the phone.

"What are you doing at a circus? I thought you were headed to the Foundling Home to search for Robert Wilson."

"That's where I am and I've got a riot on my hands. I was just about to call for backup."

"Did you find the boy?"

"He's here alright, but the kids went berserk when I tried to take him into custody."

"Custody? What were you intending to do with him?"

"I'm going to run him over to Children's Services. I'm a cop, not a babysitter."

"There's no need to take him anywhere. I've already filed papers to keep him right where he is." Jensen started to protest, but Stevens talked right over him. "It's too easy for a child to get lost in the State system. He's my only evidence of criminal wrongdoing and I can't afford to have him go missing. We know where he is and he's receiving adequate care. I want him left alone."

"But this is a job for Children's Services," Jensen shouted over the rising din of the youngsters.

"I won't take the risk," Stevens shouted back. "Your work there is done. On your way out, tell the administrators I'll be over shortly to interview Robert Wilson."

₧₧

Jensen shoved his phone into his pocket, turned and shuffled back down the hall. They didn't pay him enough for this, he thought, smoothing his hair. He took out his handkerchief and wrapped it around his bloody hand, wondering if he'd need rabies shots. He tucked in the ragged ends of his shirt and tossed the wadded remains of his tie aside with a groan.

Jensen waved the Head Mistress away when she caught up to him. "Don't bother; I know the way out." He handed her the crumpled photo of Robbie. "Give this to the prosecuting attorney. He said he's on his way to see Robert Wilson." Jensen limped away toward the exit.

She smiled. "Have a nice day. I hope you enjoyed your visit."

"I never want to set foot in this place ever again," he mumbled without a backward glance.

The children watched in silence for a moment then broke into a rousing cheer.

CHAPTER TWENTY-SEVEN

Mira entered her outer office with her briefcase tucked under one arm and a multi-colored stack of bound reports in the other. As she hurried past, her secretary waved a pink *While You Were Out* phone message in the air. "Got something for you."

"Now what?" Mira gave a frustrated sigh and dumped the stack of reports on a nearby table. She leaned her briefcase alongside the precarious pile and reached for the note. "I just spent the entire morning listening to each department head plead for additional funds. I don't need any more grief."

The secretary watched her boss's expression harden as she scanned the message. "I tried to tell him you were in a time crunch to get the departmental budgets submitted and had meetings all afternoon. He kept insisting this was more important."

"For him maybe." Mira looked at her watch, wadded up the note, and threw it into the wastebasket. "Would you take those reports and the briefcase into my office and put them on the credenza? It's been a long time since breakfast. If I'm to meet with the Assistant District Attorney, I'd better run down and get a sandwich out of the machine before he arrives."

₤)(ℂ

Grayson Stevens was waiting when Mira returned. He smiled. She stared ... then silently gasped. She recognized him as the handsome man from the Deli who'd bought her croissants.

Tall and lean, he wore a dark blue three-piece wool suit and carried himself well. He moved with the confidence of a man accustomed to being in control. Seeing his face register the same surprise and recognition, Mira knew she wasn't the only one who remembered that morning at the Deli.

He extended his hand. "Ms. Hastings, I'm Grayson Stevens with the District Attorney's office. I believe your secretary informed you of my visit."

"Yes, about five minutes ago." She shook the hand he offered, very aware of the warmth and strength of his touch. Seeing a hint of gray at his temples led her to speculate on his age. Near her own, she guessed.

At the Deli she had wondered where he worked. Now she knew. He was part of the political clique of powerful interests who profited from the elimination of *useless* children. She considered telling him he should've kept his lousy croissants. They weren't that good anyway. Instead, she gave a pained smile and asked, "Are you here to serve me with a subpoena?"

He chuckled. "We generally don't announce ourselves when handing out subpoenas. But since you asked..." His hand slipped into his jacket and emerged with a folded legal form. "I wanted to discuss the upcoming Grand Jury hearing regarding Robert Wilson and this FFU."

"I see." She turned to the secretary and, in an icy voice, said, "Jackie, I'll be meeting with Mr. Stevens this afternoon. Cancel my *scheduled* appointments." She turned in his direction and arched her eyebrows. "My note said 1:00."

"I arrived early thinking we might talk over lunch."

Mira raised her hand, displaying the vending machine package with her turkey on white sandwich. "I brought mine; where's yours?"

Caught by surprise, he hesitated for a moment. "I, uh ... hoped we could go to a nearby restaurant."

"So you can ply me with gourmet food and loosen my tongue with spirits? C'mon in. You talk. I'll listen while I chew." She moved her lunch to her left hand and opened the door. "My office is through here."

Grabbing his briefcase, Grayson Stevens moved around her and held the door back so she could enter first.

Mira plopped her sandwich on her desk, pointed him to a chair, and sat down. She absentmindedly grabbed the sandwich and tried to open the wrapping. After several unsuccessful attempts she'd have used her teeth on the package if she'd been alone. Frowning, she put the sandwich down.

"Let me try," Stevens said.

"That's okay. I have scissors in my desk drawer."

He leaned forward in his chair and gently picked up the sandwich. Turning it slightly, he pinched opposite sides of the wrapper and gave them a sharp tug. The seam separated neatly. "It's all in the wrist." He placed it back on the desktop with a flourish. "Bon Appétit."

Mira removed half of the sandwich and took a small bite. "So, does Mrs. Stevens know you go around opening sandwiches for other women?"

"Why should my mother—" He stopped as a grin transformed his face. "Little slow on the uptake there, wasn't I? There is no Mrs. Stevens; I'm not married."

Mira slid the bag containing the other half in his direction. "In that case, lunch is on me today."

"Mmm...my favorite, turkey and wilted lettuce on dry white bread." He studied the sandwich for a second before taking a bite.

Mira went to a small refrigerator and returned with two bottles of soda. "What's so important that you came to visit ahead of the Grand Jury?"

"There are certain inconsistencies I need to discuss with you."

"Dare I ask who you intend to prosecute and why?"

"At this point, I'm not sure. That's the reason for the Grand Jury. We can investigate anything and everything related to the case before deciding if there's anything deserving of prosecution."

"In other words, things are so slow down at the District Attorney's Office you have to beat the bushes to find something to keep you busy."

"Hardly." His eyes sparkled when he laughed. "As an officer of the Court, if I suspect criminal activity, I'm required to follow up on it. By taking this matter to a Grand Jury, all aspects of possible wrongdoing can be explored."

"What makes you think this FFU has done anything to merit your scrutiny?"

"Suffice it to say, there are several aspects to this Robert Wilson affair that don't feel right to me. I'd be remiss not to follow-up on those concerns."

"Such as?"

"For instance, is it merely coincidence that one of your employees has gone missing? Is there a link between Aranda Blackthorn's disappearance and little Mr. Wilson's unusual survival?"

Mira took a sip of her soda, waiting to hear what else he would say.

༺༼ༀ༽༻

Giles fingered the front of his green coveralls and scowled at the subpoena in his hand. Anger and frustration made his pulse pound. Deciding it was time to check in with Helen and Barnard, he jogged over to the Security office.

Helen raised an identical form and waved it at him. "Barnard and I both got a subpoena too. It doesn't change anything. As long as we stick together, we have nothing to worry about. You'll back us up, right?"

"I ain't crazy 'nuf to be the Lone Ranger out there on my own. Aranda? Aranda who? I don't know nothin' about Aranda." He smiled and pretended to tip a hat as he left her office.

As he closed the door, the smile left his face and his brows knitted together. *Yeah, Helen, I'm going to cooperate. What choice did you give me when you dumped Aranda in with the kiddies and left me to deal with it?*

CHAPTER TWENTY-EIGHT

"Value, that is, the impulse to virtue is rooted in nature. Hence, things may be either good or evil, actions moral or sinful, men wise or foolish." ~ Arius Didymus

Mira found a parking spot a block from the courthouse and walked toward the imposing building. She rounded the stone perimeter wall and climbed the curving white steps up to the arched portico above the entrance.

She grasped the polished brass handle on the entry door and hesitated. Grayson Stevens' visit had left her feeling uneasy, inwardly restless. They'd interacted twice now and she found herself drawn to him, yet couldn't decide if he was friend or foe.

She pulled the door open. The courthouse was a beehive of activity. People scurried across the large public area, disappearing down hallways that branched in multiple directions. The clickety-clack of all those shoes on the shiny marble floor echoed off twelve-foot-high ceilings. She was tempted to cover her ears.

Pushing up the sleeve of her jacket, she glanced at her watch. She'd deliberately arrived early to give herself time to find the Grand Jury room. As she walked, her thoughts returned to her meeting with Grayson Stevens. This Grand Jury was ostensibly why he showed up at her office, yet he'd spent very little time discussing it. She could easily convince herself his visit was a ploy to get to know her better...or was that her imagination running wild?

A touch on her shoulder startled her. An image of the handsome prosecutor crossed her mind. However, when she turned she was disappointed to find herself gazing into the earnest face of a short young man.

"You look a bit lost; may I help you find your way?"

Her gaze moved from his clear blue eyes to a patch of bare scalp peeking through thinning blond hair.

"I'm Dixon," he said, adjusting thick glasses. "I'd be delighted to show you the way to the Grand Jury Room, Ms. Hastings."

How does he know my name and where I'm going?

He touched her elbow. "It's this way."

Mira jerked her arm back and glared at him. "Do I know you?"

"Of course, I just told you my name is Dixon. Actually, it's Arius Didymus Dixon. My mother was a fan of the first century Stoic philosopher, Arius Didymus. Remember that book about the Indian fellow who didn't want to be known as Piscine Patel and changed his name to Pi? Well, everyone calls me Dixon." He winked up at her. "You can too."

"Uh-huh. That's what I thought." She brought her purse up to her chest, prepared to bop him if needed.

"Ms. Hastings, you don't have to fear me." He placed a hand over his heart. "I had hoped to walk you to the Grand Jury Room, but if you don't want me to, I won't." He took two steps back and pointed. "It's the fifth door on the left down that hallway."

Feeling sheepish, she took a step in that direction. He hurriedly stepped in front of her.

Mira stopped. Glowering at him, she took a posture of defiance, chin set and arms folded around the purse in front of her chest. "What are you doing?"

Dixon raised his hands in a conciliatory gesture. "Before you run off, I want to make you an offer."

"I'm not interested."

"You can't know that. I head up *Action Group*."

She inched away. "Never heard of it."

"We arrange things. You'll be surprised how helpful we can be."

"I'll keep you in mind the next time I need someone rubbed out," she said with a scowl.

"You're not taking me seriously. Give me a few moments of your time and then I promise to leave you alone. Besides, you're early. You'll still have plenty of time to read old magazines."

Her mind raced. *How does he know so much?* "My activities are none of your business. This courthouse is crawling with cops. If you don't stop harassing me, I'll call one to haul you away."

He reached into his coat's breast pocket, pulled out a business card, and offered it to her.

She made no move to take it.

With her purse still firmly in front of her, it was easy for him to slip the card into its side pocket. "There, you have my card. Should you ever want to disclose the things that go on inside an FFU, Action Group will give you all the support you need."

His eyes bored into hers. "We can film your statements and insert them into the evening news, a popular weekly comedy, the internet ... it makes no difference. Your message will go viral."

"What are you implying?"

He lowered his voice to a conspiratorial whisper. "I believe you want to do something about the deaths of innocent children and we're here to help you."

Mira gave a quick look up and down the long corridor. Had the Home Office grown suspicious of her and sent him to test her loyalty? "What you're suggesting is risky and illegal. Even if I were interested, why should I believe you?"

"I'll give you a sample of what Action Group can do. You have a teleconference for FFU Directors this coming Friday. Tune in and see what happens."

Without taking her eyes off him, Mira reached into her purse and riffled through the pocket where he'd stuck his business card. Grabbing one of her own, she made a point of studying the card in her hand before tearing it in two.

Speaking loudly enough to be overheard, she said, "I don't want any part of whatever it is you're suggesting." She thrust the torn pieces at him and stormed away.

ஐௐ

Dixon exited the courthouse taking two steps at a time. That Mira Hastings sure is pretty, he thought. When he approached his car, the passenger side door swung open.

"Thanks Brody," he said to the man behind the wheel, and climbed inside. As he did, the door closed by itself. "This auto door thingee of yours works really well. You're almost as good at inventing computer-driven gadgets as I am at hacking firewalls."

Brody snorted. "With one important difference; hackers get arrested and inventors don't." He raised heavy eyebrows at his cousin. "So, Dix, was she interested?"

Dixon held the torn business card out for him to see.

Brody reached for the pieces and held them side-by-side. "This is a ripped up business card. What's it supposed to mean?"

"She made a big show of returning my card to me and saying she wasn't interested."

"So why the big grin?"

"Whose card are you holding?"

Brody examined the card in his hand. "It's hers."

"Right. She made it *look* like she was returning my card, but kept it. She tore her own card in two instead. What does that say to you?"

"That she grabbed the wrong card?"

"No. She was afraid someone might be watching us. She only pretended to return my card." He rubbed his hands together with glee. "We'll make a believer out of her when she sees our little demo during the FFU Director teleconference."

Brody smiled. "Sure hope you're right. We took an awful chance doing this."

"I don't think so. Carolyn Bracken vouched for her, and I've done some background checking. She's the real deal. Mira Hastings hates seeing those little kids die as much as we do. We just need to convince her to trust us."

Brody nodded. "Car start," he said, and the car's engine turned over.

"Okay, show off. Put your hands on the wheel. I'm not going anywhere with you if you insist on trying to steer by voice command."

Brody laughed and rested his hands on the steering wheel. "Someday we'll all be able to steer by voice alone." He looked over his shoulder and pulled away from the curb. "Imagine what it will mean for paralyzed people. They'll be able to talk their way through traffic."

Dixon chuckled. "After you're famous, I'll be proud to admit you're my cousin."

ℰᏀᏟᏒ

When Mira reached the fifth door down the hallway, she fought an urge to turn and look for Dixon. Listening for the sound of his footsteps and hearing none, she gripped the door handle and went in.

A receptionist looked up as she entered. "You must be Ms. Hastings," she said, checking her list.

"Yes. I'm early."

"Please have a seat. Mr. Giles is next and then you." She turned back to her keyboard and resumed typing.

Mira looked across the room at Giles fidgeting on a couch. He wore an ill-fitting suit and kept poking his finger into his collar to stretch it away from his flabby neck. His hair was slicked down and greasy looking. He tapped his foot nervously as his eyes darted about the room until they met hers.

"Helen and Barnard went in a while ago. Me next," he said with a weak smile. They continued staring at each other a moment longer before Giles looked away.

He pulled a wadded handkerchief from his pocket and wiped his forehead. Picking up a dog-eared magazine, he carelessly flipped through it. Tossing it aside, he leaned back and unbuttoned his jacket to release a bulging paunch.

Mira resisted an urge to smirk. A skilled professional like the handsome prosecutor would bind Giles up in his own inconsistencies in a matter of minutes, she thought.

ඔ

Grayson Stevens absentmindedly stared out a window. They'd taken a brief break while two jurors visited the ladies room. He speculated about his visit to the Foundling Home as he waited. When the Head Mistress called Robbie to her office he'd asked Robbie about his grandmother.

"I m-m-miss her l-l-lots," Robbie replied.

After the near abduction by Inspector Jensen, Stevens realized Robbie was afraid of him and probably viewed any person in authority as dangerous. "Robbie, if I could help you get back with your grandmother, would you like that?"

Robbie sat up straight, eyes bright. "C-c-could you r-really d-do that?"

"I can try."

"Emma too?"

Stevens raised an eyebrow at the Head Mistress. "Who is Emma?"

The prosecutor's musings were interrupted when the two jury members returned. He perused the schedule. The next person on the list was FFU Receiver & Transporter Giles.

CHAPTER TWENTY-NINE

Giles sauntered into the Grand Jury room making every effort to hide his anxiety. Even so, he stumbled on his way to the witness stand and caught himself on the railing before taking his place. He perched on the edge of the seat and wiped his sweaty brow.

Pretending not to notice, Stevens arranged his papers and quietly studied the man sitting before him. Giles appeared to be a person with something to hide.

"It's Mister Giles, isn't it?" Stevens asked as he rose.

"Do I look like somebody who's got a Mizz in front of their name?"

"No, of course not. I didn't mean to offend you. I simply wondered how you wished to be addressed."

"You can call me Giles same as anyone else."

"You appear uncomfortable. Is anything wrong?"

Giles gave a start. "Wrong? What could be wrong? I've already told anyone who'd listen I ain't done nothin'."

Though he was certain Giles had much to tell, Stevens proceeded cautiously. He needed to gather information about the FFU, but in the process didn't want a new revelation to jeopardize any child rescues.

"As you may know, we convened this Grand Jury to look into the matter of Robert Wilson."

"Can't say as I know him."

"It's your job to tend the children prior to elimination, correct?"

"I retrieve 'em, feed 'em and take 'em downstairs when it's their time, if that's what you mean."

"Robert Wilson is slightly over three years old. He came through your facility a few weeks ago. You would have interacted with him as part of your job."

Giles shifted in the chair and shrugged. "I get a new batch

every day. Ya can't expect me to remember every one of 'em. A kid's a kid. They're all the same to me."

Stevens watched Giles fidget on the witness stand. "Does your job ever cause you to suffer any mental distress?"

Giles frowned. "I ain't nuts."

"I wasn't implying you are. But you earn your living helping to kill children. I thought it might haunt you from time to time."

"I don't believe in ghosts if that's what ya mean."

Stevens decided to throw him off guard. "You've answered all of my questions satisfactorily."

When Stevens turned aside to retrieve some papers, Giles leaped up sending his chair tumbling over backwards. He picked it up sputtering, "Thank you, thank you, sir, thank you." Giles gave a curt bow to the jurors and headed down from the witness stand with a grin.

Stevens spun back around. "I wasn't finished yet, Mr. Giles. Please take your seat."

"But…" Giles' chin dipped to his chest and his shoulders sagged. He slunk back and slouched down in the chair.

Stevens crossed to stand directly in front of Giles and looked into his eyes. "Do you know a person by the name of Aranda Blackthorn?"

Giles snapped up and threw his shoulders back. "Of course I do."

"What was the nature of your relationship?"

"Relationship? Listen, I don't care what Helen told ya, me and 'Randa never had no relationship. The company's got a strict policy about fraternizing 'n' I follow the regulations."

Stevens couldn't stifle his smile. "I never meant to imply that you two had a *romantic* relationship. You are coworkers, correct?"

"Yeah, she worked at the FFU. A lotta people do. That don't mean I got *relationships* with any of 'em."

"You said, *worked* as in the past tense. Do you have some reason to believe she won't be returning?"

"How would I know? I'm no fortune teller, but it sure don't look like she'll be back, does it?"

"I can't say." Without taking his eyes off Giles, Stevens stepped closer and stared him down. "How do you feel about that?"

"Feel about what? We weren't involved or nothin'. She did her job and I did mine. Why should I have any feelings about her one way or the other?"

"I'm just surprised that a coworker of yours, and a young woman at that, disappeared under mysterious circumstances and yet you don't show any feelings. Where's your empathy?"

"What's that?"

Stevens stepped back in surprise. This was a reply he hadn't expected. "Empathy means putting yourself in someone else's shoes. Trying to understand what they might be feeling."

"Why would I do that?"

"Well, at one time or another most people do."

"Well, I ain't most people; and like I told ya before, I never laid a hand on her."

Stevens turned toward the jury, but addressed Giles. "Do you know what a sociopath is, Mr. Giles?"

"Can't say that I do. I never took any of that psycho-babble in school. I live my life and let other people live theirs. "

"One characteristic of a sociopath is their lack of empathy. The feelings of other people are of no concern to them. They view them as little more than objects. The weak and the vulnerable, which they mock rather than pity, are often favorite targets."

"So now you're criticizing the way I handle the kids. What is this, pick on Giles day?" He poked a finger on the railing for emphasis. "I can tell you here and now that I follow every rule in the operations manual. I do my job, that's what they pay me fur.

As to the kids, why should I pity 'em? There's nothin' in the manual about pity. Besides, it's not like they're my kids or somethin'."

"No, they're not. Is there anything you'd like to add about Miss Blackthorn?"

Giles rubbed his chin as he thought. "Only that I never touched her. If she went and got herself killed...'n' I ain't sayin' she did or she didn't... but whatever happened to 'Randa was her own fault."

Stevens shook his head. "Before you leave, Mr. Giles, I should warn you against discussing Robert Wilson, Aranda Blackthorn, or your testimony here today with any of your coworkers."

"Why would I want t' do that?"

"I never said you would. I'm merely reminding you that there are legal penalties associated with collusion."

"Nothin' to worry about, I got a good drivin' record...never even had a parkin' ticket."

Stevens rolled his eyes. "The exit is over there. You're excused."

Scurrying across the room, Giles flung the exit door open against the wall with a bang and rushed through. Before it closed, he could be heard muttering to himself as he hurried away.

₧₧

Rebecca Stuart moved through the courthouse hallway, eyes downcast, counting doors as she wandered along. She and Giles passed one another in the hallway, but neither gave the other a second glance.

Rebecca was grateful for a subpoena to the Grand Jury hearing. It was an opportunity to tell somebody what she thought of this whole mess. How could a disinterested father steal a little boy away from his grandmother who loved him? Surely they'd sympathize with an elderly widow whose only daughter died, leaving her mother one grandchild. There was no potential for any others.

She cracked the door and peered inside.

A receptionist lifted her head. "Mrs. Stuart?"

The older woman nodded and stepped inside.

The receptionist made a notation and gestured Rebecca toward a chair.

Mira laid her magazine down and watched the gray-haired woman cross the room. It dawned on her that she must be Robbie's grandmother. Like the pieces of a jigsaw puzzle, she fit the chain of events together in her mind. Carolyn told Rebecca and Rebecca must have unwittingly alerted Robbie's father.

Mira took a second look and noticed the woman's red-rimmed eyes. No wonder she's been crying, she thought. She must feel responsible for this whole fiasco, which might still cost Robbie his life.

Rebecca looked up and gave her a timid smile.

Mira returned her smile, trying to offer encouragement. She was still wondering about Rebecca Stuart's part in this drama when Prosecutor Stevens opened the door. "Ready, Miss Hastings?"

He looked handsome in a three-piece navy suit and pale blue tie. She bit her lip, chastising herself for noticing. She still believed they were, after all, on opposite sides of a life or death issue.

He held the door open and gave her a warm smile.

CHAPTER THIRTY

"In a time of universal deceit—telling the truth is a revolutionary act." ~ George Orwell

"Miss Hastings, you are Director at the local Facility For the Useless, correct?"

"That is correct."

"How does one happen to become Director of an FFU?"

Mira sucked in a breath. "It's difficult to find qualified people willing to fill Manager or Director positions at a Facility For the Useless. So, the Home Office introduced a college tuition reimbursement program in exchange for a five-year commitment. I signed up and after graduation was assigned to FFU eleven sixteen."

Stevens nodded. "Explain to us how a child is designated as *useless.*"

"As you know, the government determined," her brows knit together as she quoted the directive, *"To be a person with all the rights of a person, a human being must be capable of rational thought and able to formulate aims and goals for his or her life."*

"And, young children are presumed to not be able to do this, so according to current standards, they are not yet a person."

She studied his expression. Did he find the whole concept as distasteful as she did? She cleared her throat. "Small children and babies are subject to the care and protection of someone who *is* a person...typically a parent. If a parent is unwilling to perform this duty, they have the legal right to bring them to a Facility to be euthanized."

Stevens leaned toward her. "For a fee, of course..."

She nodded.

He perused his notes. "Before being designated *useless,* are they given specific medical tests, examined by a physician, or any other expert?"

"No."

"In other words, a parent can wake up one morning, decide caring for their child is too much trouble, and presto!" he snapped his fingers, "The child becomes useless?"

"Yes, the law allows parents to make that determination. It's the logical extension of Roe v. Wade, which fostered the belief that women have a right to control their own body. The argument that resulted in the passage of the *after-birth abortion laws* was that, since they still aren't a person, the child remains a product of the woman's body even after birth."

A number of jurors nodded in agreement.

Stevens sighed and ran a hand through his hair. "Tell us about the process known as *final disposition of the useless.*"

Mira bit her lip. "The simplest way to describe it would be to say the children are euthanized and their bodies cremated."

"I see. Can you go into more detail? Perhaps take us through the entire process step-by-step?"

"Why is this necessary," a juror asked.

"Because," Stevens paused for emphasis, "we hope to determine how Robert Wilson escaped the process."

Mira took a deep breath. If Stevens wanted to walk her through a full recital of the elimination and disposal processes in all their gruesome detail, she'd oblige. If FFU upper management objected, she would simply point out that she'd been sworn to tell the truth. She'd maintain her professionalism, but avoid making the practice sound acceptable in any way.

After describing the check-in procedures and holding room, she moved on to the actual elimination process beginning with the valium-laced cookies and ending with the children's bodies going into the incinerator.

Stevens interrupted her numerous times. He seemed to have an inordinate desire to rehash even the most minor details. He asked about the lighting in the basement, the noise level, and the structure of what she'd called the *Good-bye Room.*

She eyed him closely, wondering if, perhaps, he was not the hard-as-nails Prosecuting Attorney he seemed to be.

At his nod, Mira continued. "And then the chamber is filled with a hydrogen cyanide gas."

"Who chose hydrogen cyanide?"

"Upper management determined it to be the best product for this use."

Stevens turned to face the Jurors. "A little background here may be helpful. Hydrogen cyanide gas was originally known as ZyklonB. Invented in the 1920's, it was initially used as a pesticide. The Nazis decided to test ZyklonB as a means of execution. In February, 1940 they used it to kill 250 Gypsy children at the Buchenwald Camp. Its first use at Auschwitz occurred in September, 1941 when they used it to murder 600 Soviets and 250 Poles. *SS-Obersturmbannführer,* Rudolf Hoess, camp commandant, and eventual director of all Nazi extermination centers, designated ZyklonB as the poison of choice for use in Nazi gas chambers."

Stevens put his hands in his pockets and turned to face Mira. "And now, based on your testimony, we learn it's still being used the same way today in our FFUs."

The only sound in the room was the jurors re-adjusting their chairs as they squirmed in their seats.

Stevens quickly shifted gears. "Each child, or rather *eliminated uselessee,* is tracked and accounted for, correct?"

"Yes. As you know, under the Uniform Registration Act, attending physicians now procure DNA samples at birth. This becomes part of an individual's record in the National Data Base." Mira cleared her throat. "During an FFU intake process, all FFUs access and verify each child's records. They match DNA samples taken after death to those taken at birth. Then an FFU Population Accountant notifies the National Data Base that a particular individual has been eliminated."

"Have you had instances where the samples didn't match?"

"I'm not aware of such an occurrence."

"This is somewhat confusing. Your facility listed Robert Wilson as eliminated when, in fact, he's still alive. How can that be?"

She shook her head. "I wish I could tell you, but I can't."

He opened his briefcase wide. After leafing through his papers, Stevens turned and pointed a finger at her. "Can't or won't? You are, after all, the facility's Director. Surely you must have some thoughts on the matter."

She straightened and glared at him. Feeling cornered and not wanting to lie under oath, she mentally sought a loophole. Then realized she knew nothing about how they tested for DNA in the lab. "I've no idea."

"In other words, you don't know what goes on in your own facility?"

"That's very rude, Mr. Stevens."

"Sorry, Ma'am. I apologize." Stevens tapped a pencil against the palm of his hand. "And despite the gruesome nature of the process you just described, the children suffer no pain, correct?" Steven's quiet question boomed in the room's stillness.

Mira sucked in a breath and waited a moment for emphasis. "No, that's not correct. I'm told the dead often foam at the mouth or bleed from their ears. The children's skin is mottled with deep pink or green spots due to the chemicals they've inhaled."

Even the most stoic members of the jury appeared distressed. One of the women rose and ran from the room covering her mouth.

Stevens watched her leave then reached inside his suit coat. He took out a small handheld device and selected an image on its surface. Aiming it, he projected a photo onto the wall. "Is this Robert Wilson?"

"A policeman showed me Robert Wilson's photo a few days ago. That's the boy in the photo."

Stevens beamed a second picture. The same boy was in a swing. "We took this a few days ago in the playground at the local Foundling Home of Future Contributors." The next one showed a child's hand. "Do you notice anything unusual about this hand?"

"Yes. Half of the little finger in missing."

"That's Robert Wilson's hand. I propose to you, that to provide the necessary DNA verifying his extermination, someone sliced off half of his finger while he was still very much alive."

When she didn't comment, Stevens let it drop. "Ms. Hastings, before you go I wonder if you could tell us how one acquires ZyklonB?"

Mira appeared confused. "I'm not sure what you mean?"

He tossed a hand in the air. "The FFU can't euthanize children without a continuous supply. Does someone run down to the nearest pharmacy to pick up a couple dozen tins of ZyklonB every couple of weeks? I thought it was banned after the Nuremburg trials."

"We receive ours from central supply. How it gets there, I can't say. I should also point out the product we receive is *not* labeled ZyklonB. That brand name is no longer in use."

"So do the FFUs have their own factory that cranks out *Uselessee Eradicator*, or whatever it's called now?"

"I am neither a chemist nor do I know where the FFU Home Office procures its product. I can, however, tell you hydro-cyanic insecticides are routinely available to licensed users such as pest exterminators."

Stevens let out a low whistle and rolled his eyes. "So, the guy who comes to my house to kill bugs or rodents also carries ZyklonB in his van." He shook his head in astonishment. "I have no more questions."

CHAPTER THIRTY-ONE

Rebecca watched Mira re-enter the waiting room. She noticed how the interrogation had sapped the young woman's energy, and wondered how she fit into the investigation. Mira gave Rebecca a weak smile and left. Before Rebecca could give it any more thought Prosecutor Stevens called her in.

"Mrs. Stuart, you are Robert Wilson's grandmother. Is that correct?" he asked.

"Yes, and I want him back. He never should've been taken away from me."

"Ma'am, I need you to just answer my questions." Stevens pointed a transmitter at the wall, bringing up a photo. "Your grandson, Robert Wilson?"

"Yes, of course. I took that picture of him."

"The records show he was delivered to a Facility For the Useless on—"

Rebecca didn't let him finish. "I had nothing to do with that! It was my daughter's ex-husband who took Robbie away. Frank did it without my permission."

"Do you have any idea how Robert was removed from the FFU where your son-in-law left him only later to turn up at a Foundling Home of Future Contributors?"

"Clearly, it's because Robbie is very bright."

"We've been unable to find any record of him ever being tested." Stevens leaned toward her with an intense stare. "It looks more like criminal activity."

Rebecca squirmed uncomfortably.

Stevens straightened and turned to the wall again. "I have another photo to show you. It's of Robbie's amputation. What can you tell us about this?" Robbie's injured hand flashed up.

Leaving the witness stand, she inched closer. "They hacked off part of my Robbie's finger?" She reached up to place a hand over the image. "That's why he kept his hand in his pocket; he didn't want me to see what they did to him." She touched the side of her head and grabbed a nearby rail for support. "Oh, my poor baby, how could they?"

Rebecca toppled over and collapsed into the aisle.

℘)(℘

Mira's time on the witness stand left her feeling mentally depleted. Remembering a coffee stand near the main entrance, she decided some caffeine might help.

A siren wailed to a stop outside the building as she waited for her order. The front doors sprang open and EMTs rushed in pushing an empty gurney. The noisy hallway became utterly still as all eyes focused on the emergency personnel. People backed against walls to let them pass.

Forgetting Mira's latte order, the barista stepped out from behind the counter and joined the growing crowd of onlookers. Though curious, Mira stayed back rather than join the looky-loos.

By the time the barista returned and filled Mira's order, the EMTs were coming back down the hall with someone on the gurney. Mira was startled to see them roll Rebecca Stuart past her toward the exit with Grayson Stevens trailing behind.

He stopped when he saw Mira. "Mrs. Stuart collapsed when she saw the photo of Robbie's hand." He shook his head and sighed. "I came on too strong. She obviously had nothing to do with the cover-up."

"How could you imagine she'd be involved?"

He shrugged. "It comes with the territory."

Mira paid for the latte, telling the barista to keep the change. "Mrs. Stuart's going to need someone at the hospital with her." She thrust her untouched latte toward Stevens. "This is on me. Consider it payment for the croissants." She dashed out of the courthouse to follow the ambulance with Rebecca inside.

Driving up to the hospital's emergency entrance, Mira was

surprised to see Rebecca on her feet and arguing with an attendant. She parked her car and hurried over.

"I'm fine I tell you. It's not my heart and my head feels okay too." Rebecca stamped her foot. "I don't need any expensive medical tests. What I need is a taxi to take me home." Rebecca's eyes lit up when she noticed a familiar face beyond the EMT. She waved. "Is it you?"

Mira chuckled as she approached the older woman. "Yes, I suppose it is me. My name is Mira."

Rebecca moved around the man who was trying to get her into the emergency room and took Mira's hand. "Would you be kind enough to give an old lady a ride home?"

"Shouldn't you let them check you over before you leave? I'll wait and take you home after."

"Learning what happened to Robbie shocked me and I fainted. That's all. I may only be an old woman, but I'm a healthy old woman. Besides, many of my friends have gone in there and never came out. Some people place folks like me in the same category as they did Robbie...*useless.*"

"Oh, I'm sure they wouldn't—" Mira didn't finish the sentence.

Rebecca laid a hand on Mira's arm. "Robbie's the one we need to worry about."

Mira felt the beginning of a friendship forming. "Sure, you can have a ride home. It'll give us a chance to get to know each other." She took Rebecca's elbow. "I'm parked right over here."

Rebecca grinned over her shoulder at the EMTs who watched in disbelief. "Sorry fellas. Thanks for your help, but I'm fine now." She gave them a wave as she climbed into Mira's car.

CHAPTER THIRTY-TWO

The day spent at the courthouse, and later with Rebecca, threw Mira's workweek behind. Friday rolled around far too quickly from her perspective, and the mandatory conference for FFU Directors scheduled later that morning would further delay progress on her backlog.

A sharp rap on her office door startled her.

Seconds later, the door swung open and a smiling Grayson Stevens strolled in. He had a leather portfolio in one hand and a beverage carrier in the other.

Mira gave an exaggerated sigh and closed the file she'd been working on. "Couldn't you at least have called first? I don't have time to meet with you this morning."

Ignoring her comment, he sat the 2-pack cardboard basket on the desk. He rubbed his chin in contemplation. "You strike me as a White Mocha kinda gal, but I brought a French Vanilla just in case. Take your pick."

"You're not listening to me. I have an important meeting that begins in a few minutes."

Stevens flicked his sleeve back and checked his watch. "There's plenty of time. The teleconference doesn't start for another fifteen minutes." Steam rose from the cup when he pried the lid off. He slipped a corrugated insulating band around it and slowly passed it back and forth in front of her. "White Mocha. Get it while it's hot. Going once, going twice..."

She reluctantly took the cup and waited while he opened his. He raised his cup in a salute and they each took a sip. She sat her cup down and licked her lip. Crossing her arms, she asked, "How did you know about the Director teleconference?"

"You invited me."

"I certainly did not."

"Did too." He unzipped his notepad and removed a sheet of paper. "Here's a copy of the email you sent."

Tingles marched up her spine as she took the page from him. It had the FFU's standard confidentiality statement in bold type across the top, followed by her usual salutation. Though brief, the message had an extra line between paragraphs and displayed the non-standard font she used as her default. It concluded with her signature and the required FFU boilerplate about forwarding, copying and storing of messages.

The sender's address and time and date stamp were at the top of the page. She'd prove it was a forgery. Turning to her computer, she opened the Sent Mail folder and scrolled down the archives. To her dismay, she found the email neatly filed by date and time among the others.

All her red flags went up. Despite firewalls and passwords, someone had accessed her computer and sent an unauthorized email in her name. What else had they done? There was only one person she knew who even claimed to have such abilities. *Dixon.*

"Is anything wrong?"

"No. No, I'm just distracted." Mira gave him a half-hearted smile to mask her rising sense of vulnerability. She grabbed her cup and rose from the desk. "It's time we headed to the presentation," she said and handed the email back to Stevens.

80Q3

Mira shut the conference room door silencing the noisy activity in the hallway outside. She settled into a heavily padded leather chair, and pulled herself under the polished wood of the conference table. Waving her hand, she motioned Stevens into a chair beside her.

While he arranged his notepad and took out a pen, she logged into the conference site. The oversized screen on the wall acknowledged her and flashed a message to please stand by. Moments later, the FFU logo replaced the message. Nothing to do now except sit back and wait.

She looked over at Stevens. "Was it really necessary to grill me like that on the witness stand? What did you hope to gain?"

"I wanted every gruesome fact to become part of the public record. Our *polite* society seldom gives people a chance to be as brutally frank as you were for the Grand Jury."

She shrugged and began drumming her ballpoint on the tabletop, something she never did. She couldn't get Dixon and his boast about waylaying this presentation out of her mind.

The conference video started in the usual way. Mira's anxiety levels decreased as she listened to them repeat the same tired justifications for limiting population growth by eliminating those deemed useless. She began to relax. Email anomalies aside, this promised to be nothing more than a rehash of the party line.

Everything changed several minutes into the conference. A red line appeared across the top of the scene and gradually bled down, washing over the official presentation. Seconds later, the screen filled with images of very young children, crying and wailing.

Mira snapped upright in her chair. Steven's pen slipped from his fingers. They stared at each other in shocked silence.

On the screen, someone's anonymous hand pushed and shoved children into a dark cell much like the *Good-Bye* room in the basement below them. It wasn't the same room, of course, but all FFU gas chambers – although never called that – utilized the same airtight, concrete construction.

When Mira could stand no more of the whimpering and wailing, she muted the sound of the terrified children.

The distress evident on the children's faces caused tears to well in her eyes. Our children don't behave that way, she thought. That facility isn't sedating its victims. Not providing the youngsters with valium-laced cookies saved money, but increased the children's suffering.

After the chamber's door slammed shut, the image folded over from upper left to bottom right, revealing a heavily muscled man tossing the youngster's tiny bodies into a wheelbarrow-type conveyance. The camera zoomed in on a hand. A portion of the child's baby finger was missing. From there it panned to a nearby table and scanned a row of labeled bags, each holding a tiny digit.

The man rolled his wheelbarrow of children to the furnace. Opening the metal door, he began pitching the little bodies into the roaring fire. Built to standards, it looked exactly like the one Mira had described to the Grand Jury a few days earlier. However, she'd failed to tell them that, in an effort to lower costs, little bodies burning inside FFU incinerators helped heat the buildings.

Despite her best efforts, Mira began to sob. When Grayson Stevens slipped his arm around her, she leaned into him and wept into his shoulder. He held her tightly, blotting away her tears with his handkerchief.

She wondered how this gruesome presentation affected the other FFU Directors. Clearly one of them cared enough to allow Dixon, or someone associated with him, access to their facility.

Over images of little bodies going into the furnace, words appeared on the screen. Mira un-muted the sound. A synthesized voice asked, "Should this happen? It goes on day after day in every major city. Don't allow the greed of a few men and women cause the destruction of so many innocent lives. As a Director of an FFU, you know what goes on inside your facility. Rise up against this insanity."

As the images began to fade from the screen, the voice said, "These people are not as powerful as they think they are. Grass roots movements are taking hold all over the country. May God help us protect these sweet, innocent little ones. We now relinquish control to the establishment. Never forget what you witnessed here."

The screen went black for an instant then a *Conference Over* message appeared. The whole incident had lasted only minutes.

Mira lifted her head off Gray's shoulder and straightened her jacket. She swallowed hard then patted her hair into place. She stared at the floor and dabbed at her eyes. "I...I, um, this is all very embarrassing. I don't normally lose control like that." She cleared her throat. "It was unprofessional of me. I'm sorry."

Neither of them acknowledged what had happened between them. They rose and faced each other. Rocking from side to side and ill at ease, they didn't seem to know what to do with their hands and glanced about the room avoiding eye contact.

Stevens cleared his throat. "Forget about it. That was pretty heavy stuff."

She gestured toward the screen. "I never anticipated anything like this. I'm sorry you had to witness it."

"Don't be." He scooped his portfolio off the table with a sigh. "I'd like to discuss this with you ... at a later date, of course."

"My schedule is pretty full right now."

He smiled for the first time. "Maybe over the weekend, I'll call this evening to see how you're feeling."

ℰᏅℭ℞

That evening Mira attempted to unwind by settling into her favorite rocking chair to knit. Her yellow cat snuggled against her left hip. She leaned to her right, attempting to keep the blue baby blanket off the cat.

"You're a good boy, Butterscotch. You don't try to play with my yarn." The cat looked up and meowed like he understood.

She held the blanket up and admired it. "When this one's done I'll put it with the pink one and take them to the pregnancy center downtown." She sighed and shook off the negative thoughts threatening to overwhelm her. "No sense crying over what can't be undone."

Wouldn't it be sweet if twins got these matching blankets? The thought made her smile. She was still smiling when the phone rang. Caller ID didn't recognize the number, but she picked up anyway.

"Ms. Hastings? It's Grayson Stevens. I told you I'd call, remember?"

"Yes, of course. Things did end abruptly after the conference."

"I also wanted to ask about Mrs. Stuart. Have you seen her since she went into the hospital?"

"Rebecca was never admitted. She's doing well at home."

"If you're on a first name basis, I take it you've kept in touch." He faltered and took a deep breath, "And, she's okay?"

Mira grinned. The self-confident, over-bearing County Prosecutor, so accustomed to asking questions, seemed to be having trouble conversing. Was he nervous calling *her?*

"She's fine. She made a fuss and refused to let them take her inside so I drove her home."

"That was kind of you."

"She's a very nice woman. Is that why you called?" She noticed his hesitation and smiled to herself again.

"I thought perhaps we could discuss the conference over dinner tomorrow."

He caught her off guard. She paused, "Okay. I recommend LaCosta. It's better than a quick burger and not a budget buster."

"Oh, I'll get the tab, but I like LaCosta too. How about I pick you up at—"

"I'd rather meet you there. How about 5:30?"

"Fine, I'll see you there. By the way, my friends call me Gray."

"Until tomorrow then," she smiled, "Gray

CHAPTER THIRTY-THREE

"Be courteous to all, but intimate with few, and let those few be well tried before you give them your confidence. True friendship is a plant of slow growth, and must undergo and withstand the shocks of adversity..." ~ George Washington

The next evening a misting rain soaked the streets and sidewalks. Mira held a small red umbrella over her head as she hurried from her car to the restaurant, high heels clicking with every step.

Gray waited under LaCosta's awning. As she approached, he stepped forward and took her elbow. She glowered down at his hand in disapproval. He quickly removed it and held the door open. Stepping into the foyer, Mira placed her wet umbrella in the stand while Gray checked on their reservation.

As the hostess led them through the restaurant's festive interior, she gave Gray an appreciative perusal. He seemed oblivious to her admiration, but Mira noticed. When they arrived at their booth, Mira gave the woman a thunderous look.

The hostess responded with a catty wink and left.

Resisting Gray's attempt to help her out of her coat, Mira tugged it off and laid it on the vinyl seat beside her. She stowed her purse under it. "You need to understand this is *not* a date. I'll pay for my own dinner."

He shrugged. "Whatever you want."

She drummed her fingers against the side of her frosty water glass. "I've updated you on Rebecca Stuart's condition and described everything about the FFUs in extreme detail at court. What did you want to discuss?"

He offered her a menu. "Let's order first, okay?"

She waved the menu away. "I don't need to look at it. I like their chicken enchiladas."

"Sounds good. How about hors d'oeuvres and a glass of red wine?"

"They bring fresh chips and salsa before the meal, and I prefer iced tea." She noticed Gray take a deep breath and sigh. Realizing she'd been unnecessarily abrupt, she vowed to be more pleasant.

"I love Mexican food, second only to Italian," Gray said when the waiter turned away.

She studied his dark eyes and hair. "Are you of Italian descent?"

"Maybe. Or, possibly Chicano. I know nothing about my birth parents."

"How's that possible in today's climate? Unwanted babies aren't adopted, they're euthanized."

"Well, it's no longer a secret; I can tell you if you really want to know." He took a sip of water.

"I'd like to hear your story. Adoption is of special interest to me," Mira said.

"I was too old to euthanize before anyone discovered I wasn't my parent's natural son. Fines and occasional bribes allowed them to keep me."

"How did they get you to begin with?"

"One hot summer day Dad left his car in the company parking lot with the windows down. He said it was an old beater so he didn't worry about leaving it unlocked. When he came back after work, there was a bundle on the passenger-side floor. He leaned over to check and the blanketed object squirmed." Gray smiled.

"That's it? Who left you? Did you cry?"

He started to answer, but the waiter appeared with identical oval platters. Steam rose from the chicken enchiladas buried under melted cheese. They'd sprinkled round slices of black olives on top with blobs of sour cream and guacamole in the middle. A generous helping of Mexican rice sat on one side, with refried beans on the other. The waiter placed salads next to each plate with a flour tortilla rolled up on the edge.

Mira closed her eyes and inhaled deeply. "Mmm, it smells really good. But there's so much. I'll have to take some home."

Gray dug into his dinner, dropping the rest of the story.

Mira's head suddenly popped up. She stared across the table. "You don't get off that easy. What did your mother say when your dad showed up with a baby?"

He gave her a mischievous glance. "While Dad told Mom the story, she unwrapped me and changed my diaper. Later she dressed me in some of the things they'd bought for their own baby."

"Wait...their baby? They already had an infant?"

"Not yet they didn't. Mom was pregnant and due very soon. I grew up with their natural son, Bryson. Since he was only a few weeks younger than me, it was almost as if we were twins." He drained his water glass and scanned the room, hunting for the waiter.

"Don't stop there." She pushed her glass at him. "Take mine. I barely touched it."

He grinned and lifted her glass, taking a long swallow. "The next day, Mom found a note tucked into the garments I arrived in."

"What'd it say?"

"I memorized it as soon as I learned to read."

He momentarily closed his eyes as if reciting in school. "It said, 'My baby's father and his parents say my son is useless and want to send him to an FFU. I'm certain Grayson will grow tall and wise if given a chance. I pray you'll take care of my baby and raise him with the child you're expecting. Please don't let him be harmed. Thank you and God bless you.'"

He paused, taking another sip of water, and looked across the table. "After hearing my story you probably wonder how I can pursue Robbie's case since he and I were both saved from an FFU."

Mira was silent, her gaze fixed on him.

෫෬

Jonathan backed the car out of their driveway.

Carolyn smiled as they pulled away. "This was a good idea. We should stay busy and it'll be good to let someone else do the cooking for a change. Where shall we eat?" She didn't wait for a reply. "How about a movie after dinner? Saturday's usually date night."

Jonathan stiffened and gripped the wheel tightly. "I don't know, Mom."

Noticing his tension, she wished she hadn't mentioned date night. "Let's see how we feel after we finish eating."

"Okay. Since this is all spur of the moment, how about the Burger Barn?"

"Someone I know is craving curly fries."

"They make the best in town," he said as he drove.

"How can I pass up a recommendation like that? Burger Barn it is."

The parking lot was nearly full, so Jonathan pulled up front to let Carolyn out. She'd get a booth for them while Jonathan parked the car. Long ago they initiated this routine at fast food restaurants. She'd find their table and he'd order since he could maneuver everything easier with two arms than Carolyn could with one.

When he entered the restaurant the warm scent of fried food made his mouth water. He'd not eaten with any enthusiasm since Aranda disappeared. He stood tall, grateful his appetite was returning. At the counter he ordered curly fries and a Barn Burger for each of them with extra bacon and cheese on his. Carrying the tray of food, he inhaled deeply as he crossed the restaurant to join his mother.

Carolyn popped a curly fry into her mouth. "Instead of going to a movie, how would you like to visit the Foundling Home?"

"That's a great idea. It'd be good to see those little munchkins again. The house has been too quiet. I'm used to the sound of children playing."

"Spoken like a full-fledged parent."

Jonathan toyed with a fry. "I just meant that I've always enjoyed interacting with the kids as they passed through the house."

She touched his hand. "Don't be embarrassed. Someday you'll make a great Daddy."

He gave her a wry frown. "Once upon a time I looked forward to that day...even imagined what it would be like." He crumpled the empty box his burger came in. "Not anymore."

"Don't give up. Detective Brinkman will find her. Until then, we have our prayers and hopes."

෨෬

Mira and Gray's waiter arrived with dessert. "Sopapilla," he said, "cheesecake squares with cream cheese filling, sprinkled with cinnamon. Enjoy."

They ate in silence for several minutes before Gray raised his eyes from his plate and cleared his throat. "I guess my brother, Bryson, got his name because of me. Later, my parents gave us a younger sister, Autumn. My siblings and I were always close, but I often wondered if Mom and Dad regretted not being able to have another child of their own. Still, Dad always told me I was their gift."

He peered across the table. "Your turn now."

Mira smiled shyly, and began telling him about her childhood, the neighborhood she lived in and schools she attended. She tactfully omitted much of her late teen years, skipping ahead to college and her life as an adult."

Blotting his lips, Gray put down his napkin. "Do you have any nieces or nephews?"

She gave him a quizzical look. "Why do you ask?"

He shrugged. "With no kids of my own I enjoy interacting

with Bryson's boys. I wondered if you did the same, and how you felt about the kids who go through your FFU."

Fear surged through her. What was he up to? Rather than give any hint of how she felt, she said nothing.

Gray frowned. "Okay, I'll lay my cards on the table. I've watched a young woman rescue small children from your facility. I ran her license plate through DMV. It was Aranda Blackthorn."

Mira stared at him, frozen in place. How long had he been spying on them? She recalled the jogger she'd seen the day she watched Aranda in the parking lot. It was Gray. He must suspect she was Aranda's inside connection. Why else invite her to dinner?

Gray touched his mouth with his napkin, his eyes never leaving Mira. "I don't believe she could have managed it without inside help."

Mira slid back in her seat as far from Gray as she could get. Realizing she'd made a terrible mistake meeting him like this, she scooped up her things and rose to leave.

"Please don't go." Catching her hand, his eyes pleaded with her to stay.

She could get lost in those dark brown eyes if she let herself. More confused than ever, she sank back onto the cushion wondering if he was toying with her.

He planted his elbows on the table, leaned forward and lowered his voice. "I believe you maneuvered yourself into a position where you can help some of these children. Now, if that's the case," he hesitated momentarily, "maybe we could help each other—"

She didn't give him a chance to complete the sentence. "What sort of trap are you setting for me? You're implying I've broken the law. You can't possibly have any proof of that." Grabbing her coat and purse, Mira swiftly rose and rushed out of the restaurant giving Gray no opportunity to stop her this time.

CHAPTER THIRTY-FOUR

Mira's mad rush out of LaCosta did not go unnoticed.

Sitting in his car across the street, Giles watched Gray and Mira through the restaurant windows. When Mira came out alone, he dropped his binoculars and started the engine. "In a hurry are we, Director Hastings?" He made a clucking noise with his tongue. "I know where you live."

Wiping spittle off his chin, he reached across the front seat for his ski mask. Next, he patted the lump in his jacket pocket where a switchblade lay hidden. Stepping on the gas, he sped away from the curb. "Race you home, Boss." Diabolical laughter reverberated throughout his car.

സ്റ

Gray wanted to rush after Mira, but couldn't leave until he paid for their meals.

Now I've gone and done it, he thought. I pushed too hard, too soon. If she'd only let me finish.

Glancing up, he found the waiter at his side. The man extended an electronic payment tablet with both bills on it. Gray took it, added a generous tip, and entered his pay code. "So much for splitting the cost of dinner," he muttered, handing the device back to the waiter.

When he reached the exit, he saw her red umbrella still in a stand among others. He recalled how lovely Mira looked when she'd arrived. Her cheeks rosy from the cool evening air with the red brolly framing her like a portrait.

If I return it, I'll have to see her again, he thought, and smiled. He gave the hostess a farewell nod as he stepped outside into the rain. He pushed the button on Mira's umbrella and it popped open. Gray whistled as he strode to his car.

സ്റ

Mira's neighborhood was awash in shadows. She pulled into her driveway and scanned the area before turning off the car's ignition and headlights. She made a fist around her keys with her house key pointing outward, a habit she'd formed after attending a women's self-defense class.

Seeing no one lurking about, Mira exited the car and jogged to her front steps. The possibility of an intruder wasn't uppermost in her mind. Her thoughts focused on her questions about Grayson Stevens. She paused on the small, covered porch and groped for the lock. An errant breeze tousled her hair and the nearby hydrangea bush rustled. The sound of shifting leaves through the pitter-patter of rain failed to register as she fumbled with her key.

As the door swung open, a shadowy figure crept up behind her. Her keys were still in the lock when an arm encircled her.

Mira gasped. A cold metal blade lay against her neck.

The man tightened his grip and kept the flat of the knife firmly pressed against the side of her throat. "Don't make no sound." He leaned close and whispered, "Jes' do as I say and ya won't get hurt."

A quiver of fear danced along her spine. The man's rancid breath nearly made her gag. She took shallow breaths and was silent. *This couldn't be happening. Where did he come from?*

The intruder snickered beneath his ski mask.

Fear must excite him, she thought. I mustn't let him know how afraid I am.

"Get inside," the man growled. He pushed her in and kicked the door shut. Not bothering to lock it, he shoved Mira in the direction of the bedroom.

"There's a little money in my purse and change in a drawer in the kitchen." She struggled to keep her voice from breaking. "You don't have to hurt me. Take the money and leave."

He scoffed. "Take yur coat off."

She awkwardly shrugged her way out of it, avoiding the knife near her throat. "I don't have anything of value, only cheap costume jewelry. Please take the money and leave while you can."

"Enough about money. I'll get yur dough later." He laughed and shoved her into the bedroom.

She stumbled forward, catching herself on the bed's footrest.

He removed the knife from her throat long enough to slice through the waistband of her skirt. It fell in a tangled heap around her ankles, leaving the lower half of her body nearly naked. Her skin crawled as she felt his eyes move over her lacy undergarments.

He isn't here for my jewelry or a few loose coins from a kitchen drawer.

Stifling a shiver and ignoring her rising panic, Mira forced herself to concentrate. Her assailant's demeanor, poor grammar and speech seemed eerily familiar. Raising her eyes, she studied the man's reflection in the dresser mirror. Even though a ski mask hid his face, his height and build convinced her it was Giles.

Would he have bothered to hide his identity if he planned to kill her? So long as he felt safe beneath his ski mask she had a chance. She didn't dare let him know she'd recognized him.

In spite of an intense desire to put distance between herself and Giles, she decided offense might be the best defense. She spun around and raised her knee, thrusting it toward his groin.

He side-stepped and her knee barely brushed past his thigh. Terrified now, she snatched a lamp off the nightstand and hurled it across the bed at the window. She listened for the sound of breaking glass. Instead, the lamp hit the frame and fell harmlessly to the floor.

She sobbed.

Giles was behind her in an instant.

Something hit her in the lower back, sending pain shooting up her spine. Mira crumpled to her knees. "You stabbed me!" she screamed.

"Shut up bitch, or next time it'll be my knife in yur back, 'stead uh my knee."

Despite the pain, relief flooded through her. He didn't stab her. At least not yet.

For the first time since her attacker forced his way in, Mira reached out to God. A comforting presence surrounded her. The terror she'd felt washed away like water flowing down a drain. Peace replaced her fear and her mind began to function again. She'd handle this situation by trusting in a power greater than herself.

"What do you want me to do?"

"It's party time 'n' we're gonna have us some fun. Take off yur clothes and get on the bed."

As Mira approached the side of her bed, she thought she saw a shadow slide past the bedroom door. She remembered Giles hadn't locked the front door. *"Oh God, please let there be someone in the hallway and let it be someone to help me. Make this end safely and quickly.*

Mira walked to the head of the bed and spun to face him. She needed to buy time and keep Giles' focus away from the doorway. She slowly undid a button and dropped the shoulder of her blouse.

"Hurry it up!" he shouted.

"Don't be in such a rush. You did say you wanted to have fun, didn't you? How about a little striptease?" She undid another button. "I saw a dancer do this in a movie once."

"I'm not interested in waitin' 'n' watchin'." Giles grabbed her wrist and slammed her against the wall. He pointed his knife at her. "I'm losing my patience. Unless you wanna bleed all over your frilly things, you better get 'em off. Now!"

His eyes glinted through the mask. The evil in them horrified her.

CHAPTER THIRTY-FIVE

"Your friend is your needs answered." ~ Kahlil Gibran

"How did you like Mrs. Stuart's stories everyone?" The Head Mistress lifted her hands to lead the children's clapping. They were seated on the carpeted library floor in a semi-circle around Rebecca. Robbie was snuggled under Rebecca's arm with Emma pressed next to him and Mandy next to Emma. Robbie's grandmother held a large illustrated children's book in her lap.

When the children's applause died down, Emma pointed to the door. "Look. It's Aunt Carolyn and Jonathan!" Before Robbie could untangle himself, Emma had grabbed Mandy's hand and the two girls ran to the doorway.

Carolyn knelt and swept her arm around Mandy as Emma leaped into Jonathan's arms. Robbie-come-lately stood and stared. Jonathan winked at him. He kept an arm around Emma and opened his other arm for Robbie, who raced into it.

The Head Mistress joined them with Rebecca trailing behind her. "Mrs. Stuart, let me introduce Carolyn Bracken and her son, Jonathan Bracken. As you can tell, they've been instrumental in caring for these three and many of the other children here."

Robbie took his grandmother's hand and led her to Carolyn. "We s-s-stayed with Aunt Carolyn and Jonathan 'fore we c-c-came here."

Rebecca began to extend her hand, then hesitated.

"Oh please," Carolyn said, with a big grin. "I have a hand to shake with. I don't even miss the other one."

Rebecca took her hand and smiled. "Thank you. Thank you for all you've done for my grandson, and for all the children. You too, Jonathan. I'm thrilled to meet you both." Still holding Carolyn's hand, she stepped aside and whispered, "Could I ask you something? Robbie never stuttered like that at home. Do you know when he started doing it?"

Carolyn sighed. "Severe emotional trauma can cause

stuttering. It's known as *psychogenic stuttering*. If Robbie didn't do it before, it's probably because of his frightening experiences at the FFU."

"I thought it might be something like that. Do you think it will go away?"

"Most children outgrow it. Once he feels safe again, it will most likely subside. Don't let it bother you."

Rebecca squeezed her hand. "I appreciate hearing that."

The Head Mistress joined the three adults with their entourage of children. "Mrs. Stuart has begun reading to the children almost every evening since shortly after Robbie arrived. We were about to move to the cafeteria for a bedtime snack before tucking the children in. I hope you'll join us."

"We'd like that very much," Carolyn said.

৪০৫৪

"I said take 'em off!"

Mira stalled, willing the dark fog of evil surrounding her to lift. She backed away from him, trapping herself in the narrow alleyway between the wall and the bed.

Giles came at her. "Okay, I'll do it myself." The blade of his knife slowly swayed from side to side like a cobra preparing to strike.

She raised her arms, crossing them over her chest, and covered her face with her hands. Peering between her fingers, she thought she saw a blurry figure rush into the room.

After that events spun out of control.

An unseen thrust sent her toppling onto her bed. The momentum carried her across it and onto the floor. Hearing a yelp of pain from the other side, she cautiously peeked over the edge of the mattress. Giles' knife lay abandoned on her flowery bedspread.

Dazed, she pushed herself up and rubbed a bruise on her

elbow. The rest of her seemed none the worse for wear.

Sweet relief flooded through her as she tiptoed around the end of the bed and saw Giles laying face down on the carpet. Her rescuer had both of Giles' arms twisted behind him with a knee in his back while Giles thrashed around like a beached fish. Ignoring her attacker's whimpering she focused on the man restraining him and rubbed her eyes in disbelief.

Grayson Stevens glanced back at her over his shoulder and winked. "You left your umbrella at the restaurant. I came to return it. Are you okay?"

"I am now, thanks to you." Realizing she was half undressed, she hurried to her closet and grabbed a robe.

"We need something to truss this guy up with while we wait for the police."

"I'll happily sacrifice my drapery cords." Mira tightened her robe and gingerly picked up the discarded knife. She climbed onto a chair and gathered the cords. The sharp blade easily cut through them, reminding her of how different the evening's outcome could have been.

She carefully sat the knife on the sill. "Here you are ... Gray," she said offering him the cords. After what he'd done, his first name just felt right.

Gray coiled the thin ropes around Giles' wrists. "You miserable piece of crap. What kind of coward forces himself on a woman? I'll see you don't ever try anything like this again."

When Giles tried to resist, Gray pressed his knee deeper into his back. While Giles moaned in pain, Gray quickly ran connecting loops around his neck and ankles.

Mira regarded Gray through moist eyes. "How did you manage to be right outside when I needed you?"

"When I came to return your umbrella something didn't look right. I saw a man follow you into the house as I pulled up."

"So what took you so long?"

"From my vantage point I couldn't see he had a knife on you. For all I knew, you were meeting a lover."

"Him, a lover? Not in this lifetime."

"Maybe a surprise visit from a brother or a cousin, for all I knew." He waved a hand in the air. "I didn't want to do anything until I was sure. The clincher was seeing your keys still in the lock."

A sigh escaped her lips. "Well, I'm glad you were here. Thanks for hanging around and saving me from being raped..." her voice quivered, "or worse."

From the floor Giles grunted and muttered, "*How about a little striptease,* my eye. Shoulda kilt 'er 'n' been done with it."

"Did you have something to say?" Gray grabbed the cords and raised Giles off the floor.

He shrieked in pain.

"I'm sorry, did that cause you discomfort?"

Giles nodded vigorously.

"Life's tough. Maybe you should have stayed home tonight." Gray looked toward Mira. "Let's unmask our pervert."

Mira grabbed Gray's hand to stop him. "I don't want to look at him right now."

Gray shrugged and gave her hand a quick squeeze before pulling his away. "If you want to wait, we'll wait." His eyes searched the room. "Phone?"

Mira walked around the bed and picked up her phone from the floor. She'd knocked it off the nightstand in her tumble across the mattress. Walking back, she pushed the pre-programmed number for the Police Dept. "I keep them on speed dial," she said as it rang, "but I don't know why. If I called a taxi, it'd get here faster than the police."

Gray took the phone from Mira as someone answered. "This is Grayson Stevens with the District Attorney's Office. We need a patrol car immediately at ..." He handed the phone to Mira and she gave them her address.

He nodded approvingly and took the phone back. "We have a breaking and entering, menacing, kidnap and attempted rape." Gray was silent for a moment as he listened. "Right. The attacker is restrained and in my control."

Giles made an angry growl.

Gray handed the phone back and glared at Giles. "One more sound out of you and we'll conduct a test to see how sharp that knife of yours really is."

He grabbed the cords binding Giles and dragged him through the house, out the door, and bounced him down the front steps. Leaving him in the rain, Gray stepped under the porch to wait.

A police car arrived several minutes later. While Gray spoke with the officer, Mira changed into loose fitting jeans and an oversized sweatshirt. She came out in time to watch the policeman shove Giles into the back of his patrol car.

He slammed the door and returned to the porch. "Good job. You made my work easy." Flipping open a report folder, he turned to face Mira. "You must be Ms. Hastings. I just need to get a few preliminary facts."

As the officer recorded her statements, Gray placed a reassuring arm around her shoulder.

The officer gave her a sympathetic look and closed his folder. "Ma'am, since it's the weekend you won't hear from a detective until Monday. I know it's hard after what you've been through, but try to relax and have a good day tomorrow. Someone from the Department will be in touch."

He tipped his hat to Gray, got into his car, and drove off. Mira and Gray stood side-by-side watching the police car's taillights disappear in the distance.

"Should I have gone to the station?" Mira asked.

"No need. I expedited the process. You've nothing to do now except wait for a detective to call you." He ran his tongue across his lip. "I'm sorry about this whole nasty business. If you'd feel safer, I could spend the night."

She shook her head and gave a thin smile. "Thanks, but no thanks. I've already had one close call this evening."

"No, that's not what I meant. I'd sleep on the couch."

Images of snuggling up to Gray filled her mind. It isn't *him* I don't trust, she thought. But, I don't want him to know that.

She took his hand in hers. "I understood what you meant. I'll take a sleeping pill and it'll put me right out. Thank you for everything. I don't know what I'd have done without you. "

He started to leave, then turned back and gave her a tender look.

"What is it?" she asked, her voice quavering.

Before she knew it, he was beside her. "I wouldn't be able to live with myself if something had happened to you." Without warning, he pulled her into his arms, hugged her tightly and whispered, "Thank God you're okay."

He gently kissed her when she looked up at him.

Though she longed to stay in his arms, she forced herself to pull away. "Good night, Gray." She paused in the doorway as her yellow cat shot past her and into the house. She smiled and waved. "Thanks again. See you soon."

After closing the door she looked through the peep hole. Gray remained there on the porch until she pushed the dead bolt home. At its loud click, he turned and walked to his car.

CHAPTER THIRTY-SIX

After Gray left, Mira went room to room methodically checking and re-checking each window to be sure it was closed and latched. Next she double locked her outside doors. She didn't turn on the TV, radio or music. Without admitting it to herself, she wanted to be alert to any unusual sound in the night.

Afraid to go to bed, and still fully dressed, Mira curled up in an overstuffed chair. Her cat jumped onto her lap and she wrapped her arms around him. "Oh Butterscotch, I'm so glad you were outside when that terrible man came." Tears rolled down her cheeks as she stroked the cat. "We're safe now. Everything's secure and we're okay." She buried her face in the fluff at the cat's neck, and continued to softly weep.

They slept in the chair together until the next morning when a ringing phone startled her awake. Butterscotch leaped off Mira's lap. Straightening in the chair, she rubbed the back of her neck and reached for the phone.

"Ms. Hastings?"

"Who is this?"

"It's Dixon. I would have waited for you to call me, but I saw the police report about an intruder last night. Are you all right?"

Him again.

"How did you find out?"

"I set a tickler for you."

"A what?"

"My partner and I regularly make automated sweeps through the government's communications and databases. I programmed our computers to send me a notification any time your name pops up."

"Look, I don't know what you think you're doing, but this is none of your business."

"Please, Ms. Hastings. Let me help you."

"Why and how?" She jumped when her doorbell buzzed. "I can't talk right now, there's someone at my door."

"Don't worry. It's only me."

She slammed the phone down and hurried to the door. Opening it a crack, she peeked out over the safety chain stretched across the narrow slit between the jamb and the edge of the door.

The same short, young man from the courthouse stood on her front stoop smiling up at her. He touched the brim of his ball cap in greeting.

Crossing her arms, Mira frowned down at him. "You've been spying on me."

Dixon made a soothing motion with his hands. "Spying is such an ugly word. We were monitoring you for your own protection."

"What if I prefer not to be *monitored*?"

He stared at the ground. "If you really feel that strongly about it, I can change the programming."

"What makes you think I believe anything you say? I have no idea what you're up to."

"I wouldn't lie to you. I'm on your side. We're fellow warriors in the fight for a moral society."

"I suppose you left your superhero cape in the car?"

Dixon gave a low whistle. "My but we're touchy this morning. I suppose I can't blame you. I understand your reluctance to trust me after what you went through last night."

He shifted from one foot to the other. "Look, my cousin and I monit...um, we sort of keep an eye on things. Most of what we encounter is routine, everyday stuff. But sandwiched between the bureaucracy's mundane ramblings can be tidbits of priceless information. When unraveled, these hints reveal their plans with startling clarity."

"So like a prospector, you swirl your pan in the creek searching for a golden nugget in the sand."

He grinned. "Exactly. May I come in? I've got lots to tell you."

"No, you may not come in. If you really do what you say, prove it. Give me an example of those mundane ramblings."

Dixon bit his lip as he thought. He snapped his finger**s**. "Last Tuesday you requested three hours of personal leave to go to the dentist."

Mira's eyes widened. She thrust the door shut, double locking it. Leaning against the door she took a deep breath to quiet her hammering pulse.

"Please, Ms. Hastings," Dixon pleaded through the door. "Remember your FFU Director's conference? Didn't that prove Action Group can deliver?"

She opened the door a tiny crack. "What does Action Group, whoever they are, want from me?"

Dixon leaned into the narrow opening and lowered his voice. "Think of Action Group as a government watchdog. Our goal is to end the taking of innocent lives. For the past month, we've been monitoring the production of a propaganda campaign the government intends to release soon." Dixon turned to check behind him before continuing. "We want to counter it with honest information of our own."

"And how do you expect to come by this so-called *honest information?*"

"I'm looking at an excellent source right now. Let us give you a platform. With our help Mira Hastings, a mild-mannered FFU Director, can change the world. You'll have an opportunity to expose the horrible things happening inside FFUs. You can tell the citizens of this nation how dishonest and greedy those in power are, and how their motives aren't for the public benefit at all. It's only what they want everyone to believe."

"Do you have any idea what my career would be worth if I did that? My very life could be in danger."

"We have contingencies in place for your protection. Let me tell you about them."

At that moment, all she wanted was a hot shower and a cup of coffee … and maybe not in that order. "Look, Dixon, if that's really your name, I'm not up to this right now. Give me a few days."

"Right you are." He dipped his head. "Think about it. I know you'll make the right decision. Until next time." He turned and walked away.

Mira sighed heavily, leaned into the door as she closed it, and double locked it again.

Parked on the street outside her house, Brody waited behind the wheel of a plain gray van. Dixon climbed into the passenger side and nodded at his cousin. He punched a number into his cell phone as Brody started the engine.

"Carolyn? Dixon here. I just left Mira Hastings' house. I'm concerned about her mental state. She could really use a friend right now. Let me fill you in on what's happened," he said as they pulled onto the highway.

ৰেওল্প

Giles lifted the sleeve of his jail uniform and wiped the blood running from his nose. Once he had the nosebleed taken care of, he tugged up the tail of his shirt and gingerly blotted his split lip. Staggering to the bars of the jail, he began shouting to anyone within hearing. "Git that detective down here. Tell him I got somethin' he's gonna wanna hear."

To Giles' relief he was ushered out of the cell and into an interview room.

The detective he'd spoken to the night before soon joined him. He sat down and frowned. "I was on my way out of the building when you started caterwauling. What do you want now?"

Giles patted his lip again and winced. Grimacing, he pointed to his eye which was nearly swollen shut. "Do ya see what they done t' me? Ya gotta move me outta that holding cell."

"Yeah. They don't much like rapists in there, do they? Coulda been their sister you picked on."

"Well, what're ya gonna do about it?"

"I already made him write, 'I must not hit the other prisoners' a hundred times.' Good enough?"

Giles sneered at him. "You better show me some respect or I might decide I don't wanna talk to you after all."

The detective shrugged. "No problem. I'll have the guard take you back to the cell." He leaned over and opened the door, preparing to yell for the guard.

Giles grabbed the man's arm. "Okay, okay! Ya made yur point." He exhaled noisily. "Somewhere around here there's a missing person's report on Aranda Blackthorn sittin' in a drawer goin' stale. How'd ya like me t' solve that sucker for ya?"

The detective pushed Giles' hand away and rose. "Sit tight. I'll get somebody from that department down here to talk to you."

CHAPTER THIRTY-SEVEN

Brinkman strode into the interrogation room, a dog-eared file under his arm. Glaring down at Giles, he worked his cigar around the side of his mouth. After a moment or two, he jerked out a chair, spun it around and straddled it. "This better be good. It's my day off." Brinkman opened the file folder and pulled a pen from his pocket. "So you're the guy who kidnapped poor Aranda Blackthorn. Probably killed her too. Why'd you do it, huh? Wouldn't she put out for you?"

Giles straightened in his chair. "I never said I did nothin' like that to nobody. I only said I can tell ya what happened to her."

"And to Amelia Earhart and Jimmy Hoffa too? If you know what happened to Aranda, then five'll get you ten you're the one who made it happen." Brinkman took a long puff of his cigar and the tip glowed bright red. He took it out of his mouth and blew smoke at Giles.

Giles wheezed and fanned at the cloud, his swollen eye blinking. "I tell ya I had nothin' t' do with it. I never hurt her."

Brinkman studied his cigar as he thought. When he jammed it back in his mouth, Giles hunkered down for another onslaught of smoke. Instead the detective cupped Giles' chin and stared him in the face. "For the moment we'll pretend you're telling the truth. Where is she? What happened to her? And who did it?"

An evil gleam of vengeance flickered in Giles' eyes. "I can tell ya. Just cut me a fair deal."

"What is it you expect to get for this information?"

"I wanna walk outta here a free man like last night never happened." Giles paused for a moment. "And I don't wanna go back to that holding cell." He dabbed at the stream of tears dripping from his blackened eye. "I need to be someplace safe."

"Let's hear what you have to say and then we'll consider your demands."

Over the next thirty minutes Giles assured Brinkman he knew

all about Aranda's disappearance and implicated two unnamed security guards in her death. He grinned as he fingered them, laying it on thick. He said the guards threatened him if he didn't help them. Expressing grief over Aranda, he implied she was dead, but refused to confirm or deny it. Giles withheld just enough details to bargain for his freedom.

Brinkman snatched the folder off the table and rose. "I'll have to clear any deal with your victim," he glanced down at his notes, "a Mira Hastings." He chewed his cigar. "I see she's your boss; this oughta be interesting."

Giles leaned forward, "Remember," he said, his voice quavering, "I can't go back to the same cell."

Brinkman signaled to the guard that he was finished. "See if the penthouse suite is available for this man, please." The guard let out a hearty belly laugh and Brinkman left snickering.

৪০৫৪

After Dixon's worried phone call, it didn't take Carolyn and Jonathan long to rush to Mira's and rap on her door.

At Carolyn's shout from the porch, Mira finished buttoning her blouse, grabbed a pair of slippers, and hurried to open the front door.

"Don't get me wrong, I'm happy for your support," Mira said after listening to Carolyn's explanation. "But, I think Dixon's way too interested in my life." She readjusted the towel around her wet hair. Thanks to him, she'd barely made it out of the shower before they appeared at her door. "How is it you know Dixon?"

Carolyn gave Mira an indulgent smile. "He's been a Life Chances supporter for several years. He approached me when he was still in college. It scared me to death how much he knew about our activities. Fortunately he's on our side."

"I thought Life Chances stayed under everyone's radar."

"We do our best, but Dixon's special. Don't know how he does it, but he seems to have an inside track to all kinds of information. Technical communication is his specialty."

A sudden banging on the door made them all jump. Mira looked from one to the other and raised her hands in a gesture that meant, *I don't know who it could be.*

"I'll get it," Jonathan said.

Mira nodded gratefully.

He opened the door and exclaimed, "Brinkman?"

"That's *Detective* Brickman to you." He marched through the open door. "You sure get around, don't ya kid?"

Jonathan frowned. "Are you working this case too? Shouldn't you focus your attention on finding Aranda?"

"That's why I'm here. Your friend Giles says he can tell us what happened to Aranda."

Jonathan's fingers tightened into fists. "I told you it was Giles! I'd like to strangle the little weasel." He suddenly stopped. "What about Aranda? Was she a hostage? Is she okay?"

"Keep your pants on kiddo. Ms. Hastings has some decisions to make."

৩৮৩

Rebecca was in a melancholy mood that Sunday morning when she returned home from the early service at church. Following her set routine, she ran water into a kettle and sat it on the stove to heat, then put two slices of bread in the toaster and pushed the handle down.

The previous evening, the Head Mistress called her aside to alert her of their intention to disperse some of the easily-identified children to safer locations. It made perfect sense. Given all the turmoil surrounding the FFU, it was only a matter of time before the Foundling Home came under greater scrutiny. Rebecca decided to take Robbie out of the home and asked for a few days to make arrangements.

While the water heated and the bread toasted, she laid a teabag beside her cup. She removed a tub of butter from the refrigerator. Her hand automatically went for the jar of homemade strawberry jam, but drew it back. Robbie was the one who loved strawberry jam.

Rebecca felt regret over not saying good-bye to longtime friends. That was, after all, what one did when moving. To offer good-byes would lead to questions. Where are you going? How can we get in touch? Where will you stay? The truth was she didn't know, and couldn't allow them to talk her out of it. I don't plan to relocate, she thought. Robbie and I must *disappear*.

She broke a piece of toast in half and took a bite. No, she thought with a resolute nod, far better to handle things this way. Ideally, her exit would be as seamless as a finger pulled out of water. She'd leave no mark behind.

Rebecca knew it couldn't happen without a plan, and a good one at that. She opened a pad and began a to-do list as she ate breakfast. First up, she needed to call Carolyn Bracken. The Head Mistress suggested that Carolyn could provide any connections she'd need.

She scrutinized the room. What about all my stuff? I can't make an escape in a moving van. The answers came quickly. The rescue mission must know of people who needed furniture and clothing. Her eyes went to the open cupboard. The soup kitchen could use the dishes, silverware, pots and pans.

There was the untouched settlement from Veronica's death. Not wanting anything to do with that money, she'd put it away for Robbie's future. Veronica would surely want her to use it now. If she didn't hide him, Robbie might not have a future. The more she thought, the more confident Rebecca felt and the longer her list became.

ഇൻ

Mira choked back a sob. "How can you ask me to drop all charges against Giles? He can't go free. He could come back and kill me." Her eyes went from Brinkman to Carolyn seeking guidance.

Carolyn's eyes met Mira's. "If what Detective Brinkman says is true, that he believes Aranda is no longer alive…" Carolyn held her breath and looked at Jonathan who sat slumped forward, his face covered by his hands. "We all want to know what happened to Aranda, but at what cost? We can't put any more women at risk."

"It won't be like that," Brinkman said. "We can drop all of Ms. Hastings' charges and still keep Giles in jail."

The three of them gawked at him, waiting for an explanation.

"The detective who booked Giles did some checking. He's already tied Giles to several other rapes in the area. We'd have had him sooner if we'd had his DNA. But, the Uniform Registration Act wasn't in effect when he was born. All the women had pretty much the same story. He jumped out of the bushes and held them at knifepoint."

Brinkman turned to Mira. "Regardless of the disposition of your case, he won't get off. But, no one's going to tell him that until we get the scoop on Aranda."

Mira sighed with relief. "He is a cruel, heartless and dangerous person. Thank goodness we can find out what happened to Aranda without releasing him to prey on anyone else."

"Does this mean you'll go along with the plea deal?"

"Of course." Her eyes narrowed with determination. "But, I want to know everything he tells you."

CHAPTER THIRTY-EIGHT

"The life of the dead is placed in the memory of the living."
~ Marcus Tullius Cicero

They arrested Helen and Barnard based on the information Giles provided. The disclosures gradually leaked out over the following weeks. Sensing a scandal in the making, the press jumped all over revelations of criminal behavior at FFU-1116. The resulting press coverage made life difficult for Mira. Laboring under a burden of intense grief over Aranda's death, the daily turmoil became more than she could bear.

She was secretly relieved when her District Supervisor placed her on Administrative Leave. With no schedule to order her day Mira slipped into a self-imposed isolation. She only roused herself from the dark pall of grief long enough to attend the memorial service Carolyn and Jonathan arranged for Aranda.

Sitting in the church's quiet interior with sunshine lighting the stained glass windows, Mira experienced her first inkling of peace. As she gazed at the crucifix behind the altar, she felt someone slide in beside her and take her hand.

When she turned her eyes met Gray's.

"I've missed you," he said.

"I needed time alone."

"There's so much unfinished business between us." He gently squeezed her hand. "I'd also like to discuss our relationship."

Mira stared straight ahead. "We have a relationship now?"

"A friendship, if you prefer." Getting no response, he added, "Our association, the fateful entanglement of our lives, call it whatever you will."

She gave him an apologetic smile. "I'm not at my best today."

"No more restaurants. Come to my place and I'll cook dinner. How's this weekend?"

"Life's been crazy. I'll have to let you know."

Gray contemplated the pews up to the bare altar. There'd be no coffin for Aranda. Not even an urn of ashes, he thought with a sigh. "My heart goes out to Carolyn and Jonathan. I've had cases in which they never found the victim's remains. It makes it so much harder on friends and family."

Mira acknowledged the pain with a nod. "I've had a special arrangement with a man who owns a local cemetery. He provides a receptacle for the children's ashes and replaces it with a new one every month or so. He's created a hidden *Garden of Innocence* where he inters them. I provide him with the children's names and he records them in a large ledger."

She met Gray's eyes. "He started with one book. It resembled an old family Bible, with parchment pages and a tooled leather cover of burgundy and gold leaf." She sighed. "He's filled it and is over halfway through another. He stores them in the cemetery's chapel so our FFU children won't be forever forgotten."

She dabbed at her eyes with a tissue. "Since the ashes hadn't been removed yet, I offered to place a small portion in an urn as a memorial to Aranda. Carolyn and Jonathan considered it and decided Aranda should remain with the youngsters she loved. Her name will go into the ledger along with those of the children."

"You're amazing."

She shook her head.

"Let's move forward," he whispered, leaning close. "There probably won't be many people here today."

They walked up the aisle together, taking places nearer Carolyn and Jonathan. Others drifted in, forming a tight little knot near the front of the church, while an organ played softly in the background.

ℰⳳ

Mira put off accepting Gray's invitation for a week. Though her mind had often returned to Gray and their *relationship*, she felt a certain ambivalence. When she arrived at his condo, loud, deep-throated barking greeted her as her foot hit the front step.

"Deeohgee, quiet!" A yellow Lab rushed out when Gray opened the door. The dog ran excited circles around Mira then bounded into the house ahead of them.

"Sorry about Deeohgee. He has a hard time controlling his enthusiasm."

"I understand." The dog hurried to her side as she entered the living room. Mira bent down to look him in the eyes and scratched behind his ears.

Tail thumping, Deeohgee whimpered in pleasure.

"He likes you," Gray said.

Deeohgee flopped on his back to get his tummy rubbed.

She dropped to one knee to oblige. "You think?" she asked, peering up at Gray.

"He's friendly, but discerning. He won't roll over for just anyone."

"And such an odd name." She tested the sound of it as she rose. "*Dee-oh-gee*. Is it Oriental?"

He shook his head and smiled. "No, no, nothing foreign. You just spelled it." He drew the letters in the air with his finger, as if writing on a blackboard. "D-O-G."

Mira giggled. "You named your Labrador, *Dog*? I feel like the straight man in a comedy routine."

He pretended to be insulted. "What's funny about that? Deeohgee is a perfectly respectable name." Try as he might, he couldn't contain the smile that edged its way onto his face.

She grinned back. "Smells like dinner's almost ready."

Gray took her elbow and she let him. "We're eating on the patio. I need to pick up a few things in the kitchen on the way."

§∞⁂

Their arms were full of condiments, so Gray used his foot to open the sliding glass door. He motioned Mira through. Before either of them could get outside, however, Deeohgee squeezed between them and rushed out.

Stepping onto the deck, Gray set trays of condiments and side dishes on the table. While Mira arranged things, he rolled back the hood on the barbecue to inspect the ribs. They were perfect and he put several saucy ribs on each plate.

"I had no idea your barbecue would be this elaborate."

He gave her a thumbs-up gesture at the compliment before adding grilled veggies to their plates.

Mira gazed across the small yard as she waited. The red brick patio held an outdoor table and chairs as well as the barbecue. Budding pink azaleas surrounded a patch of emerald green grass. Wisteria vines partially covered the wooden fence, framing the area. They also climbed a trellis and onto the lath roof above the patio, shading it with cascading purple blooms.

"Dinner looks wonderful," Mira said, sliding onto the chair Gray pulled out for her.

The table was already set. A ruby red glass lamp sat at its center with a glowing votive candle inside. It cast a warm blush on the tabletop. A narrow red vase with three white roses sat beside Mira's silverware. She leaned over to smell them. "This vase looks like cranberry glass. Is it an antique?"

"It was my mother's. She said my great grandmother received it as a wedding gift. It's one of the few family mementoes I still have. Since my brother and sister are both married, I felt they should have them for their kids. What about you? Any family treasures you've held onto?"

Mira thought a moment then shook her head. "Nope, Butterscotch is my only treasure. I never thought a pet could mean so much to me, but he does."

"Yeah, I know what you mean. Deeohgee is the family I come home to every night."

She watched him tear open a foil-wrapped baked potato and butter it.

I wonder if he ever wishes he had someone else besides a dog waiting for him at home.

"You're awfully quiet. What deep thoughts are you contemplating?" he asked with a wink.

"I was thinking that with this giant meal we should invite your neighbors in to help us eat it all."

"Not tonight. This evening is ours and I won't share it with anyone else." Gray picked up a juicy rib. "I hope you don't mind me using my fingers. It's the best way to get the meat off."

His laid-back manor diffused the tension she'd felt about coming. She answered by picking up an equally juicy rib and taking a bite.

"Remember telling me you ran Aranda's license plate through the DMV? Why didn't you ever do anything with it?"

He took a deep breath, hesitating. "If someone is willing to risk themselves to rescue a child, I want to help, not hinder them."

She smiled. This was a Grayson Stevens she wanted to get to know much better.

„)ಠ

As evening crept up, they moved inside. Gray lowered the lights and lit a small fire. Deeohgee padded over and stretched out in front of the hearth. After a big yawn, his head sank onto the rug.

Gray joined her on the couch. "You know, we never did get around to discussing the strange goings on during the Director's Conference. Or why you invited me in the first place. Given everything that's happened, those few weeks seem like a lifetime ago."

"I've already told you, I didn't invite you."

He chuckled. "I've still got your email around here someplace. Shall I go get it?"

"Oh, you received an email alright, but I didn't send it.

Someone, and I'm pretty sure I know who, hacked into my computer and sent it."

Gray crossed his arms and thought for a moment. "Would this unnamed hacker also be the individual who interrupted the presentation?"

"I'm certain of it."

"I thought so. That little interruption during the conference had Dixon's fingerprints all over it."

Her jaw dropped. "You know Dixon?"

"In a manner of speaking. About 18 months ago he was caught trolling classified files and the case landed on my desk. How do you know him?"

"Dixon introduced himself in the courthouse. He claimed he'd demonstrate his computer prowess during the conference."

Gray frowned. "He needs to be more careful. Dixon's good at what he does, but he can be a bit reckless at times. His Achilles' heel is youthful over-confidence. I won't be able to sweep things under the rug if he gets himself into trouble again."

"You let him go?"

"I declined to prosecute citing insufficient evidence."

"But there's still a record of the charge."

"There would be if I hadn't removed the file from the database. As far as the system is concerned, the event never happened."

Mira pondered what Gray said then turned to face him. "Why put your career on the line for Dixon?"

Gray's fingers drummed the arm of the couch. "Now and then events need a little nudge in the right direction. When it comes to the FFUs, the bad guys have already stacked the deck in their favor. Without a little surreptitious help now and then things will never change."

Mira gave a happy sigh and scooted closer.

Gray welcomed her by slipping his arm around her shoulder.

"You ran out of the restaurant when I mentioned seeing a young woman with a laundry cart. That young woman was Aranda, wasn't it?"

Mira acknowledged him with a glum nod and brushed away a tear.

He shook his head. "It's nearly unbelievable to imagine Giles incinerating Aranda's body along with the children. There seems to be no end to the depravity."

"She died to protect Carolyn and Jonathan and the rest the Life Chances program. If she had revealed their network, there's no telling what harm it might have caused."

"The bitter irony is that in doing so Aranda also protected Giles and the guards who killed her."

The memory of Giles's attack sent a shiver through Mira. "Thanks to your rescuing me, their crimes didn't remain hidden. The truth came out in all its ugliness and brutality."

"They won't be doing much of anything for a long, long time."

She sighed and let her head rest on his shoulder. "At one time I believed I could change the system by becoming part of it. Now I'm not so sure."

CHAPTER THIRTY-NINE

"To understand the heart and mind of a person, look not at what he has already achieved, but at what he aspires to."
~ Kahlil Gibran

Gray rose from the couch, crossed to the fireplace and prodded half-burned embers.

"I got a piece of good news last week," he said as he settled back onto the sofa next to Mira. "Little Robbie Wilson's grandmother is doing story hours for the children at the Foundling Home. She volunteers so there's no record of her involvement, and it gives Robbie time with Gramma."

Mira smiled. "I loved your story of how all the children banded together to protect Robbie from that investigator."

"Circumstances make them wise beyond their years." His hand rested on her shoulder and he checked his watch. "Tomorrow's Monday. I'm not keeping you too late, am I?"

Mira snuggled closer and shook her head. "You're the one who has to worry about the time. Tomorrow I'll be searching job websites. I'm on Administrative leave, remember?" She tugged at her earring. "Not that I didn't deserve it. Three of my employees are in jail. Two charged with murder and conspiracy, while the third, who happens to also be a serial rapist, confessed to incinerating a coworker's body."

Giving Gray no chance to comment, she added, "Meanwhile, the District Attorney's office is investigating an incident in which a child scheduled for elimination turned up alive and well in a Foundling Home. On top of that, the child's father is suing for Breach of Contract and Non-Performance while half-a-dozen auditors from the home office snoop through every file drawer, desk and computer to see what else they can find." She sucked in a deep breath. "Let's face it, the only time I'll ever see the inside of that FFU again is when I go back to clean out my desk."

He gave her a gentle squeeze. "The FFUs are designed to do horrible things, so is it any wonder that other horrible things happen there?"

"One has to wonder how our society's craziness was allowed to go as far as it has," she said.

"One thing leads to another." Gray chewed his lip, thinking. "To protect women from dangerous, illegal abortions, they legalized them. The fact that more women have died since they became legal, is hidden from the public."

He sighed heavily. "It wasn't long before doctors withheld treatment for children born with disabilities, letting them die instead. Parents and nurses had to watch babies suffer through days of dehydration. This led to choosing a quick *more merciful* euthanasia for all those they deemed *imperfect*."

Mira grimaced. "With abortion centers so profitable, it didn't take long for the greedy to lobby for FFUs. They started with children under two then moved it up to four. Yet, they're still not satisfied." She leaped up. "When will it end?"

Awakened, Deeohgee swiveled his head and gave a low woof. Verifying everything was okay, he put his head back down and resumed napping.

Gray reached for Mira's hand and pulled her back to the sofa, placing his arm around her shoulders. "In spite of everything, I'm grateful we met."

Staring into the fire, they quietly mused on the strange series of events that drew them together. After a long silence, Mira rocked forward, preparing to rise. "I should help you clean up the rest of the dishes."

"They won't go anywhere." He gazed into her eyes. "Besides, I'm happy here. What about you?"

She reached over and stroked his cheek. "I'm *very* happy here." She rested a hand on his knee and sighed. "I can't believe anyone would tolerate FFUs if they truly knew what happens inside them."

"Wasn't that the motivation behind Dixon's interruption, to remind everyone of what actually goes on within their facilities?"

Mira's brows puckered. "The problem is, he's preaching to the wrong crowd. I think most FFU employees enter the system expecting to provide a service. But two or three things happen. Decent people recoil in horror, beat a hasty retreat and spend the following months and years trying to rid themselves of the memory. The experience leads many of them into organizations such as Life Chances."

She opened her hands and gestured outward, "Those who stay fall into two categories. First, there are those so desperate for the income they ignore their conscience and never tell a soul where they work. These people typically end up in record keeping or intake...as far from the actual killing as possible."

"That leaves just the final group. Who are they?"

"They're the FFU's dirty little secret. People who see opportunity in a job most others find repulsive. Just as the Nazis depended upon the SS and their cadre of psychological misfits to run their concentration camps, the FFUs couldn't function without sadists and sociopaths like Giles and Bernard."

"Not unlike an abortion center depending upon someone who's willing to mutilate unborn infants," Gray said.

She nodded and continued. "At the other end of the spectrum are the careerists, folks who've made a pact with the Devil. They're so thoroughly corrupted by greed that they'll do or say anything to advance their career. Upper management is composed of nothing but such people."

Gray lifted her chin. "There's a group you overlooked."

A quizzical expression crossed Mira's face.

Gray brushed her hair aside and kissed her forehead. "People like you and Aranda who willingly go into the belly of the beast and risk their life to rescue a child. I bet there are others, more than you imagine."

"I agonize for Aranda and the children, especially those she would have saved." Mira brushed aside a tear. "Not only is it cruel and inhumane, it's just plain wrong. I'm tired of saving one here and one there; I want to save them all."

"You're talking about upending the entire system. A lot of us dream of turning back the clock and starting over again, but how do we accomplish it?"

"By letting people know the truth." The resolute tone of Mira's voice said as much as her words. "Dixon is urging me to film an exposé about the FFUs. He says he can insert it all over the place and it'll go viral. You know Dixon better than I do, what do you think?"

Gray ran his tongue around the inside of his cheek. "As an attorney I advise caution. Dixon will want an FFU Director, not an amorphous figure in a hooded cloak. And, those careerists in upper management won't take kindly to you shining a bright light on the workaday world of an FFU."

"It's just a matter of time until they fire me. Why should I worry about what they think?" Mira said with a shrug.

"I'll tell you why. The flow of innocent children through the FFUs is making them rich. They're happy to see Helen and Barnard hauled up on charges so long as they can distance themselves from their actions. There have been no statements of regret from management about anything that happened. Aranda's death made it abundantly clear how far they'll go if threatened. I don't want you to suffer a similar fate."

"If Dixon's plan succeeds, it's worth the risk. My question for you is, can he pull it off? Is he really as good as he says he is?"

"From what I've seen, I'd say yes." Gray grasped her arms and looked deep into her eyes. "Even though your bravado frightens me, I want you to know one thing. I'm in your corner. Whatever you decide and no matter what the consequences, I'll support you one hundred percent."

"Thanks, I needed to hear that," she whispered.

He leaned forward to kiss her. She wrapped her arms around him and returned his kiss...again and again.

CHAPTER FORTY

"Courage is not simply one of the virtues, but the form of every virtue at the testing point." ~ C.S. Lewis

Buoyed by Gray's vow of support, Mira contacted Dixon and made arrangements to record an exposé.

Blinking and yawning, she tightened her grip on the steering wheel. She'd risen at 3 a.m. to get to Dixon's headquarters by daybreak. The first inklings of morning sun edged over the horizon as she traveled the country road watching for the turnoff.

She checked her rearview mirror again. No one behind her. "Getting close," she mumbled when she spotted a stake with a ribbon of pink surveyor's tape fluttering from it. She lifted her foot from the accelerator, letting the rise of the road slow the car. When an opening in the trees appeared on the opposite side, she applied the brake and quickly turned onto a gravel track.

It was indistinguishable from any of the dozens of roads she'd passed. Only the presence of rusting mailboxes on weather-beaten posts promised that it actually went somewhere. About a half mile later she saw a drive between the decaying remnants of a white board fence. She turned in, cautiously following it. Moments later she rounded a cluster of oaks and saw Dixon tossing hay over the fence to a pair of horses.

He waved at her and hurried to an aging red barn. He swung open the wide doors and motioned her through.

Mira drove in. When Dixon closed the doors behind her, rusty hinges squealed. She gingerly stepped out of the car onto the dirt floor wishing she hadn't worn heels. "Horses?" she said with a laugh. "I didn't imagine you as a ridin' and ropin' cowboy."

"They're part of our persona. Just a coupla good ole boys livin' the simple life out here in God's country." He lowered his voice. "We didn't arrange things to make ourselves easy to find."

She glanced around the barn's weathered timbers, noticing dust motes drifting in the shafts of light filtering through cracks in the board siding. "This certainly isn't what I expected. How do you survive out here?"

"Our firm designs and maintains websites for a number of small businesses, and Brody does programming for a software company in Florida. It keeps food on the table and provides us with a cover." A nervous look shadowed his face. "Did you check to be sure you weren't followed?"

"Once I got off the Interstate I was all by myself. I'm getting rid of the car in a few days anyway; Carolyn has arranged a swap."

"Great, then let's get to work."

She struggled to keep up as Dixon headed toward the back of the barn. He stopped beside a rickety stairway. Her eyes followed the steps up to a hay-filled loft. "Certainly, not up there?"

Stepping under the loft, he shoved aside several bales of hay covering a dusty trap door made of weather-beaten planks. "It's over here." Dixon lifted it, revealing a steel underside and a prefabricated steel stairway leading to a room beneath the barn. "If anyone ever notices, we'll tell them the previous owner feared tornadoes and built this underground shelter."

Dixon stepped aside, letting Mira descend the sturdy stairs. She followed them to a small, bare room and waited while Dixon closed the hatch above. A dim bulb dangled from the ceiling on a cord that barely cleared Mira's head. She could make out several fearsome cracks in the barn's old foundation and shuddered at the thought of spiders and worse.

"Not to worry. All is not as it seems." Dixon reached into one of the cracks and pressed a release. After a loud click he swung aside a portion of the wall, revealing a doorway.

Mira found herself entering a brightly lit office. A red-haired young man twisted around from his computer. He rose with a smile and approached her, extending his hand. "I'm Brody Branigan, Dixon's cousin. Welcome to the Inner Sanctum."

Mira ran her eyes around the brightly lit, carpeted space as she shook Brody's hand. Shelves packed with electronic gear lined both side walls. A large green screen completely covered the back wall. Long-armed lights and reflectors on tripod frames stood on both sides of a comfortable set with a couch, coffee table, matching chairs, end tables and lamps. The arrangement felt eerily familiar until she realized many talk shows employed a similar set.

Brody pointed to the filming area. "Ready for this, Ms. Hastings?"

Mira swallowed hard. "As ready as possible, I suppose."

Dixon joined them carrying a stack of poster board sheets under one arm and a magic marker in his other hand. "Take a seat over by my desk and we'll get started." He sat the poster boards on a corner of the desk and reached for a sheet of paper. "First, we'll flowchart your main points and then I'll transfer them to these cue cards. I'll stand behind Brody while he films and hold up the cards to help you stay on topic. Give me an idea of what you plan to say."

As Dixon and Mira discussed the nuts and bolts of her presentation, Brody moved around the set adjusting the lights and aligning the camera.

Dixon laid down his pencil and picked up the marker. "I think that about covers it. I'll number the cards, enter the main talking points and create a list of bullet-pointed key phrases beneath each one. The cue cards should aid the flow, but it's no problem to stop and do something over if you're not satisfied."

Mira nervously watched him work.

Dixon looked up at her. "I'm sorry. You probably want to spend a few minutes getting ready. There's a restroom with a mirror over there. You'll find a bottle of eye drops there too. They'll get that *I didn't get enough sleep last night* redness out."

CHAPTER FORTY-ONE

"Just imagine you're sitting in your living room having a discussion with friends," Dixon said before the filming began. "And don't worry about the background. The green screen allows us to chroma key in special effects during the post-production and editing process. At times it will look like a family den complete with walnut paneling, fireplace and picture window. As your narrative moves to the FFU's methods of operation, we'll switch to footage illustrating the actual events."

Brody directed his gaze at them and raised bushy eyebrows. "We can start filming whenever you're ready. After the shoot, Dix and I will need time to merge the images and complete the editing. Once that's done, it's just a matter of having you disappear."

She raised her eyes from Dixon's cards and gave Brody a confident smile. "I won't need much time after I leave here. I spent the last week getting packed and ready. The sooner you release the tape, the sooner it can have its impact. If this saves even one child..."

Dixon scratched the back of his neck and straightened his stack of poster board cards. "Has Carolyn Bracken and the Life Chance's group covered everything? You can still back out."

"They have and I won't. It's time someone exposed the money -hungry cruelty driving FFUs."

"You'll be at great risk once this begins to circulate. The powers that be will do anything they can to silence you. Trust me; they won't risk letting you do an encore." He led her to the couch. "Good luck," Dixon whispered and squeezed her shoulder before taking his place behind Brody.

At Brody's signal, she took a deep breath, threw her shoulders back and began.

Mira repeated what she'd disclosed before the Grand Jury, but in greater detail. She described some of the little ones who'd captured her attention and who, try as she might, she couldn't forget. She spoke of their fears and tears, hoping to touch the hearts of those who saw the broadcast.

She explained in graphic detail what the children endured. She spoke of Giles' mistreatment and neglect of the children prior to their exposure to toxic gas. Authorities and the news media insisted it was a painless procedure. She assured her listeners it definitely was not.

Next she described the *Good-Bye* room and the incinerations that followed the deaths there. She likened it to the crematoriums used by the Nazi's in the 1940's. "It's been written that 'the largest mass murder in the history of humanity occurred at Auschwitz.' As terrible and shocking as Auschwitz was, the numbers killed in all the Nazi concentration camps doesn't compare to the number of babies and children that our own country has thoughtlessly destroyed." Mira started to sob.

"Time for a break," Dixon said. Brody poured her a glass of ice water while Dixon fetched a box of tissues.

She dried her eyes and stiffened her resolve. She *would* get through this. After checking her makeup, she took a deep, cleansing breath and started. "Since child genocide was introduced... No, let's go all the way back to the beginning. It was 1973 when seven men made abortion legal. They spoke of back-alley butchers and promised to use abortion only in extreme cases. Yet in no time, abortion became a method of birth control, sacrificing millions upon millions in the process."

She sucked in a breath. "Once late-term abortion became legal for fully viable little humans, the push began for after-birth terminations. Soon they were eliminating children in their first year of life. The age gradually crept higher until we reached the point where we are today."

Dixon gave her a thumbs-up sign and brought up the next card. Mira paused for a moment, reminding herself to look into the camera, and then continued. One by one she worked her way through the stack of cards until they lay on the floor beside Dixon in a careless heap.

Mira rose and stood behind her chair as she began her concluding remarks. "The bottom line is every human life matters. It's not about you or me; we're survivors. It's about your children and your neighbor's children. It's about every baby's future. If you have a heart, stand up and stop the blood bath that profits a few at the expense of many. Additional lives are lost every passing day; precious lives that, once gone, can never be reclaimed. This craziness must end."

Despite her best efforts, tears rolled down Mira's cheeks. She turned away and ran a hand across her face. The lights dimmed and the camera quit rolling. Dixon and Brody hovered in shadows, silent and still. She hoped for a similar effect on other viewers.

Drying her eyes, she grabbed her purse and hurried toward the stairs.

Dixon followed after her. "Ms. Hastings, you don't have to run away. Why not stay for lunch? We fix a mean TV dinner or, since you're a celebrity, we could break out the grill and roast weenies."

Mira shook her head. "I want to get as far away as possible and forget the last few hours. Rehashing my life at an FFU has left me feeling grungy."

"I understand. Be reassured we'll burn all cue cards and other notes as soon as you leave. After Brody downloads the files, we'll transfer everything to servers in Eastern Europe. There'll be no records of you ever having been here."

"And then what?"

"We'll insert the full tape all across the internet, giving people an opportunity to copy and disseminate it. I'll insert smaller segments into various programs and sporting events."

"They're going to let you waltz in and do that?"

Dixon shook his head. "The media world is highly automated. People envision scads of people...producers, directors, camera men and what not scurrying around the studio like in the olden days. There's none of that now. The shows, commercials and station breaks are all digitized and automatically fed into the broadcast sequentially."

He gave her a wicked grin. "It works like a charm unless someone slips something into the mix. I'll simply replace a piece of their programming with another file and let nature take its course. It beats the heck out of schlepping in the front door with half a dozen canisters of film."

"There must be security protocols, firewalls?"

"As long as human beings design the systems, other, smarter human beings can crack their codes."

She nodded and climbed into her car.

Dixon passed a manila folder through the open window. "Here's your new identity with birth certificate, driver's license, and so on. Your financial documents are also in there. I transferred most of your money into a new account so you can access it. I left a little in each account so it didn't throw up red flags."

She studied the contents of the folder. "Is this some kind of joke? You made me Maude Hoople?"

"Has a nice ring to it, don't you think?"

"And I'm five years older!" Mira shrieked.

"Because of the Uniform Registration Act, I couldn't make you younger without inputting the genetic profile they now require. Notice that you and Maude were born on the same day...just different years. I kept your initials and retained your middle name so it'd be easy to remember."

Leaving her to fume, Dixon opened the barn doors. "Where will you go from here?" he asked. "We can help."

"It's all taken care of." She knew exactly where she was going, and didn't feel the need to share her plans with Dixon.

"If you have television access, flip to the local channel this evening. Brody and I will put your first airtime out there tonight." He stepped back as she rolled past.

Mira unexpectedly stopped her car halfway out and waved him over. "Before I leave there's something I want to ask you about. Why did you hack my computer and send an email to Grayson Stevens?"

Dixon tried to appear confused. "Email to whom? What email?"

"Don't try to play dumb. I know all about the incident with the Government Database. I don't care; I just want to know why."

"I felt Stevens was someone you should get to know."

"So in addition to espionage you also dabble in matchmaking?"

Dixon grinned with satisfaction. "So you and Stevens have ... um, become friends?"

"That's none of your business." She rolled up her window and headed down the gravel drive.

CHAPTER FORTY- TWO

Gray frowned at the nondescript blue sedan in one of his parking spaces.

Someone's probably having a party.

The management of the complex provided each resident with two adjoining parking slots. Gray's were at the end of the row and he always parked on the left, giving him a grassy median on one side and an empty space on the other. He didn't want anyone dinging his sports car.

Gray eased in, staying as far to the left of the blue car as possible. He got out, paused to buff a smudge off his fender, and headed up the walk.

His skin prickled when he reached the door and all was quiet on the other side.

Where was Deeohgee?

Stepping in, he glanced down the hall and noticed the bedroom door ajar. He always shut it to keep the dog out, yet it was wide open. He ran his eyes around the room, searching. Everything seemed fine, but a chill ran up his spine.

Did it have anything to do with that blue car? And where's the dog?

Leaving the lights off, he silently crossed the living room. His hand slipped into his jacket and removed a small pistol from his shoulder holster. After his encounter with Giles, he'd obtained a concealed carry permit. Finding himself unarmed was an experience he never wanted to repeat.

He leaned around a kitchen corner. Found nothing and moved on. Gray pressed his back to the wall and inched his way to the bedroom. He drew a deep breath and spun into the bedroom doorway, gun raised.

The thumping of Deeohgee's tail on the bed greeted him. A closer look revealed a lump beside the dog, covered by a thick blue quilt. Gray flipped on the overhead light. The bed's startled occupant jerked up, threw back the quilt, saw the gun, and screamed.

Deeohgee leaped off the bed and raced down the hallway barking loudly. Holstering the gun, Gray approached the bed. "What are you doing here?"

Mira rubbed sleep from her eyes. "Gosh, it's good to see you too."

"I'm surprised to find you here, that's all. Did I forget to lock my door this morning?"

"Nope, everything was locked up tight as a drum. You even had the deadbolt thrown. When I came for dinner I spied a suspicious looking rock beneath your bushes. I thought, 'that looks like one of those *Hide-A-Key Rocks* they sell on cable TV.' Sure enough, it was." Lifting her hand, she mimicked a TV pitchman. "Never worry about being locked out again. Spin the top aside and presto, a waterproof compartment for a spare key."

"We both know locks only keep honest people honest," Gray said. "My real deterrent has always been Deeohgee. How did you manage to get past him?"

The dog smiled when she reached over and ruffled his ears. "Piece a' cake. I said, 'Hi, Deeohgee,' and he rolled over for a tummy rub."

Gray glared at him. "What kind of watchdog allows just anyone to waltz in when I'm gone?"

"Hey, wait a minute, fella. Since when am I *just anyone*?"

He shook his head. "I didn't mean for it to come out that way. Deeohgee's only met you once. He's normally more cautious."

Mira gave him a sultry wink and smoothed her hair. "With my charm, sometimes once is enough." She rocked her hand in the air. "For others...well, it takes a bit longer."

Gray sat on the corner of the bed. "You still haven't told me why you're here."

"I recall someone saying, '*Whatever you decide and no*

matter the consequences, I'll support you one hundred percent.' Of course, that's when I counted for something." She turned aside, pretending to pout. "Now I'm just anyone." She glared at him. "It's not likely the government watches Grayson Stevens, so this is a good place to be when the storm breaks."

He was still digesting what she said when he heard a plaintive mewing in the corner of the room. A pair of yellow eyes stared at Gray through the wire squares of a cat carrier. Gray shot Mira a questioning look.

"I gave up my car, my furniture and most of my clothes. I won't lose Butterscotch too."

Gray slid closer. "You mentioned a storm. What storm? Why are you hiding?"

"According to Dixon, I might be the lead story on the evening news." She gave a slight bow. "I'm about to go viral, become an instant celebrity."

She looked so sexy with hair flying around her head and her sleepy-eyed, just woke up look. Gray couldn't resist putting an arm around her shoulders. "Do you realize you're asking me to harbor a fugitive?"

Mira threw her feet onto the floor and slipped them into her shoes. "Fine, if you want me to leave, I will. I can probably find a sheltered spot and a cardboard box in an alley downtown."

"That isn't what I said."

"Sure sounded like it to me."

"It's almost time for the evening news," he said. "Let's see if Dixon's done it."

Mira stretched and yawned. "I haven't slept so well since before I decided to publicly expose the activities at the FFUs."

Gray's expression darkened. He grabbed the remote from the bed's nightstand and turned on the set, muting commercials as they waited for the news to begin.

Mira leaned back against the headboard, snuggling closer.

He grinned and wished he didn't have a newscast to watch. But, when Mira's face lit up the screen, he turned up the volume to listen. By the time the spot ended he was terrified for her. Leaving his arm around Mira's shoulders, he reached across with the other and picked up her hand. Touching it to his lips, he said, "What were you thinking? You've declared war."

"I was thinking babies are dying every day and it has to stop."

"It's been going on for decades. What makes you think you can change it?"

"What makes you think I can't? People need to be shocked out of their apathy. Conception is the beginning of a human being as a rational organism. This single fact undermines every justification for abortion or FFUs. The reality is all people are human from conception to death."

Gray's voice took on a pleading tone. "This plan of Dixon's, if you can call it that, is dangerous." He sucked in a deep breath. "Think about ants at a picnic. If they come up on the table, they get smashed. Meanwhile, hundreds of them safely feast on the crumbs that drop to the ground. By coming out in the open like this, you've painted a bull's eye on your back." He swallowed hard and chewed his lip. "I couldn't bear to see something happen to you."

"Even if it means harboring a fugitive?"

He nodded.

She smiled. "Good, I've gotten pretty fond of you too."

Gray pulled her closer and kissed her. Once they started, neither of them wanted to stop. They kicked off their shoes and slid down onto the bed. For the next several hours they forgot about the world and all its troubles.

CHAPTER FORTY-THREE

The ringing of Gray's phone awakened them. He rolled back the covers, wondering why sunlight streamed between slats in the blinds. A quick check of the clock on the nightstand answered his question. By now, the sun had been up for hours.

Mira lifted her head off his shoulder and gave him a questioning look. He leaned over and kissed her forehead. They'd loved each other and talked late into the night before settling into a deep, sound sleep.

"It's probably the office wanting to know where the devil I am." He picked up the phone, deliberately letting his sleepy voice work for him. "Yeah?"

He listened for a moment. "Sorry. I should have called, but I slept right through my alarm. You'd better not expect me in today." He ran his fingers through his hair. "Based on the way I feel, I'll likely be out for several days. Postpone or reschedule this week's calendar. I'll call when I'm feeling better." He listened a moment. "Yes, I promise if it gets worse I'll see a doctor. No, no, Jacqueline, I can manage; don't bother to bring me anything."

Glancing back at Mira, he rolled his eyes and shrugged. "I gotta go. I'm starting to feel bad." Gray quickly hung up and frowned at the phone. "My Administrative Assistant wanted to bring me chicken soup."

"Uh-oh, did I take someone else's place?"

He looked stunned. "I told you I'm not dating anyone. There's nothing going on between Jacqueline and me. She's just...um, overly helpful at times."

She lowered her eyebrows and crossed her arms. "Overly helpful?"

"What can I say? I've been too busy for, for *attachments*." He put his arm around her and pulled her to him. "I was waiting for someone like you to enter my life." He kissed her and nuzzled her neck, inhaling her scent with a happy sigh. "And here you are."

"Yep, here I am." She danced her fingers along his ribcage.

He laughed and squirmed away when she tickled him.

They stared at each other, both grinning. A second later, immersed in laughter, they fell into each other's arms.

Mira watched the muscles move in his bare back as he rose. He was more muscular, than she'd realized. She sighed, realizing he cared for her as much as she cared for him. She felt comfortable trusting him with her life. After all, he'd saved her once already, hadn't he?

୫୦୦ଓ

Crumbs tumbled onto the dining room table when Mira bit into a chocolate drizzled croissant. Food was sparse in Gray's bachelor kitchen, so he'd thrown on a sweat suit and jogged down to the nearby Deli.

Her cheeks colored when she noticed Gray watching her. She licked the chocolate off her lips and raised her right hand. "I swear I don't usually eat like this, honest. For some reason, everything tastes especially good this morning." She looked at the half eaten croissant on her plate and shook her head. "You're a bad influence. If I eat like this all the time, I'll be twice my size."

"Once in a while can't hurt." Gray picked up another glazed donut, eyeing it with anticipation. "I'm not usually this hungry in the morning either," he said with a wink.

She winked back.

Feeling joyous, he flicked a crumb off her chin. "I wish you could have heard the buzz at the Deli. What you did has had a national impact. Dixon's right, you're going viral."

Mira was shocked and pleased at the same time. "I expected the government to squelch it."

"It's out of their hands. Every time they smack it down in one place, it pops up in two more. You're unstoppable."

He reached across the table and took her hand. "Mira, will you marry me? Now, right away, just as soon as possible."

Her eyes went to the table. "I'm not much of a marriage prospect. I'll probably be on the run for the rest of my life."

"Then we'll run together. I'll be your protector."

She started to object, but he placed a finger over her lips. "Let me finish. I've given this a lot of thought."

"When?"

"On my way to the Deli."

"The Deli's no more than five minutes away."

"I had to go both ways and, besides, there was a long line."

She checked an imaginary watch. "Okay, instead of five or ten minutes of deliberation we'll credit you with a full fifteen minutes of deep thought. Regardless, it's still not a good idea. You'd lose everything by marrying me."

"But look what I gain."

"Yeah, a life on the run spent watching your back."

"It's a risk we'll take." Too excited to sit still, Gray rose and began to pace.

Mira scooped crumbs off the table and onto her plate. Picking up their dishes she carried them to the sink. "You're really serious about this, aren't you?"

"I am." He took her is in arms and kissed her.

A sudden knock on the front door caused them both to jump. Gray pointed across the kitchen to the walk-in pantry. Mira tiptoed over and slipped inside. He waited for the pantry door to close before peering through the peephole.

A slow smile curled his lips. He threw back the bolt and opened the door wide. Carolyn Bracken entered carrying a large shopping bag. Jonathan trailed behind with a large box.

"What have you got there?" Gray asked.

"Disguises. Mira can't stay cooped-up here for long, and she shouldn't be identifiable when she leaves. I have wigs for her to switch in and out of, along with various outfits to match."

"I get the picture." He turned toward the kitchen. "Mira, come on out. It's Carolyn."

The two women exchanged hugs. Mira couldn't control her curiosity and began riffling through the bag Carolyn brought.

Carolyn took a second bag from Jonathan and handed it to Gray. "Both of you may end up on the run. I brought a few things for you as well. It made sense to bring them now while it's still safe."

He rubbed stubble on his jaw. "You must be psychic. I'd already decided to grow a beard." Gray reached over and gave Carolyn a peck on the cheek. "We were just talking about the same thing. Bless you."

Mira shook her head. "No, we weren't. Maybe *you* were, but *we* weren't."

Gray walked over and lifted her off the ground. "It's out of your hands," he said, and kissed Mira firmly on the mouth.

Noticing the shocked look on Carolyn and Jonathan faces, he smiled and said, "I'm going to marry this girl."

A bemused smile crossed Carolyn's face. "That quick? My, how...um, nice."

Mira stepped between them. "Ignore him. He has an imaginative fantasy life."

Gray moved to her aside. "She doesn't know what she's saying. It's a done deal. She's a damsel in distress and I'm her White Knight."

"In that case, there's something I want to talk to the two of you about," Carolyn said.

CHAPTER FORTY-FOUR

"A man of courage is also full of faith" ~ Marcus Tullius Cicero

Carolyn gathered Gray and Mira around the kitchen table. "Like most people about to be married you're probably thinking about having a family."

"Sure, someday. Right now, our plate's full." Gray gave a noncommittal shrug. "There's plenty of time."

Caroline rested her arm on the table and leaned closer. "Maybe there is for you. Not everyone has that same luxury. Look, I know I have no right to ask this, but I'm going to anyway."

Gray's expression reflected his apprehension. "What exactly do you have in mind?"

Carolyn took a deep breath, arranging her thoughts. "Mira, do you remember Emma, the little girl you rescued?"

Mira smiled and nodded.

"A young couple came to the door at Bright Minds the day I tested Emma. They wanted me to test their daughter, Mandy. You see, in addition to Mandy they also have a set of twins and learned another child is on the way."

Gray glanced around the room, looking grim.

"Three children and another on the way is a dilemma no one should have to face," Mira said, wringing her hands. "Even Solomon couldn't solve this. What are they going to do?"

"They refuse to consider abortion and won't send one of their children to the incinerator. That's why they came to Bright Minds. If the family has to separate they felt that Mandy, as the oldest, could best cope with a change." Carolyn's eyes darted between Gray and Mira. "She's currently at the Foundling Home with Robbie and Emma."

"What a sad story. Fortunately you were able to provide a solution. Not a perfect one, but a solution," Gray said.

"Wait, it gets worse."

"What could be worse than having to send one of your children away to make room for another one?" Mira asked.

Carolyn lifted an eyebrow. "How about finding out you were carrying twins again?"

Gray sighed. "So, instead of a family of four, they've become a family of five. Placing Mandy in a Foundling Home didn't resolve their problem."

"You've pretty well summed it up, Counselor."

"Why are you telling us this?" Mira asked.

"The twins were born at home a couple of days ago ... a boy and a girl. The mother's doctor is a friend of mine. He held off filing the birth certificates to let them come up with a solution, but he can't stall forever. The Abramson's feel it would be traumatic to separate the older boys. If a loving couple adopted the newborns, then Mandy could come back home."

Carolyn's raised hand stifled Gray before he could comment.

"Here's what needs to happen. Get married right away and I'll provide a marriage license back-dated to last year. Your names will appear on the birth certificates. No one need ever know the children aren't yours." Carolyn rose before they could reply and headed for the door. "Promise me you'll think about it. Call me tonight with your decision."

ℰᏜ

"My God, she doesn't ask much, does she?" Gray sputtered as soon as the door closed. "Not only does she assume we don't want to have three children of our own, she also wants us to take responsibility for two children sight unseen."

"Isn't that sort of what your parents did?"

"They'd been married for several years."

"There's something I've never told you," Mira said softly.

Gray didn't acknowledge her. "The children must look something like us," he said, thinking out loud. "Carolyn thinks we could pass them off as our own. She's got it all worked out…a fake marriage license, a doctor who'll put our names on the birth certificates. Hell, she's probably *already* got our names on them."

Mira touched his shoulder. "Don't get so excited, nothing's decided yet."

He gave her a sullen look and continued grumbling about Carolyn under his breath.

She didn't try to make out what he was saying. Lost in her own thoughts, Mira's emotions were racing. *What would it be like to actually be a mother?* She bit her lip. "Gray, what if we couldn't have children of our own?"

His expression changed as he looked at her. "Then we'd view this as an opportunity, wouldn't we? Are you suggesting we forego having children of our own in order to save two babies at risk of being destroyed?"

"Possibly. How would you feel about it?"

"If that's what you wanted, I'd go along with it."

Mira clenched her fists so tightly that her fingernails bit into her palms. "Even if it meant never having offspring of your very own?" She willed herself to relax, but couldn't. Tears formed in her eyes. "Tell me what you truly think."

Gray shrugged. "My brother has taken care of extending the noble Stevens genome into the next generation with his boys. Besides, if you want to split hairs, he's the one with the Stevens genes, not me." He picked up her hand. "After all, I wouldn't be the one getting pregnant. It's really up to you."

"I wish I could have a child with you more than anything in the world. But I'm not able to have children."

"How would you know that?"

"I just do."

He took a deep breath. "Sounds like maybe there's a reason this happened to the Abramson's. Don't Christians talk about 'invisible hands' being in control?"

"Aren't you a Christian, Gray?"

"You're changing the subject."

"No, this is important. Are you a Christian?"

"Of course, I'm a Christian." His cheeks colored. "Just, um, not a very good one. But I'm working on it."

"Truth be told, we all are. I need to tell you about my past. But, it's hard for me to do it."

He slipped an arm around her shoulder. "I'm listening."

She took a deep breath. "I was 17 and dating a jock. One night when he pressured me, I didn't tell him no. Deciding that the first time was always disappointing, I gave in again. The second and third times weren't much better. One morning I woke up nauseous and couldn't even look at my breakfast."

"Didn't the jerk care enough to use protection?"

She stared into her lap. "We were young. I felt if we never planned on something happening it was somehow okay because love should be spontaneous. Anyway, I'm not making excuses for myself. I did it and shouldn't have."

"He doesn't sound like much of a man."

"We were both kids. But this story isn't about him. He dumped me after paying for my abortion."

"Your what?"

She lifted her eyes to meet his. "This is hard. Please, let me finish."

Taking her hand, he brought it to his lips.

"The end of this miserable story is..." Mira inhaled and looked at the floor. "In a first trimester abortion, if the doctor accidently leaves some tissue in the uterus, it can cause a severe infection, permanently damaging reproductive organs. That's what happened to me." She sighed. "I spent several weeks in the hospital and almost died. They did a partial hysterectomy."

Gray said nothing.

Mira kneaded her brow, and took another deep breath. "Can't you see? I've no business being part of Life Chances. I'm not the solution; I'm part of the problem."

"No, you're not." Hugging her, he whispered, "Don't even think like that. The pressure society exerts on young, single women led you to do what you did. When voices from every side urged you to do it, you weren't aware of any other options. You couldn't have known at 17 what you know now."

"There really is no one else to blame. It was my choice to make and I made the wrong one."

"And you've paid for it ten times over. Yes, it was an awful thing, and scarred you in ways I can't begin to imagine. But look at the good that resulted from it. It turned your heart. How many young lives have you saved because of it? Isn't there a saying, 'God can extract good from any bad event'?"

"I'd like to believe that."

"Let's call Carolyn and give her our decision. It'll make her very happy." Gray's brows knit together, "...and us too, I hope."

CHAPTER FORTY-FIVE

"You're never too old to set another goal or dream a new dream." ~ C. S. Lewis

"Well, Mrs. Stuart, that's the last of it." The young man in faded jeans and a worn flannel shirt jumped up to grab the canvas strap dangling from the truck's roll door, and pulled it shut. Dusting his hands, he rounded the truck with a grin.

"You can't imagine how much your donations will mean to the families we serve. I'll drop these off for you on the way." He carefully sat two boxes of dishes and glassware inside the cab before climbing in. Leaning out the window as he backed out of her drive, he called, "Thanks again. God loves a cheerful giver."

Rebecca watched the truck drive away then went back into the house. She paused in the entryway. Seeing the empty room brought back memories of times long past.

This was how it looked the first time we saw it.

The sound of Rebecca's footsteps on the bare floors echoed off the walls as she moved from room to empty room. This was their first house. Their only house, she thought, and chuckled recalling how Bob had insisted on carrying her over the threshold the day they moved in. She'd insisted he didn't have to do it; they'd been married nearly three years.

"It's not about having to do it; it's about *wanting* to do it," he'd replied and kissed her.

Starting from scratch, they'd painted and papered and gradually furnished the house over the ensuing years. Bob got a new job shortly before Veronica was born. They'd wanted more children, but it wasn't part of God's plan.

Bob was already sick when Veronica married Frank. Rebecca remembered how proud he looked walking Veronica down the aisle.

And now they were both gone.

She brushed aside a tear and took a deep breath. She raised

her eyes to the ceiling. "I wish you were here to tell me I'm doing the right thing. I'm counting on you and Veronica looking after us as we travel."

Rebecca phoned the Foundling Home and told them she'd be coming for Robbie. Though Veronica's car remained in the garage, Rebecca seldom used it. She'd decided she was too old, the streets too busy, and the reminders of her daughter too troubling when she drove it. But today was different.

She took a final look around. Then closing the door on her former life, she headed for the garage.

৪০৫৪

"I take it you've come to a decision."

Mira looked across the table at Carolyn and smiled. "We'd love to have an instant family."

"I was almost certain you would." Carolyn rested her hand on theirs. "God bless you both. It may seem presumptuous, but I've been gathering up loose ends in anticipation. Eileen and Jacob, the children's parents, will provide you with most of the equipment you'll need — bassinets, a double stroller, baby outfits, and an initial supply of diapers."

"Speaking of loose ends. Would you consider adopting Butterscotch? He hates being in the car and it looks like we may do a lot of driving. I'll miss him terribly, but he'd be so good with the kids you rescue."

"Not sure how many youngsters there will be now that Aranda's gone," Carolyn said. "But I'll be happy to take Butterscotch. I love cats. I promise to dote on him."

"Thank you." Mira reached to hug Carolyn.

Carolyn turned to Gray. "I put some feelers out and found a nice van for you."

"A van? Thanks, but no thanks." Gray frowned and rubbed his nearly bald head. In an effort to disguise his appearance, he'd shaved the front and top, leaving a two inch ring of hair above the ears and around the back to make it look like natural hair loss.

"With small children you'll need the extra space for the babies' things when you travel. It's very low mileage and the dealer will make an even swap."

"I guess he would. My car's a classic; do you have any idea what it's worth?"

"He already has a crew detailing the van for you."

Gray looked like he might weep. "Carolyn, I'm just not a van kind of guy."

She frowned. "You planned on cramming a wife and two kids into that low-slung, two-seater you're driving?"

"To be honest, I expected children to come later. You might as well paint a sign on the side of the van saying, 'Hen-pecked family guy.' Why not a nice four-door sedan? It's more fuel efficient and retains a smidgeon of sportiness."

"I worked really hard to locate this van for you."

Gray started to object, but stopped when Mira kicked him under the table.

"And we owe you a debt of gratitude for finding it." He cleared his throat. "I... um, can hardly wait to see our new van."

೫ CR

Robbie and Emma's classroom door opened and the Head Mistress entered. "Robert Wilson, please come with me. Bring your things with you."

Emma's eyes immediately went to Robbie. She saw him tremble. Sensing his fear, her hands began to shake.

Robbie picked up the picture book he'd been flipping through and grabbed the blue flannel shirt draped over the back of his chair.

Emma knew Robbie had been cold at his father's house. The shirt was the one thing he still had left from his Gramma's. He took the shirt everywhere he went, even on warm days when he didn't need it. Not knowing where they were taking him, she was glad he'd have it with him.

Emma stared at the door after as it closed behind Robbie.

What if the inspectors came back for him?

"Okay, class," the teacher said, "let's get back to work. Robbie will be fine, you needn't worry about him."

But Emma did worry. What if he was right about the other children there at the FFU with them? Were all of them really dead?

Will I ever see Robbie again?

It was no use trying not to sob. Folding her arms on the desk, she rested her head into on her arms and let the tears flow.

A few moments later, the classroom door sprang open and banged against the wall. Emma jerked up.

Robbie raced into the room looking as if he was being chased. He scurried to the back of the room and grabbed Emma by the hand. "Come on!" he said, tugging at her arm.

She was shocked and held firm. She cared more for Robbie than anyone else in the world, but the prospect of meeting the inspectors was frightening. Why would he put her in jeopardy too? But then her love for Robbie won out. Whatever it was, she wouldn't let him face it alone.

When Emma rose and followed Robbie out of the classroom, the other children silently watched with apprehension. Two of Emma's friends began to cry.

℘ℭ

The instant she and Robbie stepped into the hallway, Emma's fears dissolved.

"See Emma, it's Gramma!" Robbie yelled and ran into her waiting arms.

The Head Mistress stood beside his grandmother holding a white plastic bag knotted at the top. It held all of Robbie's things.

Rebecca held out her hand to Emma. "Hello. Are you going to wish Robbie good-bye?" Without waiting for an answer, Rebecca gave the Head Mistress a quick thank you, and took Robbie's hand. As happy as Robbie was to see his Gramma, he resisted when she started to lead him away.

"What's wrong, honey? Did we forget something?"

"Yes. We can't l-leave Emma here. She d-doesn't have anybody else. Can she come l-live with us? She's really, really nice, Gramma. Honest."

Rebecca's face reflected astonishment before softening. She grinned at her grandson. "That's up to the school. If they'll let her go, then..."

Three pairs of eyes implored the Head Mistress. She placed a hand on Emma's head and smiled down at her. "Emma Spencer also came from the FFU. Having her far from here is to her advantage and the Foundling Home's as well. If you're willing to take her, do so with our blessing and prayers for your safety. It'll only take us a few minutes to gather her belongings. "

"Thank you." Rebecca started to shake the woman's hand and hesitated before hugging her instead.

"You'd better hurry," the Head Mistress whispered in Rebecca's ear. "Two masked men are about to arrive and whisk Robbie away." She winked. "At least that's what I plan to tell Children's Services." She placed a slip of paper in Rebecca's hand. "Here is Carolyn Bracken's address. Go there. She'll help you."

Rebecca folded her hand around it. "I'll be sure to destroy this when I find her." She smiled down at the children. "Then I guess everything's settled. Emma, if you want to come with us, I'd be proud to be your grandmother too."

Emma smiled. When Rebecca knelt and opened her arms she raced into them and embraced her new grandmother's neck.

CHAPTER FORTY-SIX

"We did it!" Rebecca shouted as they drove out of the Foundling Home's driveway.

"What did we do, Gramma?"

She surprised herself by laughing out loud. "You're both safely away and we're back together, Sweetie." She reached over and squeezed Robbie's hand.

At the courthouse Rebecca had realized even before the hearing ended that there might be trouble brewing for the Foundling Home where they'd sent Robbie. At that moment, she'd resolved to get him away from there one way or another.

Under her breath, she muttered, "Things would've been fine if Frank Wilson had only left well enough alone." As much as it hurt to admit it, however, she knew she shared some of the blame. She never should have called him. He hadn't even known about Robbie's rescue from the FFU until she opened her big mouth. Shame colored her cheeks. Had she truly expected him to cooperate, or did she ring him up just so she could gloat?

Anger quickly replaced shame. How could anyone deliver their own flesh and blood to such a place? She gave Robbie a quick inspection as she drove. He smiled up at her.

She smiled back, but her brow furrowed in concentration. She hadn't planned on ending up with two children instead of one. Keeping them hidden would be a problem, and she'd need help.

§∞൭

After parking the car, they approached Carolyn's brown stucco home. Emma and Robbie didn't recognize the house. They'd never been out front before, only in the sheltered backyard.

Rebecca held the children's hands, loving the feel of a small hand in each of hers. Reluctant to let go of either child, Rebecca said, "See the button next to you, Emma? It's a door bell, push it."

Emma obediently pushed the bell on the wall and they listened to a lyrical chime echo inside. There were approaching footsteps before the door opened a crack, and then flew wide as Carolyn Bracken gave them a broad smile. "Come in, come in!"

Robbie jumped for joy. "It's Aunt Carolyn, Emma!"

Emma walked over and wrapped her arms around Carolyn's waist, hugging her.

Carolyn dropped to her knees and swept her single arm around both children. "It's so good to see you both," she said, kissing their cheeks.

Carolyn observed Rebecca closely. "How did you know to bring them here?"

"The staff at the Foundling Home suggested I come to you. They gave me your address and said you might be able to help us find a safe place."

Carolyn grinned. "Absolutely! As you can tell, Robbie and Emma are familiar with this house."

Carolyn took Emma's hand. "Robbie, take your grandmother's hand and we'll all go to the kitchen for a bite to eat."

Rebecca checked her watch. She hadn't bothered to keep track of the time, and was surprised to see it was well past the lunch hour. The children were probably hungry. For that matter, so was she.

After turkey sandwiches and creamy tomato soup, Emma turned to Jonathan who'd joined them for lunch and asked if they could play Go Fish. It was her favorite card game. Jonathan smiled and nodded to his mother as he scooted the children out of the kitchen, giving the two women an opportunity to speak privately.

Carolyn crossed the kitchen, took down two mugs one at a time, and filled them with coffee. She placed them on a tray. "Would you carry these to the table for us?"

Rebecca hopped up and retrieved the tray.

Carolyn carried a package of cookies to the table and settled into a chair across from Rebecca. "Robbie talked about his Grandma all the time when he was here."

"I can't thank you enough for saving Robbie's life."

"I'm only one link in the chain." She studied the swirls in her coffee. "The young woman who secreted Robbie out of the FFU was named Aranda."

Rebecca's shock was apparent. "Was?"

Carolyn blinked back tears. "Yes. A short time after she brought Robbie home the security guards caught her with a child in her laundry hamper."

"What happened after that?"

"They questioned her, beat her, and threw her into the Goodbye Room with the youngsters. Afterwards they incinerated her body." Carolyn sobbed, tears spattering the tabletop. "She lived here with us, but even under torture she never gave them any names."

Rebecca gasped. "She put her life at risk to save my Robbie." Reaching across the table, she took Carolyn's hand in hers.

"Aranda's with the children now. I'm sure she's never been happier." Carolyn sniffed. "Better we savor our victories than mourn our defeats. The momentum for change is growing nationwide. For now, most supporters remain anonymous for their own safety. Someday the truth of what's happening will be known, the mood of the nation will shift, and this whole ugly nightmare will go away, including those equally dreadful abortion clinics."

"But abortion isn't as horrible as killing a little child," Rebecca said.

"Isn't it? We know babies in the womb react to stimuli of any kind ... touch, sound, light. They suffer as much or more trauma than Aranda did."

Rebecca's forehead wrinkled. "That's not what we're told. Why would our government lie to us?"

"It's lucrative, and you aren't told because they don't want you to know. I've witnessed ultrasound films of abortions. The unborn instinctively understand something awful is about to happen and struggle to get away from the abortionist's instruments. They suffer all the fear and pain associated with any other brutal death."

Rebecca slunk down in her chair. "I'd like to help, if I can."

Robbie's shout of "Go Fish!" filtered into the kitchen followed by Emma's laughter.

"You're already helping by shouldering the responsibility of protecting those two precious youngsters." Carolyn patted Rebecca's hand. "Earlier you said you wanted to go into hiding with the children. I can get you the assistance you'll need."

Carolyn reached into a side pocket. Pulling out her cell phone, she input a number. "The first thing you'll need is a new identity," she said, waiting for the call to go through.

ଛଠଔ

The Head Mistress brought her people together for an emergency staff meeting. They walked into the conference room and at each place found boxes of large white plastic bags, printed lists, and bold markers.

"We've got some work to do, folks. In front of you is a list by name and room number of children rescued from FFUs. Move down the halls as quickly as you can. Empty their dressers and re-arrange the furniture so their absence isn't noticeable. Gather each child's possessions into a separate bag, tie the top, and label it with their name. Leave the bags in the hallway beside the door. A custodian will come behind you with a cart to collect them."

"What do you plan to do with the children?" one of the workers asked.

"Why clear out their possessions?" asked another.

"It won't be long before government people come knocking at our door. Children with missing digits might as well scream, 'I escaped from an FFU.' We'll load the children and their belongings onto school buses and relocate them to safer places. I want one of you on every bus to keep order."

"What about their belongings?"

"Load the bags through the back door of the bus they're on. Keep your list so you can check off the children as they enter the bus and match them with the bags."

"The children will want to know where they're going."

"Tell them they're off on a special field trip. The busses are all going to different safe locations. Some of you may not know of them, but your bus driver can tell you all about the one he's driving toward. When you arrive, explain to the children why they're there before they exit the bus. Hurry, and Godspeed."

Staff personnel hurried from room to room emptying the dressers of children who'd been marked for extermination. In short order white bags littered the hallways. Later that morning several school buses pulled into the parking lot. An hour later they rolled out filled with children heading for a new life.

CHAPTER FORTY-SEVEN

"Men stopped slavery. Men gave up their seats in the lifeboats of the Titanic. It was men who ran up the stairs in the Twin Towers to rescue people. Men are made to take risks and live passionately on behalf of others." ~ John Eldredge

As Gray and Mira traveled a busy interstate following Carolyn's directions to the Abramson's home, Mira suddenly asked Gray to pull off the highway.

Finding a place to park, he glanced over at Mira who'd grown very quiet. "Is something the matter?"

Tears glistened in her eyes. "We're taking a big step."

"Are you having second thoughts? There's still time to back out. Carolyn might be upset with us, but we can change our mind and head down the road by ourselves." He reached back to pat Deeohgee squeezed in the narrow space behind their seats.

"I wasn't talking about the babies. I have no reservations about them. It's you and me I worry about."

He felt flutters in his stomach. "Sweetheart, everyone's life has ups and downs. We will too. Will we disagree? Of course, all couples do. We'll be challenged by each other and by our children as they grow up. That's part of life. It's always full of challenges, sorrows and joys. I only know that I'd rather face the ups and downs of life with you than without you." He reached to take her hand. "Please marry me, Mira. Don't turn me down."

She looked into his eyes and smiled for the first time. "If you can stand to put up with me, I won't have any problem loving you."

Gray pulled Mira into his arms to kiss her, but Deeohgee didn't give him a chance. Pushing his head between them, the dog excitedly licked their faces.

ೞೞ

Mira began calling out street names as they got closer. "Apple, Cherry, Huckleberry, Peach. You better slow down,

Plum's probably next."

Gray slowed and signaled a turn. As they rounded the corner, the sports car's powerful engine revved when he downshifted. A moment later, they pulled up in front of a small white house. Neat and well kept, it looked much like the others on the street.

He double checked the address. "This must be it." Gray scanned the street then got out. None of the other cars parked along the curbs seemed to represent a threat.

"It's all clear. Before we go inside, how do you intend to resolve your worries about getting married?"

"I can't." She leaned over and kissed him. "Like every other couple, we'll just have to make it up as we go along."

As soon as they opened the car door, Deeohgee leaped over the seat and out of car. When they reached the porch, the door opened and Carolyn emerged, smiling. Deeohgee plowed ahead and into the house. Carolyn jumped aside and then laughed. Mira also chuckled as Gray apologized for the dog's exuberance.

"By the way," Carolyn said. "Butterscotch is doing well. It's the first time I've shared my bed, but I've gotten quite used to his purring beside me as we go to sleep."

Hearing an approaching vehicle, all three turned. A white, 7-passenger van pulled in behind Gray's sports car.

"That's your van, right on time," Carolyn said.

Gray reluctantly headed back down the steps. He met the driver halfway and signed the necessary paperwork. Removing the sports car's ignition key from his key ring, he replaced it with one to the van. The man nodded and jogged back to the curb.

Gray listened to the familiar throaty growl of the engine when the man turned the key. Then he grimaced when the driver ground the gears as he put the car into reverse. He stood with his hands on hips watching his beloved car slowly vanish in the distance.

"The poor man's just lost his favorite toy," Carolyn whispered to Mira as they watched through the front window. "It's good that he'll have something else to keep him occupied."

"Don't worry, I plan to keep up with my wifely obligations," Mira replied.

"Oh, I meant the children."

Mira gave her a wry wink. "Of course you did."

ഇര

Jonathan met Gray on the porch to get the van's keys from him. He drove the van around to the alley in back of the house so he and Jacob could load it.

When Gray came inside, Carolyn took his hand and tugged him over to the side of the room. "There are some extra license plates wired to the underside of both middle seats. Each of them has a title and registration. It might be good to swap plates every day or two. There's also a kit to convert it from a passenger van into a panel van under the back seat."

Gray nodded. "Gotcha."

"Jonathan put a box of cheap cell phones in with your luggage. Dixon sent them. This way you'll have a new phone every day. If anyone calls you, they should first say, 'Have you ever considered refinancing your home?' That'll be our code. Don't answer if they say anything else. Get rid of the phone the first chance you get. Dixon says dispose of them where they'll never be found."

"Our Dixon's quite the 'I Spy' sorta guy isn't he?"

"Be grateful he's on our side," Carolyn said. "Now let's get you two lovebirds married."

ഇര

Mira gasped in surprise when they led her into the dining room. They'd strung white streamers and other festive decorations. A 3-tiered cake adorned with fluffy white frosting and pale pink roses sat in the center of the oak table.

A young woman walked up to Mira and extended her hand. "I'm Eileen Abramson, my husband, Jacob, is out back helping load your van." Eileen swallowed, blinking back tears. She dropped Mira's hand. "This is so difficult for us."

Mira put her arms around Eileen and embraced her. "I have no words for what you must be going through."

Eileen sniffed and straightened. "Despite the pain of saying good-bye to the twins, you've enabled us to bring Mandy back home where she belongs. I can't tell you how grateful we are." She reached into her pocket, drew out an already damp handkerchief and wiped her eyes.

"Time is short," Carolyn said, grabbing Mira's hand. "This is Dr. Clancy. While the Reverend hears your vows, Dr. Clancy will finish the birth certificates. They'll list me as his nurse. Since we're close friends, it isn't unusual that I might attend a home birth."

Next, she led Mira to the minister. "This is Rev. Crenshaw. He's going to marry you and Gray, and backdate the wedding certificate." She stared into Mira's eyes as Gray joined them. "That's okay with both of you, right?"

Gray and Mira each nodded.

"Jonathan and I will sign as your witnesses. We don't want Eileen and Jacob's names appearing on any records connected with you." Carolyn's gaze bounced around the room. "Where are the men?"

As if on cue, a door squeaked and Jonathan and Jacob strode in.

Gray took his place and reached for Mira's hand. Together they answered the Reverend's questions, said their *I do's*, and kissed each other at the end. It was all over very quickly.

As the magnitude of what she'd done suddenly sank in, Mira felt dizzy and a little overwhelmed. She took a wobbly step and grabbed a chair for balance. Gray put a solid arm around her.

"Thank you," she whispered, realizing she'd just entrusted her life and future to him. Despite her fears, the thought thrilled her.

Jacob Abramson wheeled a double-wide stroller into the

room. He'd laid it flat for the newborns and closed its cover. A convertible model, it would also adjust to hold toddlers when the twins were older.

Eileen took Mira's elbow and led her over to the stroller. She lifted the covering and let Mira peek inside.

"O-o-oh," Mira exclaimed and motioned to Gray. She reached for his hand with a smile. "Look at them. Just like two peas in a pod. Aren't they adorable?"

"They'll be a week old tomorrow."

Curious, Deeohgee poked his nose into the pram, sniffed and wagged his tail.

"Looks like they already have a friend and protector," Eileen said, smiling through her tears.

"I'm sure they do. He's a big lump of love." Mira tried not to appear overly happy, but couldn't hide it. "Thank you. I know it's a terrible sacrifice for you." She opened her arms and Eileen fell into them, softly weeping against Mira's shoulder.

Gray looked at the two women hugging and crying, then over at Jacob. He appeared stricken. He crossed the room and shook Jacob's hand. "I promise we'll do all we can to ensure your children receive proper care and lots of love."

As Mira lifted one of the sleeping babies out of the pram, Dr. Clancy handed Gray a large manila envelope. "Inside are their completed birth certificates and your marriage license. I'll file the birth records the first of the week."

Mira stared down at the infant in her arms, and realized she was celebrating her wedding day, her first anniversary, and new motherhood all on the same day.

What a wedding present.

CHAPTER FORTY-EIGHT

Carolyn took Mira aside. "Eileen has prepared a cooler with several bottles of her breast milk. There's also formula for when it runs out." She took Mira's hand in hers. "There's something you may not have thought of," Carolyn's eyes moved to Mira's chest, "*breast feeding*."

Mira stared at her. "Milk production is a side effect of the drug Domperidone, but it's not safe for nursing mothers. I'd better stick with formula."

"I'm not suggesting drugs. You have two hearty babies willing to suck, and sucking is the best way to induce lactation. You'd need to drink lots of liquids, and oatmeal is supposed to help. I don't know if it does or not, but it can't hurt."

Carolyn touched her forehead to Mira's, and reached into a pocket. "I brought some herbs." She handed her a plastic bag. "Fenugreek Seed has been used since Biblical times to increase a mother's milk flow. Gradually increase the dose. You're taking enough when your urine and sweat begin to smell like maple syrup." She chuckled. "Don't be surprised if Gray develops a sudden yearning for pancakes."

Mira's cheeks turned pink.

Carolyn smiled and pulled out a second packet. "This is Blessed Thistle herb. In addition to regulating hormones and stimulating a mother's milk, it also settles an upset stomach. By combining the two, you get the best of both worlds. I listed the standard dosage on each label."

Mira stared at the bags of herbs. "Thank you. I'll try them, but if the best way to promote lactation is feeling motherly, then I'm already there." She took a deep breath. "Between these, the babies' efforts and my desire, maybe I'll actually be able to breast feed."

"I know you'll be successful, especially since there are two of them." Carolyn pointed to a large white box encircled with yellow ribbon. "Here's something else you should have for the babies.

Take it with you and open it later when you're settled somewhere safe."

Tears of gratitude welled in Mira's eyes.

"You and Aranda are both like daughters to me. Be safe," Carolyn whispered as they hugged.

෴

Jonathan Bracken stood watch at the front window while the others celebrated. Letting the curtain drop, he caught Gray's eye. "A black SUV just pulled up across the street."

Gray rushed to the window, took one look, and said, "We've got to get out of here. Somehow they found us."

"Quick! Out through the backyard," Jacob said. "Jonathan and I have already loaded everything in your van. The car seats are ready and waiting. Grab the babies and go. I'll be right behind you with the stroller."

With Deeohgee at their heels, Gray and Mira rushed out the back door each carrying a newborn.

There was a loud banging at the front door as Jacob folded the stroller.

Jonathan hurried to Jacob's side and grabbed the stroller. "You live here. Answer the door. After I help Mira and Gray get the babies into the van I'll hide in the alley. Go. Now." Jonathan tucked the stroller under his arm and raced to catch up with Gray and Mira.

Eileen, Carolyn and the others quickly cleared the dining room of all indications of a wedding celebration. They removed half the plates and silverware, leaving only four dirty plates on the table. Carolyn tucked the cake box under her arm and headed out the back door.

When Jacob opened the front door, two armed men shoved him aside and barged into the house. After surveying the living room, one of the men cornered Jacob. "Where are they?"

"Where are who?" Jacob swept his arm in a wide circle.

"Since you apparently feel you have some legal right to be here, go ahead and look around. But could you holster the weapons? You're scaring my wife and guests."

"What guests?"

"This is our friend, Dr. Eric Clancy, and our pastor, Reverend Gerald Crenshaw."

"The man put his gun away. We're going through every room in this house." He paused on the stairway and glanced back at Jacob. "We hear you have twins."

"Yes. The children are with their grandmother at the moment. There's a picture of our three children on the mantle over there."

"Three, huh?"

"That's the legal limit."

"Sure, you don't have any more?"

"I think I'd know if I did."

The other man came into the room with a box of diapers. "What are these for?"

Jacob smiled. "Didn't your mother ever tell you?"

Even the man's partner laughed.

"Our twins wear diapers to bed at night. They size them by age. You can check the package." Jacob stepped toward the man offering to show him.

Instead, he tossed the box aside in disgust.

While the two men searched the house, Jonathan and Carolyn followed the alley to the next cross street. From there, they strolled to the local park where they'd left their car, got in and drove home.

Gray and Mira sped north while the babies dozed in matching car seats Jacob had strapped into the van's center seats. Deeohgee stretched out along the bench seat in back. A happy grin expressed his pleasure at having more space than he ever had in Gray's sports car.

ౚౢఆ

It was dark when Gray pulled into the motel parking lot.

"Mira, honey, wake up. I need to go in and register."

She stretched and yawned. "All I want is a hot shower and a soft bed."

When Gray opened the van door, the dome light came on. A baby woke and began to whimper. It wasn't long before the other started to cry too.

Mira touched Gray's arm as he exited the vehicle. "They probably need a diaper change and want to be fed. Once we're in a room, I'll change the one in pink if you take the one in blue."

Gray agreed and headed for the office. He returned with the receipt and a room key, frowning. "I'd like to strangle Dixon for calling me Gus Steinway! Whenever someone sees my new name they invariably say, 'Oh, Steinway like the piano.'"

Mira snickered. "I like it better than Maude Hoople."

"I'd love you no matter what your name was; although Mira suits you best." A baby started to whimper again. It dawned on Gray that he hadn't thought about the babies. What was wrong with him anyway? In all the excitement, he hadn't bothered to even ask their names. He considered them for a moment then snapped his fingers. "Something just occurred to me."

"What?"

"No one will be looking for a married couple with two children. Having the babies with us works to our advantage."

"All you can find to say about them is they're good cover?"

"No, of course not." He parked the car and gaped at the crying twins. Both of them had red, scrunched-up faces. He knew he should say something nice about the two of them, but found it hard to think of anything right then.

They changed and fed the babies and bedded them down in the double stroller which served as a temporary crib.

Gray did a quick survey of the baby supplies on hand. "How long before the formula is gone? Shouldn't we find a place to buy more?"

"We'll see." Mira ignored the questioning look he gave her.

He yawned and stretched. It could wait until morning. He kicked off his shoes, stretched out on the bed and sighed deeply. He rolled onto his side to watch Mira as she undressed. When she headed for the shower, he decided he wasn't too tired to join her.

⁊⊙ℂℜ

A baby's wail shocked Gray awake early the next morning. He rubbed the sleep out of his eyes, reminding himself they were parents now. Mira was already walking the floor with one of the twins. She nodded toward the other baby. Still groggy, he slid his feet into slippers and rose to comfort the tiny infant.

"This parenting stuff isn't easy, is it?" he asked as he joined her in random steps around the room.

"It's a labor of love." She nuzzled the baby in her arms. "Don't they smell wonderful? There's nothing like the scent of a newborn."

Gray took a little sniff. He only smelled baby powder, but knew better than to say so.

"I fed them both and bathed them in the bathroom sink while you slept."

"Why didn't I wake up?"

She winked at him. "You were tired and they're still newborns. They don't cry that loudly. They'll probably nod off in the car when we leave."

"You're amazing." He folded back the blanket hiding the baby she held. It seemed so tiny. When two blue eyes stared up at him his heart melted. "Her eyes are so blue."

"This is the boy, silly. And they're too young to know if their eyes will stay blue. They could change."

The baby in his arms settled and he put her in the middle of the bed. Gray grabbed his shaving kit and headed for the bathroom. "Did you happen to ask what their names are?" he yelled through the open doorway.

"The boy's name is Alexander Brian and the girl is Leila Ruth."

Gray dropped what he was doing and rushed into the bedroom. "That's remarkable. My two grandfather's names were Alexander and Brian."

Mira smiled. "And my grandmother's names were Leila and Ruth."

He returned to the bathroom shaking his head. "Unbelievable. It must be a sign by those invisible hands again." He thought about it for a moment then stared around the corner. "Or not."

"Eileen said they decided we should name them ourselves so we'd feel like they're truly our children. You were busy so I told Dr. Clancy what to put on the birth certificates."

His eyes narrowed. "What about the last name?"

She bit her fingertip. "Well, it starts with S."

He put a fist to his forehead. "Please tell me not a lifetime of 'Steinway like the piano?'"

Crossing the room, she kissed him and playfully tugged his short beard. "They're Alexander and Leila *Stevens*," she whispered. "And I liked you better with more hair on your head and none on your face."

CHAPTER FORTY-NINE

Gray and Mira were driving out of the motel parking lot when a cell phone rang.

"Have you ever considered refinancing your home?" Rebecca asked.

Mira immediately recognized her voice and chuckled. "What can we do for you?"

"I wondered if you'd be kind enough to give an old lady another ride."

"What do you have in mind?"

"Carolyn said you and Gray are heading west with an empty seat in your van."

Mira twisted to look down the aisle between the two middle seats that held the twins in their car carriers. Deeohgee was stretched across the bench seat behind them. "Yeah, in a manner of speaking."

"Could you squeeze Robbie, Emma and me in the back? I promise we won't be any trouble."

Mira covered the mouthpiece and explained to Gray.

He gave a thumbs up. "Deeohgee can lay all the way in the back on top of the luggage. We'll make it work."

"Gray says the more the merrier. Where should we pick you up?"

"It's best you not come to Carolyn's. The Eastside Mall has a carnival this weekend. We'll meet you by the Ferris wheel at 10:00 o'clock."

୬୦୯౩

"Do you see them?" Gray asked as he scanned the mall parking lot. He circled the lot looking for a parking space, but couldn't find any. The traveling carnival covered a large portion of the parking area.

Mira shaded her eyes against the sun. "Rebecca said they'd hang out around the Ferris wheel. We need to find a parking place and walk over."

"Do you think that's wise? I'd rather we kept the car running. I don't think anyone is tailing us, but you never know. Look what happened at the Abramson's."

"Drop me off in front of the carnival. I'll go find them. Just keep circling and we'll flag you down. Okay?"

"I don't like you putting yourself in harm's way. Better you drive around with the babies while I go inside."

Mira sighed. "It has to be me. I'll be better able to recognize them."

"Be careful." He reached for her hand as she prepared to get out. "Kiss me before you go."

She leaned back and kissed him. "Don't worry if this takes longer than you expect. We're 15 minutes early. They may not even be here yet."

"Then don't get out of the car for another 15 minutes."

"You're being silly. We're at a carnival. Why are you so jumpy?"

"Lately I've had this crawly feeling about everything. I won't feel secure until we're safely out of sight."

"What? You don't think my short blond wig and sunglasses are enough to conceal how I look?" She tickled his ribs. "I think your beard and bald head make you look quite gussied up. You look nothing like a musty ol' prosecutor."

"Who're you calling *old*?"

She winked. "Certainly not the man who kept me up half the night."

"I don't remember you complaining."

"At least not until the twins woke us at 5:30 this morning."

Gray nodded. "Yeah. We need to do something about that."

"You can't blame them, they're only babies. They'll eventually start sleeping longer hours."

"I meant *we* need to start earlier," he said with a wink.

As they came back around to the entrance, Mira pointed. "I see them. They're at the gate and ready to go inside. Let me out quick so I can catch them."

As Mira watched the trio enter, Gray noticed something that sent a shiver racing up his spine. He grabbed her arm. "Wait. Who are those two suits wandering in behind them? They're not dressed for a carnival. Two men with no kids spells trouble."

Her fist shot to her mouth and she bit a knuckle. "We have to get them out of there."

"We put the twins at risk if we expose ourselves." He checked the rearview mirror, looking for anything suspicious. "Call Carolyn. If Rebecca has a cell phone, she'll know it."

෨෬

Emma skipped over to the Ferris wheel. "I wish we could ride it."

"I know sweetheart, but not right now. Remember what I told you to say?"

At the top of her voice, Emma yelled, "I gotta go to the bathroom."

At the ladies room door, Robbie pulled away and exclaimed loudly, "I'm not going into no girls' bathroom!"

His shout gave Rebecca an excuse to turn toward him and look over his shoulder. It appeared she was simply reasoning with a three-year-old. She scanned the area behind them and saw the two men in dark suits and silvered sunglasses. She and the children disappeared into the ladies room.

She bent down to quietly tell Robbie he'd done a good job. In his excitement he hadn't even stuttered. Glancing around, Rebecca directed the children into the larger, handicapped stall with a prayer of gratitude that it was empty.

Once inside, Rebecca quickly reached into the large handbag over her shoulder. She removed their pre-arranged disguises and hastily helped the children into them. Robbie became a little girl who would hold her big sister's hand. A long brown wig covered Emma's blond hair. Adding some lipstick and ear-rings made the tall youngster resemble a pre-teen trying to look grown up.

Rebecca tucked her own dress into Carhartt overalls; concealing it and making her look heavier than she really was. She added a red kerchief that completely covered her hair, and then knelt in front of the *girls*.

"I'm going out first. Wait a little while and come out together. Wander back over to the Ferris wheel. I won't be there so don't look for me. Just stare at the wheel like you're two sisters wanting to ride it. If Ms. Hastings shows up, call her *Mom* and whine about how you want to ride the Ferris wheel. Be a good little actor and actress."

From the handbag she pulled out pieces of a cane and screwed the threaded ends into each other. She filled her pockets with personal items and stuffed the big purse into a wastebasket. The only thing that hadn't changed was their shoes, though she doubted anyone would pay attention to their feet.

She gave the children last minute instructions, hugged them both, leaned on the cane and limped out. Once outside, she moved off to the left and out of view of the men who kept watch on the restroom's exit.

Inside, Emma silently counted to one hundred. "Okay, Robbie, it's time to go."

Robbie gripped her hand. "I'm sc-sc-scared."

"It'll be okay. Aunt Carolyn's very good at making disguises for people. I've seen her do it hundreds of times." Emma knew it wasn't true. Not *hundreds* of times, but at least once or twice. And Robbie needed reassuring. "Nobody will know who we are."

"Then how will the good people find us?"

Emma frowned. She was worried about that too.

"Remember, Aunt Carolyn said she'd have short blond hair and sunglasses. Try to spot her. If you see her, squeeze my hand two times." Emma studied Robbie and smiled. He really *did* look like a little girl. "We've waited long enough. Let's go."

Robbie still hesitated. He felt safe in the restroom. After all, no man would enter a ladies bathroom; or would they? Just then one of the men stuck his head inside the door.

Two teenage girls pushed past him. "Geez Mister, whatcha think you're doin'? You a pervert or somethin'? Our dad's waiting outside. If you try anything, he'll come knock your block off."

Emma recognized an opportunity when she saw it. Keeping Robbie with her, she slipped out while the two girls distracted the man. She walked briskly, tugging and pulling the terrified Robbie toward the Ferris wheel. Any enthusiasm they'd felt about the carnival had vanished. All they wanted now was to get as far away from the two men as possible.

Some distance away, Rebecca stood in line at a concession stand keeping a watchful eye on the two *girls* hurrying toward the Ferris wheel. As she waited to buy chocolate-covered pretzels, she continued to monitor the men in dark suits. They had begun following the children as soon as they left the restroom.

Without warning, one of the men ran toward the children. He grabbed Emma's arm, spinning her around.

"Ow! You leave me and my sister alone," she screamed. "Help! Help! Somebody help us."

CHAPTER FIFTY

"Family means no one gets left behind or forgotten."
~ David Ogden Stiers

"Good girl," Rebecca thought as she noticed Emma struggling with the government agent. She grabbed the bag of pretzels she'd paid for and left the line. Still leaning heavily on the cane, she hobbled over to a man wearing a mall security uniform and pointed out what was happening near the Ferris wheel.

Fearing a possible child abduction, the security guard rushed to the Ferris wheel, shouting as he ran. "Hey, Buddy, what're you doing? Leave those kids alone!"

The man in the black suit continued holding onto Emma. "Butt out of this; these are my kids."

"Bloody hell they are!" Mira ran up beside Emma and Robbie. "This is my Maggie and my Sherry." She spoke in her best approximation of an English accent. "They're my daughters, and I have no idea who this pervert is."

The security guard twisted the man's arm behind his back, preparing to cuff him.

"Let me go. I'm a Federal agent."

"Yeah," the guard replied, "and I'm the Green Hornet."

Mira leaned down and lifted her sunglasses, winking at Emma.

"Mom," yelled Emma, hugging her. "Can we ride the Ferris wheel now?"

Mira couldn't imagine why Emma would ask such a thing, but she looked her straight in the face and said, "Absolutely not. We are going straight home. This isn't a safe place for children."

Robbie turned to her, and began to cry in a high pitched voice, "I wanna go on the Ferris Wheel, Mom. I've never been on one before. Pleeezzze Mom."

She found his whining annoying until it dawned on her that

they were both role playing.

The security guard turned to Mira. "I'll call the police so you can sign a complaint."

"I'd rather you bonked him on the noggin with your nightstick. People like him shouldn't be walking the streets."

"I'll let the police deal with him."

"We must go. My mum is waiting for us. She's elderly and mustn't be alone too long. Getting a bit daffy, you know? And automobiles become stifling when left in the sun." Mira took the children's hands and headed for the exit.

The man thrashed and hollered, "You're letting them get away."

"But you aren't. I'm callin' the cops."

Hidden in the shadows, Rebecca watched everything as it played out. She'd considered running over and bashing the guy with her cane when he grabbed Emma. Thanks to Mira's timely arrival she hadn't had to get involved.

She scanned the parking lot, looking for the van Carolyn said they'd be driving.

⁕⁖

It puzzled Gray to see Mira approaching the exit with two little girls. *Where was Robbie?*

Through the carnival gate he saw one of two men they'd identified earlier. He was on the ground wrestling with a security guard. Gray's chuckle died in his throat when he noticed the other man running after Mira and the children. Honking the horn wildly, he pulled onto the sidewalk by the entrance and hit the automatic open button for the van's side door. It slid back just as Mira and the children rushed up.

They scrambled in, and Mira hit the close door button. Not waiting, Gray pulled away while the door was still sliding shut.

The man ran alongside the van, grabbing for the door handle, shouting and pounding on the window.

Emma and Robbie shrieked in terror, dropped to the floor and crawled to the back seat.

Gray noticed a telephone pole several yards ahead and aimed for it. With certain disaster looming, the man let go of the door handle. He ran away from the car, lost his balance, and cartwheeled across the dirt lot.

The car skimmed past the pole with mere inches to spare. Gray took a quick backward glimpse over his left shoulder and, seeing his opening, tromped on the accelerator. The vehicle shot off the sidewalk and bounced onto the pavement. Their pursuer picked himself up and dusted off as they disappeared into traffic.

Emma buckled herself in as the carnival disappeared from view, but Robbie knelt on the seat, staring out the back window. "Gramma, Gramma. You left Gramma!" he cried.

On her knees between the twins, Mira made Robbie sit down and buckled him in. "Robbie, we didn't see her and we couldn't wait. I'm sorry." Mira blotted tears from Robbie's cheeks and patted his hand. He continued to quietly sob as Mira turned around to squeeze between the center seats where the twins slept and into the front passenger seat.

"It's your call whether we go back for her," Gray said. "Keep in mind they know what the van looks like now."

"Oh God, I don't know. All I can think to do is pray."

"Why not call Carolyn and tell her what happened. Maybe she can contact Rebecca and arrange another pickup."

&)(&

Rebecca felt elated seeing Gray drive up onto the sidewalk. She'd started toward the van, expecting to have more time, but knew she had no chance when she saw the man in the dark suit racing toward it. The agent was closer to the car than she was and gaining on Mira and the children with every step. If they'd waited for her, they'd all be in custody now.

With them safely away, Rebecca turned her attention to the man who'd chased the van. He went back into the carnival to help his partner with the security guard.

Broken glass clinked beside her when she moved her foot. Reaching down, she scooped up several thick, jagged shards and casually walked over to their oversized black vehicle. She cast a wary gaze back over her shoulder, then wedged glass into the tread of the SUV's front tires and strolled away.

She crossed the parking lot, breaking down the cane as she walked and entered the enclosed mall. Rebecca watched through a department store window as the two men ran back to the car and jumped in. They rolled forward and pulled into the exit lane. Meanwhile, both front tires flattened against the pavement as they waited for an opening in traffic.

Rebecca turned away from the window and walked into the mall, looking for a secluded spot to call Carolyn. The bag of chocolate pretzels brushed against her leg as she walked. She looked down at it with sadness. She'd bought them as a treat for Robbie and Emma. Her shoulders drooped as she trudged through the mall.

When would she see her grandchildren again?

CHAPTER FIFTY-ONE

Gray and Mira decided to gas up before heading to the Interstate. It also gave them all an opportunity for a restroom break and diaper changes.

While Gray pumped gas, Mira settled the children and babies back into the van. She went back into the convenience store to pay and noticed warm fresh pizzas under a glass case. She bought two and sliced them into manageable squares for little fingers. She also got bottled water, packaged sandwiches for later, milk for Robbie and Emma and soft drinks for Gray and herself.

Her arms were full as she carried it all back to the car. She handed the largess to Gray to hold while she carefully distributed it.

"Yum." Emma licked her lips. "That smells so good. Thank you, Miss Hastings."

"Sweetie, I'd love it if you'd still call me Mom. It will help with our disguise, and I'm not Miss Hastings anyway; I'm married now." She pointed a thumb at Gray. "Maybe you should call him Dad as well."

Emma grinned as she took another big bite of pizza.

With the food balanced in everyone's laps, Gray got behind the wheel. He drove until they saw a freeway ramp and immediately took it.

Mira looked up at the compass above the mirror. "Why are we heading north?"

"I'm more interested in putting distance between us and that pair in the SUV than which way we're headed. Besides, I don't want to get too far away until we hear from Rebecca."

Gray reached for Mira's hand. "We're suddenly in the same predicament that Jacob and Eileen were in. What if someone asks why we have four children?"

"Robbie," Mira called to the back of the van. "Do you think you could remember to call us Uncle Gus and Aunt Maude?"

"Cool," said Emma. "That makes Robbie and me cousins. I'd rather have him for a cousin than Aunt Reeta's kids, Raylene and Rhonda."

Robbie looked at Emma and gave a half-hearted smile. "Okay. Uncle G-g-gus and Aunt M-m-mood. I'll 'member."

Emma munched her second piece of pizza and took a swig from her carton of milk before glancing over at Robbie. His chin rested in his hand and his pizza square sat untouched on a paper plate beside him on the seat.

She watched the adults and frowned. Was she the only one who cared that Robbie wasn't eating?

"Robbie, this pizza's really, really good. You should have some."

Robbie slowly turned in Emma's direction and shrugged. His red, swollen eyes and forlorn look said it all. "I'm not h-h-hungry. When are we g-g-gonna get Gramma back?"

She pointed toward the adults. "They said not to worry, that she'd be all right."

"Then w-w-why isn't she here? What if those bad men catch her and s-s-send her to an FFU? What if they b-b-burn her up?"

Emma's hand began to shake. She didn't want to think about the bad stuff. Not now ... not ever. She gave a small cough to get the adult's attention. When they didn't respond she tried again, louder. Gray's eyes darted between the mirrors to check both sides as he changed lanes. Head down, Mira was focused on the map in her lap.

Emma wadded her napkin into a ball and lobbed a soft arc over the middle seats. Mira's head snapped up when the missile bounced off her hair. She swiveled in her seat to glance back.

"Robbie won't eat," Emma said.

"It'll be okay," Mira bent to return to the map.

Emma pounded her fist on the armrest beside her. "I *said* Robbie won't eat anything. He just sits there looking all mopey."

Mira called to Robbie, but he ignored her. She caught Emma's eyes. "Robbie is very upset about his grandmother. He'll feel better once we know she's safe."

"When will that be?"

"We're working on it."

It didn't look like they were working on it to Emma. Whenever Mira wasn't staring at the map she was fussing with the babies. All they talked about is how fast they could go and how far away they'd be. Didn't they know they were also getting farther and farther away from Gramma?

ৡ৹ଔ

Traffic thinned once they passed under the outer beltway. Gray set the cruise control and relaxed for the first time. "I'll take some pizza now," he said with a tired sigh.

Mira lifted the lid and held the box out to him. She was closing the box when the cell phone vibrated in her pocket. She answered and a familiar voice asked, "Have you ever considered refinancing your home?"

Mira grinned. "How are you?"

"I'm back at Carolyn's and no worse for wear." Rebecca sounded happy and upbeat. "Can I speak with Robbie?"

This time when she called his name Robbie looked up, "Someone wants to talk to you." Mira extended the phone.

He unbuckled his seatbelt and hopped down. Stretching between the middle seats, he took the phone and put it to his ear. An instant later, he smiled for the first time since they'd left the Mall.

"Gramma! I was 'fraid those bad g-g-guys g-g-got you." He began to tug at his lip and nod as he listened. After a minute or two he said, "Okay. I will, Gramma. I love you too." He handed the phone back to Mira.

Robbie climbed back on the seat and re-buckled his seatbelt. He grabbed his slice of pizza. "She made the b-b-bad guy's tires go flat so they c-c-couldn't chase us. Then she ran away and went back to Aunt Carolyn's house," he said as he chewed.

After pausing for a sip of milk, he asked for more pizza. "Gramma said not to w-w-worry about her. She and Aunt Carolyn and Jonathan are gonna run away like us, only they're takin' a plane. Somebody named Dixie's helping. They're going to the same p-p-place we are so we'll all be together s-s-soon." Robbie smiled and took a big bite.

ৎ৹১

It was getting dark by the time they pulled into a motel. A neon sign glowed *vacancy* in the window of the small office. Off the beaten track and tending to dowdiness, it sported a sign that read, *Tourist Cabins, Monthly Rentals Available.* Gray parked the van out of sight and walked back to the office.

He returned a few minutes later muttering about the desk clerk. "I'm going to strangle that Dixon if I ever get my hands on him. I can't go anywhere without someone saying, "Steinway, like the piano?" The next time it happens I'm going to say, "No, Steinway like the refrigerator.""

Mira giggled and patted his hand. "Were you able to get an isolated cabin?"

"We're down at the very end near a grove of trees. The cabins have two doors. The owner said I could park around back."

Both Mira and Gray carried a baby in. Robbie and Emma followed rubbing sleep out of their eyes with Deeohgee bringing up the rear. When Gray snapped on a light, Mira studied the worn carpet and sagging chairs. "These cabins were probably quite nice when they were new."

"Yeah," Gray said with a sarcastic laugh, "when our parents were Robbie and Emma's age." He continued hauling in luggage while Mira got the older children ready for bed.

Robbie looked up at her as she tucked the covers around his chin. "Do I have to wear a dress again tomorrow?"

Mira hadn't given a thought to Robbie's situation. Rebecca

turned him into a little girl at the Mall and in their mad rush to get away they hadn't gotten any of the children's things. All either child had were the clothes they'd worn all day.

After giving them both good-night kisses, she sat on the edge of the bed. "You'll both have to start the day wearing what you have. We'll stop somewhere and get you some more clothes once we're on the road. I'm sorry, but that's the best we can do."

Robbie stuck out his lower lip, flipped on his side and pulled the blanket over his head.

₭₧

Jonathan yawned and absentmindedly gazed through the dining room doorway as he stirred his coffee. Carolyn and Rebecca mirrored his fatigue. The three of them had spent the afternoon and evening sorting and packing.

He eyed the neat row of suitcases waiting near the front door with a caustic expression. "I never realized how going by air limits what you can take with you. I feel like I'm leaving my life behind," he said, clanking his spoon onto the table.

"You can always pay excess baggage fees," Rebecca suggested.

Carolyn laughed. "With all of his stuff it would be cheaper to charter a cargo plane. After all, we do want the plane to be able to get off the ground."

"It's not like I haven't struggled to pare things down. All day I've been weighing *this or that*. Every time I put something in, something else comes out."

"I know it hurts," Rebecca said. "I went through the same process, so did Mira and Gray. If you recall, I showed up here with two suitcases and the children's meager possessions stuffed into a couple of plastic trash bags." She paused, "And thanks to that melee at the Mall the children left without so much as a teddy bear."

She leaned forward, staring into his eyes. "There's a message in all this, Jonathan." Rebecca swept an arm in a wide circle. "These things that mean so much to us ... are just *stuff*. One way or another it's all going to rot or rust. People matter, not stuff."

He gave a rueful nod.

Carolyn carried dishes into the kitchen and looked back from the sink. "Or as Job put it, 'Naked I came from my mother's womb and naked shall I return.'"

For an instant Rebecca appeared as though she might tear up. "For me, the hardest part of this whole process is leaving my daughter behind. I'd give anything and everything to have her for just one more day."

"At least she has a grave." Jonathan rose to his feet, hurried to his bedroom, and closed the door behind him.

Rebecca looked at Carolyn and gave a disheartened shrug. "I'm sorry. I should have kept my big mouth shut. I've had longer to deal with my grief than he has with his."

Carolyn shook her head. "It's nothing you did. Aranda is the first loss he's ever experienced. He'll eventually work through it."

Their heads snapped around when the bedroom door opened a few moments later. Jonathan emerged in pajamas and a robe. "I'm going to Dixon's first thing tomorrow. We can't do anything until I pick up our new IDs."

"Sounds like a plan," Carolyn replied.

He remained in the doorway, chewing his lip and rocking from one foot to the other. "Well then. Busy day tomorrow; I'll turn in."

CHAPTER FIFTY-TWO

Early the next morning a baby's whimper woke Gray and Mira. He left to secure breakfast for his new family while she sat on the bed feeding one of the babies. Emma wandered into the bedroom, noticed Mira's open blouse, and stopped.

Mira smiled at her. "It's okay, Sweetie, we're both girls. I hope we'll all become like a family someday." Her gaze returned to the infant in her arms.

Emma checked to see that Robbie was still sleeping before stepping into the room and closing the door behind her. She scurried over to the bed, shoved the rumpled covers aside, and plopped down beside Mira to silently watch her nurse the infant. When Mira finished, she returned the child to the bassinet and put the other baby to her opposite breast.

"Does that hurt?" Emma asked.

Mira shook her head. "Nope, it feels very pleasant. After all, this is what we're made for."

"Aunt Reeta used a bottle. I thought that's what you were supposed to do."

"A bottle works too, but breast milk is healthier."

Emma snuggled beside her and held the baby's fingers.

Mira's mind wandered as she watched Emma play with her new little sister. On the day they married, she didn't think she could be any happier, but she was. Only the night before she'd watched Gray in a rocker with a twin in each arm. His fatherly cooing to them unleashed an astonishing depth of emotions in her. Despite changes in their circumstances, and the tension of being on the run, there was no place she'd rather be. And no other people she'd rather be with. She leaned over and softly kissed the top of Emma's head.

If only it could stay like this forever.

෨෬

Jonathan was up and out of the house before Carolyn and

Rebecca woke. They were still eating breakfast when they heard his car returning.

The door opened and Jonathan stumbled in ashen-faced. He opened the coat closet and shrugged off his jacket without a word. A hanger quivered in his hand.

"That was quick. Did you see Dixon?" Carolyn asked without looking up from her paper.

He attempted to jam both arms of the jacket onto the hanger without success. Frustrated, he flung it all into the closet and slammed the door. Turning, he tried to answer, but his trembling lips didn't work. He finally mumbled, "He wasn't there."

"If he wasn't in the house, you should have tried the barn."

His fingers sank deep into the upholstery when he gripped the back of the couch. "I said, *He* wasn't there."

"You could have talked with Brody, you know."

Rounding the sofa, Jonathan collapsed onto a cushion. He shook his head and ran his fingers through his sweat-soaked hair. "How many times do I have to tell you HE wasn't there?"

"We're right here in the room with you. There's no need to raise your voice."

He muttered an apology. "Dixon wasn't there. Brody wasn't there. The horses weren't there. The barn wasn't there." He threw his hands into the air. "It's gone, everyone and everything is gone."

"Country roads can be confusing, perhaps you took a wrong turn," Rebecca said.

His withering glare told her the suggestion didn't merit an answer.

Carolyn took him a glass of cool water. "You look like you're running from the Devil himself. Here, drink this down and then tell us what happened to upset you so."

Jonathan up-ended the glass, gulped it down and sat it on the table beside him. "I left here and drove out there, okay? And before either of you asks, yes, I *do* know where Dixon's place is. His rusty mailbox with the faded lettering was still on a post by the highway. Going down the road, everything looked the same as always...the same dusty, rutted road, the same broken down white board fence, the thicket surrounding his driveway. Everything was all the same."

"And then what?"

"Do you remember the corral where he kept two horses?"

"As I recall, the horses were right beside the barn," Carolyn said.

"Not anymore they aren't. Oh, there are some smashed and broken pieces of the posts and rails scattered about the area, but the horses and corral aren't there. They're...just gone." He swiveled his head, looking from one woman to the other. "Dixon had a big old barn with peeling paint next to the corral, right? Two stories, the upper part served as a hay loft. Underneath the back portion he had a secret office where he and Brody worked. He took us down there once."

The memory brought a smile to Carolyn's face. "It has a steel stairway with rails on both sides, overhead lighting, and all kinds of computer stuff. He jokingly referred to it as his *bomb shelter*."

Jonathan pounded the chair arm for emphasis. "The barn, if you can still call it that, is nothing but a crumpled heap of splintered timber. A bulldozer or...or something shoved everything back into the field. Meanwhile their supposedly secret office is nothing but a big hole in the ground. I looked down into the crater. There were chunks of broken concrete lying on top of wall panels, pieces of desks and God knows what else. It looked like a bomb went off in Dixon's bomb shelter."

After a long silence Carolyn whispered, "Did you go up to the house?"

"I did. All the front windows are knocked out." He slowly waved his hand back and forth. "The front door was hanging half off its hinges and swinging in the wind. All the cupboards and closets were thrown open. Tables were overturned, drawers pulled out and dumped. Everything scattered across the floor. All the walls have big holes where someone smashed into them with a sledge hammer and ripped the plaster off. Probably to see if anything was hidden in them."

Jonathan lowered his head. "I figured I better get the heck out of there before whoever did it came back."

"That was the wisest thing to do," Carolyn said.

"When was the last time you interacted with Dixon?" Rebecca asked them.

Carolyn hesitated a moment. "Umm, I'd say it's been a week or so. Why?"

"I'm thinking about the men at the fair."

"What about them?"

"If the government raided Dixon's place a week ago, they could have known about our plans to meet Mira and Gray," Rebecca said.

Jonathan's eyes nervously darted about the room. "That could be how they found us at the Abramson's." He swallowed the bile rising in the back of his throat. "What if they're holding Dixon and Brody? There's no telling what they know. This could be worse than anything we ever imagined."

Carolyn scoffed. "Don't be hysterical and let your imagination run away with you."

"Me hysterical? Face the facts, Mother. They could know about the Abramson's children, Rev. Crenshaw, and Dr. Clancy. The kids at the Foundling Home are at risk. What if they have the license number of the van Mira and Gray are driving and the aliases they're using. They might have gotten the names of other Life Chances members too. What about Bright Minds?"

Carolyn's blood ran cold. "You're right. There's no limit to the damage this could do."

"We've got to let Mira and Gray know what's happened." Rebecca sobbed and buried her face in her hands. "They could get my Robbie and little Emma too."

"We're all at risk. How soon before they come for us?" Jonathan's eyes widened. "Aranda died to protect us. What guarantee do we have that Dixon and Brody will do the same? How soon before government agents are pounding on our door?"

Rebecca reached for the phone to call Mira when six hard raps shook the front door.

CHAPTER FIFTY-THREE

"C'mon, Robbie, time to get some clothes on." Gray tossed him the dress he'd worn the day before with his Gramma.

Robbie folded the dress and handed it back. "Boys aren't supposed t' wear dresses."

"It's all we've got. You can't go outside in just your undies."

Robbie's lower lip quivered. "It makes me feel funny."

Gray rested his hand on the little guy's shoulder and drew him closer. He peered at the bedroom door before whispering, "I don't blame you. I wouldn't want to wear a dress either. But if I had to, I'd tell myself, 'A dress doesn't make me a girl. Underneath I'm still wearing boy's underpants.'"

Robbie gaped at his Fruit of the Loom briefs, thought it over, smiled and raised his arms for the dress.

"Good boy," Gray said, spinning him around to button the back. "We won't make you wear that wig when we go out this morning." He swiped Robbie's hair down onto his forehead. "We'll just throw a scarf over your head. No one will ever know."

ഇരു

As Gray entered the motel's small office, the proprietor lifted his head over his newspaper. "Here comes the piano man," he said with a grin. He thumbed through the previous day's tickets and pulled one out. "Was everything okay?"

"Just dandy," Gray said and paid for their rooms with old-fashioned money.

Opening a cash drawer, the owner counted change out onto the counter. "With a name like Steinway you must take a ribbing," he said without looking up.

"Every once in a while," Gray replied with a shrug.

"Stop by anytime you're in the neighborhood." The man handed him the bills and wished him a good day.

After they left the aging motel, Gray took the children into a nearby donut shop. While Mira waited, she noticed a full-service drug store across the street. Gray and the kids ate their donuts while she hurried in and purchased packages of underwear and socks for Robbie and Emma.

Mira kept watching and, on their way to the interstate, a secondhand clothing store caught her attention. At her request, Gray pulled in. With Robbie on one side and Emma on the other, Mira circled the car and leaned in to kiss him good-bye. "Keep the engine running while we shop," she said, "just in case."

Gray found a spot next to a nearby oak and let the spreading branches hide the van in their shade. After checking the babies, he reclined the seat. He tugged down the brim of his ball cap and folded his arms behind his head. Looking like a man without a care in the world, he warily monitored the passing traffic through narrowed eyes. Even though he'd changed the van's license plates in an alley after they left the carnival, this waiting process evoked unsettling memories of the day before.

ഇരു

Inside the store, Mira selected several pairs of jeans while Robbie and Emma rummaged through a long rack of T-shirts.

"Robbie, let's go try these on." Mira took him into the dressing room first and selected several outfits for him. "Keep that one on," she told him when they finished. "I'll put the dress and scarf in my purse."

He waited outside the door while she repeated the process with Emma, who also preferred jeans to a dress.

"Don't forget to ring up the clothes the children are wearing." Mira smiled. "They liked them so much they wanted to wear them home."

The clerk's eyes registered surprise when she looked down at Robbie. "I could swear you had two girls when you came in."

Mira leaned close and whispered, "It's the chemotherapy. Her hair hasn't completely grown back yet."

After bagging the clothes the chagrined clerk removed two

caramel bars from a box on the counter. "Would you girls like a treat this morning?"

Mira nudged Robbie. "Isn't that sweet? Go ahead, dear, you can have one."

Robbie took the candy without a word.

⊱⊰

When the insistent raps at their front door didn't cease, Jonathan cautiously peeked between the slats of the blind. "It's only a bum," he said with a sigh of relief. "What should I do?"

"Open it, I suppose." Carolyn joined him in the living room. "If he's looking for a handout, we can surely find a little something for him."

Carolyn opened the door and scrutinized the short young man with rumpled clothes, matted hair, and a scruff of untrimmed beard. He looked as if he hadn't bathed in at least a week. The longer she stared the surer she became. After several moments Carolyn quietly said, "Dixon?"

He gave a rueful nod. "Can I come in?"

"Of course, of course ... by all means."

"I went out to your place to pick up our IDs and saw the mess," Jonathan said, closing the door. "I thought you and Brody were arrested. Or possibly dead."

Ignoring Jonathan, Dixon turned to Carolyn, "Do you have space in your garage for our van?"

When she said she did, Jonathan hurried out to open the garage door and wave to Brody. A minute later Jonathan returned with a disheveled Brody.

"You know we wouldn't have come if we had any other place to go," Dixon said. "A shower and something to eat and we'll be gone."

"I'll reheat some leftovers if that's alright," Rebecca said.

"Anything's fine when you've lived in your car for a week," Dixon said, taking a seat at the table.

Brody sat beside him and Jonathan and Carolyn joined them as Rebecca rattled pots and pans. "When Jonathan told us about the state of your house and barn we assumed you'd been taken into custody."

Pretending to raise a sword in the air, Dixon patted Brody's shoulder. "Fear not, m'lady. The good Friar and I evaded the evil Sheriff of Nottingham. Though bedraggled, we remain undefeated. Verily I say, we shall rise again to fight another day!" He hung his head. "Assuming they don't catch us first."

⁊ᘓᘓᘗ

Between bites, Dixon opened an expanding folder. He removed an envelope and handed it to Carolyn. "Here are the IDs I promised you."

He reached for another slice of bread and began smoothing a glob of butter across it. "Since you haven't purchased tickets yet," he said, concentrating on the bread, "I suggest you take the train instead of flying. It'll cost more, but security's not as tight. They have suites that sleep four and during the day you can stretch your legs and watch the country glide by."

Dixon reached down to pet the yellow cat winding around his ankles. "Some even let you take a small pet. Who knows, you might even see Maude and Gus zip past on the Interstate." He winked and took another bite.

Jonathan dragged his chair over beside him. "How can we go anywhere now that our cover's blown?"

"What do you mean? Those IDs I gave your mother are rock solid."

"I saw what the government guys did to your office and home. Nothing's secure now that they have your files and records."

"They got our *physical* possessions...the house, furniture, a pantry full of food with expired use by dates, some office supplies...a hamper full of dirty clothes. It's a setback, not the end of the world." He scooped up a spoonful of peas and popped them in his mouth.

Dixon's confident reply didn't satisfy his young inquisitor. "Why did black SUVs show up at the Abramson's house? Also two guys came to the local carnival when Rebecca took the kids to meet Mira and Gray. They must've found out about it when they raided your house."

Brody rubbed his chin. "We go to great pains to cover our tracks. Like Dix said, what they got was physical. They were after the ephemeral stuff, the bytes and bits at the heart of our operation, stuff that lives in cyberspace." He rapped on the table. "It's time to ditch your cell phones."

Carolyn frowned. "Oh my goodness. We have met the enemy and it is us?"

Rebecca gasped. "I've gotten so used to just punching in a number. It never occurred to me that anyone might track my calls." Tears began to roll down her face.

Jonathan put a hand over hers. "Whoa, none of that. You couldn't know. Mom and I didn't think of it either." He opened a paper bag and held it out. "Give the phones to me and I'll take care of them. Meanwhile, we need to get out of Dodge ASAP."

After disposing of the phones, Jonathan went to the train station where he booked a suite aboard Amtrak leaving later that evening. He bought three tickets, and made arrangements for Butterscotch the cat to accompany them.

He knew Dixon and Brody would be able to deal with the house and furniture for them. Once the two men had established a new base of operations, they could donate whatever they didn't need to the local homeless shelter just as Rebecca had. He smiled to himself. They'd be on their way west shortly after dusk.

CHAPTER FIFTY-FOUR

"War is evil, but it is often the lesser evil." ~ George Orwell

Citing the possibility of the babies bothering other lodgers, Gray always asked for a room as far from others as possible. Each time he returned to Mira's side, he muttered about desk clerks asking, "Steinway, like the piano?"

They'd fallen into a routine of long days spent driving. They varied the route alternating between state highways and Interstate. They headed northwest one day and southwest the next as they zigzagged across the country's midsection in a generally western direction. They seldom pulled into a motel before dark and got underway again in time to see the sun come up. Most of their meals came from takeout restaurants.

Both Mira and Gray developed an appreciation for Dixon in the days and weeks following the filming of her exposé. They came to look forward to his daily morning calls from the home refinance network and the cryptic messages he provided. Faced with an implacable foe, Dixon's updates provided a measure of comfort. It was good to know they had someone watching their backs.

೮೦೦೪

The uniformed operator studied the image on his monitor with a satisfied smirk. "I don't know where you've been, but I've got you now." Glancing up from his console, he swiveled his chair and looked across the room at his supervisor. "I've got a positive ID on that vehicle they're after."

"Let me have a look." The supervisor crossed the room and stared over the man's shoulder.

The operator made a slight lens adjustment, realigning the drone's airborne camera with the highway. In the center of his screen a white van traced an arrow-straight path along the Nebraska Interstate.

"How many people inside?"

He zoomed in for a closer look and shook his head. Sun shade film applied to the interior of the van's windows made them opaque from the outside. "I can't see inside. No way to tell."

"How can you be so sure it's the one?"

"The description matches the van at the carnival where they picked up those kids."

"It's a big country. There are lots of white vans."

The van's license plate suddenly filled the screen. "I've identified a white van licensed in the same state where they had the fracas. That narrows it down." The operator leaned into the screen. "Hey *little white van*, how'd ya like a rocket up your tailpipe?"

"Keep your hand away from that launch button before you start an incident. The public's not ready to have us blowing vehicles to smithereens as they drive along the Interstate. If it is them, they've got nowhere to go. Monitor their behavior for a little while." The supervisor walked back to his desk.

Pulling back the focus until he had the entire highway in view, the operator leaned back in his chair with a shrug.

೮೧೪

Gray yawned in the mid-morning sun and glanced over at Mira. She was slumped against the window with her eyes closed.

He gently poked her and she jerked up. "What is it? Where are we?"

"We're somewhere in the middle of Nebraska. With nothing to look at but an occasional cow wandering the driest landscape I've ever seen, and endless highway stretching out in front of me, I'm about to doze off. You'd better talk to me."

Her cell phone beeped before she could say anything. She pushed a button and a voice asked, "Have you ever considered refinancing your home?"

"What's up, Dix?"

"Tell Gray to set the cruise control if he doesn't already have it on. Also tell him to stare straight ahead. Under no circumstances should either of you look up at the sky."

"Why all the orders?"

"A drone's got a fix on you. If they see you rubber-necking, they'll know you know."

Mira fought the urge to peer into the sky. "I haven't seen anything."

"It's there; trust me."

She pressed the phone against her chest. "Dixon says to set the cruise control and don't look around; a drone has a fix on us."

"What does he want us to do?"

Mira relayed Gray's concern then held the phone between them so they could hear Dixon and he could hear both of them.

"It's about ten miles to the next exit," Dixon said. "Maintain a steady speed and don't do anything that would indicate you know they're watching you. Take the exit when you come to it. Head north and turn right on the first crossroad you come to. Drive a mile or so then pull over. Raise the hood like you've broken down and wait for help to arrive."

Gray's grip on the steering wheel turned his knuckles white. "What about the drone? It'll track us."

"Not when we get finished with it."

ℴℂℝ

Dixon looked askance at Brody sitting a few feet from him. "Everything set?"

Brody nodded and snapped his fingers.

"Good. Set your timer. I want to take that *mosquito* out when they're about three miles from the exit."

Hundreds of miles away, the drone's operator planted his elbows on his desk. Resting his head on his hands, he watched the white van continue down the highway toward the horizon.

It took the operator several seconds to respond when the

image on his screen suddenly showed nothing but cloudless sky. "What the…" He grabbed the controls and tried to bring the drone's nose back down.

Instead of leveling out, it yawed hard left. Farm fields, rusty windmills and cattle swept across the screen in rapid succession. The operator muttered a curse and tried to force it back to its original heading. The highway now ran across his screen instead of up and down. The drone was heading south instead of west.

Hearing his mutterings, his supervisor and several coworkers gathered around his station. The operator gaped at them. "I don't know what's wrong. I've lost all control."

The directional indicators across the bottom of the screen were going mad. The drone went up, then descended, then went up again. Images of dry grass filled the screen. "It's going down," his supervisor shouted.

Before the operator could respond, the image began to spin as the drone fell into a death spiral. An instant later the screen went black. In desperation, the operator tried to reboot. The room became ominously still when the words *No Signal* appeared on his screen.

CHAPTER FIFTY-FIVE

"Never give up, for that is just the place and time that the tide will turn." ~ Harriet Beecher Stowe

Off to their right Mira saw a slender cloud of gray smoke and dust rise in the air. "Looks like we're clear," she said.

Gray continued checking his mirrors. At the last possible moment he turned onto their exit. Nervously following Dixon's instructions, he drove about a mile and a half and pulled under an oak that shaded the narrow country lane. After raising the hood, they all sat back to wait.

A short time later a tow truck with *Karl's Garage* painted on the door pulled up behind them. "Howdy, neighbor. Looks like you're having some trouble," he called as Gray exited the vehicle.

Gray gave the stranger a cautious nod.

The burly man in gray, grease-stained work clothes approached with hand extended. "My name's Karl Wright. By any chance, have you ever considered refinancing your home?"

Gray clasped the man's hand and grinned. He introduced himself as Gus Steinway and winced when Karl said, "Steinway like the piano, huh?"

After he met Gus' wife, Maude, Karl walked to the front of the van and bent over to peer into the engine well. After a few seconds, he tapped the brim of his hat and said, "Looks like what you need is a new set of license plates."

It only took him a couple of minutes to install the plates Gray removed from under one of the middle seats. Karl rose from a squat and dusted his hands. "California," he said, studying the new plate. "My wife, Delores, and I went out there for our twenty-fifth anniversary. She really enjoyed Disneyland. Why don't you stay with us for few days? Let 'em wonder where you went."

"That's very kind of you."

"Delores loves company. I'll pull around you. Drop in line and follow me home." He headed back to his truck whistling and flipping the screwdriver in his hand.

❧❧

Spending several days on the Wright's farm refreshed everyone's spirits. Gray had time to decompress after his long days behind the wheel and Mira enjoyed having a seasoned pro assist her with the babies. Karl's wife, Delores, helped bathe and change the twins and generally played Grandma.

With Delores being watchful, Mira grabbed a few extra minutes to open the white box with yellow ribbon that Carolyn had given her. What she pulled out surprised and delighted her.

"Are those matching pink and blue knitted blankets?" Delores asked. "They're sure lovely."

"Thank you. I made them. As I knitted these, I imagined them for a boy and girl, possibly twins. I gave them away to a Pregnancy Shelter as I'd done with other baby blankets, but these two are special." She gave a satisfied smile. "Carolyn somehow retrieved them and gave them back to me."

Mira had to stop herself from saying, *as a wedding present*. There were some things she couldn't share. Becoming a wife and mother on the same day was one of them.

From outside happy sounds echoed through an open window. Turning, she watched a laughing Robbie and Emma chase baby chicks in the barnyard. Deeohgee gave a cheerful bark as he romped with the Wright's three Border Collies.

Karl said he'd let the children bottle feed calves tomorrow, she thought. Maybe they'd also like to help Delores and me pick and shuck sweet corn for dinner. She sighed happily.

❧❧

By the end of the week, Gray and Mira announced they should be on their way.

After supper, Karl and Gray retired to the hay barn to refit the van. At the Abramson's, when they'd picked up the babies, Carolyn said there were materials to redo the van if needed. But, she didn't elaborate on exactly what they were.

"Do you need a large pair of wire cutters?" Karl asked as Gray leaned into the back of the van groping under the wide back seat.

Gray cut the last of the retaining wires and a large flat cardboard package attached to the underside of the seat dropped to the floor. He clambered out of the van and reached back to retrieve it. Laying the kit across a pair of sawhorses, the two men opened it.

"What exactly do we have here," Gray asked, eyeing the shiny white rectangles with rounded corners.

"These," Karl said with a flourish, "are going to convert that van of yours into a FedEx truck. Don't worry; it'll make more sense once we sort the panels by size."

After they'd grouped the panels into pairs Karl picked one up and held it over the appropriate window. "Each one of these is sized to cover one of the van's windows. We'll attach them with super strong double-sided tape, making it into a panel van."

Gray hesitated a moment. "Won't that make the interior awfully dark?"

Karl nodded. "That's an unintended side effect, nothing we can do about it."

Gray moved around the van carefully washing each window with alcohol then drying it. Karl came behind outlining the windows with heavy duty, double-sided tape.

Going to the sawhorses, Gray picked up the panels and brought them to the van. One-by-one the two men pressed the panels against the tape's fresh adhesive. By the end of the evening they'd been completely around the van. What Karl said was true. From a distance you couldn't tell the van had windows.

"What about weather?" Gray asked as they returned to the house.

"The film is waterproof. Some moisture will wick in around the edges over time. Even though it's not a permanent fix, it'll last more than long enough to get you where you're going."

The following day they completed the job by applying the FedEx decals they found in the box. There were large decals for each side and smaller ones for the front and back.

Gray and Karl made a trip to an outdoor outfitters shop and bought several battery-powered lamps to combat the darkness inside the van. Their round base fit into the children's cup holders providing the equivalent of an end table with a lamp. Whenever they grew tired they could click off the light, close their eyes and drift off to sleep.

They rose early their last morning with the Wrights. After a hearty farm breakfast everyone helped carry things out to the van. The children stared in amazement and asked, "Where did our van go?"

With everything stowed and the children all belted in, Gray and Mira thanked their hosts. Karl led them back to the Interstate, giving them a farewell wave as they continued on their way.

སྐ

"New drone looks like it's working okay. Seen anything out there?" the supervisor called across the room.

The computer operator shook his head. "Everything's quiet." He leaned to one side, giving his supervisor a view of the screen. "Nothing anywhere around except a FedEx truck running its route." The supervisor watched the delivery van disappear over a rise and turned back to his desk with a grunt.

སྐ

Gray and Mira relaxed a bit once they left the barren stretches of Nebraska and Wyoming behind. The time spent driving grew shorter and they began stopping at deserted pullouts to enjoy the view and let the children stretch their legs.

Several days and hundreds of miles later, their route gradually led them into mountainous regions. Snow-capped peaks loomed in the distance as they drove. They found winter came early to the high country. Gray now scraped frost off the van windshield at the start of each daily trip.

When they entered the forests of the Pacific Northwest, even the children sensed they were nearing their destination.

CHAPTER FIFTY-SIX

Although they didn't know its name or exact location, Gray and Mira's little band were headed for a *safe village*.

Life Chances, and similar organizations, created a variety of shelters for families seeking refuge from the government's restriction on family size. These scattered communities were camouflaged and generally self-sufficient, existing beneath the government's radar.

Traveling by train, Carolyn, Jonathan and Rebecca arrived at the same destination days before Mira, Gray and the children. Living quarters were waiting for them and they settled in, eagerly anticipating the arrival of the others.

℘℃

Rebecca was reading when her landline phone rang. Hearing Dixon claim to be the home refinance network put a sparkle in her eyes.

"I told Gray they're predicting a cold front ahead of him with possible heavy snow," Dixon said. "That's the morning weather report for your neck of the woods too."

"You managed to speak to them?"

"Yep. Robbie sends Gramma his love, by the way."

"Oh Dixon, you're a sweetheart."

"Be careful, you'll ruin my image." He cleared his throat. "I'm going to go out on a limb and say today *could* be the day ... tomorrow at the latest.'"

A shiver of excitement rippled through her. "Do you mean it?"

"If they can stay ahead of the weather they'll be there today. Mother Nature, of course, offers no guarantees. Gotta go."

He's always in such a hurry, she thought, cradling the phone.

Determined to be at the arrival point when Gray and Mira got there, Rebecca put aside her book and quickly threw some things into a small carry-on. When she finished, she peered around making a final check before tugging on a hooded parka. She zipped the bag and grabbed her purse. After sharing the good news with Carolyn and Jonathan, she headed out accompanied by one of the men from their village.

Once at the *safe house* located far above the village, he carried Rebecca's bag inside and sat it on the bench of a hall tree. All newcomers came through this massive two-story structure, staying a night or two before being relocated into the safe village below. Rebecca recalled when they first arrived being fascinated by the intricate carving of dark oak panels. She now admired them again as she tugged off her bulky coat. The man took it from her and hung it beside the bag.

Beginning with the drawing room, he walked her through the first floor to re-acquaint her with its layout. When they entered the kitchen he crossed the room and led her to a large pantry. Assured that she knew where everything was, he left to return to the village.

Rebecca headed for the library hoping she could pass the time by losing herself in another book. The eight-paneled walnut door effortlessly swung aside at the turn of the handle. A large stone fireplace dominated the back wall. Walnut shelving crammed with books lined the wall to her left.

There was a rolling ladder for access to the upper shelves. She smiled. It was something she'd only seen in movies. Similar shelves, set between high, multi-paned windows, filled the right wall. She stumbled upon a cache of Jane Austen novels, selected one, and settled into an overstuffed chair with matching hassock.

When her stomach began to rumble, she left her book face down on the side table and wandered into the kitchen. "Ah, comfort food," she murmured aloud, surveying the well-stocked shelves. Spotting a canned Danish ham, she decided it would be a quick fix.

Poking about, she also discovered several sealed tins of cookies lurking behind the rows of canned fruits and vegetables. She started to close the pantry door, but stopped long enough to reach in and snatch a tin of chocolate covered shortbread.

"These will be perfect to take to the library and nibble on after supper," she said with a guilty grin. The sound of a voice, even only her own, momentarily dispelled the house's brooding silence.

After her impromptu supper, Rebecca returned to the library. It was already dark outside. Shafts of moonlight poured in the eastern windows, giving the room an eerie cast. She turned down the radiator and stacked some kindling in the fireplace. It took only minutes to get a fire going. Taking a lap robe off the back of a sofa, she wrapped it around herself.

The old house creaked and groaned in the wind. Too apprehensive to go upstairs alone, Rebecca hunkered down in her chair. When a particularly strong gust set the fire to dancing, she jerked up. Her brow wrinkled. "Okay, Rebecca, you're alone in a big old house. So what? Count Dracula, Dr. Frankenstein and the rest of those fiends are all fictional characters. Get over it."

Yawning, she let herself drift off to sleep. The book tumbled from her lap and landed on the thickly carpeted floor as soundlessly as the snowflakes accumulating on the lawn outside.

Rebecca woke the following morning stiff and sore from spending the night in a chair. As she stretched, she vowed never to do that again.

Pulling open the window's heavy drapes, she watched the morning sun sparkle off ice crystals in the snow, turning them into diamonds. Beautiful as it was, the snowy white vista offered no sign of her loved ones. Disappointed, she shrugged and tramped off to the kitchen. After a breakfast of tea and toast, she climbed the stairs to shower. Later, with nothing else to occupy her time, she settled down into the same overstuffed chair and returned to the Jane Austin novel.

₨₧

Gray checked his watch and whispered to Mira, "Today could be the day. If we get an early start, we might beat the cold front that's forecast. With a little luck and clear roads we could be there in time for a late lunch."

Not wanting to create expectations in the children's minds, Gray and Mira chose to keep the prospect of their imminent arrival to themselves. They were glad they had when snowflakes appeared mid-morning.

By noon the storm front, combined with the shorter day length and a canopy of conifer branches overhead, made it abnormally dark. An ominous feeling crept over Mira as she nervously listened to the squish of the tires on the snow-covered pavement. Meanwhile, Gray carefully navigated the narrow road.

The branches above them sagged under the weight of accumulated snow. When the snow began, Gray had worried about leaving tracks and said he was glad the overhanging branches would shield them from prying eyes in the sky.

True enough, Mira thought, but the tall trees bordering the road also make it difficult to know how much snow has actually fallen. What will road conditions be if we drive out of their protective shield?

Mira twisted in her seat, checking the children behind her. She was pleased they all slept. Better to let them snooze away the last leg of the trip than listen to a constant barrage of, "Are we there yet?"

"I'm glad it's you driving," she whispered, settling back in her seat.

"No need to worry. The snow isn't that deep and the van handles well. Rest easy." He reached over to pat her knee.

She caught his hand and placed it back on the wheel. "I'm glad you're confident, but I feel better when you have both hands on the wheel with your eyes pointed straight ahead."

He chuckled, but did as she asked. "My biggest concern is having a deer bolt out of the forest. That's why I'm not rushing to get there. Better to go slow and have time to react to anything that runs out from the tree line." Gray's eyes swept both sides of the road as he drove, alert to any movement.

"What if they run out just as we get to them?"

"If we're traveling slowly enough, the car won't sustain major damage. Hopefully they won't either," he added.

His reassurances made her feel better. Sometimes she couldn't believe how lucky she was to have met and married such a capable man...*and handsome too,* she thought, inwardly grinning.

"I wish we'd bought some extra food when we gassed up," she said. "The babies are fed and happy, but Robbie and Emma are going to be starved when they wake up. Who knows whether there will be anything in the house to eat once we get there?"

"Maybe we should call a pizza delivery."

Making a fist, she gave him a light tap on the arm. When they arrived at their destination they both expected to find only the slightest remnants of civilization.

"Maybe I can shoot a moose," he said, reading her thoughts.

"You shoot it, you butcher it. I avoid whole chickens at the market so I'm hardly up to tackling something as big as a moose carcass."

He chuckled.

CHAPTER FIFTY-SEVEN

Gray peered through the swirling snow at the dark mountains. "High up in the forest like this, I'm thinking this place we're headed to is probably a back woods cabin.

She eyed the passing trees and nodded. "Mm-hmm, that's occurred to me too. Just as long as it's dry and warm. I wouldn't want the children to get chilled."

"Probably heated with wood." Gray's brow furrowed. "I hope there's some already chopped and split. I'll be up to swinging an axe after a good night's rest, but I'd hate to have to do any chopping as soon as we get there." He sighed deeply. "But if I must, I will; can't let my family shiver the night away."

She reached over and patted his leg. "You've been a real trooper through everything."

"Me? A trooper? Well, maybe I did ride in on my white horse and rescue everyone, but isn't that what a hero's supposed to do?"

She laughed then put her hand over her mouth afraid she'd awaken the children. A quick look over her shoulder confirmed they still slept soundly. "You're a lot of fun to be with, you know that Mr. Stevens?"

"Now, now, Mrs. Stevens is it proper to discuss our sex life in front of the children."

This time she tried hard to control her laughter, she really did.

Emma roused, stretched and rubbed her eyes. "Oh look, it's snowing. How much longer before we get there?"

"I'm sorry Mom woke you, Sweetheart," Gray said.

Mira reached back and squeezed Emma's hand. "It can't be much longer now. *Daddy's* driving slowly and carefully in this snow. He's worried a deer might jump out in front of us."

"And Daddy likes deer," Gray added.

Emma beamed. "Oh, that's nice, *Dad*. Will there be deer where we're going?"

"Deer and who knows what other types of animals. It looks like we're headed into the wilderness."

Emma stared out the windshield at the falling snow. "We're in the *wilderness*? Are there wild animals out there?"

Mira shot Gray a look. "It's nothing to worry about, Emma honey. Everything's fine; we'll be okay."

₧)₳

Rebecca didn't want the novel to end, and when it did, she found herself at loose ends. She passed her time alternately pacing and watching out the front windows. The huge house, a lumber baron's retreat built over a century earlier, offered everything she needed. But her euphoria over the beauty of her plush surroundings quickly wore thin as feelings of loneliness and isolation set in. She didn't relish the idea of spending a second night alone in the big house.

Outside, tiny snowflakes danced past the window. They seemed to come from nowhere, moved into the porch light for a brief instant, then disappeared back into the darkness. Her heart ached for Robbie and the others. Dixon said they could arrive yesterday, but they hadn't. Where were they?

Keep them safe, Lord, the roads can't be good. And please... please let them get here soon.

"Maybe they'll be hungry when they arrive." With no one around to call her a batty old woman, Rebecca had fallen into the habit of giving voice to her thoughts. "What's better on a snowy day than hot soup? I could make a pot of soup and keep it on the stove until they get here." Delighted to have something useful to do, she headed for the kitchen.

The freezer contained stew meat and the pantry held sealed cans of dried vegetables. It wasn't long before she had a large pot of thick, hearty soup steaming on the stove. She made brownies and put them in the oven to bake. She sat brown and serve rolls from the freezer on the counter to defrost, planning to heat them when they arrived.

Once the food was prepared, she searched drawers and cupboards until she found tablecloths, napkins, candles and more. She paused in the doorway to the dining room, surveying the area, then shook her head. You didn't need crystal chandeliers, bone china and hand cut stemware for a soup dinner.

Instead, she spread a gingham tablecloth over a large wooden table in the kitchen. She found practical stainless steel utensils in a kitchen drawer. Counting her, they'd need five places. To give the table a balanced look, she set a place at both ends with two on each side.

"If the kids ask, I'll say the extra place is for the man who isn't here."

Having everything ready for their arrival buoyed her spirits. Now if they would just get there. She whispered another prayer for their safe and timely arrival.

ଔଓଓ

"I think I see a faint glow of light up ahead." Gray pointed through the snow at a tiny flicker in the distance. "Maybe someone left a light on for us."

"The last time I spoke with Dixon, he said Rebecca planned to meet us when we arrived. They surely wouldn't leave her out here all alone in a tiny cabin."

"No, I think the glow indicates someone's already split wood for her." Gray nibbled at his lip. "I just hope she hasn't already burned all of it."

The glow grew steadily brighter as they drove. Eventually the shadowy outlines of a large structure gradually began to materialize in the snow-driven darkness. Gray squinted through the windshield as additional details continued to emerge. Whatever that was out there, it definitely was *no* mountain cabin.

Robbie woke up as they ascended the long driveway and

rolled to a stop. "Where are we?"

No one answered. They were all awestruck.

Surrounded by tall firs and hemlocks, the mammoth building seemed to have grown out of the surrounding hillside.

Robbie rubbed his eyes in amazement. "Look, it's a castle."

"Is not," Emma said. "Castles have moats; it's a mansion."

"Castles always have towers and it's got two of 'em."

They'd rolled to a stop in front of two pairs of overhead garage doors set into the exposed portion of the basement wall. A wide porch with stairs at both ends ran between the rounded towers, providing access to the first floor. The pinpoint of light Gray had originally spotted in fact came from a blending of multiple outdoor fixtures. Some were on posts near the stairs, others at the corners of the building and two evenly spaced between the garages.

Lamplight, muted by drapes, shone through first floor windows on either side of the double entry doors. Windows along the side of the building cast yellow bars of light onto the snow covered ground. The upper story roof had rows of dormers marching along each side marking off eight bedrooms.

"I still say it's a castle," Robbie insisted. "I bet it's got swords and armor and all kinds of neat stuff inside."

CHAPTER FIFTY-EIGHT

Rebecca heard their vehicle before she saw it. Grabbing the heavy wool shawl she left by the front door, she wrapped it around her shoulders and stepped out onto an expansive veranda. Clutching the shawl closed with one hand, she frantically waved at the van with the other. Tears of happiness, relief and gratitude filled her eyes.

Thank you, God!

Her sight followed the van's headlights as it climbed the curving drive. When it pulled up and stopped, Rebecca hurried down the snowy steps. After leaning into the van to throw kisses to Emma and Robbie, she helped Mira get the twins out of their car seats. The two women carried the babies inside.

Bending into the car, Gray kissed Emma on the head. "Let me carry Robbie inside and I'll come back and lift you over the snow too." He hefted the sleepy boy and trudged through the snow with Robbie at his shoulder, the child's soft, warm breath on his neck.

Deeohgee jumped out of the car and raced toward the front of the house. Even stopping to pee on a tree, he still beat everyone to the front door.

Emma watched Gray walk away from the car with Robbie. She cast wary glances at the dark surrounding forest and trembled. Who knew what lurked behind the trees? A wind gust sent icy fingers dancing up her spine. *There's no way they're going to leave me alone out here in the wilderness.*

Leaping out of the van, she immediately sank in the snow. Emma shrieked when ice cold wetness filled her shoes. She lifted her legs and bent her knees to slog through the deep snow, arms extended for balance. She wobbled toward the stairway, trying not to fall down or allow additional snow to find its way into her shoes.

At her cry, Gray stopped and spun around. He waited at the top of the stairs for her to catch up, and tried not to laugh. He looked down at her clambering up the slippery steps and smiled. "Sorry Sweetie. I would have come right back for you, honest. Come on, let's get inside and warm up."

Now that she was safe beside Gray, Emma took time to look around. Being on the veranda provided a panoramic view and she stared in wide-eyed wonder at the winter scene. Light from the residence's many windows danced across the snow. Tiny particles of ice reflected it back making everything around them sparkle and twinkle.

"It's like the stars in heaven are glittering on the ground," she whispered. Then turned and shouted, "Brrrr. C'mon, Dad. It's cold out here."

Emma's earlier fears vanished as soon as she entered the front door. She watched Gray put Robbie on a sofa and she plopped down beside him. Reaching over to lightly tickle his ear, she giggled when he tried to shrug away.

He bolted up and stared at her for a moment. "How come you got snow all over you, Emma?"

"You do too, Silly." To prove it, she brushed some off his head and onto his face.

He retaliated by knocking some off her hair. A moment later, both children were prancing in circles brushing flakes of snow from each others' shoulders and hair. Their exuberance mirrored everyone's relief at being reunited.

"I'd better bring in the luggage," Gray said.

"Why don't you pull the van into the garage? That way you won't have to go back and forth through the snow," Rebecca said.

"I would like to hide the van."

"Go on. I'll go open the overhead door for you."

When the automatic garage door lifted, he drove in. Although Rebecca hurried back to the others, Emma waited and held the side door from the garage to the house open for him.

Gray stepped in and dumped the last of their bags on the floor. Emma closed the door behind him. He placed a hand on her head to tousle her hair, then raised his head and took a long sniff. "Yum. I smell hot food."

"Gramma made soup."

"Then let's hurry and get some!"

As they entered the kitchen, Rebecca threw an arm around Gray's shoulder, kissing him on the cheek. "It's been on the stove eagerly awaiting your arrival."

Turning, she repeated the gesture with Mira. "I can't tell you how happy I am that you finally got here. She ran her eyes across the paneled wainscoting and up the carpeted stairs. "This place is dreadfully quiet when you're the only one in it."

Robbie jumped up. "Let's eat. Gramma's a good soup-maker."

Rebecca leaned down to hug Robbie, but before she could he and Emma bounded off toward the table and sat down waiting with eager smiles.

"Go ahead and feed those two. We should care for the babies before we eat. We'll be back as soon as we can," Mira said.

Upstairs Mira and Gray found two cribs already laid out and waiting for the babies. Dim light filtered in from the hallway as they put the sleeping babies down and pulled fluffy comforters over them.

"God bless, Rebecca, Carolyn or whoever did this," Mira said, stooping to kiss a baby on the cheek.

She switched on a night light and studied the room. The soft pastel plaid fabric on the upholstered rocking chair matched the curtains at the window. She picked up a baby monitor sitting on an end table. "We'll have to find the other unit to this monitor. Then we can take it with us from room to room as we move about."

"Let's look for it in the kitchen," Gray whispered. "I'm starving."

"You don't get away that easy, Mister. All we've done is drive; I haven't had even one big, warm hug all day."

He happily obliged.

ℰℭ

While they prepared for dinner a man in a black overcoat stepped from the woods and silently rounded the house. He'd pulled his collar up against the wind. A black tweed walking hat shaded his face. Snow slipped off the back of its brim when he tilted his head toward the lighted windows on the side of the house. He listened to the happy chatter in the kitchen for a moment then resumed plodding through the deep snow.

Rounding the corner of the house, he paused beside the stairway long enough to note the tire tracks that disappeared under the garage door. He nodded with satisfaction and headed up the stairs, his footfalls muffled by the snow.

His loud knock at the front door startled the diners.

The children's spoons clattered onto the table. The plate of brown 'n' serve rolls being passed around came to a sudden stop.

Deeohgee leaped to his feet and bounded off. His loud barks echoed through the hallway as he ran to the front door.

"Who in the world could that be?" Rebecca wondered aloud.

"Has anyone else been here since you arrived?" Gray asked.

"No one."

Signaling everyone to stay put, he rose to answer the door.

"Shouldn't you take a weapon or something ... just in case?" Mira asked.

"If someone wanted to harm us, they wouldn't knock."

"How reassuring."

Gray gave Mira a peck on the cheek, smiled at the children to allay their fear and called, "I'm coming Deeohgee." He quit barking as soon as Gray reached the door. Moving to one side, the dog took a position near the door's leading edge. Deeohgee's muscles tensed in readiness. He emitted a low, guttural growl as he studied Gray's reaction to the surprise visitor.

Bracing against the door, Gray put his eye to the peep-hole. An elderly man waited outside. He appeared to be alone, and it looked like he was wearing... a clerical collar? Gray opened the door a crack and peered out.

"Good evenin' t' ya, Grayson Stevens, or would you prefer I call you Gus? I'm Father MacBain 'ov Holy Redeemer Parish. May I come in outta the snow?"

"Of course, Father. Come in, come in." He stepped aside to let the priest enter and Deeohgee backed up too. "We were just sitting down to hot soup. Would you like some?"

"Aye, that'd be lovely. Beastly night t' be out 'n' about." The priest removed his hat and coat, shaking off the snow before hanging them up. He sat on the bench and tugged off his boots. "Best leave the wellies t' drip on the rug," he said, setting them aside.

The dog trailed the two men down the hall as they discussed weather and road conditions.

Father MacBain crossed the room and rested a hand on Mira's shoulder. "Ah, this must be your lovely wife, Maude," he said with a twinkle in his eye. He smiled at the children staring up at him from the opposite side of the table. "And this sweet lass would be Emma with Master Robert beside her."

Robbie gave him an indignant look. "She's Emma alright, but my name's *Robbie*."

"Aye, and 'tis a right fine name if ever I heard one." He reached across the table to shake the boy's hand. "Folks here and about call me Father Mac."

Straightening, he looked to his right. "Rebecca, my dear, I owe you an apology. No one down below told me you'd come here yesterday. Had I known you were alone last evening I'd come up to spend the night with ya."

His jowly cheeks glowed crimson. "Holy Mother, help me! The devil's got me tongue." He swallowed hard. "That dinna come out the way I intended. You surely understand...I meant, I shoulda... I would never..."

Rebecca chuckled. "We all know what you meant, Father. It was a kind thought, but I managed." Walking to the stove, she began ladling out a bowl of thick, hot soup for him.

CHAPTER FIFTY-NINE

"Coming together is a beginning, staying together is progress, and working together is success." ~ Henry Ford

Father MacBain attacked his bowl with enthusiasm. "I apologize for wolfin' down me food so fast. I got so busy on my rounds today that I forgot all about lunch. I feel as hungry as our dear Lord musta after his 40-day fast."

He took another spoonful of soup and smiled appreciatively. He looked up at Rebecca and gestured with his spoon, "Delicious soup, this; sticks to a man's ribs. You'll have t' make it for one of our parish suppers."

"Parish? What parish?" Gray asked. "Once we turned off the State Highway, all I saw was forest. There wasn't any sign of habitation."

Father Mac took a final swallow. Wiping his mouth, he folded his napkin and set it aside. "Appearances *kin* be deceiving. Truth is, we're not alone up here in these mountains."

With startled expressions, several pairs of eyes turned toward the dark windows.

"Nae, I dinna mean the Big Grey Man who haunts the passes of Ben MacDhui, or Sasquatch, as he's known hereabouts." He shook his head. "Not a'tall." He waved aside their questions. "Everythin' kin wait 'til mornin'. You've had a long day and should be heading off t' bed. For now, as my dear Mum used t' say, 'snuggle under them covers 'n' sleep like a *peerie.*'"

"What about you, Father," Rebecca asked as she collected their empty bowls.

"Truth be known, I plan on *bidin'* here for the night too. Bright 'n' early tomorrow we'll all take off to the glen for a tour." He turned toward Gray and Mira. "Let ya see what we have here." Rising, he walked to the window. The snow continued to blow and swirl in the howling wind. He watched for a moment then gave an involuntary shiver. "I'd rather not go anywhere on a *murky* night such as this. As we Scots say, it's *perished wi' the cauld.*"

Gray joined him at the window. Leaning close, he quietly asked, "Can I speak with you privately?"

"Aye, ye kin."

Gray asked Mira if she could manage the children without him. When she nodded, the two men headed for the library.

Emma tugged the hem of the priest's jacket as they passed. "How do I sleep like a *peerie,* Father Mac?"

He dropped to one knee putting them at eye level. "A *peerie* is a child's toy, Lass. A spinning top you set in motion by jerkin' a string." He patted her head. "It means to sleep *verra* steady and sound, as I'm sure ye will."

෧෬

"Gray, you look like a man carryin' the weight of the world on his shoulders," Father Mac said as he settled into an overstuffed chair.

"We cast our lot into this sight unseen ."

"And now that ye've gotten here, you're having second thoughts, reservations?"

"Our destination was always a safe *house.*"

Father Mac ran his eyes around the room and shrugged. "Well, you're safe here aren't ye?"

Gray bit his lip. "To be honest, what I am is confused. At dinner you mentioned a parish. That implies more than just a handful of people. We hadn't planned on joining some kind of religious cult."

"The hallmarks of a cult are heretical doctrines and a strong, authoritarian leader. Truth is we are a tad clannish. I suppose some might say, 'set in our ways,' but the only leader we follow is our dear Lord." He tapped his head then chuckled. "Rest assured, we've no Anabaptists here."

"I'm no expert on religious beliefs."

Father Mac leaned back into the cushion and crossed his legs. "As ye probably know, both the good Lord and his apostle, St. Paul, admonished the early believers t' be *in*, but not *of* this world.' This country of yours has a long and colorful history of religious sects who've attempted to follow this command by separating themselves from society."

"But why call them Anabaptists?"

"The sect known as Anabaptists originated under Zwingli in the 16th Century. Nearly all of the later separatists...the Amish, Mennonites, Moravians, Hutterites, 'n' so on, trace their ancestry back to him."

Father Mac worked his tongue around the inside his cheek as he thought. "Then again, some might file us under Religious Utopians. Rather than simply absent themselves from society, these folks set out to construct a brand new one from the ground up. The Utopian movement was short-lived, but the towns they founded still bear witness to their dream. The Amana Colonies in Iowa, for instance."

"Enough of the history lessons; let's cut to the chase. Have we joined some kind of Catholic commune without knowing it?"

"Would that be a problem for ye?"

"Mira and I aren't Catholic." Gray's expression hardened. "Do you expect us to convert?"

"The word commune, religious or otherwise, implies a sharing of goods and property. As isolated as we are, we couldn't survive unless everyone worked together." Father Mac gave him a paternal smile. "But there's no compulsion, Gray. It's simply neighborly charity."

He raised his hand to stifle any further objections. "We don't make religious demands on people. We simply have strong convictions about right and wrong, just like you and Mira. It'll all be clearer tomorrow when we go down to the glen. Awright fur now?"

෨෨෬

Gray climbed into the king-sized bed beside Mira, grateful the end of the day had finally arrived. He squinted into the darkness. "What did you do with Deeohgee?"

"I let him sleep with Robbie. They're crazy about each other."

She swept her hair aside and let her head sink into the pillow, enjoying the cool feel of the cotton pillowcase against her neck. "How did things go between you and Father Mac?" she asked with a yawn.

"I got a few of my questions answered."

"Want to talk about it?"

"Nah. *'Tis awright fur now.*" Gray smiled and rolled toward her. "We've got a big day tomorrow," he said and kissed her.

෨෨෬

The next morning, Deeohgee's head snapped up at the sound of a melodic gong.

Robbie's eyelids fluttered. He hugged his pillow and snuggled deeper into the covers.

The dog remained still as a statue on the floor in Robbie's bedroom, head cocked and alert. After the second gong Deeohgee rose to his feet and padded across the room. He scratched at the door and it was inched open to release him. Deeohgee accompanied his liberator down the hall. Each time they passed a bedroom door, he paused and struck a small bell with a wooden mallet.

Gray rolled out of bed, motioning for Mira to stay put. He cracked the door and peeked out.

"Guid mornin' t' ye," Father MacBain said and struck the bell three times in rapid succession. "Time t' be about the day's business."

Mira hopped out of bed and scurried to the closet. She cinched her robe and stepped into the hallway where she encountered two half-dressed children hurrying to finish.

The priest called back from the top of the stairway. "Since this is yur first mornin' here, I have a full breakfast for ye in the kitchen." He started down the stairs with Deeohgee trailing behind, tail wagging.

A door opened beside Mira. Rebecca stuck her head out and smiled. "I forgot to warn you about Father Mac's breakfasts. It's his traditional way of welcoming new arrivals. I hope you're both hungry. I ate until I almost burst and when I refused his offer of toast and marmalade, I thought the poor man's eyes would tear-up."

Moments later, Gray emerged sniffing the air. "Yum, is that bacon I smell cooking?" He caught Emma's hand and reached for Robbie's. "C'mon kids, let's not keep the man waiting."

"What about the twins?" Mira asked.

He looked back and grinned. "Sorry, I've already got my hands full."

Rebecca placed a hand on Mira's shoulder. "I'll help."

೫೦೧೪

Gray and the children found Father Mac in a white apron at the kitchen doorway. He shooed them into places around the table.

"Go ahead 'n' sit yourselves down. Everything's ready," he said, pouring orange juice. "We'll start the day sayin' Grace, then a wee bit of oatmeal."

The bowl of oatmeal he sat in front of Gray looked like it'd feed a lumberjack. The children received smaller portions. A tray with a pitcher of cream, along with dishes of brown sugar and golden currants went in the center of the table. A metal rack holding sliced toast, a plate with a hefty slab of butter and a squat jar of marmalade followed.

Their chef crossed his arms, smiling as he watched them eat. "I'll cook your eggs whilst ye work on the porridge. How d' ye like them?" Father Mac asked, heading for the stove.

A few moments later their happy host returned with warm plates overflowing with food. Using a fork as a pointer, he made a clockwise circuit around the plate detailing what constituted a *Full Scottish Breakfast*.

"Now here ye got yur broiled slice of tomato with some cheese on top. Next to it there's a rasher of bacon, some nicely browned *tatties*, a scone, and a *banger*. That's a sausage link," he whispered to the children. "Down here we have sautéed mushrooms, baked beans, and your fried egg."

Emma tilted her head in Robbie's direction after Father turned away and whispered, "Did you ever see so much? How could anybody eat it all?"

But they did.

CHAPTER SIXTY

Upstairs, the women changed, fed and dressed the babies. They arrived at the kitchen as Gray and the children finished breakfast.

Gray pushed his plate away and rose. "Let me take care of the babies while you two eat." He took Alexander from Rebecca and carried him over to the blue sleeper-seat. After covering him with a light blanket, he returned for Leila.

"You see," he told Mira, "there was a very good reason I came down ahead of you."

"Sure there was. You were hungry." Mira handed him the baby and gave him a playful slap on the shoulder.

He grinned at her as he fitted Leila into the pink sleeper-seat. "Isn't this convenient? You can both enjoy a leisurely breakfast since the kids and I have already eaten. No need to thank me, I'm always glad to help."

Mira rolled her eyes and shook her head.

Father Mac bustled over with glasses and a pitcher of orange juice. "Don't fret over the dirty dishes; I'll get t' 'em." He sat a glass of juice in front of Rebecca with a stern look. "House rules say one welcome breakfast to a customer." He winked. "We'll overlook it this time so long as ye don't make a habit of comin' back fur *anither*."

Father MacBain spooned up oatmeal and returned to the stove. "How do you like your eggs?"

Mira turned to Rebecca. "Anything's okay with me. You pick."

"Flipped over easy."

"A *braw* choice," said the priest. He cracked four eggs into a black cast iron skillet. "Don't dally o'er your food, ladies. We have a far day ahead 'o us."

⊱⊰

Gray knelt beside the stairway helping Emma tug on her boots while Rebecca helped Robbie. Rising, he headed for the stairway leading to the garage. "I'll pull the van out and you can meet me down in front."

Father Mac shook his head. "You'll not be needin' the van today. Won't do ye much good up here. Vehicles *kin* reach our village *awright*, but not in the straight forward manner you're imaginin'. We don't have much use for automobiles."

"How do you get around?"

"The good Lord gave us feet 'n' we use 'em." Father Mac rested an arm around Gray's shoulder. "We'll be stepping back in time to...oh, say the turn of the century."

"But they had cars in 1999."

"I shan't deny it. The problem is ye took a wee step when a giant one's called for. Try 1899."

Disappointment shadowed Gray's face. "We risked our lives driving across the country just so we could throw away all modern conveniences and have to live like our great grandparents?"

"Now there ye go frettin' *agin*. We *ah-ready* talked this out. Trust me, 'tis a good life we lead here." Father Mac winked. "Plus we got a few odds 'n' ends thrown into the mix that Victorians ne'er imagined."

When everyone had their pants tucked into their boots, and gloves and hats on, Gray and Mira strapped on baby carriers. Gray placed a drowsing Alexander into his carrier, slipped on his coat and closed it over the infant strapped to his chest. Mira repeated the process with Leila.

Dressed and ready, they followed Fr. Mac out the door and down the steps. The snowstorm had abated and crisp, cool air met them under a bright morning sun.

Gray noticed a sign beside the drive and brushed away wind-driven snow by running a gloved finger around and between its embossed letters. "Look at this," he called to the others. "I never saw it in the rush to get inside last night."

The others gathered around him, admiring the hand-carved

wooden panel. A large *Welcome* emerged from the dark background in raised letters of gold-leafed script. Carved elk, deer, bears and cougars graced the center of the panel and beneath them additional gold-leafed letters identified their safe house as the *Fireside Hunting Lodge.*

"It's a perfect cover," Father Mac said, joining them in front of the sign. "This Lodge has a national reputation as a luxury hunting resort. The fees from well-to-do visitors fund the maintenance of the building. Meanwhile, the maids, cooks, guides and so forth all come from our village. It provides welcome income."

He turned to Gray. "You couldn't have timed your arrival any better. The elk, cougar and bear rifle season all closed last week. Next week the place'll be crawlin' with bow hunters out after elk."

The old priest stomped snow off his boots. "Outside of hunting seasons, the building is ours to use as we please. "Let's get a move on. It's this way."

At the back of the Lodge, the little band traversed a snow covered yard that stretched out about 150 feet. The edge was guarded by a tall fence with sturdy wooden posts sunk into concrete. Chain link panels between these uprights provided a strong barrier.

When they approached the fence, Mira and Gray recognized the reason for such elaborate precautions. A few feet beyond it the earth dropped away, providing a heart-stopping view of the valley below. Nature had carved the plateau into the side of the mountain, offering a bird's eye view of seemingly endless forest. Far across the valley white peaks rose against an azure blue sky studded with billowy clouds.

Father Mac pointed toward the base of the forested abyss. The *glen* as he called it. "The settlement where you'll be livin' is *doon* there."

The fence gently curved to their left, following the lip of the yard. It terminated at a black, rocky outcropping beside a copse of spindly trees. Emma and Robbie pressed their faces against the fence's diamond shaped openings, searching for a glimpse of the illusive village. Seeing nothing but trees bounded by more trees, they turned to Father Mac with disappointed expressions.

He tapped a fingernail against his Roman collar. "Trust me. You'll find many a *hoose doon* there at the bottom of the *brae*."

"Well, there may be a village down there, but how are we going to get to it?" Mira asked.

"A pleasant jaunt 'n' a little ride'll take us home," he said with a smile. Motioning them to follow, he crossed the snow to a gate at the end of the fence. Pausing long enough to input several numbers into the lock's keypad, he swung the gate back and waved them through like a tour guide.

The children edged closer to the adults, hesitant to follow a path that appeared to go nowhere.

"What's keeping all o' ye? Don't ye want to see your new *hoose*?" Father Mac waited until everyone, including Deeohgee, had come through then closed and relocked the gate.

"Robbie, best take your *Granmither's* hand as we walk; she knows the way. Emma *kin* hold mine. On the way, I'll tell ye how this all *come aboot*." He headed into the trees, shoving low branches aside as he walked.

They came out of the snow-laden trees at a wide foot path. It had railings and more chained link panels bounded by old railroad ties. The path was in-filled with pea gravel, forming a gentle stairway down the slope.

"Like everywhere else in the American west, this area experienced a gold rush. A trapper, or perhaps someone scouring riverbeds in hopes of finding riches, noticed shiny specks in the river sand. Well, as ye can imagine, people flooded in soon as the word got out."

Gray nodded. "Sounds like Sutter's Mill."

"A wee bit, perhaps. Miners came with dreams of wealth. In some places those dreams came true, but here at Duncanville, as they called the place, they weren't quite so lucky. Ye might say the miners panned for gold, but their dreams ne'er panned out. The good Lord, ye see, had bigger plans for the wee settlement."

The little group continued moving in and out of shadows as they descended the pathway listening to Father Mac's saga.

"What became of Duncanville? Once the miners abandoned it, I mean?" Gray asked.

"Twas ne'er abandoned; only the *chancers* left. Those made of hardier stock, most probably a band of stalwart Scotsmen, refused t' give up. They stayed on in hopes o' finding a way t' make a livin' here."

Father Mac pointed into the deep ravine beside them. "The hills 'long side us had veins of quartz 'n' the men began mining the crystals. Thought they'd sell 'em for jewelry. It didn't take long afore they discovered gold intermingled with the quartz." He chuckled. "Never did sell many crystals, but they'd found a way to scrabble a livin' out of the hillside."

"And so Duncanville prospered after all," Mira said with a smile.

"Prospered? Nae. But it struggled on 'til the quartz and its small bits of gold ran out. That's when a lumber baron purchased the whole town, lock, stock and barrel, along with the surrounding valley. He brought in a work crew, expanded the town so they'd have a place t' live and set about logging the trees. They built a sluiceway and floated the logs down river to one of his company's sawmills. Things went along peaceful as could be until the Spruce Squadrons arrived in 1918."

Gray gave him a puzzled look. "I've never heard of a Spruce Squadron."

"Planes were all made *oot* of wood then, donna ye know. Spruce and other high quality lumber was in great demand during the First World War. So the Army sent men *oop* here to help with logging. Many a stick o' Duncanville wood crossed the channel headin' for battle." He lifted his bushy eyebrows. "Course the Brigade scrambled away soon as the war ended."

He shrugged. "Things slowed down when the Great Depression hit, but they managed to keep a few men working. Things boomed *agin* in the 40's. By the end of the second great war they'd cut most of the trees. Work came to a halt *aboot* 1956. They took the equipment out, the loggers moved on to other sites, and Duncanville faded from the maps."

"What a sad story," Mira said. "So Duncanville became a ghost town?"

"Aye, but this is where our part of the story begins. The owner's grandson, who now ran the company, decided he'd like a summer retreat perched up there on the hill overlooking the valley. He's the one who built what's now called the Fireside Hunting Lodge."

Father Mac rubbed his chin and lowered his voice. "The family still owns the land 'n' the *hoose*. The current owner, our benefactor, converted the summer home into a hunting lodge *soom* 20 years ago."

CHAPTER SIXTY-ONE

The sloping gravel path led them around a blind curve. Following it, they found themselves facing an old brown building that hugged the rock face. Having spent its life in perpetual shade, the building's metal roof was a menagerie of lichens and moss. Orange rust stains on shake-sided walls identified where the gutters leaked.

Gray studied the dented metal door in front of him. "What is this, um, this place?"

"We've reached *oor* destination," Father Mac cheerfully replied.

"You walked us down here to see an old warehouse that looks like it could blow away in the next wind storm?"

"Aye, this is where I led ye, but it shan't blow away. Recall I told ye we'd take a pleasant jaunt 'n' a little ride to get us home? We've had our jaunt. 'Tis time to take the ride." Father Mac opened the exterior door and folded back the accordion safety gate behind it revealing a small, murky room with benches along the walls.

Deeohgee whined and Robbie stroked his muzzle, comforting the dog and himself. "It sure is dark in there," he whispered.

Rebecca reached down and found Robbie's other hand. "It will be okay, honey. I've done this several times."

Taking Emma's hand, Mira led her in and they took a seat. Through the dim light, she looked into the little girl's frightened eyes. *They've both been exposed to enough darkness for one lifetime*, she thought, *now this*. Silently she tried to pray away all the darkness and fear from the children's short lives.

"Funny, it looked much bigger from the outside," Gray said.

"This is only half of it, *dinnae* ye see." The metal wall beside him gave a hollow rumble when he pounded it with the flat of his hand. "All the apparatus is *hoosed* on the other side."

Extending his arms, he lifted one hand and lowered the other.

He wiggled the fingers of the upper hand. "It's an elevator. We're up here right *noo*." He wiggled the other hand. "*Doon* in the glen there's a counter weight keepin' us here."

He moved his hands in opposite directions, lowering one as he raised the other. "As the water's let *oot*, our weight pushes the car down 'n' the counter weight rises. T' go up agin, ye reverse the process." He slowly returned his hands to their original position. "Ready?"

His nervous passengers gave tentative nods.

"Furst, we release the brake." He gave a large crank several turns. "Then we set this jitney in motion." Grabbing the handle beside him, he eased it forward with a grunt.

Metallic creaks echoed around them. Chains rattled and clunked as they moved across their sprockets. After what seemed like an interminable lull, the car shuddered and began a slow descent.

Mira gave a quiet sigh of relief when light filtered in through the heavy trees.

"Ye needn't have worried. 'Twas built by the Army Corps of Engineers... the same folks who constructed the Panama Canal. The Squadron used it t' ferry men and tools *doon* t' the worksite." Father Mac gestured over his shoulder. "Their headquarters sat where the Lodge is today."

"Son of a gun, the old relic still works." Gray sounded both surprised and relieved.

"It's like a Ferris Wheel," Emma said, grinning. She pointed at the treetops appearing outside the wide front window and giggled.

Mira's brow knitted. "Oh dear, I packed my bags like you asked, but they're still sitting in the bedroom. All I have for the babies is what's in the diaper bag."

Father Mac patted her hand. "Don't fret over it. Ye're not the only mum with a wee one. We got plenty o' nappies 'n' such in the village. A cleaning crew will be headin' up as soon as we get *doon* to make things ready for this weekend's arrivals. They'll bring all yur gear back with 'em when they come."

Everyone's head turned when the sounds around them suddenly changed. They heard movement on the other side of the wall accompanied by the sound of running water.

"No need t' fret. We're nearin' the midpoint. That's the ballast tank passin' by on the other side of the wall."

Their smooth descent continued, coming to a stop with a soft thump. Father Mac opened the door and two people were waiting on the landing platform.

Robbie shouted, "Aunt Carolyn! Jonathan!" He and Emma pushed out and raced to them, leaving the adults to disembark.

"Don't hug me too tightly," Mira warned as Carolyn approached. She opened her coat to show her why. "There's a baby onboard." Leila scrunched up her eyes against the sudden brightness and burrowed deeper into Mira's bosom. "Gray's carrying Alexander," she said as she re-buttoned the coat.

Father Mac rested an arm around Gray's shoulder. "Why not leave the wee one with the others so's I *kin* take ye on a tour."

Gray removed his coat and lifted the straps of the baby carrier off of his shoulders. Motioning Jonathan over, he helped him into it. "That's precious cargo you've got there; take care," he said as he turned to join Father Mac.

The old priest pointed to a large building perched on the edge of a fast moving stream. "We'll start here at our generating plant. During timber times they processed logs there. The *mill lade* bounded by rock walls ye see aside the building comes from a river t' the south of us. It powers our turbines for electricity 'n' also provides plenty o' fresh water t' slake our thirst."

"So you're off the grid then? Am I right in guessing it also serves the inn up above?"

The priest shook his head. "They got their own well 'n' power lines. It'd look strange if they didn't. We *dinnae* want someone wonderin' about it *noo* do we?" he said with a wink.

The two men followed a grassy strip that ran through the center of the settlement. At regular intervals paths branched off, each with rows of compact houses on both sides. They'd painted the houses in muted browns and grays to blend into the shadows. Their dark green metal roofs matched the needles on the branches that sheltered them.

It reminded Gray of a forested campground he'd once stayed in with his parents on a family vacation. He tilted his head back, staring up at the tall trees. "Now I understand why we couldn't see the houses from up above."

"Aye. Once the logging stopped and they abandoned the logging camp, the trees self-seeded themselves. Now, ye couldn't take 'em *oot* without destroyin' the *hooses*." The old priest smiled. "Best git accustomed to living with plenty o' shade."

"The houses seem small," Gray said as they walked, "and so much alike they could've been made with a cookie cutter."

"Each one's a *cottar hoose*, built for a workman 'n' his family. They have two bedrooms, one fur mum and dad 'n' one fur the little 'uns. A few have another room tacked on t' the back. Don't ye worry, they're nice enough inside. We'd not put ye up in a *brothy*."

Father Mac paused as they walked, introducing Gray to other families in the settlement. Each time they stopped, Gray noticed an occasional derelict house sitting among the newer homes. He said nothing until they turned down a lane with a freshly painted home at each corner. The rest of the lane consisted of nothing but weatherworn shacks surrounded by sagging fences.

The scene stopped him in his tracks. The comparison between these tumbled-down buildings and the sparkling homes at the corner couldn't have been starker. Their old roofs, if one could even call them that, consisted of little more than curled and tattered shingles bravely clinging to exposed lath. The original four over four windows were each missing one or more panes and years of weathering had stripped away most of the exterior paint leaving behind gray, splintered siding.

Reading Gray's disheartened expression Father Mac stepped beside him and softly said, "When a *boody's* been *oot* in bad weather, it takes some time front o' the fire afore they feel themselves *agin*. The *hooses* ye see there have been left t' the elements since the 1950's. *Dinnae* let the way they look dampen yur spirits. They built them to last, sturdy and true. Our men give 'em a good going over, fixin' what they can and replacin'—"

He stopped midsentence and stared back. "I see the women and children acomin'. Let's wait *fur* them so I can give ye all the grand tour."

CHAPTER SIXTY-TWO

"We must let go of the life we have planned, so as to accept the one that is waiting for us." ~ Joseph Campbell

Robbie and Emma broke away from the adults and ran to Gray. Brimming with excitement, they talked over each other as they told him of the *neat* things they'd seen along the way.

Mira came up beside Gray and kissed his cheek. "Carolyn says we're going to love our new home."

Gray ran his eyes down the row of weathered buildings. "Depends upon which one is ours, wouldn't you say?"

"I thought we'd left Mr. Gloom and Doom behind." Mira elbowed him in the ribs. "Now quit *yur* lookin' at them *auld hooses,"* she mimicked. "He'll not put us up in a *brothy*."

Father Mac chuckled and handed Gray a key. "Best ye decide *fur* yourself. 'Tis the corner *hoose* that has your name put upon it."

Gray hurried ahead and cautiously walked onto the covered porch, unconsciously testing its solidity as he crossed to the door. Unlike its neglected neighbors, which had narrow plank siding, the house had a new board and batten exterior with vinyl double-paned windows. When Gray opened the door, warm air mingled with a hint of fresh paint wafted out. The others quickly rushed in behind him, filling the carpeted living room.

The house's floor plan was a simple square bisected by the entry door on one end and a bedroom hallway on the other. The living room, not overly large but adequate, lay to Gray's left. On his right was an equally large eat-in kitchen with a half wall enclosing the dining area. The house had three bedrooms, the largest on the living room side. Across the hall was a bath along with a smaller bedroom. A door at the end of the hall opened into a third bedroom added onto the back.

After a quick glance into the kitchen, Mira headed down the hall with Emma trailing close behind. She opened the door on the left first. A double bed. "This will be Mom and Dad's bedroom."

Emma opened the door across the hall and peeked in. "Just the bathroom." Moving on down, she opened the other door and saw two cribs. "Here's the baby room."

Mira grasped the handle of the door at the end of the hall. "And I'll bet dollars to donuts this one is for you."

Emma gasped when she saw a twin bed with an apricot spread and lemon yellow ruffled curtains at the window. She pirouetted around the room singing, "My bedroom, my bedroom, I'm going to have my very own bedroom." She suddenly stopped and stared up at Mira. "Where will Robbie sleep?"

"At his Gramma's house," Rebecca said as she joined them. She pointed out the window. "We're right behind you; drop in for cookies anytime."

Carolyn, Jonathan and Robbie joined in admiring Emma's bedroom.

Mira turned to Rebecca. "Leila's telling me it's time to eat. I'm going into the baby's room. Could you get Alexander out of his carrier and bring him to me?"

Rebecca and Carolyn followed Mira into the room while Jonathan headed down the hall to join the men. Robbie trailed behind Emma. When she reached the doorway she spun around and spread her arms, blocking his path. "You can't come in here. This is for ladies only."

Robbie glared at her. "You're not a lady; you're just a kid."

Emma lifted her chin. "I'm a *young* lady." She reached for the doorknob. "Now leave us alone."

He gave her a nasty look before stomping down the hall to join the men.

Father Mac chuckled when he noticed Gray rocking slightly to test the strength of the kitchen floor. "Strong enough fur ye?"

He turned and gave the priest a sheepish look. "Guilty as charged. After seeing those weather beaten derelicts, I had my doubts."

"Ye needn't have worried. The building crew always pulls up

the old floorboards. They check the joists 'n' replace them if necessary afore layin' down the new floor. They rip *oot* all the old plaster and lath, replace any damaged studs, 'n' hang drywall. The *hoose* has new windows, doors and roof along with new wiring. They also take away the heat stove and chimney," he pointed at the sleek white baseboards, "and replace it with these electrical units. He crossed his arms and rubbed away an imaginary chill. "'Tis gonna feel mighty cozy on a cold winter's night."

Gray's face reflected his surprise. "But electric heat is inefficient. With so much wood available, why not burn some it?"

"Aye, there's plenty o' wood alright, but we've got other priorities."

Gray's raised eyebrows demanded further explanation.

Father Mac chuckled. "*Fur* instance, smoke rising out of the trees could lead a *boody* t' think there's a forest fire. A hot stove presents a hazard for families with wee ones crawlin' *aboot*. The bottom line is, electricity comes to us at very little cost. We generate all we can use and more." He smiled. "If *yur* wonderin' what we did with the wire; 'tis tucked away underground. Even the biggest storms *dinnae* faze us."

Gray ran his eyes around the room a second time. "How do you pay for... for all of this?"

Father Mac took a deep breath and rested an elbow on the kitchen counter. "A wee bit here 'n' a wee bit there; it all adds *oop*. The profits from the Lodge go into the community fund. Folks contribute toward the cost of their home, if they're able. Many work at the Lodge. The wood 'n' other materials come to us from one of the owner's companies. One way or another, the good Lord sees we're taken care of."

A bored Robbie tugged at Gray's shirt sleeve. "I'm hungry."

Jonathan laughed and squatted down in front of Robbie. "Mom, I mean *Aunt Carolyn*, has lunch ready over at your house. When the ladies come out, we'll go over there and eat. Okay?"

Robbie smiled and nodded. "I want to see *my* room!"

80CR

When Robbie saw his room he jumped up and down, clapping his hands. Printed on his window curtains and bedspread were fluffy brown bears. A shelf full of young boy's toys adorned one wall, but best of all, a huge stuffed toy bear sat in the center of his bed. He made a running leap onto the bed. Falling onto the giant bear, he hugged it and grinned.

Emma squirmed between the men. "Mom says lunch is ready, come get it."

"I 'spose ye'll be wantin' to bring that beastie to lunch with us." Father Mac eyed Robbie and chuckled. "Don't think he'll fit through the kitchen door though."

"Yes he will," Robbie said. He gave the bear a tug. It barely moved. "Maybe he'd be happier stayin' here."

As they ate, a sense of relief filled the house like the calm after a frightening storm.

When Father Mac left after lunch, Gray and Mira returned to their house with Emma and the twins in tow. Moments later a crew from the Lodge arrived with their suitcases and other belongings. They'd barely opened the first suitcase when they heard a knock at the door.

Gray opened it to find Jonathan and several men from the village holding large boxes of groceries. They carried the boxes into the kitchen and sat them on the counter. "This should be enough to get you started," Jonathan said after making introductions. "Save the boxes. You can return them tomorrow and get anything else you need when Mom takes you over to the store."

While the twins slept in their new cribs, Gray and Emma finished stocking the bedroom dressers and closets as Mira opened the kitchen cupboards and decided where things should go. She'd never undertaken a happier task. We've escaped at last, she thought, and the FFU and its craziness seems no more than a bad dream. She whispered a prayer of thanksgiving as she stacked canned goods on a shelf.

That evening she cooked her first meal in their new home. It was nothing elaborate, just spaghetti with a sauce made from hamburger, tomato paste, canned mushrooms and spices. She heated garlic bread in the oven, steamed fresh green beans and opened canned peaches for dessert.

Gray sat on Mira's right with Emma on her left. The twins lay in their carriers on the other side of the table.

"How is everything?" Mira asked.

Emma gave her a big smile. "This is the bestest dinner I ever had."

"My thoughts exactly," Gray said, reaching for Mira's hand.

That evening, amid yawns, the young family retired early. As they lay snuggled in bed, Mira threw her arm over Gray's chest. "Do you miss that great big bed at the Lodge? This one is so much smaller."

"Are you kidding? This is perfect. I like having you close." He kissed her forehead.

"I like it too." She sighed. "Everyone seems so friendly. I feel safe here." She tilted her chin and looked into his eyes. "Do you think you can be happy in this village? It's so different."

"I'll be happy wherever I am, as long as it's with you."

"I feel a bit guilty though. There are so many children still being sacrificed. Shouldn't we do more?"

"We'll talk to Father Mac about it tomorrow. I doubt the other villagers feel any differently than we do. They probably *are* doing something."

"You always know just the right thing to say." Snuggling against him, she whispered, "Listen."

Gray cocked his head. "I don't hear anything."

"I know. Isn't it wonderful?" She rolled in his arms to kiss him.

CHAPTER SIXTY-THREE

They settled into the village quickly, making many friends. Over the next five years their lives became more happy and peaceful than they could have ever envisioned.

The *hooses* they moved into blossomed. Mira and Rebecca created a path between their two homes and bordered the area between them with flowering plants. A lush garden provided a larder of fresh fruits and vegetables which they canned each summer and enjoyed during winter rains or occasional snowstorms.

A coniferous forest sheltered the village from above; yet allowed enough sunlight to filter through and nourish the gardens that grew well in the rich silt loam soil.

Rebecca dropped onto a backyard bench and wiped her brow. "Mira, come sit with me. We deserve a rest."

Mira laughed. "You rest," she said, patting the older woman's shoulder. "I want to hoe over here before I quit. Gray and the kids will be back soon. I have to take advantage of times when he takes them to the playground. Robbie and Emma aren't a problem, but those five-year-olds. They seem to challenge one another to see who can be the most mischievous."

Rebecca nodded, smiling. "They're loveable though, and bless Gray for being such a good dad." Watching Mira work, Rebecca longed for some of the younger woman's energy. She sighed in acceptance. "The village keeps growing and growing. So many families keep arriving with more children than the state allows. Duncanville housing must be near full capacity."

"That's what Gray says. I never thought of him as a contractor kind of guy, but he's doing a great job directing the construction crews." She heaved a sigh. "If only things could slow down. He works so many long hours and comes home worn out. But, he refuses to let the influx of people exceed the number of homes available for them."

"Well, at least he's taken the weekend off. The kids must be thrilled to have extra time with him."

Mira leaned on her hoe and winked at Rebecca. "Oh yes. And I'm happy to have a few hours for myself."

Rebecca smiled. "Are you going to the Print Shop this afternoon?"

Mira tossed a hand full of weeds on the pile destined to become mulch. "No, it's Gray's turn to go. I'll be home with Emma and the twins."

"Why not send them over to my place? Then you can go with Gray."

"Really? Would you mind? That would be so nice."

"I'm glad to help any way I can. They always need extra sets of hands to package the latest batch of Life Chances brochures on Saturdays before the truck arrives to get them. I'm not much help; I tire out too quickly."

Mira brushed off her hands and dropped onto the bench beside Rebecca. "Have you seen the recent production run of brochures? They didn't pull any punches. Color photos of cute children going into the gas chambers and another of them coming out limp and dead. It's heartbreaking."

Mira wiped her brow with the back of her hand. "But, the brochure distributions are helping. I think the tide has turned and most of the public finally objects to the insanity of it all." She bent forward, elbows on her knees and chin in her hands, staring off into space. "All these years later though. It's taking so long to end the butchery."

Rebecca placed an arm around her friend's shoulders. "It may not have ended yet, but it will. Not soon enough, but it will."

੩੦੨

Mira and Gray entered the Print Shop, letting the door slam behind them. Their neighbors moved along tables sorting and packing newly printed tri-fold brochures. An erasable whiteboard hung at the end of the room listing city names with tallies below them.

"Miami's asking for twice as many brochures this time as they did before," Gray noted. "That must be an indication that they've doubled the number of volunteers willing to distribute the bulletins. That's a good sign."

Mira nodded. "Look at Boston. Their requests have grown too. Who'd have expected that?" Her eyes scanned the board. "Oh my, almost every major city is asking for more brochures. How will we ever keep up?"

"The same way we always do. Our needs are always met." He gave her a kiss. "I think this means we're getting closer and closer to ending the government mantra of *A Planned Society Makes Good Sense*. We're actually a *controlled society* and there's no sense in that. Freedom is coming. The day is near when children will be valued and not sacrificed."

Mira was encasing a package of 500 brochures in clear plastic wrap when Father Mac ran into the Print Shop shouting and waving his hands. The background chatter of a dozen voices abruptly stopped.

"Everyone, everyone, listen!" Anxiety etched his features. "Dixon just phoned with terrible news." He stopped to take a deep breath. "Two safe villages on the other side of the country are being attacked. Right now, as I speak."

"Attacked?" Mira gripped Gray's arm for support.

Everyone began talking at once as they rushed to Father Mac's side.

"Hush now. Hush," he said, raising his hands in a soothing gesture. "Let me finish telling you all of it." He paused to catch his breath. "Dixon says few people knew aboot these villages. I'd not heerd o' 'em, but somehow the government discovered 'em. They were abandoned, forgotten resorts from the 1920's, overgrown in the Appalachian mountains, one in Tennessee and one in North Carolina. Not as forgotten as we hoped."

"My God," a man said, "They must be searching out safe places everywhere. How long before they find others? Maybe even us?"

Father Mac placed a hand on the man's shoulder and shook his head. "Being hidden from above makes us safer than most. Not everyone's as lucky. Let's pray for those they've found."

After a quick, but intense prayer, Father Mac turned toward everyone present. "We must call a meeting of our whole community and let everyone know aboot this. 'Tis possible survivors will be directed here for shelter."

"Let's hope there are survivors," Gray said. "I've witnessed how organized our government's violence can be." He lifted his hands in a gesture of exasperation. "We're already crowded, but we can't turn anyone away. We need a plan to provide for those who manage to escape. Up to now we've been rehabbing the old worker's cottages, but we've only got a few left. When they're gone, what do we do? Should we build from the ground up?"

Father Mac shook his head. "I don't think we have time."

"So," Gray said, "we need to identify housing that families can double up in."

The once spirited room became totally quiet.

ໜ

Within a few days, people began to straggle in and the villagers welcomed them, offering sympathy and understanding. The safe community, formerly called Duncanville, soon found itself inundated with refugees. They couldn't provide enough housing for everyone and many of the residents found themselves forced to make room in their homes for strangers.

Mira and Rebecca quickly decided to release Rebecca's home for the refugees. She and Robbie moved in with Mira and Gray.

"I've given the arrangements some thought," Rebecca said. "I think the two boys should share the twins' room and Leila can move in with Emma." Mira started to object, but Rebecca raised her hand. "Wait, let me finish. I'll take the living room couch."

Mira knit her brows together. "That hardly seems fair, or comfortable."

"I think it makes perfect sense. I'll have more privacy in the living room than crowding into a bedroom with the girls, or sharing one with Robbie. Why force three children into one room? They'll never go to sleep; and I'll sleep better in the living room by myself." Rebecca smiled and nodded. "It's settled."

To Leila's delight, she moved in with big sister, Emma. Robbie wasn't as happy about sharing the twins' room with younger Alexander, but knowing the circumstances, he gave in with only moderate grumbling.

ഇൻൽ

Everyone in the village hoped and prayed the violent attacks on the safe villages would stop.

But they didn't.

Believing they threatened the strength of the state, the government was determined to find and destroy all the safe villages. Gradually, the government's *internal security force* worked its way across the country, locating and attacking more and more of the hidden sites where people were living free and at peace.

The government attempted to conceal the wanton violence from the public, but Dixon and Brody wouldn't let them. The cousins managed to secure film footage of the many brutal attacks, and fed the images of killing, burning and carnage into every outlet they could.

One or two attacks might have been forgotten, but the state didn't stop with a few villages. Films of horror and death filled the air waves week after week. Faced with the reality of cruelty again and again, the public's anger and dissention began to grow.

While all of this was going on, the people in Gray and Mira's village monitored the path of destruction and held their breath. In spite of their increased numbers, the village grew eerily quiet.

Eventually, after a long lull in the violence, they started to believe they'd remained hidden like Father Mac said they would. Life in the village felt almost normal again.

CHAPTER SIXTY-FOUR

Mira wrapped a robe around herself and headed for the bedroom door.

"Where are you going?" Gray asked.

"To talk to Rebecca. We can't get much said with the kids underfoot, so we have to talk while they're asleep."

"What about talking to me?"

"We get to talk in bed every night. It's Rebecca I don't get to talk to. Go to sleep."

He rolled over and obeyed.

Mira padded out into the living room. "Rebecca?"

"Come on in. I'm more than ready for our girl talk."

Mira smiled. Having the elderly woman and Robbie move in with them wasn't a burden. Mira had grown to enjoy having them so close, sharing meals and other duties. "I think the kids need to have something to cheer them up. They need to have some fun again."

"I agree. Robbie's birthday's coming up. We could use it as an excuse to plan a party at the Lodge and invite all the young village children."

"Wow. That'd be an undertaking." A line appeared between Mira's brows as she considered it. Then she relaxed. "I'm game if you are. Butterscotch needs to come back down to the village; we could do it after the party."

"Do you mind that Carolyn decided to make your cat the Lodge mascot?"

"No. He seems happy with the assignment and makes up to every new guest. The children will enjoy having him at the party. I'll bring Deeohgee up to the Lodge too. He loves being with the kids and is always thrilled to see Butterscotch."

"The children all love Deeohgee."

"Not everyone got to keep their pets before arriving here," Mira said. "Maybe he helps fill that void a little."

ഔൽ

The day of Robbie's party arrived and the children excitedly packed as many as possible into the tram that carried them to the mountain lodge above the village. Those who had to wait, were stomping their feet and complaining by the time the empty contrivance returned for them. Only having Deeohgee wait with them soothed their impatience.

As they waited with the children, Rebecca linked her arm in Mira's. "It's so good to have something pleasant to look forward to."

"It's been a lot of work. Thank goodness Carolyn and some of the mothers helped us get it ready."

As the empty tram lowered in front of them, Mira and Rebecca climbed into it with the last of the children. Deeohgee brought up the rear.

They couldn't have asked for a more perfect, Spring day.

ഔൽ

Carolyn rushed into the house shouting Jonathan's name.

"What is it, Mom?"

"Father Mac is sending a warning throughout the village." Breathless, she gulped air before continuing. "Dixon called again. We have to get up to the Lodge and tell them!"

"Why? What's happening?"

"I'll explain on the way. We have to hurry."

Jonathan helped his mother place an arm into her sweater and draped the other side over her shoulder. He grabbed their coats before racing out the door. The tram ride to the Lodge could be chilly.

ಐ�

Children's laughter and giggles echoed through the Lodge's large ballroom.

"Thank you for making this such a great party for Robbie," Rebecca said.

"Nonsense." Mira threw an arm around Rebecca and hugged her. "I love him too, and you worked just as hard" Mira patted her stomach. "Look what's left of the beautiful cake you baked."

"I'm glad we did this," Rebecca said. "The children deserved a little joy after weeks surrounded by the tension gripping our village. But, you know this sets a precedent. We'll have to plan another huge party when Emma's birthday arrives."

"That's okay, however, we're all going to be tired tomorrow after the kids keep us up half the night. A sleepover? What were we thinking?" Mira shook her head. "Oh dear, imagine when the twins begin to expect real parties too, and not just family like in the past."

Rebecca's eyes sparkled with joy. "It's worth the work. Being so happy sometimes scares me. Outside our village, people aren't living the way we are."

"No sense worrying about an unknown future," Mira said. "Let's just be happy today."

Robbie's giggle caught their attention and they turned to watch him tear open a birthday present as children from the village crowded around him. Robbie tossed the ribbons aside, and Butterscotch happily attacked them, making the children laugh.

Given their isolation and relatively low income, there wouldn't be lots of presents and most of those were handmade. Mira and Rebecca pooled their money to buy his biggest gift and chose to have Emma present it.

Through the happy chatter, Emma shouted, "Here Robbie, open this one next."

Taking the wrapped package, he smiled as he tore off the blue paper. "Oh, combat boots, just like I wanted. Wow!" He lifted the boots out of their box and a pair of heavy socks fell into his lap. He picked them up and turned them over. "These are great too. You're the best Emma."

She grinned. "Gramma said you wanted the boots and she picked out the size, but I chose the black ones with red lightning on the sides. I knew you'd like them best. I picked out the socks too."

"I'm gonna put them on right now." As he took off his sneakers, Butterscotch tried to play with his laces and he had to push the cat aside.

"Here, I'll get him out of your way." Emma picked him up and hugged him to her. While the boys crowded around to watch Robbie put his boots on, the girls moved to Emma to scratch Butterscotch's head or stroke his back.

Gray joined the women, and nudged Mira. "Look at Robbie trying to get those boots on. I better go help him lace 'em up."

Mira shoved a lock of hair behind her ear. "I think the kids enjoyed the games, but it was the food that won them over. We're all too well fed. The party favors are a big hit too."

"The tiny flashlights on glasses frames like headlamps they can wear? Kids love that kind of stuff. They'll pester their parents to let them go outside at night to use them."

"More likely they'll use them in their bedrooms at night to stay awake longer than they should." The women laughed.

Still smiling, Rebecca said, "It's been a wonderful day, a simply wonderful day."

"Yes, it has." Mira reached for Rebecca's hand, unaware that it was the last time they'd ever touch.

₧)(₨

Robbie marched around in his new combat boots while boys oohed and aahed over them, and girls shook their heads in wonderment.

Gray stood back and admired the kind, generous boy he loved like a son. Turning toward Mira, he saw Jonathan enter the ballroom and rush toward her. *Something's wrong.* Gray raced over to them.

"Jonathan, welcome. Glad you decided to join us," Mira said. "Where's Carolyn? Is she here too?"

Jonathan paused to catch his breath. "She's coming. I ran ahead. The phones are down; we came to warn you."

Gray took him by the shoulders and began leading him toward the kitchen. "Let's not upset the children."

"They're going to be upset soon enough." Jonathan grimaced. "The authorities are doing aerial reconnaissance not far from the village. They're searching us out and will likely be here soon, very soon."

"How can that be?" Gray asked. "I watch the news and there's been nothing reported in weeks. Surely Dixon would have…"

"It was Dixon who warned us. The authorities have found a way to keep Brody and Dixon quiet for now. Dixon wants us to prepare, maybe even evacuate."

In shock, Gray didn't speak. Then the silence was broken with the extremely loud rushing swoosh of a missile, immediately followed by KA-BOOM!

They all jerked and ducked as loud booms echoed up from the village below. Frightened yells from the children carried through the ballroom as the adults rushed to them. Outside the floor to ceiling windows they saw helicopters fly past heading to the village.

"They don't know the Lodge is connected in any way to the safe village," Carolyn said. "Thank God all the children are up here."

"Not all," Mira gasped. "We left the twins with a babysitter. I've got to get to them." She ran to the exit, frantic to reach the tram.

"Jonathan, stay with Rebecca and the children," Gray yelled, hurrying after Mira. "Get them away from the windows. Rebecca take them to the shelter. Go!" Then he rushed out of the ballroom and was lost from sight.

"Children, come with me where we'll be safe," called Rebecca. They all flocked to her, except for Emma.

In the roars from the valley below, no one heard Emma. "Mom," she shrieked, and whirled to try and catch Mira and Gray.

Robbie saw Emma run off and bit his lip. *No one else sees her.* How could he let her go alone? He spun around and ran after the person he loved most in the world.

Rebecca moaned as she watched Robbie disappear. She grabbed Jonathan's arm stretching up to speak into his ear over the noise. "Please. Robbie and Emma aren't here. I can't leave the others."

He patted her hand. "Don't worry, I'll get them," Jonathan hollered above the noise. "You take the rest of the kids to that shelter and we'll join you." Realizing they must have followed Gray and Mira to the tram, he loped after them, hoping to overtake them.

CHAPTER SIXTY-FIVE

"Political language... is designed to make lies sound truthful and murder respectable, and to give an appearance of solidity to pure wind." ~ George Orwell

Some of the village children stood unmoving, staring at the large windows. Black smoke circled up from the valley below. Dark, sleek helicopter gunships sailed out beyond the windows, flames appearing to rip from their bellies.

Carolyn came puffing up to Rebecca's side. "I saw what happened. Trust Jonathan to protect them. You have to lead us to safety."

Rebecca's face was pale as she stood staring at the windows. Carolyn prepared to slap her into action, but Rebecca nodded. With great effort she turned toward the other children and away from Robbie and Emma.

As they sent up prayers for friends and loved ones in the village below, the two women gathered the children and guided them out of the ballroom and away from the large windows.

"I'll follow and make sure we don't lose any more kids," Carolyn said.

"We must get Deeohgee. Mira shut him in a bedroom when he got too exuberant."

"There's not enough time..."

"He can help soothe the children," Rebecca said, "and it's on the way."

⁎

Robbie ran as fast as he could, but he couldn't see Emma running ahead of him any longer. "Emma! Wait for me!"

Robbie stumbled to a stop at the tram entrance, trying to catch his breath. The tram's descent hummed and squealed as it moved away. Emma waved at him from inside the car where she sat with Gray and Mira. As it vanished over the lip of the hill, Robbie stomped his foot and tried not to cry. Jonathan came up behind him and squeezed his shoulder.

It was then that they heard the loudest explosion of all. It echoed through the valley as the shock wave lifted them off their feet and threw them to the ground.

Struggling up onto their elbows, they watched in horror as portions of the tram's superstructure pulled away from the mountain and slowly crumpled into the valley. The additional weight stretched the main cable beyond its limits. Suddenly severed, the thick black cable twisted in the air, its frayed ends extending outward like a snake's fangs.

Robbie leaped up and scrambled toward the hillside. Jonathan's strong arm jerked him back. Robbie struggled briefly, sobbed and went limp as a deafening roar rumbled up the hillside. Clouds of dust and debris filled the air around them.

Then everything went silent.

"My God," Jonathan murmured. He held the sobbing Robbie to his chest. He wasn't about to let go and have him suffer whatever fate the others had.

"Emma...Mama Mira..." Tears streaked down Robbie's face.

Jonathan struggled to remain calm. Did Gray, Mira and Emma reach the end of the line before the tram's structure collapsed?

If so, where are they now?

His thoughts turned dismal. It wasn't likely they survived the destruction, and that caused fresh grief over Aranda to the surface from where he'd buried it years ago. Overwhelming sorrow threatened to overcome him, but he couldn't allow it to. Not for himself, but for Robbie.

߈ࠨ

Carolyn lifted the smallest child under her one arm and hurried as quickly as she could after Rebecca. Between the sobs and cries of the children, she heard Rebecca urging them forward and through a panel in the wall. She prayed Jonathan and the others were all right as she hugged the little girl to her.

"Carolyn," Rebecca called, shoving the dog into the opening behind the children. "We're going on a short ride. You're last, so be sure to pull the panel closed behind you. Find the strap and yank it!"

"What? Wait! I don't understand." Before Carolyn reached her, Rebecca disappeared into the hole in the wall, and Carolyn leaned forward to peer inside. In the dim light she could see children, wearing their eyeglass lights, swooshing downward on a long metal slide. She gulped and cuddled the youngster to her as she sat down and bent over to fit through the opening.

"Hang on Sweetie, I've got to let go of you for a moment. Feeling around she found a leather handhold. Before she could pull it, the little girl wriggled off her lap and out the opening in the wall. "Baby, wait! It's not safe out there."

Running down the hallway, the little girl turned over her shoulder and called back, "The kitty. We can't leave the kitty. I'll get him!"

She had to go after the child. But thoughts of getting off the ground with one arm, and no one to help, alarmed Carolyn. Then the crash of shattering windows followed by a flash of flame sent an adrenalin surge through her.

They're attacking the Lodge!

She scrambled backwards, leaned against a wall and gradually shoved her way against it until she was upright.

Glass crunched beneath her feet as she ran after her little charge. She frowned that she didn't even know the little girl's name. "Sweetheart, where are you? Please call to me so I can find you." She looked under furniture and opened closet doors.

Loud booms continued echoing in the valley below. When she didn't immediately find the little girl, she wanted to weep.

The yowl of a frightened cat caught her attention. She turned to see the child scurry around a corner holding the frantic cat. It was much too big for her, but she didn't let go.

"It's okay, kitty. Don't be afraid," the little girl murmured. "We'll save you."

The huge yellow cat allowed the little girl to carry him amidst all the noise and chaos. She hugged him to her under his front legs while his back legs dangled in front of her. Carolyn couldn't believe her eyes. Although he cried, he barely struggled in the little girl's arms. It was as if her reassurances had him mesmerized.

Carolyn pulled off her sweater and draped it over Butterscotch. "Maybe this will help keep him quiet."

Dodging large pieces of broken window glass, they made their way back to the wall panel that led to the shelter. Carolyn sat down and held the sweater-wrapped cat while the little girl climbed into her lap, then the child took Butterscotch back into her arms.

Inching forward farther into the hole, Carolyn reached back for the strap that would close the wall panel behind them. Suddenly a tremendous boom caused everything around them to shake, and flames shot across the floor. Heat radiated behind them, and Carolyn yanked on the strap as forcefully as she could.

The wooden panel began to slide closed behind them as flames whipped at the opening. She felt her hair singe and reached back to be sure nothing was burning. Frightened herself, Carolyn realized the child – so brave moments before – had started to cry.

Carolyn took a deep breath and whispered, "Don't worry little one, this ride will be fun." She hoped it would be. Lifting her heels she gave a slight push forward, just enough to launch their glide toward the gloom below.

‽‽

"Robbie, we can't do anything here." Jonathan looked into

the boy's tear-stained and dust covered face. Pulling his hand into his cuff, he wiped his sleeve across Robbie's chubby cheek. "The tram is gone and we have to get back to your grandma."

Robbie's eyes were vacant, although tears continued to make tracks through the grime.

"You okay?"

Robbie didn't answer.

Jonathan lifted Robbie and turned back the way they'd come. *Robbie's in shock*, Jonathan thought. *Maybe I am too.* He shivered. He had no idea where the safe shelter was that Gray ordered the women to.

At the Lodge Jonathan continued to carry a silent Robbie while he wandered the hallways, calling out names as they searched.

"Robbie, I can't find your grandma. The shelter she took the other children to must be so well hidden that maybe we won't find it." He looked into Robbie's soft brown eyes, and saw no recognition there. "So, we're on our own, buddy. We need to leave the Lodge and hide in the woods on the other side. Do you understand me?"

Still no response.

Helicopter gunships whirred overhead and machine gun shots ripped through the front doors. Jonathan spun around and raced upstairs to put greater distance from them. On the opposite side of the building, he carried Robbie out onto a second-story balcony. He sat Robbie down near the back wall and walked to the balcony's cement railing. He traversed the length of it from one end to the other, leaning over and looking below.

Okay, there has to be a safe way to climb down off this thing. But, he saw none.

A helicopter's loud rotor blades announced its approach, and Jonathan raced back to Robbie. Joining him in the wall's shade, he hoped they could remain hidden. Jets of flame shot out from the helicopter. Explosive booms followed. *Too close.* The building shuttered, and a gaping hole appeared in the roof.

Why are they targeting the Lodge?

"Robbie, I'm going to put you on my back. I want you to hang onto my shoulders so you won't fall." He hitched Robbie around and the child grabbed his neck to cling tightly to him, so tight that it was difficult for Jonathan to breath.

Well, at least you're responding to me now.

Jonathan removed his belt and reached to secure it around Robbie's back and across his own chest. It barely reached, but he was able to hook it in the last hole. He breathed a sigh of relief. If Robbie did let go, the belt should keep them strapped together and prevent him from falling.

Jonathan approached the far side of the balcony and looked down over the cement railing. He chose this spot because there were hedges below, and he hoped they'd help if he fell.

He planned to throw a leg over the three-foot-high balcony wall where there were openings to allow water to drain off. His foot should fit neatly through the backside of one of them. From there he intended to transfer a handhold down to the floor level and allow himself to hang freely from the floor of the balcony, putting them closer to the ground when he let go. Jonathan expected to hit the ground with his feet and then lean to one side so that he wouldn't fall backward onto Robbie.

Unfortunately, they ran out of time.

Jonathan was reaching down, trying to find a decent hand hold when another helicopter passed overhead. Tingles of fear crawled up his spine as he felt the pilot's eyes scan the building.

He's seen us!

Jonathan listened to the helicopter's engine rev, and watched it rise in the sky. The chopper slowly banked into a wheeling turn.

He watched windows implode and walls blow apart. The chaos mesmerized Jonathan, feeling more an observer than a participant in this unfolding drama of death.

He snapped back to reality an instant later when he saw the craft level out for a strafing run.

"Robbie," he shouted over the pulsing thump of the approaching helicopter, "hang on. We're going for a short ride."

Jonathan threw his leg over the wall.

Sparks spewed from the gun as the first tracer rounds phosphoresced around them.

Amid an ear-splitting blast of flame with pieces of cement exploding near them, the two tumbled downward.

CHAPTER SIXTY-SIX

Carolyn zoomed down the incline with the child clutched to her chest and the cat wrapped in her sweater, struggling to hold onto them both with one arm.

How are we going to stop? I can't let go of the child.

Rebecca waited at the bottom as they careened toward the room below. A few feet from the end of the slide, Carolyn felt Rebecca's arms reach for her to slow their descent.

"I didn't think you'd want to land on your backside like I did." Rebecca took the child and sat her next to her companions. "I worried you were never coming. What happened?"

"This happened," Carolyn said, setting the cat down.

"Butterscotch!" a child yelled. The children surrounded him, kissing and petting the yellow feline. He began to purr as if this kind of excitement was an everyday occurrence.

Stepping back, Rebecca brushed singed hairs from Carolyn's back. "Looks like you had a close call."

"We survived, that's what counts. I'm still worried though."

Suddenly an especially loud boom caused everyone to jump. The two older women watched plaster dust fall from the ceiling and instinctively reached for each other's hand.

"They're attacking the Lodge?"

"Yes, they are," Carolyn said.

Six-year-old Lucy's brown eyes turned to Rebecca. "Are we okay?"

Rebecca placed a hand on the child. "We'll be safe here."

Were Jonathan, Robbie, Emma and the others okay as well?

"We're in a bunker Gray built," she told Carolyn. "Once we close off the chute with the slide, it will be fireproof...soundproof too. There's enough food and water to sustain several adults and children for a full month if necessary. He even made sure there's dog and cat food."

At mention of the dog, Carolyn spun around looking for Deeohgee. The yellow lab was sprawled in a corner on his back, legs in the air, as two little boys scratched his chest.

Carolyn moved to Rebecca's side. "I saw…" She stopped midsentence as frightened little faces stared up at her, all ears.

"Later," Rebecca said. "Kids, the 'copters can't reach us here. They're trying to make everyone leave the village. Do you remember practicing escape routes with your folks?" Heads nodded around the room.

Lucy bit her lip, trying not to cry. Rebecca gathered the little girl into her arms. Soon all the children crowded around Rebecca, who'd read to them every week at the village library.

Carolyn suddenly felt very alone. They don't know me, she thought. Then a little hand wrapped around hers. She looked down. The little girl who rescued Butterscotch smiled up at her.

℘♋

After the children were asleep on cots or in blankets on the floor, Rebecca and Carolyn made their way to a secluded corner. They spoke in hushed whispers.

Carolyn pulled her sweater over her shoulder. "There was fire upstairs when I closed the panel. How will we ever get out of here if they burn down the Lodge?"

"Gray thought of that. There's another exit that goes out the back of a hillside. It's well away from the village with a cement blast door. It's completely hidden by wild blackberries."

Leaning close, Carolyn whispered, "Listen."

The silence within the insulated bunker was almost complete. The only sounds came from the breathing and gentle snores of exhausted children. Whatever happened outside remained a mystery.

"There might be patrols in the woods looking for survivors," Carolyn said. "We should wait at least a few days before leaving."

Rebecca agreed. "We have everything we need here to keep us for a good long time."

Carolyn's gaze rested on the little girl she'd tucked in a short while ago. "The longer we stay hidden, the more worried the children are going to be about their parents."

"They're more resilient than average kids," said Rebecca. "All of them went through safety drills over and over again, and listened to stories about the government. They know they need to avoid anyone related to the government."

"What a sad way to grow up."

Rebecca looked at Carolyn. "At least they *can* grow up. For most of their lives they've had loving parents, friends, an education, plenty to eat and warm clothes. How many children today don't have any of that?"

"Right," Carolyn said, "but all children should be allowed to live without want and without fear." Her thoughts turned to her son, Jonathan, and the others. *Were they safe?* Yet, for now, her focus had to be on these children.

She watched Rebecca put her elbows on her knees and rest her chin in the palms of her hands. She began to silently sob into her handkerchief.

Carolyn reached around Rebecca's shoulders. "I know what you must be feeling. My son Jonathan is out there somewhere too."

The two women huddled closer together and gazed at the ceiling. Both became lost in thoughts of their loved ones.

හ)ଔ

As soon as Jonathan hit the ground, he leaned over and whipped off the belt strapping Robbie to his back. The youngster fell to the earth. Jonathan scooped Robbie up in his arms and ran for the woods.

A blast of flame roared out of the helicopter directly behind them. A small rocket hit the ground and exploded. Jonathan leaped forward with a cry. It scorched the back of his jacket, singed his hair and left a burn on his neck, but he didn't slow down. He ran faster than he'd ever run before.

The moment they burst into the tree line, Jonathan veered to the left. Seconds later another rocket hit the spot where they'd entered. His lungs burned, and it didn't help to have Robbie wriggle to wrap his arms tightly around Jonathan's neck. Yet, he kept pushing deeper and deeper into the forest, angling away from the sound of the loud helicopter overhead. Dense Douglas-fir and western hemlock shaded the ground below, masking their wild run. Jonathan avoided any opening where sunlight filtered through and stayed in shadow, grateful he was wearing a forest green coat. He thought the singed back might also aid in concealing them.

Jonathan stopped to catch his breath beside a huge fir tree and sat Robbie on the ground. Reaching into his pocket he pulled out two crushed hats and some stale energy bars he'd forgotten were there. They went back in his pocket for later.

He slid a green knitted cap over Robbie's head and shook out a green baseball cap for himself. Kneeling down on the soft earth, he scraped aside several inches of discarded needles exposing moist soil beneath the tree litter. Digging into it with his fingers, he scooped some up and rubbed it across Robbie's cheeks.

Robbie squirmed away. "Hey! What the heck ya doin'?"

Jonathan smiled. Robbie was speaking. "This is camouflage, like soldiers wear. Close your eyes, so I can rub some on your forehead."

Robbie wrinkled his nose and closed his eyes. Jonathan finished darkening the boy's face and turned to smear mud on his own.

"What do you think? Did I cover everything?"

Robbie snickered. "You look funny. You're all dirty."

Jonathan ruffled Robbie's hair, grateful Robbie found a bit of humor in this. "Okay, Sport, let's get moving." He took Robbie's hand, leading him out from their hiding place.

They stayed under the cover of the tree canopy above them, jogging through the trees, hopping over low bushes, and pushing aside thorny brambles.

It was dusk by the time they found a small creek where they

drank their fill and cleaned up. Jonathan worried they wouldn't find a safe, protected place to spend the night.

As Robbie chewed on his second energy bar, he looked up at the tree canopy above. "It's gettin' dark."

Jonathan nodded.

"I'm awful tired." He leaned his head against Jonathan's arm.

The young man wrapped an arm around Robbie and lifted him off the ground. "Maybe you'd like to ride for a little while." Robbie smiled and hugged him. Robbie laid his head on Jonathan's shoulder. Within moments he was sound asleep.

ഇരു

"Robbie, wake up for a few minutes." Jonathan gently sat the boy on the ground in front of a giant western red cedar.

Robbie rubbed his eyes and looked up, his gaze following the length of the tall, damaged tree. "What happened to it? It looks all burned."

"It's a 'chimney tree," Jonathan said. "It was burned by fire, maybe over and over again. Fungi invaded the damaged wood making it rot. Over time it formed a cavernous area. We're going to spend the night inside it."

"Cool," Robbie said, crawling inside the immense, hollow tree. "Come on, Jonathan. Lucky we found it, 'cuz it's not cold and windy in here."

"Right." Jonathan followed Robbie in. "Once upon a time people called these 'goosepen' trees because they made convenient places to keep animals like geese. Sometimes black bears and bats use them too."

Robbie shivered. "You shoulda told me before I went in all by myself."

"No sign of bears that I could see. Now, come here and lay down. We need to sleep." He curled around Robbie and shut his eyes.

But, Jonathan slept fitfully, and shortly before dawn, he was startled awake.

CHAPTER SIXTY-SEVEN

The sound of men's voices carried to Jonathan, lots of voices. He glanced at Robbie who slept soundly. He listened intently. They were striking at bushes. *Searching for us? And for any others who fled from the village?* Jonathan held his breath.

While Robbie slept, Jonathan listened for another two hours, but heard no more unusual sounds in the forest. There was only bird song and the wind blowing through the trees.

Jonathan gently woke Robbie then crawled out and looked around. He gestured for Robbie to follow. Once outside the tree, they traveled in the opposite direction of the searchers.

Hours later Jonathan and Robbie stumbled onto a ridge that looked down on a dilapidated farmhouse. Chipped white paint covered the old house. In the grass-bare yard a scatter of black and white bantam chickens pecked the ground. Behind the house stood a large barn, bright red and freshly painted. Staying in the cover of the forest's tree line, Jonathan and Robbie moved to a safe observation point.

"Robbie, I think we ought to sit here and watch things for a while. That barn could offer us shelter from the storm that's coming." Jonathan settled back against the trunk of a tree. He was out of sight, but could still see the barn. "Let's wait here until it's almost dark."

Robbie scrunched down beside Jonathan and leaned against him. "How do you know a storm's comin'?"

Jonathan wrapped an arm around him. "Look at the hills over there. See the big black clouds? They keep getting bigger and that means they're coming in our direction."

Robbie stared, fascinated. "Hey, I see a witch on a broom. Do you see it?"

Jonathan laughed. "Yeah, I think I do."

They spent the rest of the afternoon cloud gazing and Jonathan kept Robbie entertained making up stories about the images they saw.

Once an old woman came out of the house and walked to the chicken coop. Later, she came out with a basket full of eggs.

She didn't look dangerous, but Jonathan wouldn't take any chances. Robbie was his responsibility now and he was serious about Robbie's safety.

In late evening, a young woman arrived leading a milk cow and a mule into the barn. Jonathan surmised that earlier in the day they'd been off grazing.

When the sun finally set and the sky darkened, Jonathan woke Robbie who'd dozed. He hurried him across the clearing behind the barn, stopping only long enough to grab an armful of wrinkled apples off a tree. "These will help fill our bellies," he whispered.

Robbie held one in each hand and took a quick bite as they jogged to the barn. It was overripe and mealy, but he was so hungry he didn't care.

A small side door into the barn was unlocked. In the dim light, they made out the milk cow and she lowed softly. Bales of hay were stacked near her, and the mule in a neighboring stall turned to watch them.

"Look Jonathan, a cat!" Before Jonathan could stop him, Robbie bounded after the calico sitting on a stall wall. Before Robbie reached her she jumped down and vanished behind bales of hay.

"Heck! She wouldn't let me pet her." Hanging his head, he walked back to Jonathan.

"Little buddy, don't run away from me like that again, okay? You scared me." Jonathan urged Robbie toward the ladder that led to the loft. "I think we'll be safer up there."

The sound of heavy rain began to pelt the roof and both of them looked up. "Looks like we got here just in time." Jonathan ruffled Robbie's hair and he squirmed away.

"You keep doin' that!"

Jonathan chuckled. "You go up first. I'll be right behind you making sure you don't fall."

"I'm not gonna fall. I'm a good climber." He squeezed Jonathan's hand the way his Gramma squeezed his when she wanted to reassure him. Robbie let go, reached for the ladder and began scrambling up.

Jonathan followed Robbie up the ladder, and in the loft they pulled hay together to form a soft bed. As they snuggled in, Jonathan reflected on their good fortune and prayed it would last.

Stress and fatigue left Jonathan exhausted and he was soon asleep. On the other hand, faced with hours of boredom spent snoozing all afternoon, sleep eluded Robbie. When Jonathan began to gently snore, Robbie thought he'd never get to sleep, and the loud sound of the rain on the roof didn't help.

Being careful not to touch Jonathan, he cautiously got up and tiptoed to the ladder, boots in hand. Down he went and stepped onto the barn's floor.

The barn was dim, but not dark. He sat down to put on his birthday boots and when he finished he looked up. Something moved, sending a shiver through him. *There's someone there!* He froze. *No, it's just shadows. Gramma says there are no bogeymen.* He stood up slowly eyeing the shadow he thought he'd seen move.

"Hey there."

Robbie jumped at the sound, and quickly turned to grab the ladder. His foot hit the first rung, but slid back off. He moaned and struggled to get the other foot up on it. "I shoulda stayed with Jonathan."

"I won't hurt you, son. Don't be afraid."

Robbie twisted his head around to look over his shoulder. A little old lady came out of the shadows. The calico cat ran to her, making figure eights around her ankles. She didn't look scary.

"Is that your cat?" Robbie asked.

"She sure is. Her name's Patches. You want to pet her?" She picked up the cat and carried it to Robbie, placing it in his arms.

Thrilled, Robbie snuggled the cat against his cheek. "Hi sweet Patches." The cat began to purr, and Robbie beamed.

"You want to see something really special?" the old woman asked.

Robbie nodded.

"Come over here beside Bluebell." She gestured toward the cow.

Robbie hesitated. Bluebell looked huge.

"Don't worry, she's a sweet old cow. 'Sides we're not goin' in her stall, we'll be in the empty stall next door." The old woman reached out and opened the gate to the neighboring stall and stepped through, gesturing for Robbie to follow.

Carrying Patches close to him, he slowly approached the stall and looked in.

The old woman pointed to a wooden box against the back wall with pieces of hay spilling over its sides. In the center of the soft hay nestled five squirming kittens, their eyes still closed.

Robbie walked up to the box and gasped. He'd never seen little kittens before. Patches struggled out of his arms and immediately went into the box. The kittens, alerted to their mother's presence, began mewing as they found their way to her side to nurse. Robbie looked up at the old woman with gratitude shining in his eyes.

"Can I sit down and pet them?"

"Course you can. Best not to pick 'em up while they're eating though. Let 'em finish. Then if you're real careful, you can hold one or two in your lap."

At that moment, Robbie decided he loved that old woman, whoever she was.

CHAPTER SIXTY-EIGHT

"Out of suffering have emerged the strongest souls; the most massive characters are seared with scars." ~ Kahlil Gibran

A shaft of morning sunlight slowly edged its way across Jonathan until it reached his eyes. He woke squinting and turned to reach for Robbie. Robbie wasn't there. He sat up, searching. The loft was empty.

Jonathan bolted to his feet, heart pounding. Grabbing his shoes, he headed toward the ladder and called in a loud whisper, "Robbie, Robbie! Where are you?" As he scrambled down the ladder, his eyes searched under the loft.

Robbie wasn't anywhere in the barn. Where could he be? If he'd ventured outside, someone could have snatched him and Jonathan might never see him again. Jonathan's head began to pound; he had to find Robbie.

Crossing the hay-strewn floor, he cracked open the barn door and peeked out. Across the yard an old woman was scattering corn for the chickens. Had she seen Robbie? Did he dare approach her to ask? Or, might Robbie be hiding in the woods, and approaching her would give them both away? The dilemma didn't help Jonathan's throbbing temples.

When her voice split the morning air, he jerked his head away from the crack in the door.

"Carry them eggs careful now. Don't drop 'em." A grinning boy came out of the hen house with a basket full of small bantam eggs.

Robbie!

"Can I show them to Jonathan now, can I?"

"He might still be sleeping."

"Naw, I saw him looking at us through the barn door."

The woman turned toward the barn and Jonathan cringed. Well, she'd seen Robbie. She might as well see him too. Was she friend or foe? Vowing to find out, Jonathan stepped into the sunlight.

"Hey there," she called. "Robbie and I got eggs for breakfast to go with the pancakes we whipped up while you was sleepin'." She waved her arm, beckoning him to come. "You can wash up inside and eat hearty."

The old woman placed a hand on Robbie's shoulder to guide him to the house. He cradled the basket of eggs against his chest, struggling not to drop them.

Jonathan raced to Robbie's side. Should they trust this woman? She might have already sent for the troops. They could be on their way right now.

He grew even more concerned when a pretty young woman came out the front door. Her long chestnut tresses were damp, as if she'd recently left her morning shower. She extended her hand, clasping his in an embrace that left Jonathan speechless.

"Hi. I'm Stephanie."

As he studied her, her dark eyes mesmerized him. She was beautiful and he wanted to trust her; looked forward to trusting her. However, the recent events at the Lodge made it difficult, if not impossible, for him to trust anyone.

Robbie walked around them and followed the old woman into the house, quite at ease with both women.

"Come on inside," Stephanie said. "Robbie's already eaten, but I'll keep you company while he and my grandmother are in the garden. She promised Robbie he could help her pick beans for supper tonight."

Jonathan gave a start. *They expect us here for supper?*

At the kitchen table, Jonathan forked a bite of bacon and scrambled egg into his mouth as Stephanie sat a second plate of hot pancakes in front of him.

He smiled at her, thinking he was eating the best breakfast he'd ever had. As he studied the young woman, he felt himself warm toward her.

She pulled out a kitchen chair and sat down. "Welcome to our carefully hidden *resort.*'"

Jonathan gave a surprised snort. "This weathered farm house is a resort?"

She giggled and he laughed with her. Her joy was infectious. How long had it been since he'd laughed, he wondered?

"We saw the smoke from the village, and were worried." Sobering, she placed a hand over his. "A man named Dixon called Grandmother to ask us to watch for survivors. Of course, we'd want to help."

"I'm grateful we stumbled upon your place."

"So am I." She pulled her hand back. "The travesty of killing our country's children has to end." She sighed deeply. "Actually, the *world's* destruction of children needs to end."

೧೧೮೨

After days of being cooped up underground, the two women and the village children were eager to step into daylight again. Getting out of the bunker would also allow them to learn the fate of their loved ones.

Rebecca led the children up a narrow shaft toward the surface. She lugged a cat carrier with Butterscotch inside. Carolyn and Deeohgee brought up the rear, making sure they didn't leave anyone behind. Across Deeohgee's back they'd looped two pillowcases like saddlebags loaded with odds and ends they thought they might need later.

The women set a slow pace so all the children could keep up. There was plenty of head room, but the narrow path required them to walk in pairs, holding hands. Each wore the headlamp they received at the party.

The bright circle of Rebecca's flashlight pointed the way. She felt herself tiring and wondered how Carolyn was managing.

How much farther did they have to go?

A six-year-old boy bumped into her when she paused to look back. Rebecca reached down and took his hand.

"How long 'til we find our moms and dads?"

Her forehead wrinkled. *Had all the parents survived? Had any of them survived?*

"Michael, until we know where everyone's parents are, we'll stay at a nice farm house I know about. The lady there is kind and she has a barnyard full of chickens. You can feed them and gather eggs. Won't that be fun?"

Michael didn't reply, and she began walking forward again.

The straight path suddenly turned to the right. Ahead of her, Rebecca's light illuminated the rusty orange patina on a large iron door. She raised a hand, stopping their progress before the children began bumping into each other.

Giving Michael her flashlight, Rebecca felt for and found a latch. With effort, she managed to force it up, but the door wouldn't budge when she pushed on it.

"We've got to get this heavy door open." She knelt down in front of Michael. "Will you run back to Aunt Carolyn and ask her to come up here to help me?"

"Yes, Yes!" Michael said, eagerly bobbing his head. He stood up tall, turned and ran between the pairs of children, shoving his way through the line.

෨෬

"I'm sure Gray never expected two old women and a bunch of small children to take refuge in here alone. He could probably lean into this heavy door and force it open with no trouble, but you and I are a different matter."

The children pressed in and around Rebecca and Carolyn, wanting to see. Their excited voices echoed down the narrow passageway.

Carolyn called Deeohgee to her. She reached in the pillow case on his back, and came out with a butcher knife. "Let's run this around the door's edges and see how much rust we can chip away. It might help."

After much scraping and chipping, they tried to force the door open again. Rebecca flattened both palms against the door and leaned into it. Carolyn placed her good shoulder against the door, and some of the bigger children squeezed in to help.

"Imagine you're superman shoving a tank out of the way. Ready, set, shove! C'mon, push, push, push." They were about to give up when they heard the door creak. "Keep pushing, I think we've got it."

A tiny shaft of light came through a gap at the edge of the door. The women whooped for joy. With additional effort they got the door open a few inches. They edged it along bit by bit until it was just wide enough to slip through one at a time.

"Everybody, have a jacket and gloves on. It might be cold out there, but we want out, don't we?"

A loud, "YES!" echoed through the corridor.

"I'll try to clear the way," Rebecca said, but before she squeezed out the opening, Deeohgee pushed through. He scrambled out and began digging and pushing his way through blackberries that hid the door, making a path for them.

"Good boy, Deeohgee!" Rebecca slipped out the opening. She used the knife to hack away what remained, and patted the dog.

Gradually, one by one, the children each scrambled through, with Carolyn exiting last. Some children had scrapes and scratches, but all smiled at seeing the sun again.

Rebecca nudged Carolyn. "Look at the Lodge."

Carolyn twisted to see over her shoulder. They were farther away than she expected. The Lodge's stone walls were black with soot and little glass remained in its windows.

This is not the time to grieve for things that can't be changed, she told herself.

Carolyn wondered if they should prepare the youngsters for

the possibility that some of their parents, or maybe all, might not have survived the attack. Then she realized there was no need to say anything. They already knew.

ഇൗരു

Evening shadows were closing in on the farm house when loud barking sent everyone to windows and doors. Jonathan rushed outside, down the steps and across the yard. Deeohgee met him halfway. The excited dog leaped up, put his front paws on Jonathan's shoulders and licked his face.

Not far behind, and trudging out of the forest, came a group of bedraggled kids.

Jonathan ran to them and scooped his mother up in his arms to swing her around. Tears ran down both their faces as they hugged.

Robbie heard the commotion and hurried out of the hen house. "Gramma, Gramma!" he yelled, dropping the basket and dashing to Rebecca as several eggs flew out, smashing to the ground.

She kissed him on both cheeks and hugged him tightly against her until Robbie wriggled free. He hugged his friends while his eyes searched the group for Emma. He knew she wouldn't be there, but he still hoped.

Stephanie ran into the midst of the children. Kneeling down, she reached out to gently touch as many as she could. Deeohgee nuzzled under her arm. "Looks like we just acquired a handsome guard dog," she said.

"And a mouser," Carolyn grinned, pointing to the cat carrier one of the older girls carried.

Stephanie stood up. "I just finished frosting a cake. Who wants some?"

A chorus of little voices rang out, "Me, me, me!"

CHAPTER SIXTY-NINE

"...and there shall be no more death or mourning, wailing or pain, for the old order has passed away." ~ Revelation 21:4

Twenty years later...

The hundreds of people packed into the dimly lit college auditorium sat in stunned silence as the ceiling lights brightened.

Their presenter returned to the podium as the credits scrolled up the screen. "The video you just saw recounts only a few of the horrific events of previous eras. Much of the film came from security cameras mounted above safe villages." He ran a hand through his thick hair and sipped water from the glass in front of him. "By the way, the final segment from *The Valley of Martyrs* is well documented."

This young and ruggedly handsome speaker knew what he was about. He'd boldly charted a new direction in the field of Modern History by submitting a PhD dissertation chronicling the atrocities of the FFUs. Rather than pursue a tenured position in the crusty bureaucracy of some university, he chose to take his message to the people, declining offers of an Associate Professorship. He moved about doing short stints as Adjunct or Visiting Professor of Modern History. His controversial topic and electrifying presentation made him an instant phenomenon. Here in Toronto, as elsewhere, they'd scheduled his classes in the auditorium to accommodate overflow crowds.

"Greedy men ruled much of the world. Ignoring the common good, they promoted evil, sublimating mankind's nobler instincts. Films such as the one you just watched helped to change the course of history. Brave men like Arius Didymus Dixon and Brody Branigan risked their lives to document these atrocities. Their work fueled a rebellion, ending the wanton destruction of infants and children."

A student from the campus newspaper raised his hand. "Professor, wasn't this movie created as shock value to publicize an agenda against the former government?"

"Take note, people. This guy pops up everywhere I go." He pointed at the student. "I've encountered him in Boston, New York, Dallas, Chicago and Los Angeles."

"He's lying," the young man shouted. "I was never in any of those places." He glanced around the auditorium, seeking support from the audience. "He's manipulating things to undermine my credibility."

The Professor shook his head and chuckled. "What's your name?"

"Don Frederick."

"Mr. Frederick's right; he wasn't in any of those other cities. But a skeptical student just like him was. Someone always tries to deny reality. As George Santayana, once said, 'Those who cannot remember the past are condemned to repeat it.'"

Pausing, the Professor scanned his audience. "This really happened, people. We *must* learn from the past, and not allow those lessons to be lost to future generations. My job today is to tell you. For the rest of your lives, your job will be to tell others. The story of how a few evil men and women sanctioned the killing of the helpless and innocent must be told and retold. Knowledge of these travesties cannot, *must not*, be forgotten lest they be repeated."

He pounded the podium, driving home his point. "Since then, there's been a restoration of morality and ethics. All FFUs and abortion centers were shut down, first throughout our nation, and eventually throughout the world. We overcame the errors of previous generations. Today society encourages, respects and values life, especially that of children, infants, and those still in the womb."

The auditorium remained deathly still. Then someone in the

back shouted, "Did anyone at the final *Village of Martyrs* survive?"

"Some did. Many did not."

"But all the children made it out alive?"

"Most did," his voice softened, "but not all." The whoosh of rockets and screech of tearing metal reverberated inside his skull as he remembered the special friend he'd loved and lost that day. Lifting his chin, he stared out at the audience, hands on his hips. With fervor in his voice, he said, "One thing we know about evil. When exposed, evil slinks away and denies its existence."

Putting aside old memories, he strode back to the podium. "A few examples: The Turks slaughtered a million and a half Armenians and then claimed it never happened. The Nazis murdered eight million Jews and countless others, with over a million of those being children. He pointed into the front row. "Yet some, like our friend, Don, insist the Nazi Holocaust, or *Shoah* as it's called in Israel, never happened."

Voice rising, he wrapped-up his presentation. "Stalin starved millions of Ukrainian peasants and buried the evidence in mass graves. The Chinese tried to obliterate the Tibetans then claimed their culture was never real. The Communist Khmer Rouge attempted to hide over a million people they murdered while twice as many Cambodians died from disease and starvation. As recent as the 21st century, over 480,000 people in Darfur were slaughtered and over 2.8 million more displaced in an attempted genocide. Militant Muslims hide their faces as they behead and slaughter Christians in the Middle East, Africa and elsewhere."

Resting his hands on the podium, the Professor stared intently at his audience. He nervously rubbed the end of his shortened little finger, a habit acquired years earlier. "Never forget, like a cockroach, evil always tries to hide from the light."

                                  ဆၢ

People gathered their coats, purses and backpacks. Still mulling over the presentation, most of them exited the auditorium in silence or conversed in muffled tones. A few students drifted up to the front of the stage. They formed a semi-circle there, hoping to have some time alone with the Visiting Professor.

Midway back in the almost empty auditorium, a young woman remained in her seat. Dressed in a gray wool pantsuit with discrete blue pinstripes, she appeared more businesswoman than student. Her hair and makeup were flawless, her tailored suit and silk blouse tastefully stylish.

She paid no attention to the little cluster of eager fans milling around the front of the stage. A leather notepad lay open on her knees. She tapped her pen on the arm of the chair as she reviewed her notes. Focused on the task at hand, she ignored the stragglers who trooped up the aisle.

A bank of spotlights winked out as somewhere behind the curtains a stagehand began snapping his way down a row of circuit breakers. The woman glanced up. She flipped over the cover of her notepad, tossed it into the open briefcase on the seat beside her and snapped its latch.

The last student had finished and was turning to leave by the time she rose in the shadows and approached the stage.

A pair of volunteers waited in the wings to clear the stage and dismantle the backdrops used to augment the presentation. The diorama consisted of a series of larger than life photos gathered from a variety of sources. The centerpiece of the display was a five-paneled folding wall.

When properly lit and viewed from a distance, its multi-directional focus produced a lifelike, three dimensional feel. A special effects team of movie set designers re-created an FFU holding room complete with its gloomy gray walls and frightened victims awaiting execution.

CHAPTER SEVENTY

Returning to the podium, the presenter pulled out a stack of papers and started sorting them.

"Excuse me, Professor Wilson. May I speak with you?" a female voice asked.

"Sorry, the Q & A session ended a couple of minutes ago," he said without raising his eyes.

"I'm with CBC News in Vancouver."

He stacked the pages and tucked them away. "Well, in that case, c'mon up. We can always find time for the media." Lifting his chin, he caught a glimpse of the attractive woman negotiating the stairs. He quickly adjusted his tie and buttoned his jacket. Stepping away from the podium, he strode across the stage.

They met halfway and shook hands. She introduced herself as Jane Spencer and gave him her business card. He gave it a quick once-over and pocketed the card without comment.

"You certainly came a long way to get an interview. Why…"

One of the volunteers interrupted him by hollering, "Everything's packed and stacked, Professor. All your props are on the flatbed rolling cart. Anything else you need?"

He winked at her, "Give me just a few seconds." He spun to face his stagehands. "Great job, guys. Put the cart in the storage room. The door's open. It'll lock when you shut it." He tilted his head and looked up at the ceiling. "And leave this last row of lights on. I'll get 'em on my way out."

He turned back to her and smiled. "Sorry for the interruption. And now," he eased the corner of her card out of his pocket, "Jane Spencer, I'm ready for your interview." He ran his eyes over the empty, dark theater. "That is, if we can find a place to sit down."

She smiled. "Could we go to your office?"

He checked his wristwatch and gave a low whistle. "Wow, it's later than I thought. We could, but it's all the way across the campus. They stuck me in what must be the oldest building on campus. It's like being in a mausoleum."

"Is there a coffee shop nearby?"

"Let's go exploring and see what we find." He headed for a gap between the curtains and she fell into step beside him. Leading her to an exit at the back of the building, he flicked off the last light switch as they passed the breaker box.

"This sidewalk will lead us to the quad." He gave her a sidelong glance as they walked. "Did you fly out from B.C. this morning?"

"As a matter of fact, I did."

"Poor you." He ran his tongue inside his cheek. "Let's see, I'm guessing you live about half an hour from the airport. You had to park, get checked in, and sit on the tarmac while the baggage handlers fed suitcases into the belly of the plane. The first flight out is 6:00 a.m., which means you left home," he rocked his hand in the air, "around 4:00 a.m. No time for breakfast, so you grabbed one of those breakfast biscuit things at the airport on your way to check-in."

She laughed. "Have you been spying on me?"

His eyes had a mischievous sparkle. "Would I tell you if I had?" He snapped his fingers. "On a good day, it takes about 4 ½ hours nonstop. Then you have to land and taxi, pick up your luggage, wait at the rent-a-car counter, drive to the university, find a parking spot, and hoof it to the auditorium. It can't be done in less than seven hours, which explains why you tiptoed in after we'd started."

She winced. "You noticed?"

"That's what we spies do," he said with a wink.

They were nearing the crosswalk when he came to a halt. "I can't help wondering why we're going for coffee when all you've had today is a fast food breakfast and some pretzels on the plane. I know it's a little early, but shouldn't we go to a restaurant and get you a decent meal?"

"Great idea," she said. "I'll put it on my expense account."

They walked a few blocks to a nearby restaurant. They were the first customers of the day, and when he rapped on the glass, the hostess came running to unlock the door. As they ordered, a busboy moved about smoothing tablecloths and doing last minute setups for the dinner trade.

Their conversation consisted of open-ended comments and polite snippets of getting-to-know-you inquiries while they waited for their meals to arrive.

CHAPTER SEVENTY-ONE

Professor Wilson moved his plate aside and folded his napkin. Something didn't feel right. This Jane Spencer came on the pretense of doing an interview. Yet, this felt more like a first date than an interview.

He smiled across the table at her. "What was it that motivated you to travel so far? You could have simply asked me to go down to the local studio and set up a video link."

She shook her head. "As soon as that flyer landed on my desk's in-box, I knew I *had* to see you."

He put his elbow on the table and rested his chin on his fist. "A statement like that earns you a nomination as president of my international fan club. Though I should warn you, it only has two members, my Gramma and my Aunt Carolyn."

"How are Gramma and Aunt Carolyn?"

"Fine. They share an apartment in an assisted living complex."

"What about Jonathan? Do you keep in touch?"

"Jonathan's been like a father to me. When they attacked the Lodge, he and I escaped into the surrounding woods."

"And now you're a college professor. In spite of everything, it sounds like you had a pretty good life."

He thought about what she said for several moments. "In many ways I suppose I did. I managed to escape the grim reaper not once, but twice. That alone should be enough for anyone. Were it not for the events of the attack, it would be."

"Because that was the day you lost the best friend you ever had."

Her comment snapped him back into reality. Straightening in his chair, he glared across the table. "Who are you and what kind of game are we playing here?"

"Do the names Gus and Maude Steinway mean anything to you? What about Emma and the twins, Leila and Alexander?"

He struggled to maintain his composure. "You get an A+ for doing your research. Mean anything to me? Of course they did. I knew and loved each one of them. Is this why your boss sent you across the country, to remind me of the people I've lost? Will it add pathos to your story?" He shoved his chair back from the table. "This interview is officially over."

"*This interview*, as you call it, never began. Sit back down, Robbie, and listen to what I have to say."

"My Gramma is the only one who's allowed to call me Robbie," he muttered.

"I'll start by telling you I've had several last names."

"That's the usual fallout from multiple divorces."

She ignored the comment. "I started out life as a Spencer, Emma Jane Spencer. When we went on the run I became a Steinway. Once the air cleared, Mom and Dad dropped the aliases and went back to being Mira and Grayson Stevens. We kids swapped too. Using my birth name at work allows me to draw a line between my professional and private life."

He raised his hand, stopping her. "Let me finish this saga for you. Then all you *Stevens* went to a place where no one knew you, moved into a nice home in a middle class suburban neighborhood and everyone lived happily ever after."

She smiled. "In a way, that *is* sort of what happened. You know the chaos that followed the attacks, the lawsuits and so on. Dad formed a nonprofit, public interest law firm to assist those who were victimized by the government. His one regret was that he couldn't represent Dixon and Brody."

"I have to hand it to you, you're good," he said, nodding as he spoke. "Take some of the people I mentioned in my presentation and weave their names into your narrative. You almost had me. Do they have college courses to teach you this stuff, or do you just have a natural talent for it?"

"I'm Emma, *your Emma*. How can I convince you?"

He crossed his arms and shook his head. "It can't be done. I saw the Steinways, or whatever you want to call them, get into that tram. Emma was in the car with them. I watched the superstructure pull away from the mountain and crumple, taking them all to their death. They're dead, and nothing you say or do will bring them back."

"You know what you saw. What you didn't see was Dixon and Brody helping us scramble out of the tram before everything collapsed. If they hadn't been there, we'd have been trapped under all that falling debris just as you imagined."

"Dixon and Brody went into hiding on the day of the attack and have never surfaced again. Even though no one's heard from them since then, I suppose you can produce them as witnesses?"

She nervously tapped a manicured nail on the table. "You're not going to like what I'm about to tell you. Somehow Dixon and Brody managed to steal a government truck. They filled it with villagers; us included, and sped away. Things were happening so fast. The pilots taking part in the attack saw the insignias on the doors and left us alone."

Emma's shoulders slumped. She laid her hand over his. "After everyone got out, Dixon and Brody headed back to the village, hoping to rescue more people. But, they didn't make it the second time. They sacrificed themselves trying to save more villagers."

His expression softened a bit. "If what you say is true," he said, rubbing his chin, "it would explain why so many of us were never able to reconnect with each other. Dixon and Brody were the ones who always kept us updated. They knew where everyone was and what aliases they were using."

"What do you mean, *if what I say is true?* It's time to put your academic detachment away and embrace reality. What do I have to do to make you believe me?"

"I've already told you, it can't be done. Like it or not, everything we've talked about could be uncovered with diligent research. If you want me to believe you, tell me something that no one else would know; something only Emma and I shared."

She nibbled at her lip as she thought. After several long

moments, she raised her eyes and studied his hand resting on the table. "I'll tell you something even you don't know."

Her voice quivered as she took his hand in hers. "That afternoon, Aranda wrapped up your hand with a piece of cloth before she took you away. Giles picked up the piece of your finger he'd cut off and put it in a little plastic bag. Then he walked out, slamming the door. After all of you left the holding room, I obeyed an order from Giles and got down on my hands and knees to wipe your blood off the floor."

When she finished, Emma leaned across the table and softly kissed the long-healed stub of finger on his left hand. "It's me, Robbie," she said softly, "and I'll never forget the day they did this to you."

Lifting her chin, he whispered, "You really are my Emma. So many nights I dreamed you returned to me, and now you have." He kissed her.

When they parted he took her left hand and turned it over. "No wedding ring?"

"I've never married."

"Neither have I," he said, matter of factly. "Has there never been anyone in your life?"

"You mean, besides you?"

Avoiding her eyes, he gave a jerky nod.

"I've been seeing one of the editors at the station for about a year now." She swallowed hard. "Last week he asked me to marry him. I told him I'd let him know when I returned from Toronto."

"When do go back?"

She rubbed her temple and sighed. "I'm booked on tonight's flight."

"What about your interview?"

"The local affiliate can provide me with the visuals. I only came to see if it was really you."

He checked his watch. "We still have a couple of hours together before you have to leave for the airport."

EPILOG

Friends and guests slowly filled the pews of the small church.

In the church library, Emma squinted into the mirror giving her eye makeup a final inspection. Mandy, her best friend, and matron of honor, stood at her shoulder. Her bridesmaids milled about, making small talk and examining the spines of old books as they passed time until the wedding began.

Lifting a wisp of Emma's hair from behind her ear, Mandy tucked it under the elegant French braid cascading down Emma's back. Everyone's eyes moved toward the door when they heard a light tap.

"I'll get it." Mandy unlatched the door, smiled and opened it wide. "Mrs. Stevens, we've been expecting you. Come on in. Emma's almost ready."

"Mandy honey, call me Mira." She lifted the hand of a small child who walked beside her. "Look who I found loitering outside."

Emma turned and held out her arms. The little girl rushed into them. "Aranda, sweetheart, we thought you were with your daddy."

"Daddy's busy doing stuff to get ready. He left me with my big brothers, but I wanted to be in here with you."

Emma laughed. "Mandy, did you know that Jonathan and Stephanie had four boys before little Aranda showed up? At six years old, I thought she'd make a perfect flower girl."

"She looks beautiful." Mandy patted the top of Aranda's head. "Her mom did a great job fixing Aranda's hair. It matches yours."

"And, as it should, her dress matches yours," Emma said, admiring the subtle dark rose shade she'd chosen for their satin gowns. She turned back to the mirror and applied her lipstick, talking to Mandy in the mirror. "Stephanie is one of the most thoughtful and kind persons I've met since our families were reunited."

Mira brought over a veil. "Mandy, let's get Emma's veil attached. I want to take a quick photo of you girls all together. Then I have to go outside; they'll be seating the parents soon."

Mandy began attaching the long white veil over Emma's elaborate coiffure as Mira stretched the intricate lace atop a train of white satin.

"You are truly a gorgeous bride. I'm grateful I've had the opportunity to be your mom," Mira whispered.

Emma's eyes misted.

Mira shooed her to the other side of the room and opened the door. Hearing the organist start Pachelbel's Canon in D Major, she leaned back in and waved the bridesmaids out.

Mandy handed little Aranda a white basket filled with red rose petals. "Sweetie, you know where to begin spreading your flower petals, right?"

Her head bobbed up and down.

৪০৫৪

The vestibule became a flurry of motion as the immediate family members prepared to be escorted to their seats. The bridesmaids lined up along one wall waiting for the groomsmen. The priest, groom and father of the bride squeezed into a corner, staying out of the traffic.

One-by-one the groomsmen cycled in and out of the church escorting people to their seats. "That's the last of 'em," the priest whispered when Mira headed down the aisle on the arm of a groomsman. He gave the groom a nudge. "Tis our turn next."

When they reached the altar Robbie stepped to one side. Father Elijah MacBain continued to the altar. He turned to face the congregation, smiling as he waited to welcome the bride and groom. The years had slowed Father Mac's step and turned the priest's hair white and wispy, but even time couldn't dim the twinkle in the old man's eye.

Emma waited at the back of the church, gazing up the aisle over the rose petals little Aranda had spread. She noticed that, as

Best Man, Jonathan rested a steadying hand on Robbie's shoulder.

She leaned close to Gray and whispered, "Dad, look at Robbie. He appears as nervous as I feel. Do you think he's having second thoughts?"

Gray scoffed. "Every groom is nervous, so is every bride. It's expected."

As the organ began the wedding march, Emma took Gray's arm and looked up into his eyes. "Thanks, Dad. Thank you for today and for everything you've done for me."

Gray patted the hand on his arm. "You've been my blessing and pleasure. Here we go, Sweetheart."

Tall and proud, Gray escorted his adopted daughter down the aisle. As they walked Emma recalled a terrified young girl in a dark holding room and an equally frightened little boy who'd huddled there with her. She said a silent prayer of thanksgiving that two youngsters who'd felt so alone and unloved had found the love they needed with each other.

Gray kissed her cheek and joined Mira in a front pew.

Robbie took Emma's hand. She looked into his eyes and everything else faded away.

The wedding went just as they'd rehearsed it. Father Mac pronounced them husband and wife and Robbie kissed his new bride. When they turned to face the congregation, everyone rose clapping and cheering.

Emma's heart swelled to the sound of the applause. She stood on the altar steps beside her new husband with a smile as radiant as the noonday sun.

Everything that matters is right here, she thought, staring across the sea of faces. Her eyes lingered on the people who'd come together for this event. Aunt Caroline and Gramma Rebecca sat beside Mira and Gray in the front pews. Gray's brother, Bryson and his wife and children were behind them. They'd traveled all the way from Maryland to Canada's West

Coast to be there. Mandy's parents, Eileen and Jacob Abramson, sat with Mandy's brothers, Nathan and Noah. Alexander and Leila joined them. At the end of the pew, Mandy's husband, Brett, was gently rocking their infant son.

A momentary shiver of sadness swept through Emma as she remembered the two people whose heroism made this day possible.

Emma and Robbie started down the aisle. People began reaching out, touching their hands, congratulating them as they passed. It was then she knew that in some mystical way Dixon and Brody were with them as well.

She was all the more certain when a long-forgotten insight echoed in the depths of her memory. It's true, she thought, as fingers brushed past hers. Our lives, like everyone's, were filled with ups and downs, twists and turns, doubts and uncertainties. Though neither of us knew it at the time, each of those events was leading us to this joyful and sacred moment.

THE END

WISDOM of the AGES

It's been said that there's nothing new under the sun. From distant millennia to modern times, the tenets of all the major religious traditions have rejected the killing of children, babies and the unborn.

I encourage you to read and contemplate the following insights.

Hinduism

Visnu is "the protector of the child-to-be." ~ *Rg Samhit*, ca. 1200 BC

"Now these lead to a fall from caste: stealing, murder, abortion..." ~ *Apastamba Dharma Sutra*, ca. 400 BC

Buddhism

The Buddha Himself taught, "There are Evil Karma which are difficult to extinguish, even if one were to repent of them. The first is killing the father, the second is killing the mother, the third is abortion..." ~ Siddhartha Gautama, *The Dharani Sutra of the Buddha*, ca. 500 BC

Judaism

"Thou shall not kill." ~ Ten Commandments ca. 1450 BC

"You knit me in my mother's womb . . . nor was my frame unknown to you when I was made in secret" ~ Psalm 139:13,15 ca. 920 BC

"Cast me not away from Thy presence; and take not Thy Holy Spirit from me." ~ Psalm 51:11 ca. 890 BC

"Before I formed you in the womb I knew you, and before you were born I consecrated you." ~ Jeremiah 1:5 ca. 600 BC

"Even jackals offer their breasts to nurse their young, but my people have become heartless." ~ Lamentations 4:3. ca. 586 BC

"...these parents who murder helpless lives, you willed to destroy." ~ Wisdom 12:6 ca. 50 BC

Early Christianity

"You shall not slay the child by procuring abortion; nor, again, shall you destroy it after it is born." ~ *Epistle of Barnabas* 19:5, ca. AD 100

"You shall not kill the fetus by abortion or destroy the infant already born." ~ *The Teaching of the Twelve Apostles*, ca. AD 150

"We call it murder and say it will be accountable to God if women use instruments to procure abortion." ~ Athenagoras of Athens, ca. AD 177

"We are not permitted to destroy even the fetus in the womb." ~ Tertullian of Carthage, ca. AD 200

"Why do you sow where the field is eager to destroy the fruit? Where there are medicines of sterility? Where there is murder before birth? You do not even let a harlot remain only a harlot, but you make her a murderess as well?" ~ St. John Chrysostom, ca. AD 400

Islam

The Quran teaches that on the Day of Judgment parents who killed their children will be under trial for that crime, and their children will be witnesses against them. ~ Quran 81:8-9, ca. AD 632

Protestant Founders

"For the fetus, though enclosed in the womb of its mother, is already a human being, and it is a monstrous crime to rob it of the life which it has not yet begun to enjoy. If it seems more horrible to kill a man in his own house than in a field, because a man's house is his place of most secure refuge, it ought surely to be deemed more atrocious to destroy a fetus in the womb before it has come to light." ~ John Calvin, ca. 1550

"Do no harm." ~ John Wesley, ca. 1780

AUTHOR'S COMMENTARY

Contemporary Voices

"Sweeter even than to have had the joy of children of my own has it been for me to help bring about a better state of things for mothers generally, so that their unborn little ones could not be willed away from them." ~ Susan B. Anthony, 1820-1906.

"A nation's greatness is measured by how it treats its weakest members." ~ Mahatma Gandhi, 1869-1948.

"Let us make that one point. No child will be unwanted, unloved, uncared for, or killed and thrown away. A sign of care for the weakest of the weak, the unborn child, must go out to the world." ~ Mother Teresa, 1910-1997

"A society will be judged on the basis of how it treats its weakest members and among the most vulnerable are surely the unborn and the dying." ~ Pope John Paul II, 1920-2005

"Abortion is an attack on the family and the humanity that unites us all." ~ Alveda King (niece of Martin Luther King, Jr.)

"We're all human, aren't we? Every human life is worth the same, and worth saving." ~ J.K. Rowling (author of Harry Potter series)

"Abortion is an atrocity. Those who practice or praise it are either damn idiots, misguided fools, or treacherous devils." ~ Christopher Titus (comedian and actor)

"...abortion strips women of their dignity...motherhood is empowering." ~ Abby Johnson (former Planned Parenthood Director)

"Why do we allow the painful destruction of our most precious and valuable resource: our children, our future? Why do we have the right to live when they do not? " ~ Zara Heritage